*Make time for friends. Make time for **Debbie Macomber**.*

Dear Friends,

Welcome to the fifth instalment of the Cedar Cove series. Whether this is the first Cedar Cove book you're reading or the fifth, my hope is that you'll feel right at home.

Like some of the residents of Cedar Cove you'll find a few surprises — and a new romance in the making. And I hope there'll be a lot of smiles and a laugh or two along the way.

I always enjoy hearing from my readers. You can reach me through my website by signing the guest book at debbiemacomber.com. Click the Cedar Cove button and you're in for some fun. If you aren't online, you can write to me at PO Box 1458, Port Orchard, WA 98366, USA. Three or four times a year I provide updates on the characters — letters from the characters themselves — and they often have a recipe they want to share.

So make yourself a cup of tea and settle down with your friends from Cedar Cove. Olivia, Jack, Grace, Charlotte, Ben, Roy, Corrie and everyone else — they're all eager to fill you in on what's happening in town. They're delighted you're back. And so am I!

Warmest regards,

Debbie Macomber

Debbie Macomber

50 Harbor Street

MIRA

Published in Great Britain 2010. This edition 2011.
MIRA Books, Eton House, 18-24 Paradise Road,
Richmond, Surrey, TW9 1SR

© Debbie Macomber 2005

ISBN 978 0 7783 0342 8

59-0511

MIRA's policy is to use papers that are natural, renewable and recyclable products and made from wood grown in sustainable forests. The logging and manufacturing processes conform to the legal environmental regulations of the country of origin.

Printed and bound by CPI Group
(UK) Ltd, Croydon, CR0 4YY

To Mary Lou Carney
whose friendship and wisdom
have been a special blessing to me.

Some of the Residents of
Cedar Cove, Washington

Olivia Lockhart Griffin: Family court judge in Cedar Cove. Mother of Justine and James. Married to Jack Griffin. Lives at 16 Lighthouse Road.

Jack Griffin: Newspaper reporter and editor of *The Cedar Cove Chronicle*. Recovering alcoholic. Married to Olivia. Father of Eric, who lives in Nevada with his wife, Shelly, and their twin boys.

Charlotte Jefferson: Mother of Olivia. Now married to widower Ben Rhodes.

Justine (Lockhart) Gunderson: Daughter of Olivia. Married to Seth Gunderson. Mother of Leif. The Gundersons live at 6 Rainier Drive.

Seth Gunderson: Justine's husband. Co-owner, with Justine, of The Lighthouse restaurant.

James Lockhart: Olivia's son and Justine's younger brother. In the navy. Lives in San Diego with wife, Selina, and daughter, Isabella.

Stanley Lockhart: Olivia's ex-husband and father of James and Justine. Now lives in Seattle.

Will Jefferson: Olivia's brother, Charlotte's son. Married and lives in Atlanta.

Grace Sherman: Olivia's best friend. Librarian. Widow of Dan Sherman. Mother of Maryellen Bowman and Kelly Jordan. Involved in an on-again, off-again relationship with Cliff Harding. Lives at 204 Rosewood Lane.

Cliff Harding: Retired engineer and now horse breeder living near Cedar Cove. Divorced father of Lisa, who lives in Maryland.

Cal Washburn: Horse trainer, employed by Cliff Harding.

Maryellen Bowman: Oldest daughter of Grace and Dan Sherman. Mother of Katie. Married to Jon Bowman.

Jon Bowman: Photographer, married to Maryellen. Father of Katie.

Zachary Cox: Accountant, married to Rosie. Father of Allison and Eddie Cox, aged seventeen and eleven. Lives at 311 Pelican Court.

Anson Butler: Boyfriend of Allison Cox.

Cecilia Randall: Navy wife, living in Cedar Cove. Accountant, working for Zach Cox. Married to Ian Randall, submariner. Lost a baby (Allison). Is now pregnant.

Rachel Pendergast: Works at the Get Nailed salon. Friends with Bruce Peyton and his daughter, Jolene. Romantically involved with sailor Nate Olsen.

Bob and Peggy Beldon: Retired. Own the Thyme and Tide Bed & Breakfast at 44 Cranberry Point.

Roy McAfee: Private investigator, retired from Seattle police force. Two adult children, Mack and Lynnette. Married to Corrie.

Corrie McAfee: Roy's wife and office manager. The McAfees live at 50 Harbor Street.

Lynnette McAfee: Daughter of Roy and Corrie. Moves to Cedar Cove to work as a nurse practitioner in the new medical clinic.

Gloria Ashton: Police officer for Bremerton force. Lynnette's friend and neighbour.

Troy Davis: Cedar Cove sheriff.

Pastor Flemming: Local Methodist minister.

One

Corrie McAfee was worried. And she knew that her husband, Roy, was too.

Who wouldn't be? Starting in July, Roy—a private investigator—had received a series of anonymous postcards, and while the messages weren't overtly threatening, they were certainly distressing.

The first communication, which had been mailed to the office, spoke of regrets. During the intervening weeks, there'd been several others. Corrie had read each postcard so often she'd memorized them all. The first one stated: EVERYONE HAS REGRETS. IS THERE ANYTHING YOU'VE DONE YOU WISH YOU COULD DO OVER? THINK ABOUT IT. There hadn't been a signature then, or on any of the other cards. They'd arrived at infrequent intervals and been mailed from different locations. The cryptic messages kept playing in her mind. The passing of time hadn't helped; she was as much in the dark now, in October, as when she'd seen that first postcard.

There was a final gasping, gurgling sound as the coffee drained into the glass pot. The noise distracted Corrie from her worries for a moment—long enough to glance out the wide office window that overlooked downtown Cedar Cove, Washington. Serving as Roy's secretary and assistant had its advantages, and in this instance, disadvantages. Sometimes ignorance truly was bliss; the current situation was definitely one of those cases. She'd sleep better if she'd never learned about the mysterious postcards.

And yet…even if Roy had managed to keep them hidden from her, she would still have known—because the last message had been hand-delivered, at night, to their front door. Not to the office like the others, but to their home. Late one evening, someone had walked up the sidewalk and onto the porch of their house. As it happened, Roy and Corrie were entertaining dinner guests that night—and had opened the door to discover that an unknown person had left a fruit basket and an accompanying note. Chills raced up Corrie's spine at the thought that this person knew their home address.

"Is that coffee ready yet?" Roy called from inside his office. Apparently she hadn't delivered it fast enough.

"Hold your horses—it's coming." Corrie didn't mean to snap at her husband. Normally she wasn't short-tempered. This uncharacteristic outburst revealed how upset she was by everything that was happening to them. Sighing, she filled a clean mug for Roy and carried it, steam rising, into his office.

"Okay, that does it," she said, putting the coffee on the corner of his desk. "We have to talk."

As if he didn't have a care in the world, Roy leaned back in his chair and locked his fingers behind his head. They'd been married for twenty-seven years, and Corrie found him as attractive now as she had in college. Roy had played football for the University of Washington and been a "big man on campus," as they used to say. He was tall and broad-shouldered, still muscular, his posture as straight as ever. He stayed in good shape without apparent effort, and Corrie envied, just a bit, the fact that he'd never gained any weight. His dark hair had thinned and was streaked with gray, which only added a look of dignity to his appearance.

Of all the women he dated during college, he'd fallen in love with *her.* Theirs hadn't been an easy courtship, though. They'd broken up for more than a year, and then reunited. Once they were back together, they realized how much they loved each other; there'd been no uncertainty about their feelings. They were married shortly after graduation and their love had endured through trials and tribulations, through good years and bad. They'd had plenty of both.

"Talk about what?" Roy asked casually.

His nonchalance didn't fool Corrie. Her husband knew exactly what was on her mind. "Does THE PAST HAS A WAY OF CATCHING UP WITH THE PRESENT tell you anything?" she murmured, sitting down in the chair normally reserved for clients. She wanted Roy to understand that she wouldn't be put off easily. She was afraid he knew more about these postcards than he'd let on. It would be just like him to try to protect her.

Roy frowned. "Those messages don't have anything to do with you, so don't worry about it."

His answer infuriated her. "How can you say that? Everything that happens to you affects me."

He seemed about to argue, but after all these years, he recognized that she wasn't going to be satisfied with glib reassurances. "I'm not sure what to tell you. I've made enemies and, yes, I have regrets, but who doesn't?"

Roy had reached the rank of detective for the Seattle Police Department and been forced into early retirement because of a back injury. In the beginning, Corrie had been excited to have her husband at home. She'd hoped they'd be able to travel and do some of the things they'd always planned, but it hadn't worked out that way. Roy had the time now, but their finances had been adversely affected when he'd had to take early retirement. Their income was less than it had been by at least twenty percent. In a money-saving effort, they'd moved from Seattle and across Puget Sound to the community of Cedar Cove. The cost of property was much more reasonable in Kitsap County, which also offered a slower pace of life. When the real estate agent showed them the house at 50 Harbor Street, with its wide front porch and sweeping view of the cove and lighthouse, Corrie knew immediately that this house and this town would become their home.

They'd moved from the big city, and it hadn't been as much of an adjustment as Corrie had feared. Folks in town were pleasant, and Roy and Corrie had made a few good friends—notably the Beldons—but kept mostly to themselves. They knew their neighbors' names and exchanged greetings, but that was about it.

To Corrie's disappointment, Roy had grown restless with retirement. His moods had reflected his boredom, and he was frequently cantankerous. Everything changed when he decided to rent office space and hang out his shingle as a private investigator. It was a decision Corrie had encouraged. Soon her husband was busy and looking forward to each day. He took on the cases that suited him and turned down those that didn't. Corrie was proud of Roy's skills, proud of his success and the way he cared about his clients. Never did it occur to her, or apparently to Roy, that one day he'd be solving his own mystery.

"You could be in danger," Corrie murmured, letting her anxiety show. She refused to hide her feelings, refused to pretend all was well when it wasn't.

Roy shrugged. "I doubt I'm in jeopardy. If anyone wanted to do me harm, they would've done so before now."

"How can you say that?" she asked irritably. "Bob was followed, and we both know it wasn't Bob they were interested in. He was driving your car. They thought they were following *you.*"

Bob Beldon, together with his wife, Peggy, was the owner of the local Bed-and-Breakfast, Thyme and Tide. Bob had borrowed Roy's car and phoned in a near panic, sure he was being followed. Roy had advised him to drive immediately to the sheriff's office. As soon as Bob had pulled in to the station, the tail had left him. Only later did Roy and Corrie figure it out. Whoever had shadowed Bob had assumed it was Roy driving.

"The letter said we're in no danger," her husband reminded her.

"Of course! That's what they *want* us to think," Corrie argued. "Whoever's doing this wants us to lower our guard."

"Now, Corrie—"

She cut him off, rejecting any further attempts to pacify her. "That basket was delivered to our front porch. This… stranger walked right up to our home and left it, and now you're telling me we have nothing to worry about?" Her voice quavered, and she realized how close she was to losing control of her emotions. She was tired of being afraid, tired of waiting for the next message—or worse. Tired of waking up with her eyes burning from lack of sleep. Her first conscious thought every morning was fear of what might happen that day.

"The basket came over a week ago, and we've heard nothing since." Roy said this as if this was supposed to comfort her. It didn't.

"There was no postcard in the mail today, was there?"

he asked, and she heard an unmistakable hint of tension in his voice.

"No." Corrie had collected the mail, flipped through it and tossed the bundle of bills and circulars on her desk.

Roy nodded, as if to say *Well, then?*

"Roy," she said with deceptive calm, "I can't remember the last time I slept a night straight through. You're not sleeping well, either."

He didn't agree or disagree.

"We can't go on pretending everything's all right."

Roy's handsome features tightened. "I'm doing everything I can," he told her curtly.

"I know, but it isn't enough."

"It has to be."

Corrie wasn't an expert in the area of investigations, but she knew when it was time to seek help, and they were well past that point. "You need to talk to somebody."

"Who?" he asked.

The only person she could suggest was the local sheriff. "Troy Davis…"

"Not a good idea," Roy said. "Whatever this is about happened long before we moved to Cedar Cove."

"How can you be so sure?"

"Regrets. Every postcard mentions regrets. There isn't a cop who *doesn't* have regrets—about things we've done or haven't done or should've done differently."

She thought—but didn't say—that every human being had regrets. It wasn't restricted to cops.

"The last message said I JUST WANT YOU TO THINK ABOUT WHAT YOU DID. DON'T YOU HAVE A SINGLE REGRET? To me, that implies I did something—arrested someone, testified against someone—when I was a detective for Seattle."

Her voice fell to a whisper. "You were on the force a lot of years. Surely there's a case or two that stands out in your mind."

Roy shook his head. "Do you think I haven't thought about that? You've seen me read through my files and notes, going all the way back to my first year on the force, and there's nothing."

"I don't know... You haven't talked to me. You block me out."

"I'm protecting you."

"Don't!" she cried with barely controlled anger. "I *need* to know—I have to know. Don't you see what this is doing to me?"

Roy leaned forward then, bracing his elbows against the desk. "I'm sorry," he whispered. "I've wracked my brain and I can't think of anyone who'd come after me like this."

"But there must be some case... One you might've forgotten."

Obviously at a loss, Roy shook his head again. "Clearly I have. I've put murderers away and received my share of threats over the years, but I can't think of anyone who'd do this. Yet who else could it be?" he said, almost to himself.

"What do you mean?" She was more in control now. Clutching a wadded tissue in her hand, she inhaled a calming breath.

"The type of people I dealt with weren't subtle. If they wanted revenge, they wouldn't bother with postcards."

"A relative of some criminal you sent to jail? Or...a victim?" That was a possibility she'd entertained more than once.

He raised his shoulders in a slight shrug. "Could be."

"What are we supposed to do now?" It was this constantly being on guard, not knowing what to expect, that had driven Corrie to such an emotional extreme.

"We do nothing."

"Nothing?" This wasn't what she wanted to hear. "How can we?"

"We have to, for now, until they make a mistake. That'll happen, sweetheart, I promise you, and once it does, this nightmare will be over."

"You promise?" she repeated.

Roy's expression softened and he nodded. Offering her further reassurance, he extended his arm across the desk. Corrie reached for his hand and laced her fingers through his. Her husband gazed deep into her eyes. She felt his love, his comfort, and for now it was enough. For today, for this morning at least, she would be fine. Her problem, Corrie decided, was that she was just so tired. Everything would seem less frightening if she could get even one decent night's sleep.

The front door to the office opened, and Roy abruptly released her and stood. From his years of police work he was always on the alert, never more so than now.

"Mom, Dad?" Their daughter's voice rang from the outer office where Corrie's desk was situated.

"Linnette," Corrie cried eagerly, although her enthusiasm might have seemed a little strained. "We're in here."

Their daughter came into the room, then paused, an uncertain expression on her face. She was petite like Corrie, with dark hair and eyes. Also like Corrie, Linnette had excelled in school, and because she was the daughter of a policeman, she'd always been sheltered. Her studies had kept her from pursuing much of a social life, but Corrie hoped that would change now. Linnette had never had a serious boyfriend.

"I'm not interrupting anything, am I?" Linnette glanced suspiciously from Corrie to Roy and back again. "Is everything all right?"

"It's fine," Corrie assured her in a rush. "Why shouldn't it be?"

Their daughter was far too intuitive to be easily fooled, but thankfully she let it pass. "I've found an apartment," Linnette announced and did a small jig around the office.

"Where?" Corrie asked, hoping it was in town. Linnette had been hired by the new Cedar Cove Medical Clinic as a physician assistant, and Corrie was thrilled to have her closer.

"It's on the cove, just down from the Waterfront Park," Linnette explained. "The complex next to the Holiday Inn Express."

Corrie knew the apartment building, since she passed it nearly every day when she went for her afternoon walk. The building was close to the marina and a short distance from the library. The two-story complex had a fabulous water view of the cove and lighthouse, with the Bremerton shipyard in the distance. As far as Corrie was concerned, this was perfect.

"I hope they aren't charging you an arm and a leg," Roy cautioned, but Corrie could tell he was pleased.

"The rent, compared to what I was paying in Seattle, is a bargain."

"Good."

Roy was still protective of his little girl. Unfortunately, he had a difficult time expressing his feelings for his children—especially their son. Mack and his father were constantly at odds. In Corrie's opinion, they were too much alike. Mack seemed to know exactly what to say to irritate Roy. And Roy wasn't blameless, either; he seemed to go out of his way to find fault with their son. Because of the tension between them, they generally avoided each other. Corrie didn't like it. Most of the time, she felt trapped in the middle. Thankfully that wasn't the case with Linnette, who was two years older than her brother.

Linnette was talking about the apartment and the move-in date and her job at the clinic. Corrie nodded at the appropriate moments but only listened with half an ear. Roy returned to his work while Corrie walked back to her desk, Linnette following her.

"Mom," Linnette said as soon as they were in the other room. She lowered her voice, and her face was thoughtful. Concerned. "Are you *sure* everything's all right between you and Dad?"

"Of course! What makes you ask?"

Her daughter hesitated. "Just now, when I came into the office, it looked like you were ready to cry, and Dad... he—his eyes were so...hard. I've never seen him that intense. I didn't know what to think."

"You're imagining things," Corrie insisted.

"No, I'm not."

"It's nothing. We'll talk about it later." Her daughter could be obstinate, definitely a trait she'd inherited from Roy. The last person Corrie intended to share her worries with was Linnette. Eventually, perhaps, once this was all settled, they could laugh about it over lunch. But for now, these postcards were no laughing matter.

"You dropped a piece of mail," Linnette said, gesturing toward the desk.

Corrie froze. "I did?"

"Yes, there was a postcard on the floor when I came in. I put it on your desk."

Roy must have heard because he came out of the other office. His eyes met Corrie's. "Give it to me," he instructed.

A small protest rose from her throat as she walked over to retrieve the card. Carefully she turned it over and read the message before handing it to Roy.

It said in large block letters: ARE YOU THINKING YET?

"Mom," Linnette demanded. "You'd better tell me what's going on."

Two

Charlotte Jefferson Rhodes worked cheerfully in her kitchen, baking a large batch of cinnamon rolls, Ben's favorite. After nearly sixty years as Charlotte Jefferson, she had to think twice to remember that she and Ben were actually married. A woman her age didn't expect to find love this late in life. Like so much else in the past few years, romance had come as a very nice surprise.

"It sure smells good in there," Ben called out from the living room where he sat, feet propped up on the ottoman. The Bremerton morning newspaper was folded over as he completed the *New York Times* crossword puzzle. Charlotte was impressed by his skill with words and his wide general knowledge. She also liked his lack of arrogance—he used a pencil to fill it in.

"The first batch will be out of the oven soon," she promised. She enjoyed baking, especially when there was someone who appreciated her homemade treats. Ben certainly did, but he preferred his cinnamon rolls without raisins. She liked the raisins and Jack, her rascal of a son-in-law, did too. The solution was easy enough; she simply split the batch in half.

Her husband of little more than a month was a handsome man, a Cesar Romero lookalike and a few years younger than Charlotte. Their age difference of four years didn't bother him and it didn't bother her, either. Charlotte was a young seventy-seven. While still in her teens, she'd married Clyde Jefferson; that was toward the end of the Second World War. Women married much younger back in those days, she reflected. Together Clyde and Charlotte had raised their children in Cedar Cove. Olivia, her daughter, was a family court judge and still lived here. Her son, Will, had moved to Atlanta.

Cedar Cove, where she'd lived for most of her life, was situated on the Kitsap Peninsula across Puget Sound from Seattle, and it was a thriving community. With a population of little over seven thousand, the town was small enough to be friendly, but large enough to have its own medical facility.

The new Cedar Cove Medical Clinic was due to officially open in the middle of November. Charlotte beamed with pride, knowing that without her and Ben and her friends from the Senior Center, there wouldn't be a clinic.

Even Olivia, her own daughter, hadn't seen the need for one, since the hospital in Bremerton was less than half an hour away, and there were good doctors in town. All of that was true, but Charlotte felt Cedar Cove should have a more complete medical facility, where emergencies could be handled. Half an hour was a long time to wait if you were having a heart attack! It could make the difference between life and death. Ben had felt the same way, and the cause had bonded them, especially when they were arrested for their peaceful demonstration. That rankled even now, but nearly the entire town had showed up to support her, Ben and their comrades in court. Just remembering how her friends had gathered around them was enough to make Charlotte's eyes fill with tears.

But, she reminded herself, that was neither here nor there; the clinic had been built and the staff hired, including the McAfees' daughter, Linnette, a physician assistant.

The phone rang, and Charlotte glanced at the kitchen clock, slightly annoyed that anyone would be phoning so early on a Saturday morning. To her astonishment, it was nearly ten.

"I'll get it." As she reached for the telephone, she noticed that Harry, her black cat, was curled up in Ben's lap. Now this was progress. Harry was Charlotte's protector and he wasn't fond of visitors. It had taken him half of this first month to get accustomed to Ben's presence and that long again to have anything to do with him.

"Good morning," she said cheerfully into the receiver. Clyde used to say that Charlotte was born in a good mood. She had a natural inclination toward happiness; while some looked at the world as a place of gloom and sadness, she saw the positive things in life, even though she, too, had experienced great sorrows.

"Is my father there?" a rather pleasant male voice asked. Then, as if to clarify the point, he added, "Ben Rhodes."

"Yes, of course. Is this Stephen?"

Her question was followed by an awkward laugh. "No, it's David. I'm calling from California."

"Hello, David," Charlotte said warmly. "I'm so sorry you weren't able to make it to our wedding. You were missed."

Ben's youngest son seemed taken aback by her friendliness. "I wish I could've been there, but I'm sure Dad explained that I got tied up with a work situation."

Ben hadn't said anything about either son's absence, and Charlotte hadn't pressured him with questions. She wasn't sure what kind of relationship Ben had with his children. He rarely mentioned them and avoided the topic whenever she brought it up. And yet this young man seemed so likable and polite.

"I can't tell you how much I'm looking forward to meeting you, David."

"I'm eager to meet you, too, Charlotte. My father's a sly old fox. First he moves to Cedar Cove, when he could just as well have moved closer to either Stephen or me, and then he marries again. I don't mind telling you that was a real surprise for the family. A most delightful surprise, of course."

"I was thrilled when your father came into my life," Charlotte said, charmed by David Rhodes. When neither David nor Stephen made it to the wedding, she feared there must be some problem between Ben and his sons—a fear reinforced by Ben's apparent unwillingness to talk about them. Maybe there was no problem, after all. David certainly appeared to be an agreeable young man.

"Is my father there?" he asked again.

"Yes, of course. I'm sorry, but I do tend to chatter. I'll get him right away." Charlotte set down the phone and discovered that Ben was watching her. "It's your son. David."

Ben carefully dislodged Harry, laid down the newspaper and stood. "Did he say what he wanted?"

Ben's frown confused her. David had been gracious and warm in his manner and given no hint of any tension in the family.

Returning to the kitchen, Charlotte couldn't help overhearing Ben once he'd picked up the phone. She didn't mean to pry, but she did admit to being curious.

"Hello, David," Ben said coolly.

It sounded as if Ben and his son *were* estranged, and that saddened her. She wondered what had happened. A misunderstanding? A long-held grudge? Or simply years of insufficient contact? And why wouldn't Ben tell her? After his less-than-enthusiastic greeting, he was silent for some time. Unfortunately Charlotte was privy to only one side of the conversation.

"I believe we've already gone over this a number of times. The answer is no, so please don't ask again."

Ben's words were followed by another lengthy pause.

Charlotte joined Ben and slipped her arm around him, offering her love and support. Her husband should be grateful David had phoned and that he and Charlotte had now had a chance to meet, even if it was only by phone. The last people Charlotte had expected to disapprove of their marriage had been their children. In fact, Olivia's objection to her remarriage had caused the first major rift in their relationship. Olivia's lack of faith had hurt Charlotte deeply. Ben's son, however, didn't seem to have any opposition to her marrying his father.

"I'll check," Ben said. He held the receiver against his shoulder. "David will be in Seattle on business early next month and he wants to know if we can join him for dinner."

Charlotte smiled. "Tell him I'd love to."

Ben frowned again, as if he wasn't sure what to say as he brought the receiver back to his ear. "It appears we can make it," he said in lackluster tones.

Charlotte resisted the urge to poke him in the ribs with her elbow. This was no way to act! Despite their apparent falling out, David was making an effort; the least Ben could do was meet him halfway.

Ben reached for the pencil dangling from a string by the calendar and wrote down the date and time. "We'll walk onto the Bremerton ferry," he told his son, "and take a taxi to the restaurant. We'll meet you there at seven." With no further conversation, Ben replaced the receiver.

He turned back to her. "As you might've guessed, my son and I have had our share of differences."

"He seems like such a nice young man."

"He can be," Ben murmured, his face impassive, difficult to read. "Especially when he wants something."

"Oh." Perhaps David had more than one reason for getting in touch with his father. "Did you find out what he wants, then?" she asked tentatively. She wouldn't ask too insistently. But Ben was closing himself off from her and Charlotte found that troublesome.

Ben shook his head. "I generally don't ask David a lot of questions," he said. "I didn't question him when he left his wife of one year for his secretary—and abandoned his infant daughter. That second marriage didn't last long, either." He paused. "Frankly, David is a disappointment to me."

"I'm so sorry."

She didn't say it, but her own son was a disappointment to her, too. Olivia had never said a word, nor had Olivia's best friend, Grace Sherman. But Charlotte had caught wind of what Will had done from something Justine, her granddaughter, had mentioned. It had been a casual, offhand remark about how Grace was trying to patch up her romance with Cliff after her Internet relationship with Will. Apparently this wasn't the first time, either—at least for Will. Georgia, his wife, had hinted that Will had a problem with fidelity. Charlotte didn't know whether he'd had actual affairs or they were all e-mail relationships. She had no idea what had happened in her son's life to explain his behavior. Clyde would roll over in his grave if he learned of the careless way their son was treating his marriage vows.

"I wish now I'd said we couldn't make it," Ben muttered.

"But we can. I want to meet your son."

"He's a self-centered young man. Well, not that young anymore. He's over forty now. I suppose I'm to blame for his selfishness. Joan spoiled them both while they were growing up. I was so preoccupied with my Navy career and gone so much of the time that I didn't realize until it was too late. Unfortunately both my sons lack discipline and self-control. When I recognized what they'd become, they were already adults."

"I'm sure we'll have a perfectly lovely dinner," she said in a soothing voice.

"I'm not," Ben countered sadly. "But we've made the commitment, so we'll do as David wishes and go into Seattle. I want you to meet my children, but it's important that you know in advance the kind of men they are."

"My children have disappointed me at times, too," Charlotte confessed. She'd been mortified to learn that at one point her own daughter had hired Roy McAfee to investigate Ben's background.

Ben stared blankly out the window. When he spoke, his voice was low and thoughtful. "Sometimes I feel as if my sons begrudge me any happiness. I think they believe I'd be more use to them dead." At Charlotte's gasp, he added, "If I know David, and I do, he's counting on his inheritance to get him out of another financial mess."

"But Ben, you should've told him…" Before their marriage, Ben and Charlotte had adjusted their wills. They'd left the majority of their estates to each other. Ben had left one-third of the remainder to each of his sons, and the last third to charity.

"It's important that we attend this dinner with a positive attitude," Charlotte warned.

"I know." Ben sighed heavily and then hugged her.

"Everything will work out just fine," she whispered. She had a good feeling about meeting David. She wanted to be a peacemaker in the family, to bring Ben and his sons together, and hoped that David would eventually grow to love her.

The timer on the oven buzzed and Ben lifted his head. "Does that mean what I think it does?" he asked.

"As soon as these cinnamon buns cool down, I'll frost them and give you a small sample."

"A *small* sample?" he protested.

Charlotte raised her eyebrows. "I don't want you to ruin your lunch."

"I won't," he promised. Ben sounded like a youngster, pleading with her.

"Sometimes I think you married me because of my baking," Charlotte said, smiling to show she didn't mean it.

The laughter fled from his eyes as he gazed down at her. "Then you'd be wrong, Charlotte. I married you because I've never loved a woman as much as I love you."

Three

Cecilia Randall arrived at Smith, Cox and Jefferson Accounting ten minutes early on Monday morning. She was just as glad to get to work. Being home by herself, without her husband, was lonely, despite her friends. The weekends were the worst, especially now that she was pregnant. Ian, her Navy husband, was out to sea on the aircraft carrier *USS George Washington*. Despite her reassurances, Ian worried about her—with reason, as he pointed out. Everything in their current situation was exactly the same as it had been with Allison, their first child. And Allison had been born with a defective heart.

Ian hadn't been with Cecilia when Allison was born. Nor had he been there when Cecilia buried their infant daughter. Standing alone at the tiny gravesite had nearly destroyed her and subsequently their marriage. If not for the wisdom of a family court judge who'd denied their divorce on a technicality, they wouldn't be together now.

Pressing her hand against her stomach, Cecilia sent her unborn daughter thoughts of love and reassurance. It would be different this time, with this baby. But everything had seemed normal with Allison, too. Cecilia quickly flung aside the doubts that pummeled her. Ian had enough of those for both of them.

Cecilia was five months along now and happier than she could remember being in a long time. She desperately wanted this baby. If it had been up to Ian, they wouldn't ever have children again. He was afraid. Cecilia was, too, but her desire for a family had prevailed over her fears.

"Morning," Zachary Cox, her boss, said absently. He sorted through his mail as he walked past her desk, which was located outside his office.

"Morning," she returned.

"Allison will be in this afternoon," he said, looking up from the mail long enough to catch Cecilia's eye. "She's trying to earn money for a car. Her mother and I told her we'd match whatever she managed to save. I'm hoping there's enough to do around here to keep her occupied for the next few months."

Cecilia nodded, excited about seeing Mr. Cox's teenage daughter again. Cecilia had been hired while Mr. and Mrs. Cox were going through a divorce. The same judge who'd denied her and Ian's divorce had made the joint custody decision in their case. Judge Olivia Lockhart had stated that the children and not the adults were the ones who needed a stable life. Instead of shuffling between residences, the kids, Allison and Eddie, were to remain in the family home and the Coxes would alternate, moving in and out every few days. It had worked well—better than expected—and before long Zach and Rosie Cox were back together.

Soon after Cecilia had begun working for Mr. Cox, he'd started bringing in his troubled teenage daughter. The after-school job was an effort to keep an eye on the rebellious fifteen-year-old and to limit her exposure to a group of out-of-control friends she'd recently taken up with. Despite all that, Cecilia was almost immediately drawn to her. The fact that Allison shared the same name as her own daughter had cemented their bond.

They'd quickly become friends and Allison often confided in her or asked for advice. Cecilia had watched her blossom from an irrational, angry girl into a lovely young woman of seventeen. The contrast between then and now was striking. Cecilia sometimes fantasized that this was how her own daughter would've looked and acted at this age had she lived.

"I'll be happy to keep her busy," Cecilia assured her boss. There were always a number of small tasks she didn't get to by the end of the day, and this would help her catch up before she took her maternity leave.

"Great." Mr. Cox entered his office, still perusing his mail. "Thanks, Cecilia."

Cecilia was busy all morning with only a short break—a telephone conversation with her best friend, Cathy Lackey, whose husband was aboard the *George Washington* with Ian. The two of them had formed their own support group and relied on each other when their husbands were out at sea. Rarely a day passed that they weren't in touch with each other.

At three that afternoon, Allison Cox showed up at the office, just missing her father, who'd left to meet with a client. Allison was willowy and classic-featured, a lovely girl. She wore her dark-brown hair long, all the way to the middle of her back. As she removed her gray wool coat, Cecilia saw that she'd dressed for the office in a green plaid skirt and white turtleneck sweater. When Cecilia had first met her, Allison's favorite color was black. The girl had rebelled against the destruction of her family and lashed out at those around her. Cecilia liked to think that their friendship had helped Allison. In reality, she supposed, it was her parents' reconciliation that had changed the girl's outlook on life. Still Cecilia liked to think she'd been a good influence, and Mr. Cox had frequently made a point of telling her she had.

That was two years ago, and Allison was now a high school senior.

"It's so good to see you," Allison said, hugging Cecilia, although it'd been less than a month since they'd spent time together. "How's our baby doing?"

Cecilia pressed her hand to her stomach. "She's kicking. Want to feel?"

Allison's eyes widened. "Sure."

Cecilia held the girl's hand over her stomach and watched as Allison stared intently, bit her lower lip and then after a long moment, dejectedly shook her head. "I don't feel anything."

"It might be a little early yet," Cecilia murmured, trying to remember how far along she'd been with the last pregnancy before Ian could feel their daughter's movements.

Disappointed, Allison dropped her hand. "Well, I guess I'd better get to work."

Cecilia set her up at a vacant desk across from her own. During tax season, when the accounting firm hired extra help, every square inch of space was used by temporary employees. It got fairly chaotic from January through April of every year.

Allison had been working for an hour when Mary Lou, who staffed the front desk, hurried into their work area. "There's a young man asking to see you," Mary Lou said to Allison. She cast a doubtful look at Cecilia as if to say she wasn't sure she'd done the right thing.

"Did he give you his name?" Allison asked.

"No, but he said you'd know who he is."

"What's he wearing?"

Mary Lou edged closer and lowered her voice. "He has a goatee and has on a long black coat that's got chains attached. He's wearing a big cross, too. I don't mind telling you, he looks a bit scary."

"That's Anson." Allison stood and went out to the front. She was gone for ten minutes and was clearly pleased—no, downright jubilant—when she returned.

Cecilia was more than a little curious. "What was that about?" she asked. Without being obvious, she'd managed to get a glimpse of this Anson character through one of the office windows. Cecilia understood Mary Lou's concerns. The boy's hair was long, greasy and dark. His overcoat fanned out from his sides, as though he had weapons concealed beneath it. Presumably he didn't, but still… He wasn't the type of boy Cecilia expected Allison to be interested in.

"I barely know him," Allison claimed. "He's in my French class and he sits beside me. We've talked a couple of times and that's about it."

"How did he know you were here?"

Allison shrugged. "One of my friends must've told him."

"Did he say what he wanted?"

"Not really. He asked about our French assignment." She grinned shyly and glanced down at the floor. "That was just an excuse, though, 'cause then he asked what I was doing tonight."

Cecilia nodded, a little worried about the girl's attraction to this self-styled rebel.

"He lives with his mother," Allison added.

"Oh."

"I don't think they get along very well," she said thoughtfully.

Cecilia didn't know what to say. "Would you go out with him if he asked?" she murmured. Whether Allison admitted it or not, she was attracted to the boy. Everything about her said so.

"I...I don't know, but it's irrelevant. Anson hasn't asked and I doubt that he will. Guys like Anson don't *go* out. They hang out."

It was obvious that Mr. Cox hadn't met the young man, and Cecilia could only imagine how he'd react if he found his daughter with Anson.

"Be careful," Cecilia warned softly.

"Why?"

"Bad boys can be attractive, which translates into *dangerous.*"

Allison smiled. "Don't worry. Like I said, we hardly know each other."

Cecilia didn't mean to doubt her, but there was trouble coming; she could feel it. Cecilia just hoped Allison knew what she was doing.

She didn't have time to think about Allison after she left work because she was meeting Cathy and her three-year-old son, Andy. Cecilia drove straight to her friend's house without stopping at home. The two of them were putting together Christmas packages to mail off to Ian and Cathy's husband, Andrew. Cecilia had already filled the trunk of her car with Ian's gifts. She looked forward to the evening and to the take-out Chinese dinner she and Cathy planned to order.

"Did you get an e-mail from Ian this morning?" Cathy asked.

Cecilia shook her head. "Maybe there'll be one at home." Ian never talked about what he did for the Navy. His job had something to do with guided missile systems and involved computers and other advanced technology. Ian couldn't discuss the details of his Navy life for reasons of national security, and Cecilia accepted that. She didn't care what the United

States Navy had him do, as long as her husband arrived home safe and sound. Currently the *George Washington* was somewhere in the Persian Gulf, but exactly where was a mystery.

Ian e-mailed her at least once a day. He didn't have time to send long messages, but even a short note raised Cecilia's spirits. He insisted that he needed to hear from her, too, and just as often.

Because Cathy was a stay-at-home mom, she'd picked up the necessary mailing supplies. While Andy sat on the floor and played with puzzles, the two women packaged their various gifts.

"You won't believe what's in here," Cathy said, holding up a small jewelry-sized box.

"You're sending Andrew a ring?" Cecilia asked, puzzled.

"No, it's a sheer black nightgown—with the promise that I'll wear it for him when he gets home."

Cecilia giggled. "That's cruel and unusual punishment," she said, remembering that she herself had done something similar once…

Cathy laughed, too. "I doubt Andrew will think of it that way. I'm ready for a second child. As far as I'm concerned, little Andy needs a baby sister."

Cecilia managed to smile but quickly looked away and resumed her wrapping. Her life would be so different if Allison had lived. There were no guarantees that the heart ailment that had killed their daughter wouldn't afflict this second baby. Cecilia prayed with everything in her that the child she carried now would be healthy.

Four

Maryellen Bowman arrived home from her job at the Harbor Street Art Gallery and smiled when Jon stepped outside to greet her. She felt a sense of deep contentment at the sight of her husband. From her car seat behind Maryellen, two-year-old Katie let out a squeal of delight the instant she saw her father. She started kicking and swinging her arms, eager to escape the confines of the protective seat.

"I know, honey, I know." Maryellen laughed. "I'm happy to see your daddy, too."

By the time Maryellen had parked, Jon was waiting by the car. He opened the back door and freed Katie, who immediately squirmed and wanted down. Now that she was walking, she was impossible to restrain. Still holding Katie, Jon walked around the front of the car to hug Maryellen.

"Welcome home," he said and kissed her hungrily. He wove his free hand into her dark hair and brought his mouth to hers.

Between them, their daughter chattered insistently, seeking attention. Katie didn't take kindly to being ignored. Maryellen, however, barely noticed her objections.

"You make it worth coming home," she whispered, sighing with her eyes closed. Her husband could win a kissing contest—not that she'd let him enter even if there was such an event.

His arm around her waist, Jon led her into the home he'd built with his own two hands. The property, with its view of the Seattle skyline across Puget Sound, had been an inheritance from his grandfather, and Jon had devoted countless hours to landscaping the grounds. The house was everything Maryellen could possibly want. It had spacious rooms, high ceilings, fireplaces and balconies, and a wide oak staircase to the second floor. A sweeping panorama of the water and the city lights beyond was available from every room. Her artist husband had designed and then painstakingly built the place, at the same time he was making his mark as a professional photographer. Maryellen loved her husband heart and soul, reveling in his many talents.

"I've got dinner started," Jon told her as she stepped inside the house and was met by the scent of roasting chicken. On top of everything else, Jon was a gifted chef. Maryellen had to pinch herself every day, marveling that she was loved by such an extraordinary man.

"How was your day?" he asked, as Maryellen hung up her coat and tended to Katie.

"Busy."

"I'd rather you were home with me."

"I know—I'd like to be here, too." The money Jon earned from his photographs was impressive but not yet sufficient for all their financial needs. Then there was the question of medical insurance, which was currently provided through her employer. They'd already made one giant leap of faith when Jon left his job as chef for The Lighthouse restaurant earlier in the year. Maryellen had managed the Cedar Cove Art Gallery for the past ten years and the owners had come to rely on her. She hoped to train her assistant, Lois Habbersmith, to assume her role, but, so far, that hadn't worked out as well as she'd hoped. Lois was a good employee but she didn't want the responsibility of being manager. Only after several months had she finally admitted that to Maryellen.

"I'm planning to leave by the end of next year," Maryellen said as she reached for the mail, which Jon had placed on the kitchen counter.

"Next *year?*" Jon yelped.

"I know, I'm disappointed, too, but the time will go fast. It's already autumn." Her fingers stilled as she came across the envelope addressed to Mr. and Mrs. Jon Bowman. One glance at the return address told her the letter was from Jon's father and stepmother in Oregon. It remained unopened.

When Maryellen looked up, she found her husband watching her, almost as if he'd anticipated her reaction. "It's from your family," she said unnecessarily.

"I know."

"You didn't open it." This, too, was obvious.

"No," he said, his voice devoid of emotion. "And I won't. If it'd been strictly up to me I would've tossed it in the garbage. But your name's on it, too." Anger burned in his eyes. Years earlier, his parents had betrayed Jon and lied in order to save their younger son, Jon's half brother, from a prison sentence. In saving Jim, they'd sacrificed Jon. While Jon, innocent of all charges, served seven years in prison, his younger brother continued to abuse drugs and eventually died of an overdose.

After he was released from prison, Jon had supported himself by working as a short-order cook. When he wasn't working, he was taking landscape photographs, which began to receive good reviews and significant interest from buyers.

Among other places, his work was displayed in the Harbor Street Art Gallery, where he met Maryellen. Their courtship was long and tempestuous, and only after Katie was born did they marry.

At the time of her daughter's birth, Maryellen was convinced she didn't need or want a husband. She'd married young and unwisely while in college, and it had been a disaster. When she discovered she was pregnant with Katie, she was determined to manage on her own. Other women were single mothers; she could do it, too. She'd quickly learned how wrong she was. Katie wanted her daddy, and Maryellen soon realized she needed Jon in their lives. After their marriage, they were blissfully happy for a short time. Then Maryellen had stumbled upon a stack of unopened letters from Jon's parents.

Although she knew Jon would disapprove, she'd secretly contacted the Bowmans and mailed pictures of Katie. As Katie's grandparents, Maryellen felt they had a right to know about their only grandchild. Her letter, unfortunately, had heightened their efforts to make peace with their son, which had only infuriated him. Jon refused to have anything to do with them. And he saw her actions, in contacting them, as another betrayal. He'd been enraged with her. Her duplicity and his stubborn unwillingness to forgive had almost ruined their marriage.

At the time, Maryellen had just learned she was pregnant. She hadn't told Jon. How could she, when he shut her out—no matter what she said or did? Having failed at one marriage, she believed her actions had killed his love for her and that her second marriage was doomed, too. It was then, at the lowest point of her pain and loss, that she miscarried her baby.

That had been six weeks earlier. Six weeks during which they'd carefully avoided the subject of Jon's parents. Together they grieved over the loss of this pregnancy and clung to each other, but their ability to trust was still shaky.

Maryellen studied the envelope. Jon hadn't immediately thrown the letter away, or hidden it, as he had previous ones. That was progress, she supposed. Over the intervening weeks, they'd had numerous talks on forgiveness, and she felt he was finally willing to listen. This letter would be the proving ground.

"What would you like me to do with it?" she asked.

Jon buried his hands in his pockets and gazed up at the ceiling. "You don't want the answer to that."

"Yes, I do," she told him calmly.

"Burn it."

She'd hoped and prayed that he'd conquered some of his bitterness. "But *you* didn't burn it."

"No," he admitted reluctantly.

Maryellen noticed that he stood about as far away from her as he could and still be heard. "Why not? I need never have known about this letter. Even if my name *is* on it."

He laughed, but it was a defeated sound. "You'd know. I'm incapable of keeping anything from you."

Maryellen moved from behind the kitchen counter and tentatively stepped closer to her husband. "Jon?" she asked again, keeping her voice gentle. "Tell me what I should do with the letter."

"Don't look at me like that," he demanded.

She paused. "Like what?"

"Like I'm such a disappointment to you."

"Never that," she whispered. Maryellen wrapped her arms around his waist and lowered her head to his chest. Words weren't necessary to convey her love and her pride. He was her world, her life, and nothing, not even his relationship with his family, was worth risking the heaven she'd found in him.

It didn't take long for Jon to slide his arms around her. The tightness of his embrace told Maryellen what she already knew—that he didn't want to risk losing her, either. After several moments of holding each other, Jon exhaled a long, deep breath.

"Go ahead and read it. I know that's what you want to do."

"It is," she whispered.

"But don't tell me what it says."

His response bothered her, but she wouldn't rush him. That was the mistake she'd made earlier.

When Katie toddled past on her way to the kitchen, Maryellen left Jon to swoop her daughter into her arms. She set Katie in her high chair and handed her a graham cracker, then reached for the letter.

Jon turned away as if he couldn't bear to see Maryellen tear open the envelope.

The letter was brief. Jon's father had suffered a stroke. Fortunately, he'd received medical attention in time, so there was no permanent damage. Jon's stepmother felt Maryellen would want to know and perhaps she could mention it to Jon.

"It's about your father," she said, laying down the letter.

Jon bristled. "I told you I don't want to hear."

"But he's had a stroke."

"Maryellen, how many times do I have to say it? *I don't care.* He's out of my life. As far as I'm concerned, he's dead. That man gave up the right to be my father the day he lied on the witness stand and sent me to hell for seven years."

Katie set the cracker down in her tray and stared wide-eyed at her father.

"You talk about forgiveness, and that's real easy for you. You weren't the one in that rat hole. You weren't the one who had to endure it." His voice grew harsher with each word until Katie started to cry.

Jon's shoulders slumped forward and he hurried to his daughter, lifting Katie from the high chair and cradling her in his arms. "I'm sorry, sweetheart," he cooed. "Daddy didn't mean to shout."

Dinner was uncomfortable, but Maryellen made an effort and so did Jon. After Katie's bath, Maryellen rocked her and read a bedtime story before settling her in the crib. Once there, Katie put her thumb in her mouth and promptly went to sleep.

Jon had the television on when Maryellen walked down the stairs and joined him. She sat beside her husband on the sofa and rested her head on his shoulder. As if he felt the need to have her close, he draped his arm around her and nuzzled her neck.

Maryellen smiled contentedly. Since the miscarriage, their love life had been on hold while her body healed. Letting him know she wanted him, Maryellen slipped her hand around his neck and turned so their mouths could meet. Jon's hand found its way under her sweater to cup her breast. Her nipples instantly hardened and a sigh rumbled through him.

"Are you sure you're up to this?" he asked, between deep breathless kisses.

"You certainly are."

He smiled at her bad pun even as he kissed her.

Taking him by the hand, Maryellen led her husband up the stairway to their bedroom.

Their lovemaking was fierce, urgent, powerful. While they held each other in the aftermath, Maryellen ran her hand down Jon's back. Nothing was worth disrupting the intimacy and love they shared. She hoped that eventually Jon would be able to reconnect with his parents, but she wouldn't force him into something he wasn't willing to do.

They released each other, and her husband lay beside her, supporting his weight on one elbow as he brushed the hair from her damp face. He kissed her again, his touch tender with his love.

"How bad is he?" he asked, his voice husky in the darkness. He was referring to his father.

The question pleased Maryellen. "There's no permanent damage."

Jon sighed audibly. "Good."

Perhaps he'd come farther than she realized.

Five

Linnette McAfee stood in the middle of her empty apartment, surveying her new home. The view of the cove was spectacular, with the lighthouse far in the distance. The Bremerton shipyard lay directly across the water, its massive ships glowing in the afternoon sunlight, battleship-gray against an azure sky. Living in a small town would be an adjustment, and yet, her parents had made the transition easily enough. Linnette had every reason to believe she would, too.

"Anyone home?" There was a knock at the open door, and her mother stepped inside.

"Hi, Mom!"

"I saw your car parked outside and decided to see if you were here."

"How did you know which apartment was mine?"

Corrie grinned. "I haven't been married to your father all these years without developing a few detective skills of my own." She walked farther into the room. "The door was open and I took a chance."

Linnette spread her arms. "So, what do you think?" she asked, pleased with her new apartment. She'd lived on campus while attending the University of Washington and then later shared an apartment with a friend while she did her advanced studies.

"I think it's great," Corrie said, moving into the kitchen. The area was compact but well-designed and convenient.

"I like that it has two bedrooms," Linnette said, eagerly leading her mother down the hallway to the empty rooms. Both bedrooms were larger than the one she had in Seattle. With this new apartment, Linnette was getting double the space for half the rent. Of course, her salary wasn't nearly as high as what she would've earned had she accepted a job in Seattle. But staying in Seattle had never been her intention. From the moment she'd made the decision to become a physician assistant, Linnette had set her sights on working in a small rural community.

That description didn't exactly fit Cedar Cove, but the town was lovely and it was familiar—and she'd have the advantage of being near her parents. Which was definitely a bonus, since Linnette had always been close to them.

"I was thinking I'd set up this bedroom as an office," Linnette explained as they stood in the doorway of the second and smaller bedroom.

"When are you officially moving?"

"The first of the month. Mack's going to help."

"Your dad will, too," Corrie offered. "And of course I'll be here."

Linnette shook her head. "Dad's not helping, not with his back. Besides, you know as well as I do that it's best to keep Mack as far away from Dad as possible."

Her mother's eyes grew sad. "I don't know what it is with those two."

Linnette rolled her eyes. "I do. They're both stubborn and opinionated and too much alike for their own good."

Corrie agreed. "Mack makes an effort on holidays, but it's hard for him to hold his tongue."

The problem, in Linnette's opinion, was that her father disapproved of Mack. Her brother had dropped out of college and worked as a postal employee, a job he seemed to enjoy. Roy thought that with his brains and background, Mack could do better. His attitude infuriated her brother. Although she kept out of the fray, Linnette sided with Mack. This was his life and he should do as he pleased.

"One of these days," she said briskly, "we should lock them in a closet and force them to settle this, once and for all."

Her mother shook her head. "I absolutely refuse to get involved. I hate being caught in the middle."

Linnette felt the same. She led the way back to the living room, considering where to hang her few pictures and framed posters as she walked. Pride of place would go to a beautiful Jon Bowman photograph her parents had given her for Christmas last year—fir trees on a mountainside. The perspective made it much more than simply a pretty picture. Should she hang it between the two windows or—

"Have you contacted Cal Washburn yet?" her mother asked, interrupting her deliberations.

"Who?"

"The young man I bought for you at the Dog and Bachelor Auction last July. You know, the fund-raiser for the animal shelter."

An immediate protest rose as Linnette struggled to tell her mother that she wasn't interested in a blind date with a stranger. Okay, so her brother loved his dog, who'd come as part of the package. Cal and the Australian Shepherd Mack had named Lucky were on the auction block together. But that didn't mean Linnette was going to hit it off with this bachelor.

"I really think Cal's a fine young man," her mother said.

"Then you date him," Linnette teased, hoping to find a gentle way of getting out of this.

"The least you can do is call him. Let me tell you a bit about Cal. He works for Cliff Harding on his horse ranch. I never quite understood what Cal does, but he appears to be a trainer of some sort. I don't know that much about horses."

"I don't either." The more Linnette heard, the less enthusiastic she became. She was going to spend the evening with a man who hung around horses all day. Great.

Corrie frowned impatiently. "Don't give me that look. You might be pleasantly surprised."

Linnette had been avoiding this conversation. "I did mention that the clinic hired Dr. Chad Timmons, didn't I? We worked together while I was in school and, Mom, he's just *fabulous*."

Her mother made a dismissive gesture with her hand. "What has that got to do with anything?"

"Dr. Timmons is everything I want in a husband. He's smart, witty, drop-dead gorgeous. Plus he's kind and considerate. He's my idea of the perfect man." Linnette figured her chances of snagging him had risen substantially when he was hired to work at the medical center. She'd nearly turned cartwheels down the street in her excitement. Having Chad right there, in Cedar Cove, made her position at the clinic a million times more appealing.

"In other words, you've set your sights on this doctor?"

Linnette grinned sheepishly. "Nothing gets past my mother."

"Very funny. What about Cal Washburn?"

Linnette was putting her foot down. She wasn't moving to this town so her parents could run her life—or her love life. She'd had enough of that while she lived at home. Her father had drilled every date unmercifully. It was a wonder she'd found a boy willing to take her to the Junior-Senior prom.

"Ah…I suppose I could go out with this horse guy once, but that's it, Mom."

"That would please me, considering the amount of cash I paid for your date."

"Okay, okay, I said I'd do it." She'd postponed it as long as she could but, yes, eventually she'd get in touch with him.

"You'll call?" Corrie pressed.

"Can I move into my apartment first?"

"It wouldn't hurt to set the date now." Corrie dug around in her purse and found the envelope with Cal's information, as well as an old receipt. "I gave you his phone number already."

"I lost it," Linnette muttered. She *had* lost it, accidentally on purpose.

"Yeah, right." Corrie was busy scribbling the number on the back of the receipt.

Linnette wanted to grind her teeth in frustration. Her mother wasn't going to let this go. "Think how useful it would be to have a doctor in the family," she said flippantly.

Corrie glared at her and handed over the phone number she'd written down. "Just do it, okay? It's only the one date and it'd mean a lot to me if you followed up on this one small thing."

"Okay, okay," Linnette muttered again, feeling disgruntled about the whole situation. But then—as her mother had said—she might be pleasantly surprised.

"Promise me you'll call him right away."

"Ah…"

"Linnette, how often do I ask anything of you?"

The old guilt trick, and it worked every time. "Okay, I promise I'll arrange to meet this bachelor guy as soon as possible."

"You'll like him, Linnette, only…" Her mother hesitated, biting her lower lip as if she wasn't sure she should continue.

"Only *what?*"

Corrie sighed. "Apparently Cal Washburn has a slight… speech impediment."

Linnette's mouth fell open. If an evening with a guy who smelled like horse manure wasn't bad enough, she might not be able to understand a word he said. This was definitely more than she'd bargained for.

"Mom—"

Corrie walked backward toward the open door. "You promised, remember?"

Linnette shook her head as her mother disappeared around the corner and out of the apartment. She'd be moving to Cedar Cove the following week. She wanted this date over with as quickly as possible. She just hoped Chad didn't hear about it.

Reaching for her purse, she pulled out her cell phone and dialed the number on the slip of paper Corrie had given her. Putting this off any longer would only create unnecessary conflict with her mother.

A man answered, but he sounded perfectly normal. "This is Linnette McAfee calling for Cal Washburn," she said crisply.

"Well, hello, Linnette. Cal's been waiting for your phone call. I'm Cliff Harding. Cal works for me."

"Hi, Cliff. Is Cal available?"

"As a matter of fact, he's sitting right here."

A moment later, Cal was on the phone. "H-hello."

"Hi, I'm Linnette McAfee," she said quickly. So he had a slight stutter. But his speech was clear and intelligible. "Apparently my mother bought me a date with you last July at the Dog and Bachelor Auction." She didn't give him a chance to respond. "I was wondering when would be convenient for me to collect on it."

"Any…t-time."

"I'm moving into town next weekend, but I could meet you before then."

"How-w-w-w about nex-x-xt Friday night?"

"Okay. I'll meet you at The Lighthouse restaurant at seven." She suspected she'd have to do all the talking, since he seemed rather shy, no doubt because of the stutter. She'd probably have to pay for his dinner, too, she thought glumly.

"S-s-sure. Friday."

Linnette clicked off her cell. This was the last time she'd allow her mother to do anything like this. The very last time.

Six

Grace Sherman had been looking forward to this Friday night for a long time. Cliff Harding had invited her to dinner at his house—the first sign in months that he still had feelings for her. This was just the encouragement Grace needed. She loved Cliff, but she'd done something foolish, risking her entire future with him on an Internet relationship.

It had all started when her husband of thirty-five years had disappeared. Vietnam had changed Dan, and he wasn't the same man she'd married when he returned from the war. He'd lived a bleak, unhappy life, and often suffered from bouts of depression. After Dan's sudden disappearance, she'd spent nearly a year searching for him, exhausting what savings she had, only to discover that her husband had driven deep into the woods with a trailer she didn't even know he'd purchased, and killed himself.

In the months before she found out what had happened to Dan, Grace had met Cliff Harding. His patience and kindness had won her over and they'd started to see each other—but not until she'd learned Dan's fate. Cliff was recently divorced after twenty years of marriage and dating was a new experience for them both.

In coming to know Cliff, Grace discovered that his ex-wife had been involved in multiple affairs throughout their marriage. Grace and Cliff grew close, close enough for him to fly her to Maryland to meet his daughter, Lisa. Together they'd spent Thanksgiving with Lisa and her family. That was almost two years ago.

About the same time, Will Jefferson, her best friend's brother, had started to e-mail Grace. She'd had a crush on him as a teenager and was flattered by his attention. To this day, she wasn't sure how it happened, but soon she was logging on to the Internet at all hours of the day and night in order to "chat" with Will. He became her addiction. She was mortified now to admit that, all along, she'd known he was married. He'd fed her lie after lie, and she'd swallowed each one because she so badly wanted to believe him. And while she maintained her online relationship with Will, she'd continued dating Cliff.

Everything seemed to blow up in her face at once. Cliff found out about her Internet relationship and Grace realized that Will was still living with his wife, Georgia, and had no intention of divorcing her.

Cliff wanted nothing more to do with Grace. He'd lived with one faithless woman and wasn't about to repeat that mistake. He'd made it clear that they were through. Devastated, Grace could do nothing but abide by his wishes.

Then, last August, Lisa had flown out to spend time with her father. Grace would always be grateful to Cliff's daughter for visiting her at the library, where Grace was employed. Lisa had assured Grace that Cliff still loved her and encouraged her not to give up.

That was when Grace had begun a campaign to win back Cliff Harding. She mailed him cards, sent him e-mail messages and stopped by the ranch unannounced and uninvited. Little by little she'd worn him down to the point that he'd actually sought her out for the first time in more than a year.

When she arrived home from work, Grace tried three different outfits before she was satisfied. She modeled each of her choices before Buttercup, her golden retriever, and Sherlock, her cat. Unfortunately their opinions were less than useful, although she had to laugh at Buttercup's deep sigh. Sherlock didn't bother to open his eyes. In the end she chose a blue denim jumper with big yellow daisies painted on the bib and a yellow turtleneck underneath. It was similar to what she'd been wearing the first day she met Cliff. This was a new beginning for them and she hoped her clothes relayed that message.

By the time Grace drove out to Cliff's ranch in Olalla, her nerves were frayed. She so badly wanted to be part of Cliff's life. Somehow, she had to make him understand that she *wasn't* like his ex-wife. For thirty-five years she'd remained faithful to Dan and, given the opportunity, she'd be faithful to him too. She wanted Cliff to know she'd learned her lesson and learned it well. Never again would she risk losing him. If only he was willing to give her another chance…

There was no one about at the ranch as Grace pulled into the long drive, although another truck stood next to Cliff's newly completed barn. Parking near the house, Grace hesitated, unsure where to go. When Cliff failed to answer the front door, she wandered toward the barn. Cal lived in an apartment above, and he might be able to tell her what was going on.

She was halfway to the barn when Cliff came rushing out. He stopped abruptly, staring at her, his expression confused. He was a big man with a muscular build, easily six three in height. He wore a cowboy hat and boots and looked every bit the horseman he'd become since his retirement from Boeing.

"Cliff?" she said in a tentative voice.

"What day is it?" he asked.

"Friday."

"Is this the Friday I invited you for dinner?"

Her heart fell and she nodded. *He'd forgotten.* Still, she tried to smile as she said, "I'm afraid it is."

He was immediately apologetic. "I'm so sorry, Grace. I didn't realize it was *this* Friday. As you can see, we're having a problem here."

"What's wrong?"

Cliff shook his head grimly. "It's Midnight. He's got colic."

"Colic?" In Grace's experience, that was an ailment babies came down with during their first few months. She remembered pacing the floor with Kelly, her youngest, as the infant screamed in unrelieved pain.

"It's life-threatening in horses," Cliff explained. "The vet's here and we're doing everything we can to save him. If worse comes to worse, surgery might be necessary." He removed his hat and wiped his forearm across his brow. "I'm sorry, Grace, we'll have dinner another time."

"Is there anything I can do?" she asked, willing to push up her sleeves and help to whatever extent she could.

"I was about to make a pot of coffee."

"I'll do that and bring it out when it's ready."

Cliff nodded. "Great. I'd appreciate that."

"Don't give it a second thought."

Once inside the kitchen, Grace searched through several cupboards until she located the coffee grounds. While the coffee brewed, she brought out bread and made half a dozen sandwiches, using the ham and cheese slices she found in the refrigerator. She wasn't sure how long this crisis had been in effect, but she guessed that Cliff, Cal and the vet could use something to eat.

When everything was ready, Grace carried a tray with the coffeepot and a plate of sandwiches into the barn. Doc Newton was the first one to notice Grace's presence. As she stood, she smiled her gratitude.

"I'd love a cup of that coffee. With cream," Vicki said.

Setting down the tray, Grace filled a mug for her.

Cliff, who was on his knees beside the stallion, barely glanced over his shoulder. A large tube came out of the horse's mouth and to Grace's uneducated eye, the animal appeared to be in bad shape. Cal was on the other side, gently stroking the black muzzle as he talked in low, soothing tones. Grace realized that for the first time since she'd met Cal, he wasn't stuttering. Apparently he could communicate with horses better than humans.

Grace poured Cliff a mug of hot coffee. He took it from her with a scant nod of acknowledgement. She offered some to Cal, but he shook his head.

"It's a waiting game now," Doc Newman told Grace.

"What are Midnight's chances?"

The vet shrugged. "Could go either way."

Grace knew that Cliff had a large financial investment in this stallion, but there was more to it. He loved that horse. He'd often talked about his dreams for the ranch, and it went without saying that Midnight was the very basis of Cliff's future in ranching. She speculated that losing the stallion could set him back years. But it would be a personal loss as much as a financial one.

Not knowing what else to do, Grace stepped into the background and waited. She didn't feel she could just walk away. She might not be able to give him any real help, but she wanted Cliff to know she cared.

After an hour she saw that she wasn't contributing anything. No one wanted more food or coffee, so she returned to the house. It took her all of five minutes to clean up the kitchen. Bored, she turned on the television, flicking from channel to channel, not settling on any one program for more than a few minutes. Every half hour she went to the barn to see what was happening, but there seemed to be virtually no progress. As Doc Newman had said, it was a waiting game.

At ten Grace fell asleep in front of the television, waking with a start at shortly after eleven. She looked outside and saw that Doc Newman's truck was gone. When she hurried out to the barn again, Grace saw that nothing had changed. Cliff and Cal were still with Midnight; neither seemed to notice her. As quietly as she could, she slipped out of the barn and went back to the house to collect her things.

Not wanting to interrupt Cliff, she climbed into her car and drove home, feeling depressed. She was worried about Midnight's colic, of course, and extremely upset by Cliff's attitude toward her. She wondered if he regretted the dinner invitation. Even if Midnight hadn't taken sick, it wouldn't have mattered. Cliff hadn't even remembered this was the night she was coming to dinner. He'd made no preparations, nor had he shown the slightest interest in seeing her. If anything, he seemed happy to avoid her.

Buttercup and Sherlock were waiting when she let herself into the house and their obvious pleasure at her return comforted Grace. She saw that the message light on her phone was blinking. After leaving her purse on the washing machine, she sat down at her small kitchen table to listen, pen in hand.

A faint smile touched her lips at the sound of her best friend's voice. Olivia wanted to hear all about Grace's "hot" dinner date. "Phone when you get home. I don't care how late it is."

Reluctantly Grace reached for the telephone. Olivia answered on the first ring.

"Don't you have anything better to do on a Friday night than sit by the phone?" Grace chided.

"Jack's still at the office."

Olivia didn't sound pleased, and Grace didn't blame her. "It's almost eleven-thirty!"

"Tell me about it," Olivia muttered. "But you didn't call to hear me complain about Jack. How'd it go with Cliff?"

"Dreadful." Grace went on to fill in the details, ending with her suspicion that Cliff seemed to regret inviting her.

Olivia was silent when she finished. "So what are you going to do?"

"What *can* I do?" Grace asked, discouraged and baffled by Cliff's behavior.

"You're not giving up, are you?" Olivia challenged.

"No," but this wasn't said with a lot of enthusiasm. "I guess not. But if he doesn't—"

"He'll phone you in the morning," Olivia broke in.

Somehow Grace doubted that. It was as if Cliff had put her out of his mind.

Seven

Jack Griffin was tired and hungry. It was past nine on Tuesday and he still hadn't left the office; Olivia would be annoyed. He loved that woman, but he craved the challenge of his job as editor of *The Cedar Cove Chronicle*, too. Olivia claimed he had printer's ink running through his veins and he figured she was right—otherwise he'd resent all the hours he spent getting out five issues a week.

When he'd been offered the position of editor four years earlier, the newspaper published a single issue each week and was planning to increase that to two. Since he was in his fifties and ready to cut back on the grueling hours he put in for the Spokane daily paper, he'd willingly accepted fewer hours—and less pay. The attraction of moving to Cedar Cove was more than just working for *The Chronicle*. The real draw was being close to Bob Beldon and to Eric, Jack's son, who lived in the Seattle area, too. Ironically Eric and his family had moved to Reno three years ago.

Bob Beldon was Jack's AA sponsor and best friend. Several years earlier, Bob and Peggy had returned to the area and purchased a run-down home on Cranberry Point. Being an all-around handyman, Bob had quickly transformed the huge house into a successful Bed-and-Breakfast they called Thyme and Tide. The thyme part came from Peggy, who'd immediately planted an herb garden, along with a variety of fruits, vegetables and flowers. Her blueberry muffins were legendary.

After a single visit to Cedar Cove, Jack fell in love with the small community. He interviewed for the *Chronicle* job and got it. He found a decent rental and settled into what he assumed would be a more leisurely pace of life. He was looking forward to it, looking forward to a change.

Change had come, all right, but not in the way he'd expected. Soon after his arrival in Cedar Cove, he'd met Olivia Lockhart, and the woman had turned his world upside down.

In an effort to become acquainted with the community, Jack had visited her courtroom for a day and watched her deal out judgments on a series of cases. One judgment stood out. A young couple who'd lost their child came before her, seeking a divorce. While most people in the courtroom watched the exchange between the two lawyers presenting the case, Jack had focused his attention on Olivia. He found her mesmerizing. As she studied the couple, her eyes had filled with pain. Only later did Jack learn that Olivia had lost a child, too. Her thirteen-year-old son had drowned in 1986. Under the weight of grief and loss, her own marriage had dissolved. When she denied the couple's divorce on a technicality, in effect forcing husband and wife to reconsider, he knew he had to write about her in his column.

Unfortunately Olivia had taken exception to what Jack had written. They met one Saturday morning in the local grocery and—although she might not have realized it at the time— their courtship had begun. He fell hard for her and he hadn't recovered yet. The truth was, he didn't plan to. They'd been married for over a year and his life had never been more satisfying.

Every now and then Jack had to marvel that a woman as classy as Olivia would marry an ex-alcoholic newsman who didn't even know which fork to use if there were more than two. But marry him she had, and he considered himself the luckiest man alive.

Of course, Olivia being Olivia, she'd taken it upon herself to educate him. She felt there were some rough edges that needed smoothing out. They'd had a difficult few months in the beginning, while they adjusted to living with each other. Jack was willing to admit he was a slob. Olivia, on the other hand, had a highly developed sense of order and his slovenly habits had driven his poor wife insane.

He just didn't understand why it was so important to hang up his pants every night when he intended to put them on again in the morning. He made an effort because he knew it pleased her. The same with the peanut butter jar. According to Olivia, he was spreading germs around the entire house by leaving it open on the countertop with a knife stuck in it. So now he took out the knife, put on the lid and shoved it in the fridge. And these days, he actually hung the towel on the rack when he was done with it. He could never arrange them precisely the way Olivia liked, but she didn't complain. He rinsed off his dinner plate each night and placed it inside the dishwasher, too. Love apparently did that to a man.

The one area that still met with resistance was this diet she had him on. All right, he'd admit it; he could afford to lose a few pounds. Jack had a bit of a paunch, but it wasn't *that* bad. Every once in a while, a man needed a double-bacon cheeseburger with all the fixings. He wasn't opposed to a large order of fries with that, either. They both went well with a vanilla shake.

Just thinking about his favorite meal made Jack's mouth water as he got into his car to drive home. He couldn't remember the last time he'd eaten. Breakfast had been blueberry yogurt with something stirred into it—probably wheat germ. He hated the taste of wheat germ, so his beloved wife had taken to disguising it. He let her think he'd been fooled.

When the sign for his favorite fast-food restaurant came into view, his decision was made. The drive-through window was open and he rolled straight up to it. Sitting in the parking lot, he wolfed down his cheeseburger at record speed, hardly stopping to savor the sheer luxury of it. He washed it down with the vanilla shake and munched on salty fries. He'd be in trouble with Olivia if she found out about this, but that burger had been worth it.

Hell, he was already in trouble. He'd told her he'd be home by seven and it was nearly ten. Knowing she was probably trying to reach him, he'd turned off his cell. He felt guilty about that now. An emergency had developed when the computer system crashed and he'd had to stay until everything was up and running again. He had a newspaper to get out, and there was nothing he could do but see this crisis through.

The lights in the living room were on when Jack parked in front of the house. He'd come to appreciate Olivia's home on Lighthouse Road, which had a wonderful view of the cove. Jack enjoyed sitting beside Olivia on her wide front porch, watching the sun set on a summer night.

He'd wondered, when they were first married, if he'd be comfortable in a house where Olivia had once lived with her ex-husband. His fears had come to nothing. Olivia and Stan had been divorced for more years than they'd been married, and almost every trace of Stan was gone. There was the odd family photograph here and there, but he didn't begrudge Olivia that.

Hoping she was asleep, he sneaked into the kitchen as quietly as possible. But the instant the floor creaked, Olivia called his name.

"Hi, honey," he said.

Olivia marched into the kitchen like the third brigade, dressed in her thick fleece housecoat and fuzzy slippers. Her arms were crossed and she glared at him. "You turned off your cell phone."

"I know...I'm sorry."

"Not sorry enough."

"I left a message for you," he said, pleading his case. "There wasn't anything I could do." He explained the computer situation, repeating the message he'd left on their answering machine, and hoped she understood that he just couldn't answer questions at the time.

She hesitated, and he could see her weaken. "Sometimes I wonder why we ever got married. I see less of you now than I did while we were dating."

Sometimes Jack felt the same way. "It seems like that, doesn't it?" He brought her into the circle of his arms. He loved the smell of her hair and breathed in the scent that was distinctly hers. "There are other advantages to being married, though," he whispered, slipping his hand inside the front of her housecoat. To his delight she wasn't wearing her long flannel nightgown, but the silk one that offered him easy access to her breasts.

"Jack, honestly," she protested, but not too loudly.

"Come on, honey, I'm tired. Let's go to bed."

"Are you hungry?"

"Famished." Her nipples were hard and he felt the stirrings of desire. Ten minutes ago he didn't think he had enough energy to do more than undress and fall into bed. But now... Well, Olivia had that kind of effect on him.

"I can warm up dinner in the microwave."

He nuzzled her neck. "I ate on the way home," he whispered as he brought his mouth to hers. The kiss was long and deep.

Olivia was the one who broke it off. "Jack Griffin, what did you have for dinner?"

"Ah…"

She pulled away from him, shaking her head in disgust.

"Come on, honey."

"Don't 'honey' me. Don't you realize what you're doing?"

"I was hungry and a cheeseburger sounded so good."

She wouldn't look at him.

Jack eased her back into his arms. "I have an idea that might wipe out all the evil traces of that sinful dinner."

"What?"

He slid his hands back inside her warm housecoat, weighing the bounty of her breasts in his palms. It didn't take much for his desire to be rekindled. "Can't you guess? I think a little exercise might do wonders for me."

Her eyes were closed and she let out a soft sigh in response.

"You're always telling me how good exercise is."

"That's true," she agreed. "But I thought you were tired."

"I was," he admitted, his voice sinking to a murmur as he led her toward their bedroom.

"Oh, Jack," she whispered, climbing onto the bed. "I was so angry with you this evening, and now look at me. I'm like…like mush in your arms."

This was why he loved her so much: She was as vulnerable to him as he was to her. Kneeling on the bed in front of her, Jack peeled off her nightgown and gloried in the sheen of her bare skin in the room's faint light.

He was ready for her, painfully ready, as he stripped off his pants and let them drop to the floor. He doubted Olivia would object if he didn't hang them up tonight.

Eight

"Let me look at you," Corrie McAfee said as Linnette headed toward the front door of the house on Harbor Street, ready to leave for her dinner date with Cal Washburn. She'd stayed with her parents for the last few nights.

"Mom," Linnette protested. It wasn't as if she cared whether or not she made a good impression on this blind date. The fact that she was stuck going out with Cal was irritating enough without having to withstand her mother's scrutiny.

Corrie stepped back to inspect her daughter's appearance and smiled approvingly. Then, apparently noticing a speck of lint, Corrie brushed it away from Linnette's shoulder. "You look lovely."

"Thanks, Mom." Linnette hadn't gone to any effort. The long black suede skirt and white sweater weren't new. The knee-high boots were from last year and her jewelry was a simple locket and gold earrings. She was presentable, and that was good enough. The last thing she wanted to do was impress this cowpoke.

Her intention was to fulfill her obligation and, if possible, enjoy the meal. If Cal asked her out again, she'd simply have to explain that she needed time to settle into her new home. In other words, she'd contact him when and if she was interested. She didn't want to lead him on; as far as she was concerned, this was one date and one date only.

"Have a wonderful time," her mother said.

"Mom, don't!" Linnette groaned. "I hate it when you look at me like that."

"Like what?" Her mother frowned, her expression completely baffled.

"You have all these expectations about me and Cal, and it's so unfair."

"What is?" Roy asked, walking into the living room where the two women stood.

"Both of you," Linnette cried.

"Hey, what did I do?" Roy asked, glancing at Corrie.

Linnette gestured at them. "It's like you've got me married to…to some man I haven't even met. Is it any wonder I don't want to go on this stupid date?"

Her father reached for *The Cedar Cove Chronicle* and shrugged. "Then don't go."

Corrie gasped. "I paid good money for this dinner. I want you to go out with him at least once. It would be rude to phone at the last minute and cancel."

Linnette had thought of that herself. As much as she wanted out of this, she refused to be unkind about it. But now that she had her parents' attention, there was another matter she needed to bring up.

"I want to know more about those postcards you've been receiving."

Her father's eyes narrowed accusingly on her mother.

Before he could blame Corrie for betraying confidences, Linnette explained how she knew. "I found one, Dad, so don't get all bent out of shape. She tried to keep your scary little secret, but I read one of those postcards."

"We haven't had any more in the last week," Corrie added quickly. She hesitated, then turned to Roy. "Have we?"

Roy's frown darkened his entire face. "No. And the subject is closed." With that, he sat down and hid behind the newspaper.

"But…"

"It won't do any good to question him," her mother whispered. She silently pleaded with her to drop the subject.

Linnette already knew how stubborn and unreasonable her father could be. She was furious that he'd excluded her like this. He did the same thing to Mack. Linnette found it chilling that her own father could pretend she wasn't there, seeking answers, needing reassurance. He didn't seem to understand that she wasn't asking these questions because she was intruding on their business. Her concern was genuine.

"I'd better leave now," she said, retrieving the suede jacket that matched her skirt.

Cal had agreed to meet her at The Lighthouse, the finest restaurant in town, at seven. Linnette was prepared to pay for the dinner if it came to that, but she hoped Cal would offer, since she wasn't on the clinic payroll yet. Her mother had paid big bucks for this guy, although Linnette wasn't sure precisely how much. She knew it was over four hundred dollars each for Cal and the dog, who was definitely worth her share of the money. In Linnette's humble opinion, Cal should be the one paying the tab for tonight's dinner. Nevertheless, she had enough cash to cover it, unless he ordered expensive drinks.

"Have a good time," Corrie said again as she walked Linnette to the door.

Linnette didn't think that was possible. "Any words of wisdom?" she asked in a resigned voice.

The question appeared to please her mother. "I don't know much about Cal. However, Grace Sherman at the library says he's a wonderful man but shy, so you might have to carry the conversation."

Linnette had already figured that. With his stutter, it might be difficult to have much of a conversation at all. Linnette was afraid this evening would be torture. She knew it was going to be a struggle not to finish his sentences for him. Doing that would be terribly impolite and, of course, Cal would resent it, with good reason.

Linnette wasn't looking forward to going home that night, either; her mother would almost certainly be waiting up to interrogate her about the evening with Cal. But Linnette had a few questions of her own. She hoped to learn more about these postcards so she could tell her brother. Linnette felt they had a right to know that their parents were in potential danger.

If her father's reaction to a simple question was any indication, she could forget about any hope of shared information from him. He wasn't talking, but she might be able to persuade her mother to drop a few hints.

When she reached the restaurant, Linnette parked in the only available spot and walked up the steps to The Lighthouse foyer. Funny, she'd never thought to ask Cal what he looked like. Now, standing in a foyer crowded with people, all waiting to be seated, she glanced around, hoping she'd somehow recognize him. Unfortunately, there seemed to be a number of single men milling about.

Wanting to avoid the embarrassment of asking strangers their names, Linnette decided there must be a logical way to do this. Cal would probably be wearing cowboy boots. Unfortunately, that meant she was walking around with her head down, staring at everyone's feet.

She found a man with a polished pair of boots and raised

her head. She immediately dismissed him as a possibility. He was far too old. Her survey continued. Scuffed boots—too young. Snakeskin boots—nope. Too urban.

"Linnette?"

She abruptly looked up and nearly collided with a lean, wiry man of about thirty-five. He wore a cowboy hat and western-style jacket with leather patches on the sleeves and—yes, indeed—cowboy boots. Linnette's expectations hadn't been high, but if this was Cal Washburn, he far exceeded her hopes. He was a pleasant-looking man, not striking, but obviously in good shape. Brown hair and eyes, prominent cheekbones, a solid jaw and surprise of surprises, a warm smile.

"Cal?"

He nodded. "I h-have a reservation." With his hand at the small of her back, he directed her to the desk.

The woman behind the counter looked at them expectantly.

"W-Washburn," Cal said.

She scanned the list and scratched out his name when she located it on the reservation sheet. Reaching for two menus, she said, "Your table is ready."

Linnette had no idea The Lighthouse restaurant did such a rousing business. It hadn't occurred to her to make reservations, and she was grateful Cal had.

Once they were seated, Linnette opened her menu, studied the selections and chose the seafood fettuccini with clams, scallops and Hood Canal shrimp. It sounded appetizing—and was affordably priced. She'd stick to the free rolls for her appetizer.

The waiter came for their drink order and Linnette decided on iced tea. Cal asked for a whiskey sour. Remembering that her funds were limited, Linnette opened her menu again to see if there was a price list for mixed drinks. Yes—to her horror, it was made with premium whiskey and cost almost ten dollars.

After their drinks arrived, they made small talk, with Linnette doing most of the talking, just as she'd assumed she would. Cal seemed interested in her work as a physician assistant and was impressed that she could prescribe medications and treat minor injuries. She described the first times she'd sutured a wound and put on a cast and how nervous she'd been.

The waiter returned for their meal order and it was as if Cal had only recently discovered food. He ordered a crab-and-artichoke dip for an appetizer, plus a dinner salad with shrimp. The seafood topping cost extra. For his entrée, he chose a T-bone steak.

Linnette casually looked at the menu a second time and checked on the price of the steak. According to her calculations, his tab alone would add up to all the cash she carried.

"Is s-something wr-rong?" Cal inquired.

She leaned closer and tried to figure out a way to explain that she was on a limited budget, but couldn't. It was just too humiliating. "N-nothing," she assured him.

"You stutter?" His eyes widened as though he'd met his soul mate.

"No." She shook her head. "Cal, I—" She began to explain that they might need to split the bill, but just then the waiter delivered the rolls and the appetizer.

Despite her predictions, Linnette actually had an enjoyable time. She relaxed after she started eating. Cal insisted she have a glass of wine with her meal; the expense was more than she could afford, but she let him talk her into it. When she tasted the chardonnay, she was glad she'd succumbed. The wine was not only delicious, it went a long way toward calming her nerves.

She shouldn't have been surprised that Cal ordered dessert—New York-style cheesecake, no less. He also requested two forks.

"I couldn't," she insisted, placing both hands on her stomach.

"One taste," Cal said.

"We bake it here at the restaurant," the waiter told her. "It's our most popular dessert."

"All right," she acquiesced, "one taste."

Linnette ended up eating most of it. She didn't normally like heavy desserts, but this was exceptional—the best she'd ever tasted.

They lingered over coffee, and then the waiter brought the bill, tucked inside a leather sleeve. It stood in the middle of the table, impossible to ignore. By her estimate—she'd kept a running total in her head until the wine, at which point she'd lost count—the tab far exceeded her cash. Granted, she had her VISA, but she was already close to her limit on that. For a long moment, Linnette stared at the bill, still concealed in its folder, and prayed this man her mother considered such a paragon would reach for it.

He didn't.

Linnette was beginning to worry. "Shall we split this?" she suggested.

Cal picked up the bill and looked it over. He didn't say what her half would be. "I'll t-t-take care of it on the way out," he said.

Linnette nodded.

"I had a nice time." He seemed as astonished as she was.

"I did, too."

"You aren't l-l-like I ex-x-x-pected."

"Neither are you."

He glanced at his watch. "Can I w-walk you to your v-v-vehi—car?"

She shook her head. "You go on, while I pay my half of the bill. Thank you, Cal, for a most enjoyable evening."

"Y-y-you're welcome." He dropped his napkin on the table and stood.

The restaurant wasn't as busy as it had been earlier. Several couples sat with their heads close together, enjoying each other's company. Some evening Linnette hoped that would be Chad Timmons and her.

Once Cal had left, Linnette sighed deeply and decided she'd better figure out what she owed. She reached for the bill and was shocked to find it had already been paid. Frowning, she motioned for the waiter. "This is completely paid? The tip, too?"

"Yes, the gentleman made arrangements with the restaurant before you arrived. He left his credit card with the hostess."

"Oh." He might've said something. Still, Linnette felt she should thank him. However, when she hurried out to the parking lot, Cal was already gone.

Nine

It was the first Tuesday of November, the day Charlotte and Ben were having dinner with his son. That afternoon, she sorted through her closet in search of a dress to wear. She finally decided on the pink-and-white one she'd purchased for her wedding reception. With its row of tiny ribbon rosebuds edging the collar it made her feel feminine and attractive. Although the outfit was better suited for spring than autumn, she hoped to make a positive impression on David.

"How do I look?" she asked Ben, stepping out of the bedroom and brushing the wrinkles out of her skirt. She waited for her husband's approval.

Ben glanced up from the television set and frowned.

"What's wrong?" Charlotte asked, crestfallen. She wanted to do her husband proud.

"You went to far too much trouble. You don't need to impress David."

"But... I want your son to like me."

"I know, dear, and I appreciate that, but it isn't necessary. I suspect the only reason David asked us to have dinner is to see if I'll give him another loan." Ben's face hardened. "I refuse to do it. I told him that the last time and I'm not going to change my mind." He shook his head. "Just watch. We'll get stuck with the bill, too."

"Oh, Ben, I'm sure that's not true. Anyway, he invited us."

"Yeah, but you can bet I'll be paying the tab."

"Oh, Ben, don't be so negative."

Ben didn't argue with her. She could tell he was nervous and that he regretted agreeing to this. He revealed no pleasure at seeing David or the prospect of a rare evening out in downtown Seattle.

While it was still daylight, Ben and Charlotte drove over to Bremerton and walked onto the Seattle-bound ferry. During the hour-long commute, Ben was uncharacteristically silent. They held hands and sipped coffee, and Charlotte watched Bainbridge Island fade into the distance as the Seattle skyline came into view. It really was a lovely time of year in Puget Sound. By the end of the month, Christmas decorations would be up, and a festive spirit would suffuse Cedar Cove.

Once the ferry docked in Seattle, Ben ushered Charlotte down the ramp and out of the terminal. They took one of the taxis waiting on the street outside and rode up to Martini's Steakhouse, the restaurant David had chosen.

Ben led Charlotte to an elevator that brought them to the lower floor. As she stepped off, her interest was immediately captured by the signed photographs of famous people who'd dined at Martini's.

A man who could only be Ben's son sat in the restaurant foyer. He was handsome, a younger version of his father with dark hair and a strong presence. He glanced up and smiled when he saw Ben and Charlotte.

"Hello, David." Ben spoke without emotion.

"Dad," David said eagerly, standing. He hugged his father

and slapped him affectionately on the back. When he'd finished, he gave Charlotte a warm smile.

"This is Charlotte," Ben said, placing his arm protectively around her shoulders.

David held out his arms and drew her into an enthusiastic hug. "I am so delighted to finally meet you," he said. "You've made my father a very happy man."

Charlotte was instantly charmed. Ben didn't have a thing to worry about, she decided; this was certain to be a wonderful evening. When David released her, she looked at Ben and found him scowling. She couldn't imagine why he was being so unpleasant.

David's smile dimmed slightly as he regarded his father. "Come on, Dad," he said. "Relax. Let's enjoy the evening."

"Yes," Charlotte chimed in. "I'm meeting your son for the first time and we're going to have a great meal. Let's enjoy ourselves."

David directed his attention to her as they waited for the hostess to return from seating the couple in front of them. "I can't tell you how sorry I was to miss the wedding," he said, avoiding his father's eye.

"I'm looking forward to introducing you to my children," Charlotte told him happily. "I'm sure you'll get a chance to meet them soon."

"I'm sure I will, too. Again I apologize about missing the big day but summer's an especially busy time for me."

"What do you do?" Charlotte asked, and refrained from reminding him that they were married the first week of May, which was actually spring.

"I work in insurance," David said. "It's difficult to explain but I deal with actuaries and statistics."

"Oh, yes." Charlotte nodded. "All of that's beyond me. Clyde always took care of that sort of thing. I'm grateful he did. Clyde was my first husband," she told him. Although he'd been gone almost twenty-five years, Clyde had seen to Charlotte's financial needs before his death. She would be forever grateful.

The hostess seemed to be waiting for them to finish their conversation.

"Our table's ready," Ben said, steering them toward the young woman.

They were quickly seated, and Charlotte took the opportunity to look around. A single glance convinced her that this was one of the finest restaurants she'd ever been inside. To date, the most elegant restaurant she'd eaten in belonged to her own granddaughter, Justine. Justine and Seth owned The Lighthouse in Cedar Cove and had made a brilliant success of it. She was near to bursting with pride about her granddaughter, who'd had the good sense to marry a solid man like Seth Gunderson. When David visited Cedar Cove, she'd make sure he had a chance to dine at The Lighthouse.

Their waiter approached the table, wheeling a cart, and with a good deal of ceremony revealed virtually a complete menu. Her head spun as he displayed and then described each item. When he was finished, they were given a price list. Charlotte studied it and gasped aloud. But, my goodness, it all looked so delicious. She made a mental note to tell Justine every detail she could remember. Her granddaughter would want to know about this. After the elaborate presentation, she ordered the grilled swordfish and both men ordered steaks.

The meal was superb and so was the service. The conversation, too, was enjoyable. David had an engaging manner and did most of the talking. He chatted about the weather and recent movies and how he planned to go to Vegas for Christmas. Ben remained stubbornly quiet, as he had before; it was up to

Charlotte to respond to his son's questions and remarks. The one irritation was David's cell phone, which rang four times during the course of their meal.

After the fourth call, Ben snapped, "Turn that damn thing off."

"Sorry." David did look apologetic as he reached for his cell and pushed a button. The telephone sang a brief song and then went silent.

Charlotte breathed a sigh of relief and smiled at the waiter who brought coffee to their table with several varieties of sugar from which to choose. Charlotte was quite taken with the hard candy sticks that looked like something out of a confectionary store.

Over coffee, David grew quiet. "You might've guessed why I wanted to meet with you, Dad," he said as he stirred in the cream.

"David, if this is about money—"

"Dad, I'm in a tight spot."

"I can't help you."

"Can't or won't?" David asked with barely suppressed anger.

Ben's shoulders heaved as if he'd inhaled sharply in an effort to control his own annoyance. "Since you put it like that, the answer is *won't*. I refuse to give you another dime. You haven't paid back the last two loans. I'd be a fool to give you more."

"I'm good for it. I promise."

"That's what you said last time and the time before that. Why should I believe you now?"

"Because it's true. Dad, do you think it's easy, coming to you like this? Do you think I'd do this if I had any other options?"

He seemed about to say more but Charlotte could see that

his arguments increased Ben's irritation. "How much do you need?" she asked. She didn't mean to intrude, but if it was a reasonable amount then perhaps Ben wouldn't mind so much.

"Five thousand," he said after a moment. "That's considerably less than I needed before," he added with a hopeful expression.

"What do you need it for?" Charlotte asked, wanting to help and not knowing how. Her questions didn't please Ben, she could see that, but she felt badly for the young man.

David shrugged. "It's complicated."

"The usual, no doubt," Ben cut in. "His credit cards are maxed out, he hasn't paid his taxes and he's paying alimony for two ex-wives."

"I'm getting a bonus this Christmas," David said. "I only need the money for a couple of months, just to carry me through. You know I wouldn't ask if I wasn't desperate. I'm telling you, Dad, money pressures are the worst. I can't sleep nights. I can hardly eat."

"You certainly didn't have a problem tonight," Ben pointed out. David had obviously enjoyed his meal, and Charlotte was glad of that after seeing those prices. Fifty years ago, she could've fed her family for a week for the price of a single steak.

David looked hurt. "This is the first decent meal I've had in ages. You have to know how difficult this is for me. There's no one else I can ask."

"I'm sure it's painful to ask for a loan," Charlotte said sympathetically.

David thanked her for her understanding with a smile. "I swear to you, Dad, I'll pay you back. I don't know what'll happen if you turn me down."

"How old are you now?" Ben asked his son.

David straightened slightly. "Forty-three."

"Really," Charlotte said conversationally. "I would've guessed much younger."

David ignored her, holding his father's eyes.

"Forty-three is old enough to stand on your own two feet and stop expecting someone else to bail you out."

David's shoulders slumped.

Charlotte felt dreadful for him, but she couldn't advise Ben when it came to dealing with his own child. She reached for Ben's hand under the table and he gripped it hard.

"I told you the last time that I'm not lending you another dime, and I'm sticking to that. I have to, David. I'm sorry you're experiencing financial troubles, but apparently you didn't learn your lesson."

"You're telling me *no.*"

"I am. Save your breath, because no amount of talking will change my mind."

David didn't argue, didn't get upset, but nodded as if he understood.

"So far, all I've taught you is to come to me when you have money problems and that isn't healthy for either of us."

"I agree," David said reluctantly.

"You pay me back what you owe from the first two loans, and then we'll discuss future possibilities."

David pinched his lips together and nodded again. Pushing out his chair, he stood. "If you'll excuse me, I'd better get back to my hotel. Thank you for the pleasant dinner. Charlotte, I think the smartest thing my father's done in the last fifteen years was marrying you."

Charlotte blushed with pleasure. "Thank you, David."

He bowed slightly and walked out of the room.

With his exit, the waiter walked over to the table and promptly delivered the bill.

Ten

Home from work early because of her doctor's appointment, Cecilia Randall sat in front of her computer in the spare bedroom and logged on. She treasured every e-mail Ian sent, and when there wasn't one waiting for her at the end of the day, she immediately felt discouraged. To her delight, there were two messages. She clicked her mouse on the first, but before the computer brought it up on screen the phone rang.

Cecilia glanced over her shoulder, willing it to be silent. It was probably Cathy, wanting to hear how her appointment had gone. Everything was wonderful, and she had exciting news to share with Ian. She couldn't tell Cathy before she told her husband. By rights, he should hear first. If she picked up the phone and Cathy was on the line, Cecilia knew she wouldn't be able to keep the information to herself.

After the third ring, she couldn't stand it any longer and ran into the kitchen to grab the phone before the answering machine kicked in. "Hello," she said breathlessly.

"Cecilia?"

"Ian?"

"Oh, baby, I'm so glad you're home. You wouldn't believe what I went through to make this call."

"Ian, oh, Ian, it's so good to hear your voice." Tears filled her eyes. She loved her husband and missed him terribly. Every time he went to sea it was the same.

"Tell me about the doctor's visit," Ian demanded, worry in his voice. "It was this afternoon, wasn't it?"

"Yes, yes, and everything went really well." She was nearly bursting with what she'd learned.

"They did the ultrasound?"

"Yes…"

"Everything's all right with the baby?" He sounded afraid, and she didn't blame him. If they'd had more than one ultrasound with Allison, the doctors would've discovered her heart condition before the birth. "Did the ultrasound show anything?"

She leaned against the kitchen wall, almost giddy with happiness. "It did."

Ian gasped as if this was his biggest fear.

"Ian, Ian, it isn't *anything* like that. Oh, Ian, we're going to have a son!"

"What?"

"The technician had a good view this time, and she showed me his little penis. We're having a son."

Her husband was silent for half a second and then let out a yelp that must've echoed a hundred miles. Cecilia was sure everyone on the aircraft carrier had heard him. She understood; it was the proof he needed that this pregnancy was different from their first.

Cecilia laughed with joy. They'd been told this second baby was likely a girl and that had only added to her husband's fears. As Ian had said over and over, everything was the same as it had been with Allison. Cecilia was going to deliver another baby girl while he was away. Ian was so afraid for her, for them both. If they lost another baby... Cecilia couldn't allow her mind to go down those dark paths.

"They're *sure* about the baby being a boy?"

"I know what I saw."

"How are you feeling?" he asked.

"Wonderful. Ecstatic. And very much in love with my husband."

"I love you, Cecilia." His voice lowered with the weight of his emotion. "I think of you day and night."

"Me, too."

"Working isn't too much for you?"

"Not at all." Ian was such a worrier. But this job was vital to her. Without it, she'd sit at home all day with nothing to do. Using her accounting skills and providing a portion of their income weren't the only reasons Cecilia chose to be employed. "Mr. Cox is so thoughtful and Allison's coming in to the office every day after school." Ian already knew this but she told him again. She made sure her e-mails were full of news about her everyday life. That seemed to reassure him.

"Ah, yes. Allison Cox," Ian said, sighing deeply. "You're concerned about her, aren't you?"

"She has that new boyfriend."

"And you don't like him," Ian said.

"Well, I don't really know him, so I can't dislike him, but he worries me. Did I tell you his name is Anson? What kind of name is that, anyway? He's not the boy for Allison. He's one of those Goth kids, dresses totally in black and—"

Ian interrupted her. "Your father said I wasn't the right man for you, remember?"

At the mention of her father, Cecilia rolled her eyes. She'd come to Cedar Cove four years earlier in an effort to get to know her father. Her parents had divorced when she was ten, and her memories of him were vague and mingled with her mother's bitterness. Cecilia wanted to form her own impressions of him. He'd seemed eager to know her, too.

Cecilia's mother had warned her against having any expectations when it came to Bobby Merrick, but this was something she had to learn on her own. It hadn't taken her long to discover that her father was unreliable and irresponsible. When Cecilia lost her baby, his idea of comforting her was a sympathy card sent through the mail. He was sorry for her loss, he'd written. But not once had he come to see his daughter in the hospital. Not once had he offered to help her with the financial burden. He couldn't even be bothered to attend Allison's burial. The only thing her father had done for Cecilia was get her a job at The Captain's Galley, where she'd met Ian. For that one small twist of fate, she would always be grateful.

"You're the right man for me," she breathed, determined not to bring her father into the conversation. "Oh, Ian, I miss you so much."

"I'll be home soon."

Not before the baby was born, but Cecilia couldn't think about that. This time she wasn't alone. Cathy Lackey would be with her and had promised to be her birthing coach. Cecilia had signed up for classes and they'd be starting soon. Cathy would go with her.

When Cecilia delivered Allison she'd been alone, not knowing a soul other than her father. The baby had arrived several weeks early. Her mother had intended to fly out, but couldn't reach her in time. Friendless and frightened, Cecilia had gone to the hospital on her own.

"We need boy names, Ian," she said, breaking off those painful memories.

"Ah...I can't think of anything at the moment. Let me e-mail you a few suggestions. Okay?"

"Okay. But I think our son should have his daddy's name."

"Too confusing," Ian said. "Maybe for his middle name."

"That sounds fine."

"Listen, sweetheart, I have to go, but before I do I need to ask a favor for a friend of mine. He asked if you'd mind checking on a girl for him."

"Sure."

"Her name is Rachel Pendergast and she works at a beauty place in Cedar Cove called Get Nailed."

"I know it. Almost everyone gets their nails done there."

"Nate went out with Rachel a couple of times and seems pretty interested in her, but she doesn't have a computer. Apparently she writes him a lot, but it isn't the same as being able to communicate on-line."

"Couldn't she use the computer at the library?" Cecilia asked. That was the one Cecilia had used when she and Ian were separated and she needed to keep in touch with him. With all the expenses related to burying Allison and the attorney's fees for their failed divorce, she'd had no money for anything extra.

"Apparently Rachel's never been on-line and isn't sure how it works. This is all new to her."

"I'll get her started," Cecilia promised.

"Thanks, sweetheart."

"You're welcome, my handsome, wonderful husband."

"How long has it been since I told you I love you?"

Cecilia smiled softly. "Too long."

"I love you."

She giggled with sheer happiness.

"A son," Ian whispered. "A son."

Eleven

This was moving day. Linnette's brother had been a real help. He'd arrived at her Seattle apartment early Saturday morning with Lucky, his Australian Shepherd, and a couple of his friends who were volunteer firefighters with Mack. The only stuff left to move was her furniture and a few of the heavier boxes. Linnette had already taken over what she could, a little at a time, but the larger items required a truck, which she'd rented.

"I can't begin to tell you how much I appreciate this," Linnette told her brother after he and his friends had loaded up the truck. Bryan and Drew were carrying down the dining room chairs. Her roommate had left a month earlier, and the place was now completely empty.

"No problem," Mack said. He'd stayed behind. Now he wiped the sweat from his brow. "I'm glad I can help. I'm hoping the two of us will have a chance to talk later."

Before Linnette could reply, Bryan stepped back into the room. "You ready to head out?" he asked. He seemed eager to get going. Drew followed him inside, chanting, "Hey, hey, hey. We're on our way."

"I'll be down in a minute," Mack told them.

"We'll find a chance to talk," Linnette promised.

"Good. Maybe after we've unloaded the big stuff, we can chat and then I'll drive the truck back to the rental place." It cost less to rent the vehicle if it was returned to the original location. Mack had graciously agreed to deliver it to Seattle for his sister.

Just as efficiently as he and his friends had loaded the U-Haul, they unpacked it, carted everything up the one flight of outdoor stairs and set her sofa, chair, lamp, coffee table and television in her small living room. Her bed and mattress, dresser and nightstand went into the larger of the two bedrooms. Her desk, chair and computer, which she'd carefully boxed, were in the second room. Eventually Linnette planned to add a sleeper-sofa and maybe a small work table. She wanted to start doing crafts again, which was something she hadn't had time for while she was in school. The dining room table was a Salvation Army find, but it was pretty battered and Linnette hoped to replace it soon. With a regular income she'd have a few more options.

When Mack and his friends were finished, Linnette treated them to take-out hamburgers, fries and cold drinks. As soon as they'd wolfed those down, Drew and Bryan were on their way back to Seattle, with Linnette's fervent thanks ringing in their ears.

Mack sat on her sofa, leaned forward and set his wadded burger wrapper on her coffee table. Lucky, well-behaved dog that she was, had stayed obediently out of everyone's way and now rested at his side. As if gathering his thoughts, her brother waited a moment, then looked at Linnette. "Do you know what's going on with Mom and Dad?" he asked.

Her brother was astute, she'd give him that. "What makes

you think anything's going on?" She was interested in how he'd picked up on this so quickly. As far as Linnette knew, he wasn't in regular communication with their parents.

"Mom's been phoning me every Sunday afternoon. It's gotten to be like clockwork. She hadn't said anything outright, but just recently, I'd say in the last couple of weeks, she's made some remarks that don't add up."

"Like what?"

Mack hesitated. "For one thing, she casually mentioned that if anything were to happen to Dad, I should never doubt his love for me. I asked her if Dad was sick or there was something I should know, but she claimed there wasn't. I don't think she'd lie to me, but I'm pretty sure she's not telling me the whole truth."

"Go on," Linnette encouraged. Her brother had good instincts and she wondered how much information he'd been able to glean.

"Every time Mom phones, she assures me everything's fine. So, after a while, I started to think I might be imagining things."

"You aren't," Linnette was quick to tell him, and then went on to describe the postcards her parents had received.

"They aren't threatening?" Mack asked, frowning.

"I can't say for sure," Linnette said. "The only one I saw said, 'Are you thinking yet?'"

"About what?"

"According to Mom, Dad assumes this has something to do with his work on the police force."

"Some criminal he put away?" Mack speculated.

"Perhaps someone who has a vendetta against Dad. Whoever's doing this seems intent on psychologically wearing him down."

"That won't work," Mack said with a slow grin. "If this

person wants to torment our father, all he needs to do is grow his hair long, refuse to play football, drop out of college and take a job at the post office. That's enough to send the mighty Roy McAfee over the edge."

Linnette laughed, noticing anew what an attractive man her brother was. His build was similar to their father's, but as far as his looks went, he took after Grandpa Wilson, their mother's father.

"Do you think they're in any real danger?" Mack asked seriously.

"I don't know. I've tried to get Mom to tell me how long this has been going on, but she doesn't want to worry me. The fact that she won't talk about it concerns me more. I told her that, and she got all teary and said Dad's been completely unreasonable."

"That's unusual?" Mack teased.

Linnette shook her head, smiling. "Apparently there's been more than the postcards." She sat down on the sofa beside her brother and stroked Lucky's head. "Mom said something about a fruit basket being delivered."

"They didn't eat any of it, did they?"

"I don't know what they did with it. I assume they threw it away. That one really freaked Mom out."

"I can imagine. I wonder if it's part of this person's method. You know, kill them with kindness, confuse the enemy—and then move in with the real agenda."

Linnette hadn't thought of it that way. "You and Dad might not get along, but you're more alike than you realize."

Mack cringed. "Don't tell me that. The last person in the world I want to be like is my father."

"He's not so bad," Linnette felt obliged to tell him. "And neither are you. One of these days, the two of you will come to an understanding."

"Maybe," Mack said doubtfully. "I hope we do, but I'm not holding my breath."

A polite knock sounded at Linnette's door. Lucky was suddenly alert; she gave one brief bark and stared intently.

Brother and sister glanced at each other, and then Linnette went to the door. A woman, dressed in a brown sheriff's uniform, stood on the other side, holding a small pot of bronze chrysanthemums.

"Hello, I'm your neighbor, Gloria Ashton," she said as she handed Linnette the plant.

"Linnette McAfee," she said, admiring the rich color of the chrysanthemums. "Mom told me everyone in Cedar Cove is friendly. This is just so nice. Please come in." She stood aside so Gloria could step into her apartment. Linnette gestured toward her brother. "Gloria, this is my brother, Mack. Mack, this is my next-door neighbor, Gloria Ashton."

Mack released the dog's collar, then stood and offered Gloria his hand. She took a step forward and extended her own. "This is Lucky," he said. The dog waved her plumy tail, then returned to her place by the couch.

"I'm two doors down in apartment 216. I saw your brother and a couple of other guys bringing in the furniture. I thought I'd stop by on my way to work and introduce myself. I didn't mean to interrupt you, but I wasn't sure when I'd get another opportunity."

"You're with the sheriff's office here?" Linnette asked. Gloria stood with her feet braced slightly apart, hands on her belt. She was short, petite, dark-haired; her uniform fit as if it'd been especially designed for her. The belt that held her weapon and other paraphernalia only emphasized her femininity.

Gloria shook her head in response to Linnette's question. "I'm with the Bremerton office. I've been in the area a little less than a year."

Mack stared at her and narrowed his eyes, as if he was trying to place her. "You look familiar. Have I seen you somewhere before?"

Gloria studied him, frowning, and then shook her head again. "I don't believe we've met."

Mack shrugged. "I guess not. I don't visit often, but when I do I always drive the speed limit."

"Yeah, right." Linnette snickered and her brother elbowed her in the ribs.

"You don't live in Cedar Cove?" Gloria asked.

"Too close to family," he muttered. "They cramp my style." He laughed at his own weak joke and sat down.

"Could you join us for a few minutes?" Linnette asked. "I apologize—I can't offer you anything to drink. I haven't been to the grocery store yet."

"I have to go, but thanks, anyway." Gloria checked her watch. "I thought this would be a good time to welcome you to the complex. If you have any questions about the town, I'll be happy to try and answer them."

"That would be great," Linnette told her. "I'll definitely take you up on that."

"I hope you do." After a few parting words, Gloria was gone.

Linnette waited until the door closed before she turned on her brother. "Have I seen you somewhere before?" Linnette mimicked. "Honestly, Mack, that's the oldest pickup line in the world."

"I wasn't trying to pick her up."

"Mack, you couldn't have been more obvious."

"Well, she *is* cute."

"Oh, please. You're so lame."

"Me? This is the thanks I get for giving up an entire Saturday to help my sister?"

"Okay, you're right. Sorry. If you're interested in Gloria, let me know and I'll see what I can do to set you up—since you're currently footloose and fancy-free."

Mack raised his shoulders in a shrug. "Sure. But the truth is, she *does* look familiar."

Twelve

Saturday night, Allison Cox was roused from a sound sleep by a tap on her bedroom window. Her clock told her it was almost three. She turned on the small light on her bed stand, tossed aside her down comforter and hurried to the window. Opening the blinds, she peered outside and gasped when Anson smiled at her.

"Let me in," he mouthed.

She'd be in big trouble if her parents ever found out about this. Although the temptation was almost overpowering, she shook her head. "I can't."

He nodded vigorously and rubbed his bare hands together. Then he hunched his shoulders, as if to ward off the wind. His eyes pleaded with her.

"Anson, no." She shook her head again, trying to convince herself.

He paused, waited a moment and then turned around, not hiding his disappointment.

His willingness to walk away was her undoing. He'd been so good to her, so gentle and sweet. The first time they'd kissed, his goatee had bothered her and the next time she saw him, he'd shaved it off. Allison had been moved by his thoughtfulness. He cared about her more than any other guy ever had. In fact, she liked him a lot—more than she should. Her parents had no idea how often they saw each other because she hid their relationship as much as she could. Even Cecilia had voiced her concern about Anson, and she hadn't even met him. But Allison knew he wasn't what he appeared to be. The clothes and attitude were all for show.

Twice now he'd come over in the evenings, and he'd been respectful to her mother and father. That had earned him brownie points with her dad.

"Oh, all right," she acquiesced and grabbed her housecoat. She threw it over her pajamas, then slid open the window. Leaving him out in the cold was more than she could bear.

Anson crawled into her bedroom, landing on his feet with a solid thump. Thank goodness for her plush carpet, which absorbed much of the sound. His face was red from the cold, and his lips were chapped. He wore his signature black coat, a knit cap pulled low over his ears. His hands were bare. Smiling at her in the dim room, he let his eyes soften and leaned toward her, his mouth shaping hers in a long, hungry kiss. His face felt chilled and his lips, too.

Allison broke off the kiss and clutched her housecoat tighter around her. "What are you doing here?" she asked in an urgent whisper. "Do you know what time it is?"

Anson sat on the carpet, his back against the side of the bed. Allison knelt beside him. "I shouldn't have come," he whispered. "It was wrong, I know, but…" He looked down, unable to meet her gaze.

"No, it's all right," she said and reached for his hands, warming them between her own. His coat had a peculiar smell. It was as if he'd been standing next to a bonfire and the smoke had clung to him. "What are you doing out at this time of night?"

He kept his head lowered. "I can't involve you in this."

"In what, Anson? You can't involve me in what?" She touched his face, pressing her warm palm to his cheek and was shocked again at how cold his skin was.

Anson covered her hand with his own, then slowly raised his eyes to meet hers. He slid his hand to the nape of her neck and brought her mouth back to his. His kiss was demanding, desperate.

"We can't do this here...now," she said, as quietly as she could. It would be easy to let him keep touching her, kissing her, but her father was a light sleeper and the risk was too great. Besides, something was terribly wrong. She felt it, saw it in Anson's eyes, a wildness that frightened her—and yet she didn't feel she could desert him.

Once more Anson looked down, avoiding her gaze.

"Tell me what happened," she insisted. "Where have you been?"

His voice was barely audible. "The park."

"I thought it was closed. How'd you get in?"

His mouth twisted in a half smile. "All they have is a gate. It's easy enough to jump over that."

"Who were you with?" She should've realized a gate across the entrance wasn't going to lock anyone out, least of all Anson and his friends.

"It doesn't matter," he said.

"Who?" she asked again.

"I was alone, okay?"

A siren pierced the night and Anson scrambled to his knees, crawled close to the window and peered out. "Anson?" Dread wormed its way into her stomach. "What's going on?"

Again he refused to answer as he crawled back to where she knelt.

"There's a fire?"

He hesitated and then nodded.

"Does it have anything to do with you?"

He didn't answer right away. When he did, his voice trembled. "Yes."

"Oh, my gosh." She covered her mouth with both hands as she tried to take in what he was telling her.

"I didn't mean to do it. It was an accident. My mother's got some friend at the house," he said scornfully, "and I can't stand to be around when she has a sleepover." He couldn't seem to look at her. "The walls between our rooms are thin. I can hear everything."

He didn't need to say any more for her to understand why he had to leave.

He seemed to think Allison would be angry with him and when she wasn't, he added, "I just *had* to get out."

"So you went to the park?"

He nodded. "It's cold and I didn't know where else to go." Everything began to add up. "You...started a fire?"

"I was looking for a way to keep warm." He rubbed his hand down his face. "I thought I'd make a campfire, you know, but I'm no Boy Scout. I must've done something wrong, because the wind picked up and before I knew it the flames caught—near the maintenance hut."

"Is that what's on fire?"

Anson bit his lower lip. "There must've been some gasoline on the ground or something, because it practically exploded. I tired to put it out, but I couldn't. Then I got scared. The flames were too hot, so I ran. I should've stayed, should've found a payphone and called the fire department. There isn't one in the park."

Allison's heart pounded hard as she wrapped her arms around his shoulders. Anson had come to her; he needed her. They talked every day and hung out at school together. She was crazy about him, but her teachers, her friends, even Cecilia, thought he was wrong for her. Her parents were leery, too, but they'd let Anson come to the house for dinner twice. She and Anson even went to the library and studied together. Allison didn't believe that caring about someone this much could be wrong.

"What are you going to do?" she asked.

He hung his head. "I don't know."

In that case, she did. "I'm going to wake up my dad."

"No!" His response was automatic.

"My dad will know what to do," she argued. "He won't come down on you if you're honest with him. He's fair, Anson."

He still looked uncertain. "Maybe…maybe that fire wasn't as much of an accident as I said."

Shocked, Allison sat back on her heels. *"What?"*

He glanced away and she saw that his hands had started to tremble. "I didn't mean for it to get out of control like that," he whispered.

"You set the shed on fire on *purpose?* You mean it wasn't an accident?"

His nod was barely perceptible. "Your dad will want to take me to the sheriff's office. Allison, I can't. I'm almost eighteen. The prosecutor might decide to try me as an adult."

A sick feeling invaded the pit of her stomach, but she'd learned that the best way to attack a problem was head-on. She didn't have any reassurances to give him. "They might, but I'll be with you."

"Your dad won't let you have anything to do with me if I tell him what I did."

Allison already knew this was a risk. "I know, but that's a chance we have to take. My dad's fair and he'll respect you for being honest. He'll do what he can to help you."

"Why would he?"

Allison straightened her shoulders and brought her hand to his cheek. "Because his daughter cares what happens to you."

Anson's eyes locked onto hers. "You do?"

"A lot." Allison's heart swelled with the intensity of her emotions.

At her words, her touch, Anson's eyes filled with tears. "No one's ever really cared about me before," he said.

"*I* care." And to prove how much, she leaned forward and kissed him. He smiled tentatively when she lifted her lips from his. Taking him by the hand, she led him out of her bedroom and into the kitchen. By the light of the moon, which shone coldly through the window, she urged him into a chair, instructing him to wait there while she woke her father.

"You're sure about this?"

Allison wasn't sure of anything, but she trusted her father. He'd know what to do and how best to help Anson. She had no other alternative.

Her dad was sitting up in bed even before Allison reached her parents' door. "What's going on?" he asked. Her mother slept contentedly at his side, undisturbed.

"Anson needs your help," she whispered.

"Now? In the middle of the night?"

She met his stare as he folded back the covers. "I trust you to do the right thing, Dad," she told him, her voice shaking. That was all she would say. All she could do was pray he didn't disappoint her.

Thirteen

"This is such a treat," Maryellen said, slipping into the booth across from her mother at the Wok and Roll, her favorite Chinese restaurant.

"Just consider it an early birthday gift," Grace replied as she glanced up from the menu.

"So, how are things with you and Cliff?" Maryellen asked. She didn't bother with the menu because she ordered the same thing every time. She really should try something other than the chicken hot sauce noodles, but couldn't make herself do it. The small family-owned restaurant ordered the thick rice noodles from the International District in Seattle. Maryellen could slurp up those noodles every day, she enjoyed them so much.

Her mother set aside the menu and there was such a depressed look on her face that Maryellen was shocked. "Mom?"

Smiling was clearly an effort. "I've given up on Cliff," Grace said matter-of-factly.

"You don't mean that." Maryellen reached across the table and squeezed her mother's hand.

"I do. In reality, I don't have any choice."

"No." Maryellen couldn't believe it. "I thought you were going to fight for him. What happened?"

Grace told her about the night of their big dinner date. She'd since learned from the veterinarian, who'd come into the library, that Midnight had survived. Hearing this from someone other than Cliff only seemed to increase her mother's discontent with the on-again/off-again relationship.

Maryellen understood Grace's frustration. Her mother had been so hopeful about this dinner; it was going to be a new beginning for her and Cliff. And then the evening had turned out to be such a disappointment.

"It was more than Cliff dealing with Midnight. I understand the stallion was in a life-threatening situation. That I could have accepted. But Cliff had obviously forgotten he'd even asked me out to the ranch. He seemed so…indifferent. My being there meant nothing to him. In fact, he seemed grateful to get out of having dinner with me."

"Cliff's not like that."

"Normally I'd agree with you," her mother said, "but I was there, Maryellen. I've learned to trust my instincts and that was the way I felt. Much as I don't want to believe it, I know I'm right."

Maryellen hated to see this relationship end, especially since Grace had worked so hard to win Cliff back. Until now, Maryellen had found him to be thoughtful and sensitive to her mother—far more than her own father had ever been. "You mean to say that after two weeks Cliff hasn't even tried to phone?" she asked, incredulous.

Her mother shrugged. "He left messages a couple of times."

"Well?" Maryellen looked at her sternly. "Did you return his calls?"

Her mother's smile was sad. "Olivia thinks I should, too, but I can't." She sighed so dejectedly that Maryellen yearned to hug her and reassure her.

"Why *not?*" Maryellen really didn't understand this.

She recognized from the stubborn way her mother shook her head that Grace wouldn't call him. "Olivia says I'm a fool not to, but Maryellen, you have to realize how demeaning it was, how awful I felt—it's hard to explain. Sad as it is to admit, I don't think Cliff's capable of getting beyond what happened with Will." She paused; she'd never told her daughters the whole story, but Maryellen had pieced it together. "As far as he's concerned, I committed the one sin he can't forgive. He'd like things to be different, he might even want us to be together, but something inside him is incapable of forgiving me for what I did."

Maryellen disagreed. "You're wrong. He wouldn't have phoned if that was the case."

Grace shook her head again. "I'm sure Cliff regrets what happened, but there's no need to drag this out any longer. I doubt he'll phone again and after some soul-searching, I've decided that's fine."

Her mother might have talked herself into that decision, but Maryellen didn't believe she was fine with it at all. The very first time she'd met Cliff and seen him with her mother, Maryellen had felt they were meant to be together. "Do you remember when I was pregnant with Katie?" Maryellen asked.

"Of course."

"I was convinced I didn't need Jon and that I could raise the baby on my own. Remember?"

A smile touched her mother's eyes. "You were so determined to prove it."

"Yes, well... It was easy enough to think I could do everything by myself *before* Katie was born, but afterward…it was a different story." Never would she have imagined that one tiny baby could be so demanding. Most nights Maryellen had only managed to sleep in twenty- or thirty-minute stretches—if at all. A rash of ear infections kept Katie up at night screaming in pain. Thankfully Jon had insisted on being part of his daughter's life and wanted to share the responsibility of raising her. Maryellen had quickly seen that Katie needed him, and so did she. "The similarity, Mom, is that I was so sure about everything—and I was wrong. Maybe you are, too."

As Grace began to reply, Elaine, the owner's wife, came for their order and predictably Maryellen chose her chicken hot sauce noodles. Grace asked for Wor Wonton Soup.

When Elaine had left their table and gone back to the kitchen, the restaurant door opened and in walked Cliff Harding.

Maryellen leaned toward her mother. "Don't look now, but Cliff just came in."

Grace stiffened. "Did he notice us?"

There wasn't time to answer. Cliff walked directly over to their table and smiled down at both women.

"Hi, there," Maryellen said, raising her hand. "This is a pleasant surprise."

He acknowledged her, and removed his Stetson as he turned toward her mother. "Grace," he said with a curt nod.

"Hello, Cliff." Her mother's voice was calm, and she kept her eyes trained straight ahead.

Maryellen admired her poise in this awkward situation. She watched as Grace slowly glanced up and offered Cliff the scantest of smiles.

"There must be a problem with your answering machine," he said. "I've been trying to get in touch with you."

"Would you care to join us?" Maryellen asked, ignoring the daggers her mother was shooting at her.

"Grace?"

Her mother hesitated only briefly. "By all means." She looked at her watch as if to gauge how much of her lunch hour was left. "I'll need to leave in a few minutes, anyway."

"Nonsense," Maryellen challenged. "We ordered no more than three minutes ago."

Cliff sat at the end of the booth, setting his cowboy hat on the empty space next to Grace.

"It's a little early for you to be having lunch, isn't it?" her mother asked pointedly.

Cliff smiled wryly. "The truth is, I drove by and saw you and Maryellen in the window. I figured if you weren't going to answer my phone calls, the best thing to do was talk to you in person."

"Oh."

"I'm sorrier than you know about that night," he said with sincerity.

So Maryellen was right. Cliff knew what he'd done and was trying to make amends.

"I was hoping you'd be willing to give me another opportunity." His eyes pleaded with Grace. "I'd still like you to come out to the ranch for dinner," he said in a rush.

Grace seemed to waver. "I—I don't know."

Maryellen wanted to shake her mother. "I'm sure she'd enjoy that very much," she said firmly and ignored the kick as her mother's shoe connected with her shin.

Maryellen nearly laughed aloud at the shuffling of their feet beneath the table.

In the meantime, Elaine brought Cliff a teacup and a menu. He accepted the tea, but declined lunch.

The small interruption was followed by an uncomfortable

silence. "When would you like Mom to come over?" she asked.

"Maryellen!" Her mother's protest was accompanied by a glare. "I'm sure Cliff has more important things to attend to than making me dinner."

"I'd like to do it," he countered, a smile twitching at the edges of his mouth.

"What date were you thinking of?" Maryellen was finding pleasure in this. It was a fitting turnabout, considering all the times Grace had tried to match her up after her divorce. She'd resented it back then, never suspecting that the day would come when she'd play matchmaker for her own mother.

"Thanksgiving," Cliff said.

That astonished them both, and they stared at him.

"Thanksgiving," Grace repeated softly. "I'm sorry, I already have an invitation." She sent a triumphant look in Maryellen's direction.

"To my house," Maryellen said. Feeling she needed to explain the situation to Cliff, she added, "Kelly's going to be at her in-laws', so Mom was planning to join Jon, Katie and me."

"Aren't you flying out to be with Lisa?" Grace asked.

"Lisa was here earlier in the year," Cliff said, and of course Grace knew that. "I thought I'd stay home. I don't pretend to be much of a cook, but I can probably manage a turkey and fixings."

Maryellen watched the lowering of her mother's guard. No matter how hard Grace tried to convince herself the relationship was over, she couldn't do it. In a matter of minutes, her resolve was visibly crumbling.

"I appreciate the invitation," her mother said, her eyes warm with longing, "but I'm already committed to my daughter."

"Mom, it's all right, really. Jon and I won't mind."

"Nonsense," Cliff said quickly. "I was hoping Maryellen, Jon and the baby would come, too."

Grace met Maryellen's eyes.

Maryellen felt a sense of satisfaction steal over her. "I'll have to check with Jon, of course, but I imagine he'd enjoy the opportunity *not* to cook this Thanksgiving."

"Then you'll both be joining Cal and me," Cliff said, as he got to his feet. He reached for his hat and when he smiled, it seemed to Maryellen that there was a new lightness in his expression. His habitual look was one of gravity and she'd rarely seen this kind of…elation on his face before.

She noticed that her mother was smiling, too.

Fourteen

The ringing of the phone destroyed the calm of the afternoon. Corrie reached for it on the second ring. "Roy McAfee's office," she said in her professional voice.

The lack of response caught her attention. "This is Roy McAfee's office," she repeated.

Silence again.

Sighing, she replaced the phone. When she looked up, Roy was standing in the doorway leading to his office, his arms crossed. He glowered at the phone as if it were guilty of some unspeakable crime.

"How many hang-ups have we had in the last couple of weeks?" he asked.

Corrie hadn't counted them. "Two or three," she said, but she knew it was more. She shrugged, making light of it. "I think the phone company must've issued a number similar to ours to a pizza parlor or something."

"How many hang-ups did we get in October?"

"Oh, honestly, Roy, you don't expect me to remember that, do you?"

His eyes narrowed. "As a matter of fact, I do. I don't know

anyone who has a better mind for details. How many, Corrie?"

She swallowed hard. "None."

"That's what I thought."

"In other words, you think whoever's been mailing these postcards is switching to phone calls?"

"I don't know."

"Any more postcards recently?" Corrie hated to ask, but she needed to know. She hadn't seen any, and Roy hadn't mentioned getting even one in quite a while. Still, she was afraid he might be hiding them from her—for her own protection, of course.

He shook his head. "The last card arrived on October sixth."

Corrie smiled, not that she found it humorous. She did feel a little relieved, yes. But her amusement, such as it was, came from Roy's claim that she had a head for details, although he was the one who categorized every fact, no matter how minute. If it hadn't been for Roy, the murder at the Thyme and Tide might never have been solved. Little things like the date of the last postcard stayed in his mind—and hers, too. Nothing, however, had been as troubling as this.

The phone rang again. Corrie looked at Roy before answering on the second ring. "Roy McAfee's office."

"Mom," Linnette cried, "where *are* you?"

"Ah…"

"The ceremony for the clinic opening starts in fifteen minutes! I thought you were coming."

Corrie nearly laughed out loud. Only seconds earlier, she'd been congratulating herself and Roy on their memories, and they'd let the most important day of the month slip past them.

"Dad and I will be there in a few minutes."

"Hurry! You wouldn't believe all the people who are here.

Besides, I want to introduce you to Dr. Timmons. Oh, Mom, he's just so cute."

"We're on our way now," Corrie said.

"Don't even think of driving. There isn't a parking spot to be had for miles."

Corrie loved the joy and excitement in her daughter's voice. "We'll be right over."

Roy must've heard, because he'd already collected his jacket. He held Corrie's long wool coat for her. When she'd pulled on her gloves and wrapped a hand-knit scarf around her neck, they walked out the door. Roy automatically stopped to check that it was locked.

The brisk cold wind off the cove was powerful enough to make Corrie's eyes water. She shivered and Roy tucked her hand in the crook of his arm as they set off at a brisk pace toward the newly constructed clinic across from City Hall.

"I'm glad Linnette's living in Cedar Cove now," Roy murmured, surprising her. He didn't generally reveal his emotions; he was the kind of man who showed his love through the things he did, not the things he said. Corrie was pleased he had a good relationship with Linnette. But that reminded her of his conflicts with their son, which immediately saddened her.

"I'm glad she's here, too." Corrie was more than glad, she was thrilled. Ecstatic. She just wished Mack and Roy would sort out their differences. She resisted the urge to remind her husband that Mack had helped his sister move from Seattle to Cedar Cove. Roy would see through that conversational ploy instantly.

By the time Corrie and Roy arrived at the medical complex, there was a crowd, just as Linnette had said, with more people gathering in front of the big red ribbon stretched across the sidewalk. Corrie spotted Mayor Benson with several other members of the council.

Charlotte and Ben Rhodes were there. That was fitting because it was through their determined efforts that Cedar Cove had a medical facility at all. Jack Griffin and a photographer from *The Chronicle* were interviewing a group of older people, while the sheriff and his deputies scanned the crowd.

Linnette smiled and waved when she saw Corrie and Roy. She motioned with her head at the good-looking man standing on her right. This must be Chad Timmons, the physician she'd mentioned countless times.

A small podium had been erected and Mayor Benson finally stepped up to the microphone. "Welcome, welcome," he called out, and a hush fell over the crowd. "I'm delighted to see such a large turnout for this afternoon's grand opening of Cedar Cove's brand-spanking-new medical facility."

Corrie was almost deafened by the resounding cheer that followed. "This has come about as a result of the cooperation between the private and public sectors. I'm proud to have played a role in getting this facility off the drawing board."

Corrie glanced at her husband and saw that he was having a hard time squelching a smile. "The old windbag should be thanking Charlotte and Ben," he said, bending down to whisper in her ear.

"Yeah," Corrie whispered back. "He wasn't the one who risked jail time."

Mayor Benson gestured expansively. "Now, I'd like to introduce our staff members." Several other men and women had joined Linnette and Dr. Timmons, and the mayor briefly introduced each one. When Linnette's name was announced, she gave a small wave. Corrie clapped as loudly as her gloved hands would allow.

After the introduction of the staff, Mayor Benson continued to elaborate on the role his office had played in establishing the clinic.

"Just cut the ribbon," someone shouted from the back of the crowd when rain started to fall.

Mayor Benson reached for the big scissors. "Normally it's my privilege, as mayor of Cedar Cove, to cut the ribbon, but I'd like to defer in this instance." He turned to Charlotte and Ben. "Mr. and Mrs. Rhodes, would you kindly do the honors?"

The crowd roared with approval.

Blushing, Charlotte stepped forward and with Ben at her side, cut the ribbon.

"Now we'd like everyone to come in for a tour of the facility. And please, help yourself to refreshments."

The small podium was quickly moved and the double glass doors opened wide as a stream of visitors flowed in.

Corrie and Roy paused to chat with friends along the way. Jack's photographer took dozens of pictures, but Corrie was sure the photograph on the front page would be of Charlotte and Ben cutting the ribbon. She had to give the mayor credit. He was a savvy politician to surrender the honor to Charlotte and Ben Rhodes. That had probably earned him more votes than anything he might have said.

Corrie chatted with Peggy Beldon while she waited for the crowd to diminish so she could talk to her daughter. Out of the corner of her eye she saw Gloria Ashton, Linnette's neighbor, deep in conversation with Dr. Timmons. She'd recently met her when she'd visited Linnette to drop off a casserole. Corrie noticed the way Linnette's gaze followed her newfound friend, as if sizing up the competition. Oh, dear. That could be a problem. Although Corrie had only met Gloria the one time, she'd liked her and hoped that Linnette and her neighbor would become good friends.

"Who's that?" Roy asked, nodding toward Gloria.

Linnette had walked over to Gloria and Dr. Timmons and

joined in the conversation. Corrie saw Dr. Timmons's quick frown, as if he resented the intrusion. This definitely wasn't a good sign.

"Do you know her?" Roy asked again.

"That's Linnette's neighbor. She works for the sheriff's office in Bremerton."

Roy didn't say anything. "What makes you ask?" she prodded.

"No reason."

Roy was probably thinking the same thing as Corrie. Their daughter had a major crush on this doctor. Corrie couldn't remember hearing Linnette more excited than the day she'd learned the clinic had hired Chad Timmons.

"Come on," Corrie said, taking her husband's hand. "Let's go talk to Linnette."

"In a minute," Roy said, frowning as he watched his daughter interact with the small group. "What do you know about this guy she's so keen on?"

"Just what she told me. Roy, good grief, give the girl a chance. She's got a mind of her own and she isn't going to appreciate your interference."

"Is that so?" Roy teased.

"Absolutely."

Roy smiled again. "How'd her date go with that bachelor you paid top dollar for?"

His comment hit its mark. "Touché," she murmured. The dinner was a major disappointment in Corrie's view. Apparently Linnette's evening had been enjoyable enough; in fact, according to her daughter, it'd been a better experience than she'd expected. But as far as Corrie knew, Cal Washburn hadn't phoned her for a second date. Sadly, she wasn't entirely convinced Linnette would accept if he did.

"Then I guess we should make this young doctor's acquaintance." With his hand at the small of her back, Roy steered Corrie toward the group.

The three stopped chatting when Corrie and Roy approached. "Mom, Dad," Linnette said, smiling broadly. All that was missing was a trumpet fanfare. "*This* is Dr. Timmons."

The physician exchanged handshakes with Roy and Corrie. "Pleased to meet you," he said politely.

"I think Linnette's mentioned your name," Corrie told him, downplaying her daughter's interest. "Did you attend classes together?"

"Not really," Chad said. "We met at the hospital where Linnette did her practical training."

"And this is Gloria Ashton," Linnette inserted, smiling at her father. "We live in the same apartment complex. Gloria, meet my dad, Roy McAfee."

"It's a pleasure," Roy said.

Gloria nodded. "Same here."

After a moment's silence, Dr. Timmons said, "If you'll excuse me, I'd better do some more mingling." He grinned at Gloria. "I'd be interested in following up on our conversation," he said, then glanced self-consciously at Linnette. "Could I give you a call sometime?"

His question went unanswered and there was an uncomfortable silence.

"Oh—yes, I'm sorry," Gloria said. "I'd like that."

Linnette's face fell, but she recovered quickly. With a strained smile, she ushered her parents toward the interior of the clinic. "Come on, Mom and Dad. I'll give you a personal tour."

Corrie wasn't fooled. She could sense trouble brewing between Linnette and her new friend over the handsome Dr. Timmons.

Fifteen

Cecilia liked Rachel Pendergast right away. They talked for a few minutes before the beautician seated her and draped the plastic cape around her. Rachel had a friendly, down-to-earth manner that Cecilia found appealing. Ian had suggested she introduce herself to Warrant Officer Nate Olsen's girlfriend, so she'd scheduled an appointment. Cecilia was due for a haircut, anyway, and wasn't opposed to trying out a new shop, especially one with such a good reputation.

Rachel turned the chair around so Cecilia faced the mirror. She combed through Cecilia's thick hair and ran her fingers from beginning to end.

"How much would you like cut off?" she asked, meeting Cecilia's gaze in the mirror.

"About an inch," she said, "and I'd like you to trim my bangs." Cecilia guessed she and Rachel were close to the same age; perhaps Rachel was a few years older. It was hard to tell.

"When's your baby due?" Rachel asked, leading Cecilia to the shampoo sink.

"March fifteenth." The date was embossed in her mind as

she mentally counted the days before she would hold her son in her arms.

"Is this your first baby?" Rachel asked conversationally.

Cecilia hesitated. The question always stopped her cold. And it was always accompanied by pain as she faced the memory of losing Allison. "No," she whispered, trying to speak normally. "Our daughter died shortly after she was born."

"I'm so sorry." Rachel placed a comforting hand on Cecilia's shoulder and squeezed gently.

Not wanting the other woman to think she'd taken offense, Cecilia offered her a reassuring smile. "You didn't know. It's a question I get asked often enough. You'd think I'd have a standard response by now. I should." Except Cecilia didn't know what that response should be. "It'd be easier to tell everyone this is our first baby, I suppose," she said, thinking out loud, "but I can't make myself do it. Allison was part of me and Ian, and I refuse to pretend she never lived."

"You said exactly the right thing," Rachel told her. She busied herself by turning on the water and leaning Cecilia back so that her neck rested in the curve of the shampoo bowl.

Rachel worked the shampoo into Cecilia's wet hair with strong fingers, massaging her scalp. Her touch relaxed Cecilia as she lathered her hair, rinsed and then repeated the process.

By the time Rachel had washed out the cream rinse and placed a towel over her head, Cecilia had started to consider having her hair cut much shorter than she'd been wearing it. Over the years she'd had it styled a number of ways. Ian, however, preferred her hair shoulder-length, so that was how she kept it. Maybe she could have *two* inches cut off—make the change in increments.

"You have wonderful hair," Rachel commented as she guided Cecilia back to her station.

"It must be the vitamins," Cecilia said lightly. "The only times I've had hair and fingernails like this are when I'm pregnant."

Rachel directed Cecilia into the chair. She combed out and sectioned her hair, twisting each section and securing it with a clip. "Do you know if you're having a boy or a girl?"

"Boy," Cecilia said, smiling at the thought of her husband's happiness when she'd told him what she'd learned. "The first ultrasound said a girl, but in the most recent one, the baby looked very much like a little boy. I know Ian will be thrilled with either—I will, too." She rested her hand on her stomach, already loving this baby so much. She wanted the pregnancy to be perfect, her child to be healthy, and was doing everything she could to ensure that.

They chatted while Rachel expertly cut her hair, going a little shorter than Cecilia had originally requested. Her hair would just touch her shoulders. "Since you're a first-time customer, can you tell me who referred you?" she asked, clipping away. "I like to thank the person who gave me the referral."

"That might be difficult. My husband's the one who suggested I make an appointment with you."

"Really?" Rachel paused as if trying to recall which of her male customers was married to Cecilia.

"Apparently, my husband is a friend of a friend of yours," Cecilia clarified. "I understand Ian and—I think Ian said his name's Nate—are on the *George Washington* together."

Excitement lit Rachel's eyes. "Your husband's in the Navy?" Cecilia nodded.

"Did he have any news about Nate?" There was no disguising Rachel's exhilaration now. "We write to each other, but the letters take so long, and I haven't heard from him in over a week. Everything's okay, isn't it?"

"Oh, yes…. The last I heard, everything was going well."

"Oh, good." Rachel smiled in obvious relief. "I've only known Nate for a few months," she said.

"She paid good money for him, too." This comment came from the dark-haired, slightly overweight woman in the station next to Rachel's.

"Teri," Rachel said, scowling at her friend.

"You…paid for him?" Cecilia asked, intrigued.

"In a manner of speaking, yes…"

She was about to continue when Teri cut her off. "She bought him at the Dog and Bachelor Auction in July." Having said that, the other beautician turned back to her customer.

"Rach was the only one of us who plunked down her hard-earned cash for a man," the beautician across from Rachel said. "The guys were out of my price league."

"Mine, too," Teri added.

"For that matter, he was out of mine," Rachel told her.

"Then why did you bid on him?" Cecilia asked curiously. She remembered reading an article about the auction in *The Cedar Cove Chronicle*. The piece had stated that the Dog and Bachelor Auction was by far the most successful fund-raising activity ever put on by the Animal Shelter. Cecilia thought it was certainly innovative.

"I can't say exactly what appealed to me about Nate," Rachel confessed. "He was one of the last bachelors available and not a single one of us girls had bought one yet." She paused. "Although a girlfriend of mine did get a dog."

"We all had high hopes for this event," Teri said. "We went thinking this might be a good way to meet men."

"And we wanted to support the shelter," another girl chimed in. "We're all big animal-lovers here."

"It seems to be working out for Rach," a young woman with spiked hair said.

"I don't mind admitting it was the best money I've spent in ages," Rachel agreed.

"Yeah?" Teri placed one hand on her hip. "Then why are you still dating Bruce Payton?"

"We *aren't* dating," Rachel insisted, lowering her voice. "We really aren't," she told Cecilia. "Bruce is a widower and we sort of keep each other company now and then."

"Jolene wants you to be her mom." Teri said this in a sing-song voice as if she were forecasting trouble.

Rachel exhaled slowly. "I know, and that's a problem."

Confused, Cecilia glanced from one woman to the other. "Jolene is Bruce's daughter?"

"Yes." Rachel nodded. "She misses her mother. I try to do girl things with her. Bruce appreciates that, and Jolene and I have gotten to be close in the last couple of years."

"But you're interested in Nate?" Cecilia wanted to be clear on that.

"Very much." Rachel didn't bother to disguise her feelings for him.

"I gather he feels the same way about you," Cecilia was happy to report. "Like I said, my husband suggested I get in touch with you."

"That's great." Happiness radiated from her eyes.

"Um…does Nate know you're seeing Bruce?"

"Yes—no, but Bruce and I aren't actually seeing each other in the dating sense. We just do things together, mainly for the company. And for Jolene. There's nothing romantic between us." She hesitated for a moment. "At least on my end."

"And Bruce?"

"I can't speak for him, but…sometimes I think he'd like the relationship to be more than it is. Please understand, I don't encourage him," Rachel said, looking a bit uncomfortable to be saying even this much. "I haven't said anything to Nate about Bruce, because—well, because it just isn't important enough to mention."

Cecilia understood perfectly. She believed in honesty between husband and wife, but there were some things best left unsaid. Some things that were just too hard to explain. Especially when communication was limited.

"I felt terrible when I missed a phone call from Nate. I was with Jolene and had my cell turned off. We must've been in the movie theater and then I got a message that he'd called. I was sick about that. Apparently he only got one chance and he wasted his." Rachel's disappointment echoed in each word.

"Ian said you don't have a computer."

"I don't," Rachel said. "In fact, I'm a real dunce when it comes to anything technological."

"I'd be willing to help you learn," Cecilia offered. "Ian asked me to get you up and running. The request is actually from Nate because he wants to talk to you on-line. Once you're familiar with how it works, you can use one of the computers at the library. That's what Ian and I did until we could afford our own. You'd be surprised how easy it is."

Rachel beamed. "Thank you—I really appreciate this. By the way...did your husband mention that I'm a few years older than Nate?"

"No, but it didn't sound as if Nate cared."

"No, I guess he doesn't. I think about it sometimes and then I remember—"

"What she remembers," Teri inserted, "is that Nate is one hell of a kisser."

Cecilia watched as Rachel's face grew pink. "This is the problem when you work with a group of women," she muttered, glaring across her station at Teri. "They don't know the meaning of the word *discretion*."

Teri laughed outright. "I don't think I've ever seen Rachel blush before—except when she told us about the night she and Nate sat on the beach until the wee hours of the morning."

"Nate was leaving that day," Rachel added for Cecilia's benefit.

Cecilia understood the need to be close for as long as possible. It happened with her and Ian every time he was due to ship out.

"There are a few of us Navy wives who have a small support group. You'd be welcome to stop by the next evening we meet."

"I would, but I'm not a Navy wife."

"But you could be," Teri said.

"We'd love to have you," Cecilia assured Rachel. "I'll let you know when we're planning to get together. Why don't you come to my apartment first so I can show you how to send Nate an e-mail."

"Thank you," Rachel whispered. "I'm thrilled about this."

Cecilia felt good about it herself. Not only that, her hair looked beautiful—smooth and glossy—and when she went to pay, Rachel told her it was on the house.

Sixteen

Grace didn't expect anything to come of this Thanksgiving dinner at Cliff's. When he'd joined her and Maryellen at the Chinese restaurant, he'd seemed genuine about wanting another chance, but she couldn't allow herself to believe there was hope for them. Couldn't risk another bout of disappointment. It was with this thought in mind that she drove to meet her daughter's family on Thanksgiving morning. They would all arrive at Cliff's house together.

Maryellen was certainly in high spirits, Grace noted as her daughter let her in. She loved Maryellen and Jon's home, which was built in a Northwest style and only a few miles from Cliff's property. With each visit, she marveled at Jon's ingenuity and skill. While he developed his artistic career, handling the management aspect as well as the photography itself, he also worked on his house and its grounds. Each and every day Grace was grateful her daughter had met Jon Bowman—and that she'd married him.

Katie took one look at her grandma and gleefully waddled toward her, small arms held wide.

Without hesitation, Grace squatted down and scooped her

up, to cries of delight. "How's my Katie-girl?" she asked, nuzzling the toddler's face.

Katie squealed and hugged her back, both arms locked around Grace's neck.

"We're ready, Mom," Maryellen said. She opened the refrigerator and took out a molded salad. It was a recipe that had been in the family for years, made from lime gelatin, cream cheese and melted marshmallows. Grace had always associated it with Thanksgiving dinner and apparently so did her daughter.

"I made salad," Maryellen said unnecessarily. "And Jon baked an apple pie."

"I baked a pumpkin pie," Grace told her.

Maryellen laughed. "Cliff said we didn't have to bring a thing. It seems we decided he needed a little help, after all."

"I can't believe he's willing to prepare an entire turkey dinner by himself," Grace said, impressed that Cliff was taking this on. As far as she knew, he usually settled for sandwiches, canned soup or a simple grilled steak.

"Mother, you don't honestly think Cliff is going to *cook,* do you?" Maryellen looked at her incredulously.

"That's what he said. Didn't he?"

"With all these restaurants and grocery stores offering to provide an entire meal for a reasonable price?" As if she'd suddenly remembered something, she turned to her mother. "What are Olivia and Jack doing for Thanksgiving?"

Grace smiled. "How did we get from store-bought turkey dinners to the subject of Olivia?"

"By way of Justine, of course."

Ah yes, it made sense now. Restaurants provided turkey dinners, and Justine and Seth owned The Lighthouse restaurant.

"Olivia and Jack went to Reno to be with Eric, Shelley and

the twins," Grace explained, referring to Jack's son from his first marriage. According to Olivia, everyone was excited about the trip. They'd flown out on Wednesday evening—the night of the aerobics class Olivia and Grace usually attended. It was the first one Olivia had missed in months. Grace felt guilty for not going, but without the motivation of meeting her best friend, she'd ended up staying home. If not for Olivia, Grace would have given up on the class years ago. Her knees often hurt afterward and any benefit she gained from repeatedly leaping up and down was wiped out by the pie and coffee they had after class.

"Oh, yes, I seem to remember that you mentioned Olivia had plans," Maryellen said absently as Jon loaded the car. When everything was inside, including the portable high chair, he placed a bundled-up Katie in her car seat.

Grace sat in the back next to her granddaughter. Katie was a sweet child, with huge expressive eyes. She was talking now, gibberish mostly, but she seemed to enjoy carrying on long, one-sided conversations.

Grace couldn't help feeling bad that Jon's stepmother was missing out on all the stages of Katie's development. Grace knew it saddened Maryellen, but Jon had been unwilling to compromise in his attitude toward his parents—even when he'd learned of his father's stroke.

Katie was the Bowmans' only grandchild, and they'd never even seen her, except in the photographs Maryellen had surreptitiously sent. It broke Grace's heart.

Cliff was standing in the open doorway when Jon pulled into the yard. A light rain had just begun, and he hurried out to the car to usher Grace into the house, returning to carry in some of Katie's paraphernalia.

Despite Maryellen's predictions, Grace expected to be greeted by the wonderful aroma of turkey and sage; she wasn't so much disappointed as amused when there was no such smell. A fire crackled in the fireplace and the house was warm and inviting, but Cliff was quite clearly taking advantage of a precooked Thanksgiving dinner.

While Maryellen and Jon got Katie out of her jacket and settled with some blocks and a teddy bear, Grace found Cal in the kitchen. He stood by the counter making a pot of coffee. He smiled when he saw Grace. "Happppp-y Thanks…Turkey Day," he managed.

"You, too, Cal." Grace admired the young man and liked him. "Speaking of turkey and turkey day," she said, glancing around. "It doesn't look—or smell—like there's much cooking going on around here."

Cliff stepped into the room behind her. "Guilty as charged. Cal and I opted for culinary assistance."

"The Lighthouse?" Jon asked, joining them.

Cliff nodded. "They're providing a full meal—and they're going to deliver it, ready to go." He checked his watch. "Anytime," he added.

No sooner were the words out of his mouth than the doorbell rang. Cal went to answer it, and both Seth and Justine walked in, carrying their dinner. Seth held the aluminum foil roasting pan with the turkey and Justine had two large bags. They set their bounty on the kitchen counter.

"Need help?" Cal asked.

"There's more in the car," Justine said, throwing off the hood of her rainproof jacket.

"Let-t-t me." Cal disappeared to collect the remaining food.

Justine slipped her arm around her husband's waist. Seth was a big fisherman with a robust physique and hair so blond it was almost white. A few years ago, when the local fishing industry fell on troubled times, he'd taken his savings and Justine's business sense and built The Lighthouse restaurant.

"This is our last stop," Justine explained. "Seth and I decided to make this delivery ourselves so we could wish you all a Happy Thanksgiving."

"Where are you off to next?" Maryellen asked. "There's enough here to feed an army. We'd love it if you joined us," she suggested, looking to Cliff for confirmation.

"We certainly would," Cliff said.

"Seth's family is waiting for us," Justine told them. "But thanks for the invite." She smiled as Cal came in with another two bags. "And thanks, Cal, for getting those."

Within minutes they were out the door and on their way.

Cliff and Cal set the table while Grace and Maryellen arranged the feast on platters and in serving bowls. Christmas music played softly in the background, coming from a Seattle radio station. The mood was festive and joyful as they gathered around the table.

Grace sat beside Cliff and across from Cal. When they all bowed their heads to say grace, Cliff reached for her hand as he whispered a simple heartfelt prayer. The sincerity of his words touched her. She had much to be thankful for. Three years ago, on her first Thanksgiving without Dan, she'd battled depression and loneliness as she and Maryellen struggled to make the best of a painful situation. Now her daughter was married, with a family of her own. And Grace had grown in ways she'd never expected. After a difficult time, she'd been able to accept Dan's death, to find a measure of peace with it. She'd begun to reinvent her life—and Cliff had been part of that process.

There was a lot of joking and laughter as they served themselves, passing bowls and platters around the table. It felt, Grace thought, as if they were all part of the same family.

"I think we should each give thanks for one thing," Maryellen suggested. "Let's take a minute to do that." She cast her eyes down at the pristine linen tablecloth. "I know I'm grateful for so much."

"I am, too," Cliff said. He took Grace's hand again and smiled at her. "I'm most thankful that Grace is with me today. I'm hoping we can spend more time together in the weeks and months to come."

Grace bit her lip to keep the emotion at bay. "Thank you," she whispered.

"Your turn, Mother."

Still holding Cliff's hand, Grace looked around the table. "I'm grateful for my family and friends and—" she paused, swallowing hard "—for this time with Cliff." She'd thought the relationship was over and now hope had been revived. Hope that they'd be able to see past their mistakes and move toward a future together.

Seeming to understand, Cliff squeezed her hand. For a long moment, his eyes held hers.

"Your turn," Jon said, gesturing toward Maryellen.

Maryellen waited until she had everyone's attention. "Today I'm most grateful for the new life growing inside me."

Shocked, Grace dropped her fork. "You're pregnant?"

Maryellen's eyes were glistening. "I found out last week. I can't tell you how hard it was not to say anything until now."

"Maryellen?" Jon whispered hoarsely. "You're pregnant? But I thought…is it safe so soon?"

Grace knew he was referring to the fact that she'd so recently miscarried. Another pregnancy this close to the last one clearly worried him. It concerned Grace, too, but she wouldn't say anything to diminish her daughter's happiness.

Maryellen merely nodded. "I feel fine," she said. "I really do."

"Jon?" Cliff said, motioning to her husband at the other end of the table.

For a moment he seemed incapable of responding. He kept his eyes focused on Maryellen. "I'm most grateful for my wife," he whispered.

As if to protest being left out, Katie banged the high chair with her cup, making a loud noise.

"And Katie," he added, to the accompaniment of delighted laughter.

After dinner Jon tracked down Grace, alone in the kitchen as she wrapped leftovers. Cliff and Cal had gone to the barn to take care of some afternoon chores. He didn't waste time leading up to the subject. "You didn't know?"

"You mean that Maryellen's pregnant? No, and apparently you didn't, either."

His expression was tortured, his face haggard. "Grace, I have to tell you, I'm scared. It's too soon."

"Jon," she reminded him gently, "it seems to me you know what makes babies as well as I do."

"Maryellen seemed so sure nothing would happen…."

"We don't have any choice but to leave this in God's hands," Grace told him. It was the best reassurance she had to offer. She prayed Maryellen wouldn't lose this baby, too.

Seventeen

The word *sale* held a special meaning for Corrie Mc-Afee, and that was *buy.* There was a very good reason the Friday after Thanksgiving was the biggest shopping day of the year. The sales were not to be missed. Corrie liked nothing better than to hit the stores early. The earlier the better, as far as she was concerned.

The alarm rang at five and she was dressed and out the door half an hour later, on her way to pick up Linnette. Linnette had been assigned duty on Thanksgiving Day, and in exchange, had today off. Corrie had waited until after her daughter's shift to serve the traditional turkey dinner, although it hadn't felt right. Putting dinner off until late had been worth it, however, since it meant Linnette could go shopping with her now.

Thanksgiving Day had been gloomy until their daughter arrived—and not just because of the rain. Predictably, Mack had declined her invitation. He claimed he had other plans, none of which he'd described. Corrie didn't argue with him. Her son's so-called plans, she supposed, were to avoid arguing with his father and therefore ruining everyone else's holiday. Corrie wished she could shake some sense into both of them. Roy had been annoyed that Mack hadn't come for dinner; he would've been equally annoyed if his son *had* shown up. But at least Linnette's cheerful presence had rescued his mood...and the evening.

When she pulled into the apartment parking lot, Corrie saw that Linnette's lights were blazing. She didn't have to wait long for her daughter to walk outside and run down the stairs. Opening the passenger door, Linnette slipped into the front seat.

"Where first?" she asked, her eyes bright with enthusiasm.

"Wal-Mart's already open," Corrie said. "The entire store's probably been bought out by now."

"You're joking."

Corrie laughed. "I have much to teach you, my child."

This was the first time in years that they'd been able to schedule a Friday-after-Thanksgiving shopping adventure. The last occasion had been when Linnette was still in high school.

"Let's go into Silverdale next," her daughter suggested after a quick sortie through the local Wal-Mart. "The sooner we get to the mall, the better our chances of locating a decent parking spot."

"Good idea." Corrie headed out of town. There was an unusual amount of traffic for six o'clock on a holiday morning, but she knew from experience that lots of people had the same idea—get to the stores early. Hoping to bring Cal into the conversation, she tried to think of a subtle way to introduce him. She wanted to encourage Linnette to confide in her—yet she didn't want her daughter to feel manipulated. It was a tricky balance. In the end she decided not to mention Cal. She'd see if Linnette brought up the subject herself.

"Thanksgiving dinner was great, Mom," Linnette said.

"Thanks. Speaking of that, where was your doctor friend?"

Linnette tugged at the seat belt as if it was suddenly too tight. "With his family, I guess. He didn't say anything to me." This was stated with disappointment.

Corrie suspected Chad wasn't interested in dating Linnette. The one time she'd met him, at the clinic's official opening, he'd seemed more interested in Gloria, her daughter's neighbor, than in Linnette.

"I was worried for a while that he might have spent it with Gloria," Linnette continued.

"Does she have family in the area?"

"Apparently not. I invited her to come over and join us, but she couldn't. She had to work, too." Linnette paused. "I like Gloria, but I have to admit the real reason I asked her was to make sure she wasn't spending the day with Chad." Linnette heaved a deep sigh. "That was insincere of me and I regret it. I wish Gloria *had* been able to come. Dinner with you and Dad was great, don't get me wrong, but I think she would've enjoyed having it with us. Gloria and Dad would get along really well. They're both in police work and all that."

"Your father's not in police work anymore."

"I know, but it doesn't matter. He's such a cop."

Linnette certainly had her father pegged. "It was a cozy family dinner," Corrie murmured, paying attention to the road. "And there's nothing wrong with that."

She concentrated on her driving, and they didn't speak for the next few minutes.

The silence was broken by Linnette. "Any further developments?"

Her daughter didn't need to elaborate; Corrie understood what she meant. "Some," she admitted reluctantly. Perhaps if she shared what was happening, Linnette would feel freer to talk about her own life.

Linnette waited for her to explain and then nudged her lightly when she didn't. "You can't leave it at that, Mom."

"It's probably nothing."

"Tell me."

Corrie disliked this subject in the extreme, but talking to Roy about it was impossible. He kept so many of his thoughts and feelings hidden inside. She knew this came from long habit, the natural caution of a cop. And it came from his deep-seated desire to protect her. Still, after all these years of married life, Corrie sometimes found her husband a stranger.

"Mom," Linnette whined. "Tell me."

"Sorry, I was thinking." She sighed. "At work during the last few weeks I've been getting an inordinate number of hang-ups."

"What do you mean?" Linnette asked. "You pick up the phone and the person on the other end slams down the receiver?"

"No. But he or she doesn't say anything and then disconnects as soon as I start to ask who's there."

"What about caller ID?"

"That's interesting. The calls are coming from pay phones in different parts of the county. There was even one from Seattle."

"Pay phones," Linnette repeated slowly.

"Your father isn't amused."

"I can't imagine that he is," her daughter murmured. "Whoever's doing this certainly gets around."

"So it seems. And then—" Corrie stopped abruptly. She hadn't meant to let this other part slip.

Linnette was too observant not to notice. "There's more, isn't there?"

Hands clenching the steering wheel, Corrie nodded. "Wednesday afternoon, your father and I left the office early.

Shortly after we got home, Willows, Weeds and Flowers made a delivery to the house."

"The local florist?"

Corrie nodded. "Someone sent us a gorgeous floral arrangement for our Thanksgiving centerpiece."

"Who?"

"Your guess is as good as mine."

"It wasn't on the table."

"I know… Your father didn't want anything to do with it. We didn't have that arrangement one minute before he was on the phone, trying to find out who sent it. Apparently it came as an order from another florist. Your dad was out the door before I could stop him." He'd left her to worry for nearly two hours while he tried to track down this lead.

"Did he learn anything?"

"Not much. But I doubt your father will let it drop that easily."

"What *did* he learn?"

Corrie had been curious herself and it'd taken a good hour to get the information out of him. In the end, he'd told her. "He said whoever sent the flowers paid cash and apparently used a florist in another town. When he questioned the other shop, the person who'd taken the order had already gone home. No one there remembered anyone not paying with a credit card." She shook her head. "He'll probably follow up tomorrow, if he can get hold of that employee."

Linnette took a moment to digest this information. "What happened to the flowers?"

"Your father told me to get rid of them."

"Did you?"

Linnette smiled. "Sort of. I brought them down to the Cedar Cove Convalescent Center that night. They were thrilled to have them."

"That was a very considerate thing to do."

"It was either that or watch your father have a conniption."

As if the thought had just occurred to her, Linnette asked, "Was there a card attached?"

"Yes…" The gift card had infuriated Roy even more than the delivery itself. The person sending the flowers was taunting them. One look and her husband had torn it in half and tossed it in the garbage. After he'd left, Corrie retrieved the ripped card. "It said *Guess Who?*"

Linnette let out a low whistle. "I'll bet that infuriated Dad."

"It sure did," Corrie said grimly. "I don't know what to expect next—from our mysterious stalker *or* your father."

Eighteen

Cecilia had never seen Allison so nervous. She'd been up and down a dozen times in the half hour since she'd arrived at the office after school.

"Did my dad tell you when he expected to be back?" she asked Cecilia for the third time, jumping up from her chair again.

"No, I'm sorry, he didn't." That, too, was unusual. If Mr. Cox was going to be away for an extended period, he always let Cecilia know. Judging by the way Allison was behaving, Cecilia figured that wherever her employer was, it concerned his teenage daughter. And that probably meant it had something to do with Anson.

"What time is it, anyway?" Allison glared at her watch. "He should be back by now." She sat down again.

"Back from where? Does this involve Anson?" Cecilia asked quietly.

The color drained from Allison's face. "What makes you think that?"

"How long have I known you, Allison? Two years? Three? You haven't been this anxious about anything in all that time.

Do you want to tell me what's going on?" To Cecilia's shock, the girl covered her face with both hands and burst into tears.

Cecilia placed an arm around her shoulders. "Come on," she whispered. "Let's go into your father's office." She steered Allison inside, then shut the door.

Allison slumped into the chair in front of her dad's desk, and Cecilia dragged its twin close. Reaching into her pocket, she handed the girl a clean tissue, which Allison crumpled into a tight ball.

"You're right," Allison admitted. "This does have to do with Anson. He got into—he did something he shouldn't have. Afterward, he felt really bad about it and didn't know what to do, so he came to me."

Cecilia had suspected trouble the instant she'd seen the boy, and the few things she'd heard had only confirmed that opinion. Everything about Anson screamed attitude, from his street-length gunslinger black coat to the spiked bracelet. She hadn't liked the idea of Allison hanging around with him, but had kept her opinions to herself.

"Anson came to you for help?" Cecilia repeated, wanting to be sure she understood. She didn't press Allison with questions about what Anson had done, for fear she'd stop confiding in her.

The girl nodded.

"What could *you* do?" Cecilia was annoyed that the boy had expected Allison to solve his problems.

"I took him to talk to my dad," Allison explained. "I knew Dad would help and he has. Dad's been really wonderful."

"What did your father do?"

Allison swallowed hard. "Dad said Anson had to turn himself in to the police." She lifted her gaze to Cecilia's. "I know you're probably wondering what Anson did, but...I don't want to talk about it. Okay?"

"Okay."

Turning himself in was a good start, in Cecilia's view. Her mother had drilled the concept of personal responsibility into her from a young age. Her father, on the other hand, tried to avoid it whenever he could.

"Did Anson take your father's advice and go to the police?"

Allison raised her chin slightly, as though proud of her juvenile delinquent boyfriend. "It was really hard, but he was willing to own up to what he'd done. Dad called his attorney friend and then he drove Anson to the sheriff's department."

"Barry Creech?" Cecilia asked. She knew the attorney was a client of Mr. Cox's and that seemed a logical guess.

"Yes." Allison twisted the tissue in her fingers. "Dad said Mr. Creech specializes in juvenile offenses and he'd know how to handle this."

Cecilia had assumed Anson was already eighteen, but when she mentioned that, Allison shook her head. "Anson turns eighteen next month, and we were afraid the court would want to try him as an adult because he's close to legal age." Sighing heavily, she gave Cecilia a weak smile. "I know you don't like Anson."

"It isn't that I don't like him…"

"My mom doesn't, either—but Cecilia, you're both wrong about him! Anson is a good person. He hasn't had an easy life, you know. His mother's awful… I don't even want to get into it about his mother. She's evil."

Cecilia didn't want to get into it, either. Abe Lincoln had a hard life, too, but he didn't go around committing crimes. "Does Anson have a police record?"

"No," Allison said irritably, which suggested this was a question she'd answered more than once. "He's never done anything like this before."

In other words, he'd never gotten caught. "What did Mr. Creech advise him to do?"

"He said the same thing Dad did, that Anson should turn himself in to the authorities. He met Anson and talked to his mother, and she said he's on his own." Allison's pretty face tightened in a scowl. "Dad met Anson's mom, too, and after that he said he'd go to court with Anson. The judge *has* to accept the plea agreement Mr. Creech worked out with the prosecutor. He has to." Her eyes brimmed with tears. "His own mother won't even be in court with him."

"Okay," Cecilia said in a soothing voice, "so Mr. Creech was able to get a plea agreement with the prosecutor."

Allison dabbed at her eyes with the shredded tissue. "Yes, and Dad says it's a good one. Mr. Creech got the prosecutor to try Anson as a juvenile. That means this won't be on his permanent record, as long as he maintains all the terms of the plea bargain."

Cecilia wasn't convinced that keeping his record clean was necessarily a good thing. She just hoped Anson appreciated everything Mr. Cox and Allison were doing for him. Somehow she doubted it.

"The prosecutor agreed to let Anson do community service hours, plus he has to pay restitution, stay in school and graduate on time."

"He'll need a job if he's going to pay restitution." She tried to figure out exactly what kind of mischief Anson had gotten into.

"Dad helped him there, too," Allison said with such pride her eyes shone. "The Gundersons own The Lighthouse restaurant, and Dad knows Mrs. Gunderson from when she worked at the bank. He called her, and she said they needed a dishwasher and they'd be willing to hire Anson. It's only minimum wage, but Mr. Gunderson said if Anson worked hard and proved himself, he'd consider training him for other positions when they become available."

"Great."

"Anson's really excited. He doesn't have a car or anything, but he's willing to take the bus."

That sounded like a big concession on Anson's part, Cecilia thought cynically. Still this was a light sentence; having to get a job and do a few community service hours didn't seem all that harsh. "Does he have to do anything else?"

Allison put the sodden tissue in her pocket. "He has to stay out of trouble for a year, comply with everything the court ordered and the fire won't appear on his record."

Fire. The word didn't escape Cecilia's notice. So Anson had started a fire. There'd been a piece in *The Chronicle* recently about the tool shed at the community park burning down. According to the article, it had been the act of an arsonist. Cecilia wondered if that was Anson's handiwork, and guessed it was.

"Why are you so worried now?" Cecilia asked. As far as she could see, Mr. Cox had practically held the boy's hand through this entire process.

"The judge has to agree to everything the prosecution suggests and…" Allison looked up, and moist streaks glistened on her cheeks, again. "If the judge doesn't, then Anson will go to jail. And…and—" she began to sob "—Dad said, after today, I can't see him anymore."

That was the wisest thing Mr. Cox had done. None of this was any of Cecilia's business, but she didn't want Allison getting mixed up with a boy so obviously bent on self-destruction. She'd met a dozen kids just like him while growing up and, thanks to her own instinct for self-preservation, had steered clear of them.

"Dad said Anson could stop by and talk to me for a few minutes after court this afternoon, and then that's it. We can't see each other again until Anson's fulfilled his obligations."

"Did he agree to that?"

Allison swallowed hard. "No."

"No!" Cecilia was outraged.

"He couldn't." How quick she was to defend him. "He *can't* agree to that. We go to the same school and we're in the same classes every day. It would be impossible not to see each other."

"I don't think that's what your father meant."

"No, but Anson's going to do everything by the book. He said not spending time with me will be the hardest thing of all. It's true, Cecilia. Anson loves me and I love him. He said he wants to prove to my parents that he's worthy of their faith in him. After the way my dad helped him, I think Anson would've done anything he asked."

Cecilia couldn't comment. Easy enough for Anson to pay lip service now. The proof would come later, and they'd see if he was capable of keeping his word. She didn't mean to sound heartless, but Cecilia doubted it.

Peering through the office window behind her, Allison sprang from her chair. "They're back!" Without another word, she hurried out of her father's office.

Cecilia sat down at her own desk and waited. Mr. Cox greeted her absently as he walked past. He didn't say where he'd been and when he entered his office, he closed the door.

Several minutes passed before Allison returned, her eyes swollen and red.

"Is everything all right?" Cecilia asked, worried by the girl's continuing distress.

Allison sniffled and attempted a smile. "The judge went along with the plea agreement. Anson starts work this afternoon, so we didn't have any time to talk. Next spring, he has to help clean the park for his community service hours. He said he'll put almost all the money from his job toward restitution, and as soon as it's paid off we can see each other again. Oh, Cecilia, I don't know if I can do it."

"Do what?"

"Not be with Anson," she said impatiently. "I love him so much. Mom and Dad keep saying I'm too young to know about love, but I know what I feel. It's…it's like my heart's being ripped out." She shook her head angrily and declared, "You wouldn't understand."

"Really?" Cecilia challenged. "Don't you think it's difficult for me when my husband's out at sea for six months?"

Allison's gaze shot up. "Oh, Cecilia, I'm sorry, of course it is. And you're pregnant, too. I'm sorry. I didn't mean to be insensitive."

Cecilia hugged the girl, just so Allison would realize there were no hard feelings. She remembered the intensity of her own emotions the first time she fell in love. That relationship had ended badly in her senior year of high school. She hoped Allison's experience wouldn't be nearly as traumatic as hers had been.

Nineteen

Linnette had accepted a second date with Cal Washburn, and she regretted it. In fact, she'd regretted it from the moment she'd said yes. He'd phoned shortly after Thanksgiving and before she could think better of it, Linnette had agreed to see him again. Cal was nice enough. His only shortcoming was that he wasn't Chad Timmons. Besides, she felt guilty; she'd been willing to see him a second time for just one reason—to make Chad jealous. Not that she'd seen any evidence her ploy had worked.

"I should call and cancel this date right now," Linnette muttered to Gloria, who sat on the end of her bed. "I feel awful."

Gloria was on her way home from work and had stopped by to invite Linnette out for dinner. Any other night Linnette would've leapt at the offer. Being new in town, she was grateful to have a friend.

"Bet the sick feeling in the pit of your stomach has nothing to do with the flu."

"You're right," Linnette said. She slipped on her black boots and decided to add a black knitted vest over her red blouse. The vest, one of her favorites, was decorated with sequined Christmas trees. She'd hoped to wear it when Chad asked her out, but so far that hadn't happened. If he didn't show any interest soon, the holidays would be over and it'd be too late to wear the vest for another eleven months.

Linnette eyed her neighbor skeptically and wondered if Chad had called her. He'd expressed an interest in Gloria, but judging by the little she'd managed to pick up in conversation—she didn't want to be *too* obvious—Gloria hadn't heard from him. Well, maybe she had, but if so, she hadn't mentioned it.

"So you're going out to dinner alone? Does that happen often?" she asked, hoping for more information about Gloria's social life.

Gloria shrugged. "Since you're busy, I'll probably just order in. Maybe from Wok and Roll. I'm in the mood for something hot and spicy."

Linnette sighed. "Oh," she murmured, genuinely disappointed. "I love their food. I wish I could join you."

"Another time," Gloria said. Straightening, she glanced at her watch. "I better get out of here before your date shows up."

Just then the doorbell chimed.

"Too late," Linnette whispered, dreading the evening more with every minute.

"Just remember what you said earlier," Gloria reminded her. "You want to let him down gently."

"You're right, I do. He's a really nice person. Actually, I'm glad you're here so you can meet him. Then you'll understand my dilemma. He's charming and witty, but it can be hard to hold a conversation and—"

"Don't you think you should answer the door?"

"Oh, right." Linnette hurried into the other room and opened her door.

Cal stood there holding a small potted poinsettia. "Merry Christmas," he said without a hint of a stutter.

"You brought that for me?" The answer was obvious and Linnette felt even more uncomfortable. Silently she vowed she'd make sure he understood this was their last date. It was the right thing to do.

"For you." His gaze moved past her to Gloria, who stepped out of the other room.

"Cal, this is my friend and neighbor Gloria." As she spoke, she set the plant on her coffee table, where it provided a festive touch.

Gloria came forward with her hand extended. "Hello, Cal, I've been hearing a lot about you."

Cal's gaze shot to Linnette, and he seemed both pleased and surprised. "My p-pleas-sure," he said, shaking hands.

"I'll check in with you after the weekend," Gloria said as she moved past Cal on her way out the door. "Have fun, you two."

"I'll just grab my coat and gloves," Linnette said and momentarily left him. She opened the hall closet to retrieve what she needed, and for good measure, added a wool scarf. When she'd agreed to go out with Cal, they hadn't decided what to do. She'd suggested a movie. That sounded less demanding than attempting to carry on a conversation over dinner. Because she wasn't all that interested, she hadn't bothered to look at the movie listings.

When she returned, Cal's appreciative smile warmed her. He took her coat and as he held it, she slid her arms into the sleeves, almost wishing he didn't possess such impeccable manners. Not looking at him, she buttoned her coat, wrapped the scarf around her neck and put on her gloves. They left the apartment and she locked the door, testing the doorknob—just like her father always did.

"Did you decide which movie you want to see?" she asked as they started down the staircase. The wind chilled her face immediately and it seemed about to snow.

He shook his head. "Did you?"

"Oh, I didn't really look. Should I go back to the apartment and get the paper?"

He shook his head again. "H-hungry?" he asked.

"Not very. I had a late lunch."

They continued walking, and Linnette had to admit that Cal was an attractive man. She liked the way his Stetson shaded his face, giving him a mysterious look. He wore a sheepskin coat and leather gloves, and he reminded her of a young Clint Eastwood, back in his spaghetti western days.

"Let's…j-just walk," he suggested.

"Okay, if that's what you want."

Cal tucked her hand in the crook of his elbow and they ambled down Harbor Street. Linnette thought the traffic—both vehicle and foot traffic—was particularly heavy for a Saturday night, but didn't comment. Several other observations occurred to her, but she resisted mentioning them, fearing Cal would feel obliged to respond. Conversation often seemed awkward for him. After a few minutes, she came to enjoy the companionable silence.

Then suddenly it was impossible to remain silent. "It's snowing!" she cried when a fat, moist snowflake fell on her nose, surprising her. "Cal, look! It's actually snowing."

He laughed at her obvious delight. "I see."

"We never get snow…." In the light of the street lamps, Linnette saw his face break into a broad smile. "I mean, we get snow, but it's so rare, especially this close to the waterfront."

"Christmas," he added.

"Oh, I agree. It's absolutely perfect that it's December and Christmas is only about two weeks away."

They followed the sidewalk past the waterfront park and the marina and rounded the curve toward the clinic and City Hall. By that time, the snow was coming down fast and furious.

Fascinated as she was by the snow, Linnette didn't immediately notice that all the traffic was going in the same direction they were. Everyone, it seemed, was headed toward a group of carolers who lined the steps of the City Hall building. They were dressed in Victorian costume for a Dickensian Christmas, their songbooks held open. They began with "God Rest Ye Merry, Gentlemen" and followed that with "Deck the Halls."

Caught up in the sheer wonder and joy of the season, Linnette could only listen raptly. She counted three- or possibly four-part harmony. The performance was lovely in every way. The carolers in their costumes, the large decorated tree, the snow—it was about as idyllic a Christmas scene as Linnette could have imagined.

She watched the performance with Cal standing behind her, his hands resting on her shoulders, and she realized his body was blocking the wind. Once again she wished he wasn't so thoughtful.

Afterward, when the carolers had finished, and the Christmas tree was lit to an enthusiastic burst of applause, Cal suggested a cup of hot cocoa at the Potbelly Deli. Chilled to the bone, Linnette readily agreed. They were fortunate to find a table by the big potbellied stove in the middle of the restaurant. The heat radiating from it soon warmed her. She recognized several people and they exchanged smiles.

The hot chocolate was delicious and served with a candy cane, in honor of the season. She and Cal shared a plate of shortbread cookies cut in Christmas shapes—trees and bells and snowmen. Then Linnette bundled herself up again and they walked toward her apartment. Once more, Cal tucked her arm in his elbow. This was the time to tell him it was over, but she couldn't make herself do it, knowing her announcement would destroy the festive mood.

"That was just wonderful," she said, her steps easily keeping pace with his.

"Yes," he murmured.

"So Christmassy." She hadn't felt much Christmas spirit yet. She blamed Chad for her lack of holiday cheer; she'd assumed that once they were working at the same place, they'd be spending a lot of time together. But that hadn't turned out to be true; they saw each other only in passing and hardly ever had a chance to talk. She wondered darkly if he'd planned it that way.

As they neared her apartment complex, Linnette tried to decide whether it would be a good idea to invite Cal inside. Not to offer might be rude. On the other hand, if he accepted, he might want to kiss her and she couldn't let that happen.

As she knew he would, Cal walked up the stairs with her. When she removed the keys from the outside pocket of her purse, he took them from her hands and unlocked her front door—another old-fashioned courtesy.

She found herself blurting out a rather awkward invitation. "Would you like to come inside? Inside my apartment, I mean…for a few minutes?" She knew she'd suffer a sleepless night if she didn't tell him. It was completely unfair to lead him on.

Linnette stepped into the apartment and was greeted by a blast of warm air as the furnace kicked in. "Oh!" she said, pointing toward the window that overlooked the marina. With the snow drifting down, the scene could've been an illustration on a Christmas card. A number of the boats were gaily decorated with colorful lights strung on their masts. They bobbed almost rhythmically on the water, their lights reflected by its dark surface.

Cal stopped her when she moved to flick on a lamp. "Keep them off," he said—again with no sign of a stutter.

Oh, boy. Here it was. Just as she'd feared, he was going to kiss her. He turned her in his embrace and slipped one arm around her waist and the other over her shoulder. As he bent forward, there was ample opportunity to stop him. But she didn't. Why, Linnette could only speculate. Curiosity, she supposed.

Without even a whimper of protest, she tilted her face toward his, closed her eyes and waited. She wasn't disappointed. His mouth was firm and moist and surprisingly smooth. That was what shook her most. Because Cal was a man's man. A horse trainer. Before she was even aware of it, he'd coaxed her lips open. From that point on, the kiss quickly heated up. Everything did.

A few minutes earlier, they'd been standing in the cold and snow. Now heat suffused her until it was all she could do to breathe. Gripping his coat, she welcomed the exploration of his tongue, meeting his with her own, shyly at first and them more boldly.

By the time Cal broke off the kiss, Linnette felt on the verge of collapse. They edged away from each other as though they were both in shock.

Linnette staggered into the kitchen and placed her hand on the kitchen counter in an effort to regain her balance. Long before she was ready, Cal was standing behind her, touching her shoulder.

"No," she insisted, horrified that the word sounded more like a croak.

"No?" he asked.

She turned, unsure how to handle this. Sliding her arms

around his waist, she exhaled a long, drawn-out breath. Unable to resist, she kissed the underside of his jaw.

He purred as softly as a kitten. "Nice."

"Too nice. This isn't right."

His eyes narrowed. "Sooner than you w-want?"

"That isn't it," she whispered, and because she was embarrassed and more than a little confused, she buried her face in his chest. "I think very highly of you."

"Hmm…" He nuzzled her neck. "Me, too."

Shivers of desire shot down her spine as his lips explored the sensitive skin of her throat. She had to say something, and fast. "It would be wrong to let this go on."

"Wrong?" He lifted his head and looked directly into her eyes. "No." As if to prove her incorrect, he slowly lowered his mouth to hers again. This kiss was as devastating as the first. More so. She felt herself weaken.

"Cal, please," she managed when she found her voice. "There's someone else I'm interested in."

He froze and instantly released her.

Linnette lurched backward. "I'm sorry. I've known Chad Timmons for some time and well, I accepted this date to make him jealous. *That* was wrong. I apologize."

He stepped away from her as though in a daze. Because of his Stetson she couldn't see his eyes. She didn't need to. She felt his disappointment, his frustration—his pain.

"I feel dreadful." She shouldn't have told him about Chad. It was too hurtful, too cruel. "Will you forgive me?"

Without a word, he turned and strode out of the kitchen.

"I'm so sorry," she said again. But his only response was the slamming of her door.

Cal was gone. So much for letting him down gently, for not wanting to mislead him. If Linnette had been feeling sick earlier, it was nothing compared to the knot in her stomach now.

Twenty

Charlotte wasn't sure she was doing the right thing, but she wanted Ben's children to accept her—and to like her. She also wanted to reassure them that she had no intention of replacing their mother, and to convey to David and his older brother, Steven, whom she had yet to meet, how much she loved their father.

David had called her two days earlier, on Monday afternoon. That was when Ben had his monthly get-together with other Navy retirees, so he'd been out of the house. It was one of the rare times they were apart. Charlotte had been baking sugar cookies for the Convalescent Center when David called. He was in Seattle on business again, and had invited her to lunch on Wednesday. But just her—he'd made that clear. He'd asked her not to let Ben know about it. In spite of her natural honesty, she'd agreed.

Charlotte decided to meet David at The Lighthouse restaurant. She was so proud of Justine and Seth, and she felt that meeting them would prove to David that she had a good family, too. She hoped this would assuage any fears he might have about her.

When she'd made the reservation, she'd discovered that Justine was working on Tuesday afternoon and Charlotte was glad of it.

"Grandma," Justine said hurrying toward her as Charlotte waited in the restaurant lobby. "It's great to see you!" She smiled, apparently surprised that Charlotte was alone. "Where's Ben? Wasn't your reservation for two?"

That was the uncomfortable part. Charlotte hated misleading Ben. She'd said she was going Christmas shopping and it'd be best if he didn't accompany her. Following lunch with David, she would indeed do some shopping. Her Christmas buying had been completed long ago, but she wouldn't outright lie to Ben. This was merely a sin of omission. Still, small as the lie might be, Charlotte felt guilty about it.

"There's a young man meeting me here," Charlotte said, gesturing at the dining room.

"Are you stepping out on Ben?" Justine teased.

Charlotte giggled. "Oh, hardly. This is Ben's son and he asked to meet me."

"Without Ben?"

"Well, yes. I have a feeling he wants to get to know me for myself, but…" She hesitated, unsure how much information about this clandestine lunch she should reveal to her granddaughter. "David must be afraid of offending his father because he didn't want Ben to know about this."

"And you agreed?" Justine's tone made Charlotte feel like a disobedient schoolgirl.

"I did," she said, somewhat defiantly. "David's a fine young man, but he's had a falling out with his father." Charlotte didn't feel she was to blame for that. Their disagreement was over the money David wanted to borrow. As she spoke, she scanned the dining area. Sure enough, David sat at a table by the window overlooking the Cove. He stared into space, a drink in his hand. "That's him there."

Justine frowned, but said nothing. She escorted Charlotte to the table; David stood as she approached.

"David, it's lovely to see you." Charlotte kissed his cheek and as she leaned close, she could smell the alcohol on his breath. Stepping back, she introduced him to her granddaughter. "Justine and her husband own The Lighthouse," she boasted. "They've made a wonderful success of it."

David exchanged an enthusiastic handshake with Justine, who then left them to their lunch. Knowing the menu as well as she did, Charlotte didn't bother to open it.

The waitress was by a few minutes later for their drink orders. David asked for another malt whiskey and Charlotte requested hot tea. It was barely noon yet, far too early to be drinking, in her opinion, but it wasn't her place to chastise him.

After their drinks were delivered, they ordered lunch. Charlotte chose the Northwest Salad, a recent addition to the menu. This was a Caesar salad, heaped with sautéed clams, shrimp and scallops. David decided on a rare roast beef sandwich.

The waitress left, and Charlotte poured her tea. David, she noticed, had quickly gulped down his second drink and seemed ready for a third.

"I imagine you're wondering why I asked to see you," he said conversationally as he sought the waitress's eye. When he saw Justine, he raised his empty glass to indicate he'd like another. "My glass seems to have developed a leak," he teased the waitress when she promptly returned.

The woman smiled, obviously charmed by his humor and good looks.

"I think I've figured out why you wanted to see me without Ben," Charlotte said, stirring her tea.

His gaze met hers.

"You wanted an opportunity to get to know me."

"Absolutely," he said, dazzling her with a smile. "You're the first woman to capture my father's heart since Mom died."

Charlotte blushed with pleasure. "I was a widow for more than twenty-five years myself."

David nodded absently. "That just goes to show that you're never too old to fall in love."

That wasn't *exactly* how Charlotte would've put it, but she did agree. "I love your father," she said simply.

"I know you do, and it shows. I've never seen my father this happy." He gave her another warm smile. Oh, yes, this boy was a charmer, Charlotte thought. His eyes grew serious then, and he added, "There's also another reason I wanted to talk to you."

Charlotte took a sip of tea and was about to respond when Justine brought David's drink personally.

"Is everything all right here?" she asked. Although the question was directed at them both, she looked at Charlotte.

"Oh, yes," Charlotte assured her. "Everything's perfect."

Justine eyed the whiskey glass, then reluctantly left the table. As she did, Charlotte noticed that David was frowning.

"Does she always involve herself in her diners' affairs?" he asked. Charlotte could tell he wasn't taking kindly to Justine's barely disguised censure.

"No, no, Justine isn't like that," Charlotte insisted, feeling a little awkward. "She just wants to be sure the service is good. Justine and Seth pride themselves on excellent service."

"I heard what she *wasn't* saying," he muttered. "She's afraid her precious grandmother isn't safe with a man who enjoys a drink or two."

"I'm absolutely sure you misconstrued the question."

David's scowl darkened and then, as if by magic, relaxed.

"You're right, of course. I was hoping for quality time to get to know you, Charlotte. Unfortunately that wasn't possible at our last meeting."

"I did enjoy our dinner." It had been one of the best dining experiences she'd ever had—until the very end, when David left so abruptly.

"I did, too," he agreed, "but I felt badly afterward."

Charlotte nodded. David's sudden departure had been unsettling to Ben, and to her, too.

"I want to apologize for my behavior during our dinner. I was...distressed."

Charlotte patted his hand. "I understood that."

David lowered his gaze and released a beleaguered sigh. "I never did get the money I needed. I don't think my father appreciates how hard it was to turn to him for help. I have my pride, too."

"I'm so sorry about your troubles, David."

"There's nothing worse than not being able to meet one's commitments. I was raised to be responsible, and now I've found myself in a situation where my back is to the wall."

"That is worrisome, isn't it?" Charlotte had lived frugally her entire life. She'd never had many luxuries but always managed to meet her needs.

"Thank you." His face softened at her sympathy. "Who would've believed a measly five thousand dollars would do me in?"

Five thousand wasn't all that measly to Charlotte. "I'm sure you'll find a way out of this."

David shook his head and his brow furrowed. "Not this time." His voice seemed to crack with the strain.

"How do you mean?" she asked anxiously.

David shrugged. "Let's not talk about this now. There's no need to concern yourself with my problems. You're a sweet, caring woman and I don't want to ruin our lunch by discussing my troubles."

"But I think we should. Maybe I could help." She didn't know what she could possibly do, but perhaps…

"You'd be willing to do that?" David asked, relief shining from his face. "Help me, I mean?"

"If I can." An uneasy sensation settled in the pit of her stomach—the same feeling she always got when she was in over her head. "I could talk to your father."

"Don't," David insisted. "Hard as it was, I've already gone to him and he refused. I don't have much left, Charlotte, except my pride. My father knows I'm desperate, but that didn't make any difference to him. He's never given me much help." He hesitated. "I shouldn't have said that. Forgive me."

"Of course." It wasn't true either, Charlotte knew. According to Ben, he'd lent his son quite a bit of money through the years. Not once had David repaid him.

"I need five thousand dollars, Charlotte."

The sick sensation returned. "That's a lot of money."

He didn't disagree, even though he'd considered it "measly" a few minutes earlier. "Yes," he said, "but I have every intention of repaying you with interest. I explained this to my father, but he didn't want to hear it. I'm due for a big Christmas bonus from my company. I know I'll be getting a check for five grand, probably more, and it'll come in two weeks. I only need the money until then. If I don't get some cash now…" He sat back in his chair and sighed. "I can't bear to think what will happen."

"Two weeks is all?"

David leaned forward, his eyes filled with hope. "Two weeks."

"A bank won't lend it to you?"

"No. I've tried again and again, but with my credit rating, they refuse to even talk to me."

"Oh."

"Charlotte, if you could help me, I'd be forever in your debt." He picked up his drink and drained the little that remained. "It could possibly save my life."

Their lunch arrived just then, but Charlotte's normally healthy appetite had vanished. She smiled her appreciation at their waitress and reached for her tea, needing to think carefully about this. "Save your life?" she asked, resuming their conversation.

David turned and looked out over the cove. "I don't want to get into the medical aspects," he said in a low voice. "It's rather complicated...."

"No, please tell me."

"I need this money so badly, I've—I've considered—" he paused, dropping his head "—suicide."

Charlotte's hand flew to her heart and she gasped.

"If I don't have the surgery..."

Charlotte hadn't recovered from the first shock and now there was a second one. "The money is for surgery?"

David nodded. "Funny, isn't it? No one's ever asked me why I need the five thousand dollars. My father assumes it's to pay off gambling debts. That's just like him. Sad as it is to say, my own father chooses to think the worst of me."

"You need surgery?" Her mind was reeling with this information. Surely Ben would have given him the money if he'd known that.

David's eyes were weary. "I won't humble myself any more than I have already. You know what hospitals are like. They want the money up front before they'll agree to do any kind of procedure."

"But surely you have medical insurance."

"Some," he agreed. "But not enough. I need money to pay the balance."

"But, David, your father would *want* to help you if he knew the reason you're so desperate for this loan."

He smiled as if she'd made a joke. "You don't know my father as well as you think. I was never his favorite. Dad always saw the bad in me instead of the good. I suppose I gave him plenty of reason but...we've never had much of a relationship."

Charlotte could see that Ben's problems with his son were far more complex than she'd realized. For one thing, this wasn't a recent falling-out, as she'd assumed. She felt sad for them both. Considering the disappointment Will had been to her in the past few years, she understood far better than she cared to admit.

"Dad would be so angry if he knew you gave me the money," he said, dejection overtaking his voice once again. "I can't let you do it, Charlotte."

"You can't?"

"I don't want to risk damaging your marriage to my father."

"Nonsense. Once I tell him, Ben will understand. Besides, it's my money and I can do with it as I please."

David didn't respond.

Charlotte bent down for her purse and pulled out her checkbook. She'd finished writing the check and ripped it free when Justine stepped up to the table.

She glared at David. "Grandma! What are you doing?"

David raised his hand for the check. "I don't believe this is any of your concern."

Charlotte had just given him the check when Justine jerked it out of his hand. When she saw the amount and the recipient, she scowled darkly.

David stood. "Give me that," he demanded.

Then Ben was there, storming across the dining room. What happened next was embarrassing to both Charlotte and her granddaughter. Everyone started talking at once, providing a spectacle for the entire restaurant. Before she could protest, Ben was escorting Charlotte outside, David trailing after them.

"How did you know I was here?" she asked, her cheeks red with mortification. She drew her coat—which Justine had sent after her, via one of the waitresses—more closely around her.

"Justine phoned me."

"Oh, dear."

"She was worried. She said David had been drinking quite a bit. I knew immediately why he asked to see you and told her to make sure you didn't give him a check."

"But Ben, he's ill! He needs medical treatment."

Ben's eyes narrowed on his son. "It's a lie."

"But…"

"David, for once in your life own up to what you've done. Tell her the truth."

Eyes wide, Charlotte stared at Ben's son. After an awkward moment, David shrugged. "You can't blame me for trying."

Her face burned. Like they said, there was no fool like an old fool. "Oh, Ben," she whispered. "I'm so sorry, so very sorry."

"Sweetheart," he said, slowly shaking his head. "It isn't your fault. My son is a master manipulator. He fed you a lie, the same way he's been feeding me lies through the years. David is willing to say or do whatever it takes to get money. I'm ashamed to call him my son and even more ashamed that he's involved you in this."

"I feel so…so foolish."

"Don't." Ben ignored his son as David walked quickly away from them. "You're a warm, compassionate person, and he took advantage of that. Now, didn't you say something about Christmas shopping?"

When Charlotte sniffled forlornly, he arranged her scarf around her neck, then took her hand in his.

Twenty-One

Justine Gunderson's composure still hadn't recovered from the unpleasant episode involving her grandmother when Warren Saget walked into the restaurant. The afternoon was going from bad to worse. The fact that she managed to greet him with a smile was a credit to her skills as hostess.

"Hello, Warren," she said, reaching for a menu to escort him to a table. She'd dated Warren, a building contractor, for several years before marrying Seth. Warren, who was almost twenty years older than she, had pressured her to marry him. At the time, Justine was convinced she never wanted a husband or children. It had taken Seth and the love they shared to change her mind. Their three-year-old son was the joy of her life. And working with Seth to build this restaurant had been—and continued to be—immensely satisfying.

"You're as beautiful as ever," Warren murmured as he slid into the chair by the window. She'd given him one of the best tables in the house.

"Thank you." She set the menu on the table.

Warren's hand covered hers. "Stay a few minutes," he urged.

"I can't."

"Sure you can," he said. "You're not busy now. It's almost two-thirty—the lunch crowd is gone. We haven't talked in months." He lowered his voice. "You loved me once, Justine."

She'd thought she did, but Seth had shown her the real meaning of the word. What she'd felt for Warren, she realized in retrospect, was a strange mixture of affection and pity. His ego required him to have a pretty woman on his arm at social functions, but it was all for show. Unable to perform sexually, he was tender and indulgent with her. She'd needed his kindness and for a time, the relationship had suited her perfectly. Not only that, her willingness to keep his little secret had endeared her to him. Only when Seth came into the picture and Warren felt threatened had he wanted to marry her. For a while, when admitting the depth of her feelings for Seth had proved painful and difficult, Justine had actually considered marrying Warren.

That way Seth would leave her alone, she'd believed—and he had, but she wasn't free of him. Seth Gunderson was in her thoughts every minute of every day. There'd been no escaping Seth or the love she felt for him. When she'd finally agreed to marry him, she knew without a doubt that she'd made the right decision.

"Please join me," Warren asked, his eyes pleading with her. "For just a few minutes."

Reluctantly Justine sat down. After the afternoon she'd had, a few minutes' respite would do her good. It wasn't often that she encountered a man like David Rhodes. She felt a little guilty about calling Ben, but she couldn't tolerate the sight of David manipulating her grandmother like that. "All right."

"Thank you." Warren stood and pulled out the chair opposite him. His business dealings might be shady, but his manners could never be questioned.

When the waitress came for the drink order, Warren asked for two glasses of wine.

"I can't," she protested, but he refused to listen.

"You look like you need to unwind."

This was something else about Warren. He seemed, at times—like now—to discern her feelings with astounding accuracy. Granted, at other times he could be incredibly insensitive. She decided just to enjoy the moment.

The chardonnay arrived, and despite herself, Justine relaxed and took a sip. This was one of those days when a glass of wine in the middle of the afternoon was exactly what she needed.

"How *are* you?" Warren asked, leaning back in his chair.

"Good."

He sighed and looked away. "I've missed you, Justine."

She didn't respond. That period of her life was over.

"Are you happy?" he asked.

"Very much so."

He nodded and looked around. "You and Seth have done a wonderful job with this restaurant."

"Thank you." No one really knew how much effort went into their business. Seth often worked fifteen-hour days and she served as a hostess and managed the books. The Lighthouse demanded attention to detail—every kind of detail. Early that morning, Seth had been in the parking lot picking up litter and cigarette butts, and later he'd had to clean out the grease trap in the kitchen. Both unpleasant tasks. People tended to see the glamour but not the work that went into running a successful business. Most nights when Justine got Leif from his daycare, she was exhausted. She worried that her son was being raised by strangers. She wanted a second child. Seth did, too, but the timing, he felt, was wrong. Justine worried that the timing might never be right. Much as she loved the restaurant, it had taken over their lives.

"You're frowning," Warren said, breaking into her thoughts.

"I am?" She laughed, making light of it.

He leaned toward her and reached for her hand. "There's no use pretending. I want you back."

He seemed sincere and that touched her. "Warren, I'm married," she said gently.

"You're not happy."

"I am," she insisted. "It's just that Seth is working so hard." She was, too, but she didn't mention that. "I have a good marriage, and I love my husband and son."

Warren looked down at the open menu, but she doubted he was reading over the daily specials. "You can't imagine how difficult it is to live in the same town and see you practically every day. It's tearing me apart. We had something special and I haven't found it with anyone else."

She hadn't kept tabs on his relationships, but it seemed to her that Warren had gone through a number of women in the last few years. The young ones didn't last long, she noticed.

"It's too late."

"Is it?" he pressed. "I refuse to believe that, Justine."

"Warren…"

He looked up and over her shoulder. His eyes narrowed as Seth approached the table.

"Seth," Justine said, flustered that he'd found her with an old boyfriend. "Warren invited me to sit down for a few minutes."

Her husband glanced at the two glasses of wine. He offered Warren a casual smile. "How are you, Warren?"

"Lonely," he said, his gaze locking with Justine's. She swallowed uncomfortably.

Seth placed a possessive hand on Justine's shoulder. "Has Susan taken your order yet?"

"No."

"I recommend the oyster stew. It's the special of the day."

"Warren doesn't like oysters," Justine said and immediately knew she should've kept her mouth shut. Judging by Seth's expression, he didn't want to be reminded of her once-close relationship with Warren.

"Can you come and see me once you're finished visiting with Warren?" When she nodded, Seth went to his small office behind the hostess desk.

Justine stood. "I need to get back to work."

"Seth doesn't deserve you," Warren muttered. "I'd treat you like a queen if you came back to me."

She didn't even bother to reply. Justine was happy, if tired and overworked. Seth, too. They were both committed to this restaurant; Seth was determined to make good on their investment and pay back the money his father had lent him.

"Circumstances change, Justine. I'll be waiting for you when you're ready. You won't be sorry," he promised her.

Justine sincerely doubted that.

"You needed to see me?" she asked when she stepped into her husband's office.

Seth sat behind his desk. "What did Warren want?" he asked her with a frown.

"Not much." She gave him a quick shrug. "Just to say hello." It was on the tip of her tongue to plead with him not to be angry. Having a glass of wine with an old friend meant little. Warren was nothing to her anymore and certainly no threat to Seth.

Her husband regarded her a moment, then sighed. "I guess I was rude to him—and to you."

She didn't contradict him. Instead, she walked around the

desk and sat on his lap. Slipping her arms around his neck, she rested her head on his shoulder. "You're the one I love."

"I know." He kissed the top of her head. "I'm a jealous fool."

"We both need a vacation."

Seth snorted a laugh. "That's not going to happen anytime soon."

Justine knew that, but she could've done without the reminder.

"Hey," he said, as if he'd suddenly remembered something. "What happened earlier? I saw your grandmother and Ben leave, and then right afterward a younger man shot out of the restaurant in quite a huff."

"That was Ben's son, and you wouldn't believe the afternoon I've had." She described how she'd snatched the check out of the other man's hand. When she'd finished, Justine was surprised to find her husband smiling. "You think swindling my grandmother out of five thousand dollars is a laughing matter?"

"Not at all," Seth assured her. "What I find amusing is that David Rhodes took off out of the parking lot, tires squealing. He hadn't gone more than a block when I saw one of Cedar Cove's finest racing after him, siren blaring."

It seemed a fitting end to David's visit.

Twenty-Two

Ever since Thanksgiving, when the floral arrangement had arrived, Corrie had been feeling uneasy. For the first time since the postcards had begun to show up, she felt she knew who was responsible. The postcards had so far been addressed to Roy. However, she suspected they should've been addressed to her, too.

The person in question had nothing to do with Roy's police background, but everything to do with the two of them. Knowing this killed her Christmas spirit, but for Roy's sake and Linnette's, she'd made the effort. The tree was up and the house decorated. She'd even baked Roy's favorite cookies and given batches of fudge to Linnette and Mack.

On Saturday afternoon, Roy sat reading the paper and watching television at the same time, an ability Corrie didn't share.

"Would you like to go to a movie?" she asked. Today was unusual in that they didn't have weekend plans. Even more unusual, Roy wasn't working.

"Not really."

"Would you like to invite the Beldons to dinner?" Corrie

didn't feel like cooking, but she needed something to occupy her mind, otherwise she'd sink into an abyss of memories.

Roy lowered the newspaper. "Isn't that a bit last-minute?"

"I guess."

Her husband laid the paper on the floor. "Something's bothering you, isn't it?"

She nodded, hesitant even now to mention her suspicions.

Roy stood, holding out his arms. Corrie didn't need a second invitation. He hugged her hard, and she sighed contentedly as they sat together on the sofa. She couldn't recall when they'd last cuddled like this. Their lives were so busy and, with Linnette living in Cedar Cove, Corrie should be happy. But most of the time she wasn't.

"Are you thinking about those postcards again?" Roy asked.

"A little... I've been wondering about something. I realize we promised never to discuss it, but do you think—could it possibly be—"

"No." The word was clipped, abrupt, shutting her out.

"But—"

"Just like you said, Corrie, we promised never to talk about that again and we haven't. It isn't the person you think, so you can drop that idea."

"You know this for a fact?"

"No. Come on, Corrie, that was a lot of years ago."

"I know." Like dusk, sadness settled over her and she leaned closer to her husband. Roy might not want to talk about it, but that didn't stop her from remembering. All these years she'd struggled to forget and, for a while, she'd succeeded. Now...now it seemed the memories wouldn't leave her alone.

"Let's go to that movie," he suggested, pulling Corrie to her feet.

"Okay." She went to collect her coat and when she got back, she saw that Roy was ready, too. They drove to the six-plex cinema on the hill; because they hadn't bothered to check times, they chose the next available movie, which started in half an hour.

The theater was crammed; the foyer and concession stands had long lines. Everyone in Cedar Cove seemed to be out and about.

"Look!" she whispered as they stood in line for popcorn, "Grace Sherman and Cliff Harding are here. Behind us."

Roy shrugged as if unconcerned.

"This is big news," she explained, linking her arm with his and bending toward him so as not to be overheard. "The last I heard they'd split up."

"Were they married?" He sounded puzzled.

"No," she said and elbowed him for being obtuse. "But close, I think. Everyone thought Cliff was going to give her an engagement ring. Then they broke up and no one knew why."

Roy seemed uninterested, but Corrie could tell he was listening. "I saw them together one time since, and that's it."

"So they've had a change of heart. It happens."

"It happened with us," she told him.

From the way he looked at her, Corrie knew he didn't appreciate being reminded.

"Well, I hope they're back together," she murmured.

After waiting in line, Roy and Corrie reached the concession counter and ordered drinks and popcorn. They exchanged greetings, then discovered they were attending the same movie.

"Olivia and Jack were going to meet us here, but they canceled at the last minute," Grace explained. "Jack had to go into the office for some reason."

"Yeah. Know what you mean," Roy said as he paid for their popcorn. Corrie held the bucket and one drink. "See you two inside," he said. He returned his wallet to his back pocket and picked up the second drink.

"Save us a couple of seats if you can," Cliff said, eyeing the crowd.

"Sure thing."

The movie had apparently received good reviews because the theater was filling up fast. Corrie and Roy found a place to sit near the back but didn't see four adjacent seats anywhere. Christmas was only a week away and amidst all the frantic preparations, people were obviously looking for a relaxed afternoon.

Grace and Cliff entered the theater, and Corrie pointed to the two seats directly ahead of them.

Cliff and Grace made their way past several other people and took the seats in front of Corrie and Roy.

"This is the best we could do," Roy said, leaning forward.

"Hey, I feel fortunate to get a seat at all," Cliff told him. "Thanks."

Roy set the bucket of popcorn between him and Corrie, and they shared that while the music and advertisements played. Corrie noticed the loving way Grace rested her head on Cliff's shoulder. There was something so touching about this that Corrie couldn't help being affected. It had been the same way with her and Roy when they'd first reunited.

She'd been a college freshman when they met and they'd quickly fallen in love. After a while, they were constantly together. Roy was a star athlete, the football team's quarterback. He was a campus hero, attractive to all the girls, admired by all the guys. There was even talk of his being drafted professionally. He had such promise, such ambitions.

They'd broken up when she discovered he was seeing

someone else. She'd been devastated. To this day, he swore he hadn't slept with this other girl; he insisted one of their friends had lied to her. She believed him, but she also knew he'd been under tremendous pressure. In the middle of the football season, when she needed to see him, he'd made it clear he didn't have time for her. Apparently, Corrie just wasn't in his league anymore.

What she'd wanted to tell him, what he hadn't been interested in hearing, was that she was pregnant.

Rejected and alone, Corrie didn't know what to do. She turned to her parents, who gave her unconditional support. At the end of the first term, they drove up to Washington and packed her things.

Corrie didn't contact Roy again. As far as she was concerned, he was out of her life. Without telling any of her friends why she was dropping out of college, she went home to Oregon. Her parents at her side, she'd attended a series of counseling sessions. Together, as a family, they'd decided she should give up her baby for adoption. That was the most difficult decision of her life.

Her mother had been in the labor room with her. At her own request, Corrie wasn't told whether she'd had a boy or a girl. It was painful enough to sign the adoption papers, and she feared that if she knew the baby's sex she'd envision him or her growing up. Not knowing was easier.

In September of the following year, when she'd returned to college, Corrie was a different person. Her friends seemed childish and superficial. Nothing was the same. She studied hard and kept to herself. She knew that eventually she'd see Roy on campus and was mentally prepared for it.

What she hadn't expected was that he'd seek her out. In her junior year, Roy sat with her in the library one day and asked if they could talk. Even after all the time that had passed and everything that had happened, her feelings for him hadn't died. She still loved him. They'd been foolish and immature, but they'd both changed. That afternoon they'd talked for hours. Roy noticed the difference in her and claimed he wasn't the same boy she knew, either.

A new star athlete had replaced him as quarterback, and overnight he'd gone from being pro material to a has-been. It was hard on his ego for a few months, but he recovered. She'd believed Roy was out of her life for good—and then almost overnight he was back.

Not until Roy bought her an engagement ring did she tell him about the baby. At first Roy didn't believe her, then he was angry, and after that, overwhelmed by sadness. He wept with her, and held her and begged her forgiveness. He went to see her parents, and Corrie never knew what was said, but when she accepted his engagement ring, Roy was welcomed into the family. The night of their wedding, they'd made a second vow to each other, and that was never to discuss their child again. Now Corrie couldn't help wondering if it was that child who'd come to find them.

"Corrie," Roy whispered, "are you asleep?"

"Just thinking," she whispered back.

She might have been deep in thought but Cliff Harding was snoring up a storm. Grace woke him and he gave a start, then settled down to watch the movie. Ten minutes later, Cliff was snoring again. Two-thirds of the way through, Grace stood and led Cliff out of the theater. On her way to the aisle, she smiled apologetically at Corrie and Roy.

Corrie had to admit she wasn't following the movie, either. Her thoughts weren't on the rather complicated caper plot but on the child she'd never known. The child she'd given up for adoption.

Twenty-Three

"I'm ordering cheesecake," Grace said as she slid into a booth at the Pancake Palace. She and Olivia had finished their Wednesday night aerobics class and decided to talk over coffee and pie. Coconut cream, however, wasn't going to do it for Grace. She was disgruntled and unhappy, and one look told her Olivia felt the same way.

"We're *both* ordering cheesecake," Olivia said as she took the seat across from Grace.

"You first," Grace said. They'd been best friends since grade school and were still as close as sisters. She kept almost nothing from Olivia and knew her friend trusted her unequivocally. Theirs was a special friendship.

"It's Jack," Olivia said with a groan. "Does that surprise you?"

"No."

Goldie, their favorite waitress, came over, carrying a pot of decaf. "The usual?" she asked, as she filled their mugs. Olivia and Grace were creatures of habit. Every Wednesday night, they attended their exercise class and afterward went directly to the Pancake Palace for pie and coffee.

Grace hesitated at the waitress's question and shrugged. Olivia did, too.

"We've got mincemeat this week," Goldie told them in a tempting voice.

"No, thanks," Olivia said automatically.

Grace considered it for a second. "Coconut cream," she muttered, half angry with herself for being so unwilling to venture from the tried and true. If she couldn't make such a small change, then how could she manage a truly significant one?

Goldie returned a moment later with one slice of coconut cream pie and the other of lemon meringue, plus the check.

"You're upset with Jack?" Grace said, prompting Olivia to resume their conversation.

"Damn straight I am. Good grief, I hardly see him! I was so annoyed when he broke our movie date. I can't tell you how much I was looking forward to the four of us going out. We hardly ever do that."

"I was disappointed, too," Grace said. Who'd believe that dinner and a movie would be the highlight of the Christmas season for them both?

Olivia seemed to rally. "Did you and Cliff have a good time?" she asked.

"We'll discuss that later. Finish telling me what happened between you and Jack."

To Grace's astonishment, Olivia's eyes filled with tears. "We had an argument that night. Jack didn't get home until midnight—okay, ten o'clock, but it might as well have been midnight. He was at the office all day. You'd think the sun rises and falls on *The Chronicle*. It's all he lives for, and frankly I hate it." Angrily she wiped the tears from her cheeks. "I didn't mean to get emotional. It's just that we seem to be at an impasse."

"You're not thinking…" Grace couldn't bring herself to say the word *divorce.*

"No, but things have got to change. Jack works too hard, he eats mostly fast food and doesn't get any exercise. He's going to kill himself if he continues at this pace." She lowered her eyes. "He thinks this is all one big joke. He said the other day that if he keeled over, what I'd miss most was regular sex."

Grace rolled her eyes. "Leave it to a man to reduce everything to that."

"He's promised his schedule will change after the first of the year, but I've heard those promises before. I just don't want him to kill himself over a stupid newspaper."

"He loves you, Olivia."

"I know and I love him, too. I bought him a treadmill for Christmas."

"Good. Maybe Jack will take the hint."

"He's so stubborn, though."

Grace couldn't help smiling. "What man isn't?"

Now Olivia smiled, too. She reached for her fork and cut into her lemon meringue. "All right, enough about me and Jack. What's going on with you and Cliff?"

Grace sighed heavily. "Cliff fell asleep during the movie. I woke him up when he started snoring—loudly."

Olivia burst into laughter.

"Olivia Lockhart Griffin, this is not funny."

Her friend made an effort to restrain her amusement.

"Ten minutes later, he was snoring again. I'd had it, and we left the theater." In truth, Olivia should be grateful she'd missed out on their evening. Cliff had been exhausted. He'd been working with his horses all day and ended up feeling tired and cranky. Dinner after the movie had been dismal.

"I'm so disappointed I could've cried."

"What is it with our men?" Olivia asked.

"I don't know. But I'm sick of this," Grace said. "It's like I'm married with none of the benefits."

"No regular sex?" Olivia teased.

"You might be my best friend, but there are some things I will not divulge, even to you, and my love life is one of them."

"In other words, you don't have one."

"In other words, you're right."

They both laughed and it felt good. Christmas was four days away and she was supposed to spend Christmas Eve with her girls and then go to Cliff's late Christmas morning. But Grace found she was having second thoughts about seeing Cliff at all.

"What are we going to do?" Olivia asked. "Jack will think it's very clever of me to buy him a treadmill, but I can't *make* him exercise. Nor can I keep him away from double bacon cheeseburgers."

"I can't make Cliff love me."

That comment obviously shook Olivia. "Cliff *does* love you," she insisted.

Grace used to believe that, too, but these days she wasn't so sure. "We had a wonderful Thanksgiving, but now we're in a rut. Being with me seems more of a burden than a joy. Our date last Saturday was an obligation he felt he had to fulfill. I certainly didn't enjoy myself and I doubt he did, either."

"So what's next?"

That was a question worth contemplating. "I wish I knew."

"Just promise me you won't do anything until after Christmas."

Grace made a wry face. "Here's how Christmas will go. I'll arrive at Cliff's around noon, make dinner and then knit while he falls asleep in front of the television." She'd wash the dinner dishes, kiss him goodbye and let herself out. She might as well stay home with her dog and cat; Buttercup and Sherlock were frequently better company. "Some time the next morning," Grace concluded her scenario, "Cliff will phone and apologize and then we'll start all over again."

"Cliff needs his cage rattled," Olivia suggested, tapping her finger against her lips.

"That sounds ominous."

"You feel like you're married but don't have any of the benefits? Then tell him you want to marry him."

"You think I should propose?"

"Yes," Olivia said. "That should wake him up."

"I want to get Cliff's attention, not give him a heart attack."

"Force him to make a decision—a commitment."

Grace could just imagine the look on his face, but maybe Olivia was right. It was time to either make that commitment or walk away. However, Grace didn't know if she had the courage to follow through on any kind of ultimatum.

"Well?" Olivia pressed.

"I don't know."

"You've got to do *something*," Olivia said firmly, scraping up the last of her pie.

That was true enough, but suggesting marriage seemed rather drastic. "I'm afraid," she admitted after a thoughtful moment.

"What are you afraid of?" Olivia asked.

Grace set her fork aside and picked up her coffee, then put it down again. "I don't know." That wasn't the complete truth. She knew. Her biggest fear was that Cliff would tell her he had no marriage plans. Or none with her, anyway.

"Grace?" Olivia stretched her arm across the table and squeezed her hand. "You've gone pale."

She managed a shaky smile. "I'm still waiting for the effects of that pie to kick in."

"Are you going to do it?" Olivia asked.

Grace took a deep breath. "I believe I will. It's time I learned where I stand with Cliff."

Twenty-Four

Christmas morning Maryellen woke cozy and warm in bed with her husband's arms around her. She sighed happily and turned to face him.

"Merry Christmas," she whispered, and discovered that Jon had raised himself on one elbow, looking down at her. His eyes brimmed with love as he leaned over and kissed her forehead.

"Merry Christmas," he echoed. "How do you feel?"

"I don't know yet." She lifted her head tentatively and waited a moment. All seemed well. Her stomach hadn't immediately started to heave and that was a good sign. This pregnancy wasn't as difficult as the last, the infant son she'd miscarried. This time, she'd been experiencing some morning nausea but it wasn't debilitating.

Jon remained fearful that it'd been a mistake to get pregnant so soon. That was irrelevant now. She hadn't tricked him; he knew she wasn't using birth control and it was bound to happen sooner or later. He'd just assumed, as she did, that it would be later. When it turned out not to be, Maryellen was surprised herself—and overjoyed. She wanted Katie to have a brother or sister and she didn't want to wait much longer. As it was, she was almost forty.

"You'll notice Katie's still asleep."

"Little wonder." They'd gathered at Kelly and Paul's home with Maryellen's mother for Christmas Eve. Katie and Tyler had played together, racing around the Christmas tree, their laughter ringing through the house. It had been a late night, but Katie was too excited to fall asleep until almost midnight.

"I'm thinking," Jon whispered as his warm hand closed over her breast, "that we have a good hour to ourselves." He pressed his erection against her and kissed her with an urgency that spoke of his need. "Wouldn't you say this is the perfect time to begin a new holiday tradition?"

"That sounds interesting," Maryellen murmured happily. She loved this man and knew that if she'd let him walk out of her life, she would have lost herself, too—lost the woman she was meant to be.

An hour later, they sat in the living room, each holding a mug of coffee, and gazed out at the view of Seattle. It was still dark, so the lights of the city shimmered in the distance. Jon settled his arm around her shoulders.

"Do you think we should wake Katie?" Maryellen asked.

"If we do, I have a feeling we'll live to regret it."

Jon was right. Katie tended to wake up whiny, especially after a late night. Besides, Maryellen cherished this private time with her husband and didn't want to squander it.

"Let's open our gifts," she suggested. Maryellen had spent her Christmas bonus from the Harbor Street Gallery on a high-end digital camera for Jon. He'd been eyeing it for months, but couldn't justify the expense. She knew how badly he wanted it and her joy at being able to purchase it for him made her feel giddy with excitement.

"You first," he said. Getting up, he walked over to the tree and plucked off a small package dangling from one of the branches. Maryellen had noticed it there but hadn't touched it. Her main concern had been keeping Katie away from the gifts.

"I hear good things come in small packages," she teased. They were on a limited budget, so she expected something inexpensive. A token. She tore off the wrapping and found a jeweler's embossed box. She stared at Jon, and her smile faded.

"Open it," he said.

Her husband wasn't a man who smiled often. His delight at watching her open this gift was revealed by the way his eyes brightened and the edges of his mouth curved upward in anticipation.

Maryellen lifted the lid and gasped. It was a diamond wedding ring with a solitaire diamond that had to be a full carat in size. Tears instantly blurred her vision and speech became impossible. When they were married, all they'd been able to afford was a simple gold band. Not once had Maryellen even hinted that she would've preferred a diamond. Jon was her jewel, she'd told him, and the love they shared was worth far more than any ring.

"Say something," he said urgently. "Do you like it? Because if you don't, I can exchange it."

"I *love* it…." She threw her arms around his neck and broke into sobs of joy. "How?" She was sure he hadn't charged it. Jon was an excellent money manager and always paid cash. Their home didn't have a mortgage because her frugal husband had paid for each section as he built it. He hadn't finished yet, but that would happen in time.

"I put aside money all year," Jon told her, using his thumbs to wipe the tears from her cheeks. "I always intended for you to have a diamond, but it wasn't financially possible when we got married."

Maryellen took the ring from its plush bed and slid it onto her finger. It was a perfect fit. She smiled up at him, then kissed him sweetly and whispered how much she loved him. Holding her hand out to admire the ring, she saw the diamond glittering in the light. "I really do love it. But not as much as I love you."

"I'm glad."

"Your turn," she insisted and pulled the box out from behind the tree. A large paper package tumbled out with it.

"Who's that from?" Jon muttered.

He must have guessed, but still he asked. Maryellen sighed; she didn't want anything to ruin this Christmas. "It came last week from Oregon," she finally said.

The package had arrived at the gallery, addressed to the three of them, DON'T OPEN UNTIL CHRISTMAS written in big block letters across the top. Without a word to Jon, Maryellen had brought it home and hidden it behind the tree.

"Open your gift," she said, hoping to distract him.

"When did *that* get here?" he asked in a disgusted voice.

"Last week."

"You didn't mention it."

Maryellen sank into the chair. "Jon, please, don't. Katie is their only grandchild. They love her and want to be part of her life. You've made your feelings abundantly clear, but your daughter deserves to know her grandparents."

He seemed about to argue, but after a moment his shoulders sagged and he nodded.

"Now open your gift," she said, pushing the package toward him. It wasn't heavy, but she wanted to give him the impression that it was.

Jon eagerly ripped away the paper, and when he saw the camera box, he froze. Slowly he looked up, his eyes wide with shock. "You didn't."

"Yes, I did," she announced gleefully.

"We can't afford this."

"I used my bonus."

"Maryellen, that money is for you to buy yourself something you want."

"I did. There's nothing I wanted more in this world than to give my husband the digital camera he's been salivating over for the last six months."

Jon walked to where she sat and knelt down in front of her. Taking her face between his hands, he kissed her. "Thank you."

Maryellen placed her arms around his neck. "This is the best Christmas of my life," she said and meant it. She had Jon and Katie, and another life was growing inside her, evidence of the love she and her husband shared.

Katie woke then, and dropping a last kiss on Maryellen's cheek, Jon ran upstairs to get his daughter. While he was busy with Katie, Maryellen poured the little girl her morning cup of orange juice.

Opening gifts with their daughter was a pleasure like no other. Katie wanted to play with each toy and examine each gift and—like every young child—was equally fascinated with the wrapping paper. Not surprisingly, the process took several hours. It was two in the afternoon and the turkey was in the oven before they reached the last gift—the box mailed from Oregon.

Katie wasn't sure about this package without festive paper, so Maryellen helped her. Jon stood in the kitchen and watched, as if to stay as far away as possible from the gift his family had sent.

When she'd carefully removed the outer packaging, Maryellen discovered three wrapped presents inside: one for Katie, another for her and the last for Jon. She sat back on her heels and glanced up at her husband.

"What?" he asked.

She didn't answer right away. "Here, Katie," she said and handed her daughter the gift. It turned out to be a hand-crocheted white dress with a pink satin bow and it was breathtakingly beautiful. Maryellen could only imagine the time and effort that had gone into creating it.

Katie, being far more interested in her toys, quickly returned to the wooden puzzle Jon and Maryellen had purchased for her. She seemed intent on getting all the pieces back into their proper slots.

"I'll open mine," Maryellen said. Her gift was homemade, too—a knit poncho in a soft beige wool. "Oh, Jon, look what Ellen made for me."

He didn't comment. When Maryellen tried it on and modeled it for him, he nodded once, then moved away. Apparently something in the kitchen demanded his immediate attention.

Maryellen left his gift sitting on the coffee table. She wouldn't urge him to open it. That was his choice. The gift sat there through dinner, and it was only as she was readying for bed that she noticed Jon hadn't come upstairs yet. Katie was asleep and Maryellen had to work in the morning.

Looking down the stairway, she saw her husband sitting on the sofa, staring at the gift. After a while he seized the large package with its red-and-green wrap and tore it open. This was a step forward. So far, every gesture made by his family had been met with brutal rejection. Recognizing the significance of the moment, Maryellen covered her mouth. She didn't wait to see what Jon's parents had chosen for him. Afraid of giving herself away, she went quietly to bed and waited for him to join her.

A long time passed before he did. She'd turned off the light and was lying on her side, half-asleep, when Jon climbed into the bed. He moved close to her and draped his arm over her waist, flattening his hand against her stomach.

Maryellen rested her hand on his.

"You awake?" he whispered.

She sighed sleepily in response. Because he was so still, she asked, "Are you all right?"

"I don't know," came his hoarse reply. "My father's a bastard. Knowing I was innocent, he sent me to rot in a jail cell. And now…now he gives me a fishing pole for Christmas."

Maryellen rolled onto her back so she could look into her husband's face and discovered Jon's eyes bright with unshed tears. Cradling his cheek with one hand, she kissed him, not sure how else to comfort him.

"He used to take me fishing when I was a kid, before my mother died. Those were the happiest memories of my childhood—fishing with my dad."

Closing her eyes, Maryellen wrapped both arms around him. She suspected Joseph Bowman had found the one way in which he could reach his son.

Twenty-Five

Cecilia knew Christmas Day without Ian was going to be difficult. She woke feeling melancholy, but was determined to have as merry a Christmas as possible. "Next year your daddy will be with us," she assured her unborn son, rubbing her swollen belly.

As soon as she was dressed, she logged on to the computer and left her husband a long, detailed message. She sent him all her love on this most special of days and did her best to sound happy and confident. Achieving the right tone required careful thought. If she sounded *too* cheerful, Ian might think she didn't miss him. If she seemed depressed and miserable, he'd worry. As a result, she spent almost an hour composing her message. She ended by mentioning the small get-together she was having with Cathy and Carol and added that they'd invited Rachel Pendergast to join them.

A small Christmas tree sat in the window of her duplex, a smattering of gifts beneath. Ian had asked his mother to mail her a lovely gold locket; she'd opened that the minute it arrived. Her in-laws had added a gift of their own—a Pashmina shawl in a lovely shade of soft green. Her own mother had mailed a small box of gifts, mostly baby things, which Cecilia opened that morning. Sandra Merrick had recently married for the third time. Cecilia phoned to wish her a merry Christmas and was given the disappointing news that her mother wouldn't be able to visit her when the baby was due. She'd used all her vacation time on her honeymoon. They talked for about thirty minutes and Cecilia hung up the phone with mixed feelings. Her mother was happy; Cecilia couldn't remember the last time she'd felt that way after a conversation with her. She was genuinely delighted for Sandra and hoped to meet her new husband soon. Besides, she'd do fine by herself when she was ready to deliver her baby; Cecilia had her friends.

At noon, she drove over to Cathy Lackey's for Christmas dinner. She saw Carol Greendale's vehicle parked outside Cathy's place—Carol and her daughter, Amanda, had already arrived. Amanda had been born the same month as Allison. For a long time, Cecilia could barely look at the little girl without feeling overwhelmed by grief. But now, Cecilia felt only a twinge of pain when she saw Amanda.

"Merry Christmas," she sang out, letting herself into the apartment. She carried a special chicken pasta salad her mother made every Christmas. It had always been Cecilia's favorite. She also had a bag filled with small gifts; they'd decided to exchange presents, setting a ten-dollar limit.

"Merry Christmas," Cathy called from the kitchen. She wore a felt reindeer antler headpiece with bells that jingled as she walked. Cathy's son, Andy, was playing with Amanda in the living room. "I've got the bird in the oven and we should be eating in three hours—if this oven holds up."

"Problems?" Carol asked. She had on a bright red sweater with three Christmas-tree bulbs in black, yellow and green decorating the front.

"Problems with the cook," Cathy answered, poking her head out of the kitchen. "I should've cleaned the oven after Thanksgiving and didn't, and then the minute I turned it on to preheat for the turkey, smoke started billowing out."

"Mom set off the smoke alarm!" Andy shouted.

Carol's eyes widened. "What did you do?"

"What could I do?" Cathy joked. "I shoved the bird inside and closed the door, hoping the alarm would stop—which eventually it did."

Cecilia laughed. "That's exactly what I would have done."

"No," Cathy objected. "You would've had a spotless oven, so this sort of disaster would never have happened. I, on the other hand, only cook when necessary and on holidays."

What Cathy had said about her was true, but Cecilia wasn't going to admit it. She did like a clean house and took pride in her homemaking skills.

"Rachel Pendergast is joining us for sure," Cecilia said, delighted that her new friend had agreed to come. Both Carol and Cathy had met Rachel at different times, and Cecilia had gotten to know her fairly well. Cathy and Carol were perfectly willing to invite her to their Christmas party, even if she wasn't officially a Navy wife. Nate Olsen was a friend of their husbands.

"Great," Cathy said, "the more the merrier."

The doorbell chimed just as Cathy finished speaking. Carol answered, and Rachel walked in, her nose red from the cold, bearing a sweet potato casserole and a canvas bag with a few wrapped presents peaking out. "Merry Christmas," she said. "I'm not late, am I?"

"No, no, not at all," Cathy assured her. She took the casserole dish and set it on the kitchen counter.

"Welcome," Cecilia said and they hugged. Rachel shrugged off her coat and hung it on the rack by the front door, then arranged her gifts by the tree.

"I got delayed at Bruce's," she explained, glancing at her watch.

At first Cecilia assumed that Bruce was Rachel's brother or some other relation, until she remembered he was her widower friend.

"Jolene didn't want me to leave," Rachel was saying.

Cathy brought out eggnog and they all sat down in the living room to open gifts. Cecilia had bought each of the other women a tube of luxurious hand cream, and puzzles for the kids; in return she received nail polish from Rachel, in a color called "Santa's New Suit," a paperback from Carol, and, from Cathy, a pewter picture frame engraved with booties and other baby images. She suspected Cathy had gone over their price limit and felt tears well up as she caught her friend's eye and mouthed, "Thank you."

Soon after that, the two kids moved into the bedroom, where Amanda had convinced Andy to play house with her.

"I'll make you dinner," the four-year-old said smartly.

Andy looked skeptical. "Will the smoke alarm go off again?"

"Who are Bruce and Jolene?" Carol asked Rachel. "I think I missed something here."

"Well, Bruce is a…friend. A widower. His daughter, Jolene, is nine now. Her mother died when she was five. A while ago, she said she wants me to marry her dad."

"How did Bruce react to that?" Carol asked.

"Forget her father, how did *you* handle it?" Cathy wanted to know.

Rachel grimaced slightly. "It was awkward for both of us. Bruce and I see each other on occasion. Mostly for companionship. For example, Bruce asked me to go Christmas shopping with him and I did."

Cathy exchanged a glance with Cecilia. "Does Nate know about this other guy?"

Rachel nodded. "Bruce is just a friend. Nate knows that. Technically I—I've only gone out with Nate twice, and we've stayed in touch."

Cecilia knew they'd been in daily contact ever since she'd shown Rachel how to log onto the Internet and send e-mail messages. Ian had recently mentioned how much happier Nate seemed to be now that he was able to communicate with Rachel on-line.

"Nate gave me a computer for Christmas," Rachel said shyly. "I told him it was too much, but he wouldn't take no for an answer."

"Wow," Cathy murmured.

"He's got the bucks," Carol said matter-of-factly. "Or rather, his family does."

Cecilia, Cathy and Rachel all stared at her.

"What do you mean?" Cecilia asked when no one else did.

"Nate Olsen, right?" Carol said, turning to Rachel, who nodded. "That's the guy I thought you were talking about. His daddy's Nathaniel Olsen."

The name wasn't familiar to Cecilia, and she noticed the others looked just as blank.

"Who?" Cathy asked.

"Nathaniel Olsen, as in Congressman Nathaniel Olsen from Pennsylvania." She glanced from one woman to the next. "You mean you didn't know?"

Rachel looked shocked, then confused. "N-no, Nate never mentioned anything about his family being in politics."

"We're talking money. Big money," Carol continued, clearly enjoying the role of expert. "I'm not sure where it all came from in the beginning—probably coal—but there's lots of it now and Daddy doesn't mind letting everyone know."

"Nate's an enlisted man," Cecilia said. It stood to reason

that because of his father's name, he could've gone into the Navy as an officer.

"True," Carol agreed, sipping her eggnog. "But Nate and his father had a falling out a few years back. Then I heard that Nate dropped out of college and joined the Navy."

"How do you know all this?"

"I'm from Pennsylvania," she told them. "It was big news back home, and of course his daddy put a positive spin on it. He played up his family's patriotism for all it was worth at election time."

"I'll bet Nate hated that," Rachel said quietly.

"I'll bet he did, too," Carol concurred. "I don't think he has much to do with his father these days."

"Oh." Rachel had gone pale. "I can just imagine what Nate's father would say if he found out his son was dating a hairdresser."

That was met with a moment's silence. "It seems to me Nate's his own person," Cecilia felt obliged to comment. "He's the one who sought you out, isn't he?"

"Actually, I bid on him at the Dog and Bachelor Auction, remember?"

"Yes, but you two hit it off," Carol said.

"Nate doesn't have a problem with you working in a salon," Cathy added. "What's wrong with that, anyway? As soon as Carol and I found out you did hair, we were overjoyed. We've been looking for a good hairdresser ever since we moved to Cedar Cove. The fact that you do nails too is a bonus."

Rachel relaxed a bit. "I just wish Nate had said something— about his background, I mean."

"Maybe he was waiting for the right time," Cecilia offered, wishing Carol hadn't said anything now. Rachel seemed so uncomfortable.

Carol must have regretted it herself, judging by her next words. "Come to think of it, I'm sure Nate wouldn't use family money to purchase your gift," she said. "You obviously mean a lot to him."

Rachel smiled and the color rose in her cheeks. "He means a lot to me." Her smile grew wider. "I don't know anything about his family, but I will tell you that Nate's one fine kisser."

Cathy shook her head. "Well, I don't know about Nate, but I'll bet you hands down that Andrew can out-kiss him any day of the week."

"If we're going to get into comparisons," Cecilia began.

"Girls, girls," Carol broke in, waving her arms. "This is a discussion we don't want to have."

"Why not?" Cecilia asked.

Carol looked at each one and then lowered her voice. "Exactly how long has it been since any of us had sex?"

Cecilia and Cathy both giggled.

"Too long," Cecilia said. "*Way* too long."

Twenty-Six

Corrie loved shopping at all the after-Christmas sales. Next to the Thanksgiving sales, this was her favorite shopping experience. She was delighted that Peggy Beldon had agreed to join her. They'd gotten to know each other in the last year, while Roy worked on solving the murder that had taken place at Thyme and Tide, the Bed-and-Breakfast owned by Bob and Peggy.

"I love it when I can buy Christmas wrap at seventy-five percent off," Peggy said as she loaded up her cart with half a dozen colorful rolls. "Of course, Bob complains. He says I can't save money by spending money."

Corrie nodded. "Roy says the same thing." This was a ritual lament—the same conversation they'd had on previous shopping expeditions.

"Men are so unreasonable." Peggy added several strands of outdoor Christmas lights. "Look at these," she said, holding up a box for Corrie to view. "Next year when Bob goes to put up the outdoor display, he'll discover that a whole bunch of lights have burned out. Outdoor lights just aren't made to last more than a year. I'm saving him the bother of racing down to the store for last-minute replacements. But will he thank me?"

"You're joking," Corrie murmured. "Of course not."

"We're underappreciated."

They both laughed. Corrie was grateful she had a friend to share this kind of humor with, these small, amusing insights from daily life. She'd missed that when she'd first moved to Cedar Cove. She didn't make friends easily. Linnette was like that, too, and Corrie was glad her daughter had met Gloria. Linnette had made the transition from Seattle to small-town life much more smoothly, thanks to her neighbor.

When her cart was full, Corrie steered toward the checkout stands in the front of the store, with Peggy following directly behind.

After they'd delivered their bounty to the car, Peggy suggested lunch. "We should spend some of the money we just saved," she said.

"By all means," Corrie agreed happily. "I haven't been to D.D.'s on the Cove in months. How about you?"

"Fine with me."

Fifteen minutes later, they were sitting in a booth overlooking the marina. The Christmas decorations were still up but would be coming down after the first of January. When that happened, the town would look dull and drab, Corrie mused. Winter, the rainy season of the Pacific Northwest, was her least favorite time of year.

They both ordered hot tea and crab-melt sandwiches.

Once they were settled with their tea and waiting for their lunch, Peggy surprised her by asking, "Did you get a Christmas postcard?"

The Beldons had been with Roy and Corrie the night the fruit basket arrived. Peggy also knew about the mysterious postcards. So did Linnette, but only because she'd accidentally found one. As far as Corrie knew, no one else in town was aware of the situation.

"An anonymous Christmas card came on the twenty-fourth," Corrie said reluctantly. This was the last thing she wanted to discuss, and yet the need to confide in someone burned in her chest.

"Any idea who they're coming from?" Peggy asked.

Corrie didn't answer right away. She swallowed the lump that formed in her throat. "I do have an idea," she managed to whisper. It was all she'd thought about since discussing their unknown child with Roy. He was adamant; they'd vowed not to speak of it again and he was holding her to that.

Peggy, who was a sensitive woman, gave her a concerned look. "If you'd rather not say anything…"

"I…can't. I talked to Roy about it, but he won't listen. What I'm thinking of happened a long time ago, and he feels it's best to leave it in the past." Corrie realized she'd already said more than was advisable. "He's probably right."

"Let's drop the subject then."

Needing a diversion, Corrie reached for her tea. "Perhaps that would be best."

"Can you answer one question?" Peggy sounded mildly embarrassed. "I shouldn't ask, but curiosity is getting the better of me. Was there a message on the Christmas card?"

An involuntary smile came to Corrie. "Nothing cryptic, if that's what you mean. All it said was *Merry Christmas.*"

"None of these messages have been threatening, have they?" She held up her hand. "Don't answer that. We're changing the subject."

The waitress brought their lunch, a hot crab and cheese mixture spilling over both halves of the toasted English muffins. This was one of Corrie's favorite meals, a specialty at D.D.'s. She wondered why she hadn't been here in so long.

Mostly, she decided, because of her daughter's work schedule. They enjoyed meeting for lunch, but Linnette's shift changed every week and—

Corrie's thoughts came to a grinding halt as she saw Linnette's neighbor in a booth across the restaurant. Gloria was sitting there with Chad Timmons.

"Oh, no," she whispered, setting her fork down.

"What?" Peggy asked, looking around for whatever had alarmed Corrie.

"Over there," she whispered, bending toward her friend. "See that couple on the other side of the room?"

Peggy's eyes narrowed. "Isn't that Dr. Timmons? Bob and I met him the day the clinic opened."

"The one and only," Corrie muttered. "The woman with him is my daughter's neighbor. Gloria something. I can't recall her last name." Corrie's heart raced with anxiety. "Linnette really likes her, and I'm pleased about that. A friend is exactly what she needed to feel comfortable in Cedar Cove."

"I agree."

"The thing is, Linnette has a crush on this doctor. She's turned a blind eye to anyone else."

"By anyone else, you mean Cal Washburn."

"Exactly," Corrie said more loudly than she'd intended. Heads turned. Unfortunately, some of the attention came from the other side of the room. Flustered, she immediately focussed on her meal, lowering her head and not looking up.

"She saw you," Peggy said.

"Oh, great."

"What do you want to do?"

"Nothing," Corrie muttered. "It isn't like she's trying to hide the fact that she's having lunch with Dr. Timmons. Besides, Linnette has no hold on this man. In my opinion, she's being utterly foolish." What Corrie hated most was the possibility that Linnette's friendship with Gloria might be threatened by this. Corrie certainly wasn't planning to mention it to her daughter.

"So what happened with Linnette and the horse trainer?" Peggy inquired.

Pinching her lips together in irritation, Corrie shook her head. "She told him she was interested in someone else."

"That's too bad." Even Peggy was disappointed.

"It's her decision, of course. I just wish it had worked out. I like Cal."

"I do, too."

They were so involved in their conversation that Corrie didn't notice Gloria walking across the room. Not until her daughter's neighbor reached her table and spoke did Corrie glance up.

"Hello, Mrs. McAfee."

"Hello, uh, Gloria," she said, startled. She smiled brightly to compensate for her awkwardness. "Have you met Peggy Beldon?"

"No, I don't think so."

The three exchanged small talk for a few minutes. Corrie noticed that Dr. Timmons had already left.

"I didn't want to give you the wrong impression," Gloria said, after a brief silence. "Dr. Timmons and I aren't seeing each other."

"Why would it matter?" Corrie said blithely. This really wasn't any of her business.

"He had a question for me, about a police matter, and wanted to take me to lunch. I wouldn't have gone, but he insisted. I know how Linnette feels about him."

Half the town probably knew of Linnette's feelings toward the doctor, since she hadn't made the slightest effort to hide her attraction. But Corrie figured that if Chad Timmons was interested in her daughter, he would've asked her out by now. He'd obviously set his sights on Gloria, not Linnette.

"Linnette is a good friend," Gloria went on to explain, "and I don't want to do anything to put our friendship at risk."

"That's very considerate, but I don't think you should worry about it."

"Perhaps not, but my friends are important to me, and I've come to treasure Linnette."

Corrie just hoped her daughter appreciated what a good friend she had in her neighbor.

After a few words of farewell, Gloria departed.

"She really is very nice, isn't she?" Peggy said when Gloria was gone.

"She is." Corrie nodded.

"Did you see how they were looking at each other?" Peggy asked. "I could feel the electricity all the way over here."

Corrie frowned at her remark. This was even worse than she'd thought. All she could do was hope that Linnette came to her senses and realized she was on a path that led to heartache.

Twenty-Seven

Grace Sherman had seriously considered Olivia's advice and decided to take a stand with Cliff. It was time to end this erratic relationship. She never seemed to know whether they were on or off, casual friends or practically engaged. It varied from one encounter to the next.

In her heart, she believed Cliff loved her. But he wasn't sure he could trust her, despite everything she'd said and done since her Internet dalliance with Will Jefferson. Still, Grace was secure in her own feelings for Cliff. And she wanted to be with him, as his wife. She'd seen the difference in Olivia since she'd married Jack; she'd seen the changes in Jack, too. Grace decided that if Cliff loved her, he'd agree they should be married. If he didn't feel he could move forward in their relationship, then she needed to know that now. Yes, proposing might be outrageous, maybe risky, but Grace wanted to discover his feelings—and his intentions—once and for all.

Never having asked a man to marry her before, she wasn't sure how to go about it. Her first inclination was to invite him to a fancy restaurant, the way she'd seen it done in the movies. That would create the requisite romantic setting, with champagne and classical music, but it wouldn't allow them much privacy. And if they went to The Lighthouse, elegant though it was, she'd be sharing one of the most intimate moments of her life with far too many of her friends and neighbors.

So, no restaurant, which left one other option. Fortunately Grace loved to cook. She enjoyed every aspect of it—choosing the recipes, the trip to the grocery store, the preparation itself. She didn't even mind washing the dishes. She felt comfortable in her kitchen. So—in an effort to start the new year right—she invited Cliff to dinner on Sunday.

"Any particular reason?" Cliff asked when she phoned him at the ranch. He seemed to guess that this wasn't an ordinary invitation.

"It's New Year's Day." Grace couldn't very well admit she planned to propose to him. That would come over thick slices of homemade apple pie served with French vanilla ice cream, his favorite. Or maybe she'd do it during a romantic champagne toast…

"You've got yourself a deal."

Grace just hoped he'd be as easily persuaded when she asked that all-important question.

Not wanting to speak without forethought or reflection, she carefully wrote out what she intended to say. She wanted to review their relationship, starting with the early days when they'd first begun seeing each other. They'd met due to a credit card mix-up three years ago—had it really been that long? After thirty-five years as Dan's wife, she'd been nervous and uncertain about entering into a new relationship, and in some ways she still was.

She remembered how gentle Cliff had been with her. Following Dan's memorial service, she'd collapsed from grief and fatigue, and Cliff was the one who'd stayed with her, who'd comforted her, who'd encouraged her to grieve for her husband. She'd buried Dan that day, and so much more—all the memories, good and bad. Through it all, Cliff had been at her side, a constant support.

They'd been separated for a while and during those long, lonely months Grace had understood how foolish she'd been and how much she loved Cliff. She'd made an error in judgment. She was sorry about it. Either Cliff accepted that or he didn't; it was time to find out.

For dinner Grace went all out. The most elaborate meal she could think of was individual Beef Wellingtons, along with a baked potato casserole and fresh young asparagus shoots. The salad was a special recipe from the Food Channel, with greens, blue cheese and roasted spiced pecans. She blew a good third of her monthly food budget on this meal alone, but it would be worth it.

Cliff was to arrive at six. The table was set with her mother's china, used only on the most momentous occasions. The wine—a French Merlot that came highly recommended—was open and breathing. She hadn't spared any expense on that, either. The candles were ready to light.

"What do you think, Buttercup?" she asked the golden retriever, who lay on her dog bed in the kitchen. Buttercup wagged her tail enthusiastically—approving, Grace was sure, of her plans. Sliding her hand inside her apron pocket, she fingered the half-dozen index cards she'd placed there. These cards were her security and her talisman. On them she'd written her feelings—her love for Cliff, her hopes for them both.

At ten minutes after six, Grace stood in the living room looking out the window, waiting for Cliff's truck. Sherlock, her cat, lounged on the back of the couch, undisturbed by Grace's nervousness.

Every thirty seconds, she glanced at her watch, wondering

what had held him up. When Cliff was twenty-five minutes late, she was convinced he'd had an accident on his way into town. Black ice often covered the roads in the winter months; he could've hit a patch and driven into a ditch.

At six-thirty, she couldn't stand it any longer and phoned the ranch. Cal picked up on the second ring.

"Grace?" He sounded surprised.

"Cal, I'm sorry to disturb you, but I'm worried about Cliff. He isn't here yet. Can you tell me when he left?"

"Cliff is-s here."

"He hasn't left yet?" Her heart sank to her knees and stayed there.

"Here," Cal said, "talk-k-k to him."

Oh, she'd talk to him, all right.

"Grace?" Cliff was on the other end of the line. "Dinner was tonight?"

Closing her eyes she tried to quell her anger. "Did you forget?" she asked ever so sweetly. "Again?"

"I'm afraid I did. I hope you didn't go to any trouble."

She wouldn't lie. "As a matter of fact, I did." She restrained herself from telling him she'd been cooking for two days, although she should probably let him know. "When *did* you think dinner was?" she asked instead.

"I thought I'd written it down, but apparently I didn't. I'm sorry, Grace. Is dinner ruined?"

In more ways than the obvious. "Yes, I believe it is."

"I'm sorry."

"Sorry?" she repeated. "Sorry! That doesn't even begin to cover it."

"You're angry and—"

"I'm *angry?* What gave you that idea?" The man was nothing if not perceptive.

"I'll drive into town so we can talk."

"Don't bother," she said forcefully. "It doesn't matter... It just doesn't matter." Unable to say anything more for fear she'd burst into tears, she replaced the receiver.

She was too furious to sit still. Pacing helped. He'd forgotten dinner on New Year's Day! That took effort on his part. Real effort. She'd taken her stand and she had her answer.

Collapsing into a chair, she hid her face in her hands. Buttercup came to lie on the carpet next to her, gazing up piteously, as if she understood how Grace felt.

All at once, Grace was angry again—only this time it was with Dan, the husband she'd buried. She *hated* this, hated living alone, hated all the adjustments his death had forced her to accept. Her marriage had never been completely happy, but at least she'd been contented. Over the years she'd learned how to deal with Dan's mood swings because, underneath it all, she'd recognized that he loved her and their daughters. In that moment she would've given anything to have her husband back, anything for her life to return to the way it was before his year-long disappearance...before she found out he was dead.

The doorbell chimed and she glared accusingly at the front door. Cliff. He'd made record time driving into town. Perhaps they should have this out now, face-to-face. It would be over then, and they could both go back to their own lives.

Grateful that she hadn't given in to the compulsion of tears, she walked to the door and opened it. As she'd suspected, Cliff Harding was standing there.

"Let's talk," he said. With a repentant look, he removed his Stetson, holding it in both hands.

"Yes, I think we should," Grace agreed, stepping aside to let him in.

Cliff surveyed the dining room table, set with china, crystal and candles, and exhaled slowly. "I can see I messed up big-time."

"Yes, you did," she said, "but the truth is, I'm just as glad." She swept into the kitchen.

Cliff was right behind her. "Glad?"

Opening the oven door, she took out the Beef Wellingtons, warming on a cookie sheet, and unceremoniously dumped them in the garbage. Buttercup's big round eyes followed Grace's movements, silently pleading with her to consider the dog dish instead.

Cliff squatted down beside the golden retriever. "I think I'm in the doghouse now, girl," he whispered loudly enough for Grace to hear.

She wasn't amused.

"Are you going to toss anything else? Because I was just thinking that dinner looks too good to waste."

Grace planted one hand on her hip. "I'm not going to be cajoled into forgetting this."

"Come on, Grace," he argued. "It's just a dinner. I blew it, but I'm genuinely sorry."

"Wrong!" she cried. "This *wasn't* just a dinner. It was far more than that." Her throat was clogged with tears, and she paused in an effort to regain control. "Perhaps you should sit down for a minute so I can explain."

He did as she suggested and chose the sofa. Grace sat in her favorite chair. Buttercup trailed them into the room, but seeming to sense their mood, she paused, then returned to her bed in the kitchen.

Grace knew what had to be said; inhaling, she tried to work out how to begin. Her index cards were no use now.

"I can't tell you how sorry I am," Cliff said again.

She waved aside his apology. "I know. I don't mean to be flippant but, Cliff, I'm past that. This—forgetting din-

ner with me, and not for the first time, either—is very indic-
ative of your true feelings."

He shook his head. "I should've written it down on my calendar. I don't know why I didn't. I could kick myself."

"Stop." She didn't want to hear it. "I had a lot of expectations for this dinner. But I guess that's my problem, not
yours."

He frowned. "What kind of expectations?"

"You might find this laughable.... I probably shouldn't tell
you, but I planned to set the stage by serving you the dinner
of your life. I was hoping to soften your heart toward me so
I could—propose."

His eyes widened. "Propose...marriage?"

"It's rather comical, isn't it? Me cooking for two days, a
nervous wreck, seeing to every detail, practicing how to tell
the man I love that I'd like to spend the rest of my life with
him. I'd hoped you'd feel the same way, and we could set a
date for the wedding." Her voice did crack then, and she
struggled for composure.

"Grace," Cliff whispered, his eyes warm, "I love you, too."

Afraid of embarrassing herself further, she swiped at the
tears that were running down her cheeks. "Don't worry. I'm—
I'm not going to propose." She pulled the index cards from
her apron pocket. "Look, I even made notes in case I got too
nervous to speak. Funny, huh?" She didn't give him time to
respond. "There was no need for any of this. No need what-
soever."

Cliff's shoulders slumped forward. "I don't know what
to say."

"You don't have to say anything." She took a deep breath.
"Something occurred to me recently. You and Dan are actually more alike than I thought. He did this, too, you see."

"Forgot dates?"

"No." She attempted a smile. "He had a way of letting me know how he felt without saying a word. A counselor once explained that it's passive-aggressive behavior."

"I'm not like that," Cliff insisted, stiffening at the implication.

"You've forgotten dinner dates. When we do manage to go out, you fall asleep during movies, and whenever I visit the ranch—generally at your invitation—you've got more important things to do than talk to me. Okay, there was a real emergency that one night, but what about the other times? Except for Thanksgiving, you seemed completely indifferent to my being there. Well, I got your message, Cliff, loud and clear. You haven't forgiven me. And maybe you never will." She stood then, her heart heavy. "You don't have the courage to do this, so I'm going to. I didn't lie when I said I love you, but for your sake as well as mine, it's over."

He looked stunned and remained speechless.

"This isn't a ploy. It isn't a game. I'm sincere when I say it would be best if we didn't see each other again."

He sat where he was for another few minutes. "Will anything I say change your mind?" he asked quietly.

She shook her head.

"I see." He reached for his hat.

"I wish you nothing but good things, Cliff."

He nodded.

"Goodbye." She opened the door for him. He walked past, then stopped, bringing his finger to her cheek. She didn't close the door until he was off the porch and down the steps. A shudder went through her as she sagged against the wall and waited for the pain to pass.

Twenty-Eight

Roy McAfee said little to Corrie, but he knew she was right, felt it in his gut. These mysterious postcards had come from the child he'd never known. It wasn't as if he'd *forgotten* there was a baby. The fact that he had a third child was always with him, hidden in the back of his mind.

When Corrie had told him, all those years ago, that she'd given birth to his baby, he'd been shocked, then angry. Later, he'd experienced deep sadness and a sense of bereavement. He felt that same emptiness now. He'd never blamed Corrie, and he still didn't. His own insensitivity and arrogance had led to this, had forced Corrie to make the decision she had.

There was nothing she could tell him about the baby. Not even if they'd had a son or a daughter.

He recalled the year after she'd left him—over a rumor about another girl, a rumor that was only half-true. Her loss, he'd figured. And then there'd been his sudden fall from favor, when the pros were no longer interested and the scouts stopped talking to him. His decline had been rapid and humbling.

Before their reconciliation, he'd seen her in the library one day and remembered all the things he loved about her. Her honesty. Her warmth. Her beautiful dark-brown hair, falling thick and straight to her shoulders. The way she used to kiss him...

The next day he was back, hoping to see her again. If she happened to be there on two consecutive days, he decided, he'd consider it fate.

Sure enough, at the same time as the day before, he saw her outside the library, walking with another girl. It took courage to follow her inside, to call out her name. Roy wondered if she'd ever realized what it had cost him. He'd put every bit of his remaining pride on the line that day. But whatever the price, it was nothing compared to the value she'd given his life.

Roy recognized that he wasn't an easy man to love. He tended to be stubborn; admitting he was wrong didn't come easy. Not then and not now.

He'd never forget the day Corrie told him about the baby. He'd wanted to rant at her for withholding the information; he'd had a right to know she was having his child. But he soon acknowledged that he hadn't given her much choice—and that he wouldn't have had the maturity to deal with the situation.

Still, he hated the fact that she'd been left to make these life-altering decisions on her own. When he thought about what Corrie and her family must have endured, it made him ashamed. The girl he'd loved and used had given birth to his child alone because she knew, even if he didn't, that he couldn't cope with a pregnancy.

Having the baby had changed Corrie. She was as beautiful as before, perhaps more so. However, the changes had come about not in her appearance but in other subtle ways. She'd matured. Already miles ahead of him in that area, she'd developed a dignity and a gentle wisdom that made him yearn to be with her even more.

She didn't tell him about the baby until they were engaged. He used to wonder why she'd waited. But now he understood that if she'd told him before, she'd never be sure whether his proposal had been offered out of love—or guilt and regret. Waiting until she was utterly convinced of his love might have saved their marriage.

Roy leaned back in his chair and propped his feet on the desk. His best detective work was done in this old chair, a relic from his police days. The department had wanted to toss it, but Roy had saved it from a junkyard death, rolled it out to his car and brought it home. He'd been sitting in this chair ever since. Corrie hated it, pleaded with him to get rid of it. He wouldn't.

The office door opened and then closed. "Dad?"

Roy let his feet fall to the floor. "In here," he called out to his daughter.

Linnette walked into his office and threw herself onto the chair opposite his desk. "Where's Mom?"

Roy had exactly the same question. "Apparently she took an extended lunch hour. I guess that's what I get for hiring family," he joked.

"Oh." Linnette looked as if she wanted to weep.

"You need to talk to her?"

His daughter nodded. "Dad," she said, straightening, "did you always love Mom? I mean, was there ever a time you had questions about the way you felt?"

"Sure," he admitted, a little taken aback by the question, so close to his own recent thoughts. "Just the other day," he teased, trying to lighten the mood. He wasn't much good at giving advice. That was Corrie's specialty.

"Dad, I'm serious."

"I know you are," he said, somber now. "Relationship problems?"

Linnette shrugged. "I screwed up."

Roy hated to turn his daughter away, but he wasn't comfortable with this heart-to-heart stuff. "You'd better talk to your mother."

"She isn't here. You are."

"In other words, it's any port in a storm?"

She gave him a half smile. "You could say that."

"All right." He tried not to sigh. "Tell me what's on your mind."

Pulling off her gloves, Linnette stood up for a moment and removed her coat.

"I did something I regret," she said bluntly.

"What?"

"Mom bought me a date with this guy in that Dog and Bachelor Auction last summer. Cal, his name is, and he's a horse trainer. We went out, mainly because Mom pressured me into it. I didn't want to, but I finally agreed."

"Was it so bad?"

"Not at all. I enjoyed dinner and later, I went out with him again. I had an even better time, and then he kissed me and—"

"Hold on a minute." Roy raised one hand. "I don't want to hear any of that. Otherwise, I might be tempted to bash his teeth in."

Linnette looked up and smiled. "You're such a father."

"Sorry, can't help it. You're my baby girl."

"I am not a baby."

"All I can say is wait until you have your own children and then decide." He gestured for her to continue.

"I liked the way Cal kissed me—don't worry, I'm not going to say any more about it, except that when he kissed me I got scared."

This got Roy's attention. "Did he try any funny stuff?"

"No, nothing like that. He didn't *scare* me—I'm explaining this badly. What I mean is, I knew that if he kept on kissing me, I'd want to see him again, and I couldn't because there was someone else I liked better."

"Hmm?" That was about as profound a comment as he could make. He was finding all this a bit difficult to follow. So she liked this horse guy but she didn't? And who was the "someone else"?

"I wanted to be available for Chad," she elaborated, "and I didn't want to get sidetracked."

Okay, now he got it. Sort of. "This is that doctor fellow?"

Linnette nodded. "The problem is, it didn't work."

"You mean the doctor fellow isn't interested? Or you've been thinking about Cal?"

"Both. But I was incredibly rude to Cal, and I keep wondering, you know, what would've happened if we'd continued dating. I wonder if I might've let a wonderful man slip through my fingers—and all for nothing."

"What's happening with Chad?" Roy needed all the facts, logically presented.

She shook her head. "No movement there. He's handsome and sophisticated, and at one time I would've given my eyeteeth to go out with him, but he's never asked. I doubt he ever will, and you know what? That's fine. I'm pretty much over him. It's Cal who interests me now. Except I'm not sure what I should do."

Okay. Scratch the doctor. But Roy had no idea what he was supposed to say next. He was clean out of romantic advice.

"I wonder if I should phone Cal and apologize or just let it go." She raised expectant eyes to him. "What do you think?"

That was the million-dollar question, all right. "What do

I think?" he repeated slowly. "You may not know this," he began, "but your mother and I dated for a while and then split up." He paused. "After almost two years, we met again. I've always felt fate put her in my path that day."

"In other words, if it's meant to be, I'll see Cal again?"

Roy nodded. "Something like that."

Linnette seemed to be mulling over his words. She stood up, her expression thoughtful, and reached for her coat. "Thanks, Dad."

"You're welcome." He leaned back in his chair and placed his feet on the desk once again, crossing his ankles. "Any other problems you want me to solve?"

"Not this afternoon. Tell Mom I came by, okay?"

"Will do."

Linnette left and Roy was settling down to a short nap when the door opened and Corrie burst into his office. Roy took one look at his wife and dropped his feet to the carpet for the second time. "Corrie? What's wrong?"

Tears shone in her eyes as she sat in the chair just vacated by their daughter. "I—" She swallowed hard, fidgeting with a tissue.

"What is it?"

"You refused to listen. You refused to consider what I said, so I took matters into my own hands." She was so pale, he felt suddenly terrified.

"What did you do?" he asked, frowning.

"I—you aren't the only one in this family capable of doing detective work. I have my own resources."

"Corrie? *What did you do?*" he repeated.

She finally met his gaze. "We had a daughter, Roy. I gave birth to a little girl."

Roy came around from his side of the desk and placed his hand on her shoulder. Bending down, he looked into his wife's eyes, loving her so intensely he felt a physical pull toward her. "I know," he whispered.

"You know?"

"I found out, too."

Twenty-Nine

Rachel tried, but she couldn't stop thinking about what she'd learned from Carol Greendale on Christmas Day. Nate was the son of a powerful East Coast politician. She was living in a dream world if she had any hopes for this relationship. The sooner she cut her losses, the better. And she decided to do just that, sending Nate a terse but perfectly polite e-mail. She hadn't turned on her computer since.

Friday night, Bruce phoned her at the salon and suggested they get together. Rachel's first inclination was to decline. She wasn't in the mood to be sociable, but on second thought, she didn't go out that often. Bruce was usually good company.

"What do you have in mind?"

"I don't know." He didn't seem full of enthusiasm, either.

Half the time Rachel figured the only reason he called her was that he didn't know any other women. But that wasn't true; he knew plenty of women. She suspected he had an ir-rational fear of unmarried females trying to trap him into marriage. That wasn't an issue with her and he knew he was safe.

"Want to go to a movie?" she asked.

"We could."

"Where's Jolene going to be?" She tried to think of something that might appeal to both of them.

"Slumber party."

"Dinner?" Rachel suggested.

They didn't even talk in full sentences anymore. They were like an old married couple so attuned to each other that their communication was a form of shorthand.

"Sure."

That was fine with Rachel, too. "Where?"

"You choose."

"Taco Shack."

"Meet you there?"

"Fine. Six?"

"Great."

By the time she left the salon and drove out to the Taco Shack, Bruce had arrived and scouted out a table. The Taco Shack was a popular Friday-night spot. The food was good and plentiful and, best of all, cheap.

"I already ordered for you," he said when she joined him.

"How'd you know what I wanted?"

"Cheese enchiladas. That's what you order every time."

"I do?" Rachel hadn't realized that. As a matter of fact, she read the entire wall-mounted menu on each visit. Apparently she was even more predictable than she'd known.

She got herself a Diet Coke—Bruce had a bottle of water—and their dinner was delivered two minutes later. If she ordered the same thing every time, then so did Bruce. Without instructions, the server set the cheese plate in front of her and the chicken enchiladas in front of Bruce.

As though synchronized, they both reached for their forks. "Do you want to watch a DVD later?" Rachel asked between bites.

"What have you got?"

She named a few movies that had been going around the salon. The girls at Get Nailed had a better system than most rental places, and if a DVD didn't get returned in a timely manner, the teasing was ruthless. Rachel had borrowed several for the weekend, a couple of comedies and an emotional drama, reputedly a tear-jerker.

"I haven't seen any of those."

They decided on one of the comedies, then ate in silence for a few minutes.

"Have you heard from lover boy?" Bruce asked, picking up his water.

"If you mean Nate, then no, I haven't."

"No?" This seemed to surprise Bruce.

"I ended it."

Bruce set down his water and studied her. "This is news. What happened?"

"Nothing."

"Don't give me that. You didn't write this guy a Dear John letter for no reason. That's not like you."

"I e-mailed him."

"Okay, a Dear John e-mail. Tell me what's going on."

Bruce was right; she hadn't done this lightly. She'd thought about the situation for almost two weeks and concluded that it couldn't work. "If you don't mind, I'd rather not discuss it."

"All right."

Rachel's appetite was gone, and she pushed her food around while Bruce finished his. He moved his empty plate aside. "This is bothering you, isn't it?"

Bruce was stating the obvious, a typical male trait in her experience. Because she found it impossible to conceal her emotions, she simply nodded.

They left, and he followed her back to her rental house, parking at the curb. She unlocked the front door and let him inside. The first thing she noticed in the dark foyer was the red light flashing on her answering machine. Instead of listening to her messages, she turned on the house lights and drew the living room drapes, then brought out the DVD they'd selected.

While he put the disk in the slot, she poured them each a glass of wine. He liked the reds, especially merlot, and so did she. Tucking her legs under her, Rachel sat on the sofa. Bruce sat next to her.

The previews had just started when the phone rang. Unfolding her legs and setting her wineglass on the coffee table with a sigh, she hurried into the hallway to answer it. She wasn't expecting any calls, but there was always the possibility that Jolene might be trying to get in touch with her father.

Using the remote, Bruce sped ahead to the movie portion and hit the pause button.

"Hello," she said, slightly out of breath.

"Rachel, it's Nate."

"Nate?"

Bruce's eyes flew to hers and she whirled around, unable to look at him while talking to another man. She instantly felt guilty, although she told herself there wasn't a single reason she should.

"Thank heaven you're home. I've been trying for the last half hour. Where were you? Damn, I wish you'd turn on your cell phone."

"Did you call to yell at me?"

"No, no. I just want to know what the hell is going on." His words were followed by a slight echo. "Why won't you answer my e-mails?"

"I've already said everything I feel is necessary. I think we should end this right now."

"Fine, whatever, but the least you can do is tell me why."

Rachel didn't want to talk about this now, especially with Bruce listening to every word.

"Is there someone else? It's that Bruce guy, isn't it?"

"No."

"Did I do anything?"

"No." She twisted the cord around her elbow.

"Do I have to play a guessing game with you?"

"No… I found out you're Congressman Olsen's son."

Her announcement was met with a brief hesitation. "That's a problem?"

"Yes!" she cried. "It's a very big problem." He needed to understand what that information had done to her. And if it wasn't a problem, why hadn't he told her himself, instead of leaving her to discover it on her own?

"Does this change who I am?"

"No," she acknowledged reluctantly.

"Then I don't see why it's a problem."

"I do," she said. "You're a congressman's son and I work in a salon doing nails and hair."

"What's that got to do with anything?"

"If you don't know, then I can't explain it."

"I'm Nate Olsen, a Warrant Officer in the United States Navy. Why can't you accept that and that alone?"

"Because."

"That doesn't tell me anything."

"Why did you enlist?" she demanded.

Her question seemed to take him off guard. "I had something to prove."

"It's the same with me, isn't it? You're using me in the same way."

"No."

"I'm just one more stone to throw at your father. I can just imagine what he'd think if he learned about me."

"I don't give a damn what he thinks."

"Well, I do," she said forcefully.

"Then you aren't the woman I thought you were."

She braced herself against the wall. "No, I guess I'm not."

He didn't have anything more to add, it seemed. She heard a soft goodbye, followed by a click. He'd disconnected. The phone droned in her ear, and a long moment passed before she replaced the receiver.

When she turned around, Bruce was standing in the doorway. "You okay?" he asked.

She was going to lie, to shrug it off, but couldn't. "No, not really," she finally said.

He slipped his arms around her for a gentle hug and she rested her head against his shoulder.

Thirty

"Jack!" Olivia complained, sitting on the end of their bed. "When are you going to start using that treadmill?" She hated to nag, but he'd been procrastinating ever since Christmas morning, when she'd unveiled her gift. Although he'd made an effort to look pleased, she'd seen the disappointment in his eyes.

"I will," he said, sauntering out from the bathroom in his underwear. "Soon."

"You promised to start last week."

"I know, I know." He had the resigned look of a convicted man on his way out of the courtroom and into jail. His eyes brightened. "I don't have anything to wear."

"Jack, you know darned well that I got you a pair of sweats. Don't tell me you forgot, either."

"I didn't forget," he admitted, "but I don't feel right sweating in brand-new clothes."

"Jack Griffin, that's the most ridiculous excuse I've ever heard. Enough. Exercise."

"Now?" he gasped.

"Now!"

"But I've got to get to the office."

"Not until you've walked a mile, minimum."

"A *mile?*"

"You'll be too tired tonight after work."

"I might not be," he said hopefully, looking more than a little ridiculous as he pouted while standing in their bedroom wearing only his underwear and dark socks.

"You're walking, Jack."

Olivia was through listening to his excuses. The week following Christmas was too soon, Jack had said, but right after New Year's, he'd be on that treadmill every morning. Olivia had foolishly believed him. It was already the second week of January and he had yet to plug it in. Olivia wasn't leaving this room until he began walking.

"I'm actually not feeling that well."

She rolled her eyes.

Grumbling under his breath, Jack opened his bottom drawer and pulled out the gray sweatpants and shirt. "I hope you're happy," he muttered as he returned to the bathroom.

"You'll feel much better when you finish."

"If I live."

"Very funny," she said. "Start slow and increase your speed gradually. Don't overdo it," she advised. He refused to look at her, but Olivia felt only mildly guilty when she followed him into the bathroom. "Grace and I complain every week about aerobics class, but we both feel good afterward. You will, too."

"If you say so." Jack sat on the edge of the bathtub to lace up his sneakers.

"Tell you what," Olivia said. "I'll make you breakfast while you're walking."

Jack smiled for the first time that morning. "Bacon, eggs, two slices of toast. Wheat," he added, knowing she disapproved of white bread.

"Oatmeal."

"Oatmeal," he spewed back.

"With raisins, but only if you stop your complaining."

The grumbling was back and, despite herself, Olivia laughed. He was being so childish about this.

"Call the office for me, would you?" he said as he walked back into the bedroom, giving her a list of instructions. One would think he was going to be away for a week instead of an hour. Standing in front of the treadmill, he stared at it, as if searching for one last chance to avoid this.

After a moment, he apparently reached a decision and plugged it in, then stepped onto the flatbed. Frowning at the display panel, he began pushing buttons.

"Don't you want to read the instruction book first?" she suggested.

He ignored her. The machine made a loud humming noise and started moving, nearly throwing Jack off his feet. Olivia swallowed a hoot of laughter, knowing he wouldn't appreciate her reaction.

Given no option but to move with the machine, he began walking. But after a few minutes, he was huffing and puffing, reconfirming the fact that he was in terrible shape. Olivia wanted to tell him to slow down, but she could see Jack wasn't in a listening frame of mind.

Retreating to the kitchen, she heard the hum of the treadmill in the background as she put water on the stove to boil for his oatmeal. He might complain, but she noticed that he'd finished the entire bowl the last time she'd made it.

Next, she reached for the phone and called the newspaper office. When Steve Fullerton, the assistant editor, answered, she rattled off the instructions Jack had given her. By then, the water was bubbling and she added the oats and turned off the burner to let them cook slowly.

Wondering how Jack was doing, she went back to the bedroom. As she rounded the corner, she realized he'd quit already. He'd only been at it for fifteen minutes. She hoped that in time he'd increase his stamina. She also hoped it wouldn't be a battle every morning the way it had been today.

When she entered the bedroom, Olivia found Jack sitting on the treadmill, dragging in deep breaths. His color was a sickly gray and he was sweating profusely.

"Jack?" she whispered and hurried toward him. "Jack? Jack, are you all right?"

He pressed his hand over his heart, shaking his head.

"I'm calling 9-1-1."

"No," he gasped. "I'll be all right. In a minute."

Olivia wouldn't chance that. She ran into the kitchen and grabbed the phone. She punched out the three numbers.

"9-1-1 Emergency," a woman's voice answered.

"This is Judge Olivia Lockhart," she said as authoritatively as she could. "I need an aid car at 16 Lighthouse Road. My husband is having a heart attack." She heard the panic in her own voice but couldn't restrain it. It felt as if her own heart was in danger of failing.

"Judge Lockhart, please stay on the line."

"No—my husband needs me. Just hurry! In the name of God, please hurry." She dropped the phone, remembering something she'd read months ago—that an aspirin might help a heart attack victim.

Her hands trembled as she took the aspirin bottle from the kitchen cabinet and shook it into the palm of her hand. Several tablets tumbled out and in her panic, she flung what she didn't need onto the floor.

Jack looked bad when she returned, lying prone and gasping for air. "Jack, oh, Jack," she sobbed. She managed to get him to swallow the aspirin. A siren wailed in the distance, and she ran to unlock the front door.

An aid car parked outside the house and two EMTs dashed toward the front steps, carrying their equipment. Olivia's relief was so great she nearly sank to her knees.

From that point on, events blurred in her mind. Both men worked on Jack for the first few minutes. He was unconscious by then and for one horrifying second she thought he'd died. Terror gripped her. She couldn't breathe. Before she'd even noticed what was happening, Jack had been loaded onto a gurney and transported to the aid car.

"We're losing him!" one of the technicians shouted.

"No!" Olivia screamed as she stood in the middle of her yard. "No—" Unable to watch, she covered her face. The aid car sped off.

She went back into the house, found her car keys and realized how badly she was shaking. In this condition, she'd be incapable of driving. It took three tries to dial Grace's home number correctly.

"Olivia," her best friend said when she answered. "I was almost out the door. You're lucky you caught me."

"Jack—heart attack." The three words fought their way through the tightness in her throat.

"Where are you?"

"Home."

"I'll be there in five minutes."

It was the longest five minutes of Olivia's life. All she could think about was the day her son Jordan had drowned. She remembered what a lovely August afternoon it had been when the sheriff's deputy came to the house. At first she didn't believe him—didn't *want* to believe him. Then she'd wanted her husband with her as quickly as possible.

The officer had called Stan, but her husband worked in Seattle. It took him nearly two hours to get home. Two hellish hours as the reality of their son's death started to set in. Olivia remembered how she'd gathered Justine and James around her. The three of them had sobbed and clung to one another. Grace had been the first person Olivia had phoned that day, too. She'd come over and sat with her and the children until Stan arrived.

Olivia would never forget the wrenching ache in her stomach that horrible day in August and now she experienced it all over again. She didn't know if Jack was dead or alive.

Jack hadn't wanted to get on the treadmill. He'd tried every excuse, but she wouldn't hear of it. Oh, no, she knew best and she wasn't going to let him off. Then she remembered that he'd claimed he wasn't feeling well. She'd insisted despite that. In fact, she'd badgered him into it.

Grace pulled up, and the moment Olivia saw her friend, she sprinted across the lawn, weeping and nearly hysterical.

"Get in," Grace said. "We can talk on the way to the hospital."

"I—I don't think he made it," she sobbed.

"We won't know until we get there."

Her dearest friend was the voice of reason, but Olivia was afraid to hope, afraid to believe that Jack would be given a second chance. Losing him now, so soon after finding love again, was unthinkable. Surely God wouldn't be so cruel to her.

"Did they take him to Harrison?" Grace asked as she negotiated the curves on the winding road at well above the speed limit.

"I—no, the new medical clinic, I think." All of a sudden she didn't know. The Emergency Medical Technicians must have told her, but at that point she'd been beyond comprehension.

Sure enough, the aid car was parked outside the new Cedar Cove facility. Olivia hurried inside and to the front desk. "My husband is here—Jack Griffin."

"Yes, Mrs. Griffin, the doctors are working on him now. If you'll have a seat, they'll be with you as soon as they can."

"No," Olivia argued. This woman didn't seem to understand that the man behind those closed doors was her *husband*. Damn the rules and regulations! Jack could be dying and it was her right as his wife to be with him. In all the years she'd served as a family court judge, Olivia had never used her position for personal gain. In this instance, however, she didn't care. She refused to remain silent.

"I'm a judge. And I need to be with my husband."

"I'm sorry, but we can't allow that."

"You don't understand," she said, her voice raised and nearly hysterical. "I need to be with my husband!"

Grace stepped up to the counter and placed her arms around Olivia. "The doctors will be out shortly," she said.

Olivia stood her ground. "I want to be with him."

"You will be," Grace promised in soothing tones.

"He needs me."

"Right now he needs those doctors more. It won't be long, Olivia." Grace led her back to the waiting area and with only a token protest, Olivia sat down.

An eternity passed. Two eternities.

Charlotte and Ben arrived.

"Ben has a police scanner," Charlotte explained. "When we heard the dispatcher say 16 Lighthouse Road, we knew it must be Jack."

Charlotte sat next to her on one side, Grace on the other. Each held her hand.

When the physician finally emerged, Olivia saw that his name tag said Dr. Timmons. He walked over to her.

She stood, mentally preparing herself for the worst.

But Dr. Timmons gave her a reassuring smile. "We have him stabilized."

"Thank God." Her relief was so great she felt her knees buckle. Thankfully Grace was there to support her.

"He's a fortunate man. Another five or ten minutes, and there would've been no saving him."

Olivia stared at the physician blankly. "What do you mean?"

"Without the medical clinic here in Cedar Cove, your husband would have died on his way to the hospital."

"Oh." Olivia was only beginning to grasp the implications of what he was telling her.

Dr. Timmons continued. "We'll need to transport him to Harrison Hospital, where he can be examined by a heart specialist."

"Of course."

"There'll be some paperwork for you to sign before we do that."

She nodded, and remembered how embarrassed she'd been when her mother and Ben and their friends from the Senior Center had been arrested for unlawful assembly after demonstrating for a medical clinic.

Little did Olivia realize that her mother's demand for a medical facility in town would one day save Jack's life.

Thirty-One

Corrie had been melancholy all day, but she didn't want to mention it to Roy. Telling him the reason for her sadness wouldn't help. On this date in 1975, she'd sat in the office of her father's attorney and signed the adoption papers for her baby. In those days it wasn't necessary to get the father's permission to release the child; if it had been, Corrie would've been forced to lie and list the child's father as unknown. That would have mortified her in front of her family and her father's friend, but she would've done it rather than involve Roy.

Holding a just-brewed mug of coffee, Corrie watched her husband as he sorted efficiently through the mail, setting aside bills. Roy was so used to her presence at work that he usually didn't pay much attention to her when she came into his office. This time, he looked up and frowned.

"You coming down with the flu?" he surprised her by asking.

"I don't think so. Why?"

He shrugged off the question. "You're pale."

"I am not."

"You also seem mighty quiet all of a sudden. That's not like you," he said, trying again.

"Count your blessings."

A half smile came and went in the blink of an eye. "Perhaps I should, but if you're not feeling well, go home. It's a slow day."

"Maybe I will," she said, thinking about it as she returned to the front office. Roy had been hired to do a background check for a Seattle friend, Joe Landry. Joe had recently hired a new assistant and suspected the woman had lied about her employment history. He'd asked Roy to check her out, which he'd been doing for the last couple of days. These small jobs were their bread and butter.

After about half an hour, Roy came out of his office and sat on the corner of her desk. "You're still here. Corrie, if you're not feeling well, go home." When she merely shrugged, he asked, "You talk to Linnette lately?"

"Not really." Corrie had assumed that with her daughter living in Cedar Cove, they'd spend a lot of time together. That hadn't been the case. They both led busy lives and sometimes a week went by before they saw each other or even spoke.

Her answer seemed to astonish her husband. "She was by recently and had a couple of questions regarding a, uh, dating situation. That horse guy you were so keen on."

"*You* gave our daughter romantic advice?" This was frightening.

Roy bristled. "I didn't really want to, but she needed help."

"You didn't say anything about this."

Roy rubbed the side of his face. "The fact of the matter is, it slipped my mind until just now. You might want to talk to her."

Corrie agreed and reached for the phone. Checking the time, she hoped she wasn't waking Linnette. Because of her changing shifts at the clinic, it was difficult to remember the hours she worked.

"Why don't you take her to lunch today? Do that mother-daughter thing?"

Corrie removed her hand from the phone. It occurred to her that her husband seemed awfully eager to get her out of the office. First he'd urged her to go home for the rest of the day. Now he was more or less telling her to take an extended lunch break. Something was going on and she wanted to know what.

Crossing her arms, she stared at him. "All right, what are you up to?"

His look of bemused innocence might have fooled some, but she'd been married to the man for nearly twenty-seven years.

"Nothing!" he declared, apparently shocked that she'd suggest otherwise.

"You'd better tell me, Roy McAfee."

"What makes you think I'm up to anything?"

He wasn't going to talk his way out of this. "Because I know you."

He frowned and then shook his head. "You're a suspicious woman."

She wasn't arguing with him. "That's what being married to you has done for me."

Roy slid off the edge of her desk and sauntered back into his office, as if he didn't have a care in the world.

Corrie followed him and sat in the chair normally reserved for clients. "Do you remember what the first post-card said?"

Roy didn't bother to pull it out. He'd apparently read it so many times that he was able to quote it verbatim. "EVERY-ONE HAS REGRETS. IS THERE ANYTHING YOU'VE

DONE YOU WISH YOU COULD DO OVER? THINK ABOUT IT."

"We've both been doing a lot of thinking the last few weeks," she said softly. Her heart was filled with love and, yes, regrets. She'd never even held her baby but she'd loved her. Signing those adoption papers, she'd felt she was giving away a piece of her soul. Her parents would've helped her, had she decided to raise the child on her own. But young though she was, Corrie had understood that it would've been unfair to them, unfair to her and unfair to her child. A loving family had been waiting, eager for a child, and as emotionally painful as it had been, she'd signed her name and released her baby.

"I'd like to tell you that if I'd been told about the pregnancy, I would've stepped forward and done the honorable thing. But I just don't know...."

Corrie didn't, either, which was the main reason she hadn't informed him.

"I think it's time we were honest with each other," she said.

Her husband's eyes flared. "I've never been dishonest with you."

"Perhaps not openly, but it's clear you were trying to get me out of the office this afternoon and I need to know why."

Roy sighed deeply. "Okay," he said with resignation. "I wanted to make a few calls and find out what I could about our...other daughter."

"Without telling me?"

He shook his head. "I was going to let you know what I found out."

"Eventually," she said.

He hesitated, then admitted it. "Eventually," he echoed.

"That's what I thought. But why? Do you think I'm emotionally unstable? Did you assume I couldn't deal with whatever information you unearthed?"

"No," he denied hotly. "That's ridiculous."

"Then what possible reason is there for keeping me in the dark?"

"We have a daughter who's thirty years old," he said thoughtfully. "A daughter we know nothing about."

She stopped herself from reminding him that, until recently, they hadn't even known their first child was female.

"All these years, I worked hard at pushing every thought of her—the baby—from my mind. I was comfortable doing it. I didn't *want* to know—and yet I did. We'd vowed never to mention it again but now…now she's out there and she refuses to be ignored."

That was painfully obvious to Corrie, as well. "You wanted to find her yourself. Contact her and then bring me in on what you'd done."

"I need to find her," he corrected. "I've gone into the adoption registries and entered our names."

"Why exclude me?" Corrie blurted out.

"I'll explain that in a moment. Like I said, I went on the Internet."

Confession time for her, too. "I did the same thing."

Her husband's eyes connected with hers. "She hasn't registered."

Corrie knew that. She didn't understand it. By whatever means, their daughter had been able to track them down without any of the adoption advocacy groups. And yet…

"That's why you've kept me out of it," Corrie murmured. "Because you're not sure of her motives."

Roy nodded. "If she wanted us to find her, she would've registered, but she didn't. That tells me all of this isn't as innocent as it might seem. She found me, but doesn't want to be found herself. She's content to mail anonymous postcards, send flowers. She's taunting me. This is all one big game to her, and for some reason she seems to have more of a problem with me than with you."

"I wonder why," Corrie mused aloud, "but I think you may be right." Her husband had always been cautious, and perhaps more importantly, suspicious. He considered every angle of a situation, methodically catalogued each detail. The way he worked reminded her of people who did jigsaw puzzles, carefully studying every piece.

"The adoption laws in California are different from those in Washington," Roy added. "I was thinking—"

"California?" Corrie broke in.

Immediately Roy had that chagrined look—he'd said more than he'd meant to. "Yes, California. That's where the final adoption took place."

Corrie hadn't noticed where the baby's home would be as she signed her name. Perhaps the attorney had told her, but if so, she had no recollection of it. "I don't suppose you happened to notice the date, did you?"

"No, why?"

She swallowed hard and shook her head. "No reason."

"Corrie?"

She glanced down, forcing back emotion, unwilling to say.

"I was wrong not to tell you everything I found out."

"You mean there's more?" she snapped. She felt angry that Roy had gone about this investigation and left her out. Yes, she was guilty of the same thing. But she had a good reason. Roy had claimed he didn't want to know; he'd refused to discuss the subject, so she'd had to learn what she could on her own.

"No. I couldn't find anything else. I've hit a brick wall with the California records. Only Alabama, Alaska, Kansas and Oregon are 'open records states.' The reason I was able to find out as much as I did was through an old friend who works for the California state government." Looking at Corrie, he narrowed his eyes. "How did you discover we had a daughter?"

She gazed down at her folded hands. "My mother's diaries. I have them and I looked up the year and month. She knew. She never said a word to me, but she knew we'd had a daughter."

"We'll find her, sweetheart, and when we do we'll explain everything."

Corrie just hoped it was enough for this child to know she was loved and always had been, despite the fact that she'd sent her out of their lives.

Thirty-Two

Allison Cox marched into the living room and sat down across from her father, who was in his recliner reading the paper. She waited patiently for him to lower it, which he did after a few minutes.

"Is there something you want to say?" he asked.

She nodded, and looked down at her hands, struggling to find a way to broach the subject of Anson. He wasn't her first boyfriend, but he was special, and she needed, somehow, to convey that to her father.

"Does this have anything to do with Anson?"

"Yes." She wondered how he'd figured that out. Or maybe she was more obvious than she thought.

Her father frowned darkly. "He hasn't broken his word, has he?"

"No…"

Her mother stepped out from the kitchen and her parents exchanged glances. They did that a lot lately. Maybe it'd been going on a long time and Allison hadn't noticed. She did now, because she and Anson communicated in the same way. He hadn't talked to her since his court date, not even once, but they spoke with their eyes each and every day in French class.

His gaze told her he loved her, and Allison wanted him to know she shared his feelings. Not that she'd ever let her parents find out. They'd say she was too young and insist Anson wasn't right for her. They'd be wrong, but it was a waste of breath to argue. She knew she loved Anson and would for the rest of her life.

"Do you want me in here, too?" her mother asked.

Allison had never intended this to be such a big deal. "Ah, sure."

At least her little brother was in his bedroom. Eddie was mostly a pest, but he had his uses.

Rosie sat on the arm of the recliner and placed her hand on Zach's shoulder. "You were saying?" her mother gestured toward Allison.

"I hadn't really started," she explained. "Dad asked if Anson's been talking to me." Righteously, she added, "He hasn't."

"Good."

"It hasn't been easy, you know." Both her parents seemed to take it for granted that she'd kept her promise. She had, but it'd been the hardest thing she'd ever done. The temptation was so strong because she loved Anson so much. He was the resolute one, not her, and she wanted her parents to appreciate him.

The next part was important. "Dad, I know you helped him get the job at The Lighthouse and I'd like to thank you."

Her father shrugged, as if it was a small thing. "I checked with Seth Gunderson, and Anson appears to be a good employee."

"Really?" Allison was sure this was true. She felt it in her heart, but having her father verify it made everything seem better.

"Yes." Her dad smiled slightly. "According to Seth, Anson shows up early and works hard. He doesn't drive, so he walks to the restaurant after school and pitches in until his shift starts. The only problem Anson had was with another kid who works there named Tony."

Allison bit her lower lip. "What kind of problem?"

Her father shrugged. "Seth didn't really say, but I got the impression that this Tony seems to think Anson makes the other employees look bad because he's so eager to do a good job."

Anson's attitude pleased her. "If he walks from school to work, how does he get home?"

Her father shook his head. "Seth didn't say, but I suspect one of the other crew drops him off."

"Not Tony," she said, musing out loud.

"Probably not," her father agreed.

Allison hoped someone was giving Anson a ride. It had to be two miles between The Lighthouse restaurant and the trailer court where his mother lived. She knew for a fact that his mother wouldn't come and get him. Anson had said enough for Allison to know the woman possessed virtually no maternal instincts.

"Maybe you should tell her what the attorney said," Rosie advised, sharing another of those looks with Allison's father.

Zach nodded. "Anson's turned every paycheck over to the city as reimbursement for the shed that was destroyed."

"That's wonderful." Allison clasped her hands. She was so pleased, it was difficult to hold still. "As soon as it's paid for, he can see me again, right?"

Her father grinned. "That was our agreement."

The doorbell rang, and before anyone could move, Eddie tore out of his bedroom and raced to the front door. They could hear him talking as he stood with the door open for a minute or two. Then he closed it and came into the family room. He looked around and saw everyone watching him.

"Who was it?" Rosie asked.

"Allison's boyfriend. He says he wants to talk to Dad."

"Anson?" Allison was immediately on her feet. "You left him standing out there in the cold?"

"He said that's where he wants to wait, so don't get all bent out of shape."

Zach set aside the newspaper and stood. He exchanged yet another glance with Rosie, arching his brows in obvious surprise. "I'll be back in a moment." He pointed his finger at Allison. "And no, I'm not letting him in the house. A deal is a deal."

Allison felt the room close in on her as her father stepped outside. "Mom?" she cried, hardly knowing what she wanted. She found it torture to sit in the same classroom with Anson five days a week and not be allowed to speak. Now this. It killed her to know that the boy she loved was on the other side of the front door, talking to her father. She had no idea what their conversation could possibly be about, and that made it even worse.

"Everything will be fine," her mother assured her as Allison sat down again.

"Dad's not going to do anything, is he?" So far, her father had been cool. He'd been the only one willing to stand up with Anson in court, and he'd helped get him a job, too.

It seemed forever before her father came back in. The instant he did, Allison jumped up and hurried over to him. "What did Anson say?"

Her mother joined Allison and slid an arm around her shoulders.

"It was man to man," Zach said.

"Dad!" she cried in frustration.

He smiled then, and she knew he was teasing her.

"Anson wanted to give you a Valentine card," he explained.

Allison pressed her hand to her heart. This was so incredibly sweet and romantic she could hardly believe it.

"He felt he should talk to me first. He did promise not to have any contact with you and didn't want to go back on his word."

"I can have it, can't I?" She'd die, simply die, if her father said no.

Her father hesitated. "I was impressed that he'd come and ask my permission."

"He respects you, Dad." She knew that just from the way Anson had said her father's name after they'd gone to court. "You told him I could have the card, didn't you? Oh please, it would mean so much." She hated to plead, but this was quite possibly the most important moment of her life.

Her father pulled a thick envelope from inside his jacket and held it out.

"Oh, Daddy, thank you! Thank you so much."

"He said I could read it."

Allison's gaze flew to her father's. "He didn't?"

"Zach," her mother said. "Don't tease."

Her father grinned and handed Allison the envelope. She needed every ounce of restraint not to rip it open right then and there. Instead, she took it to her room. She sat on the end of her bed and very carefully opened the envelope. The card was expensive and romantic, and the second she caught the word *love,* she thought she might cry.

Inside the card was a letter, consisting of four sheets of paper, folded into fourths. Before she read it, she studied the inside verse and blinked back tears at the sentiment.

"Soon," Anson had written at the bottom of the card, "we'll be together again." Then he'd signed his name.

Allison devoured the letter, reading it as fast as she could. When she'd finished she went back and read it all the way through a second time.

Anson told her about his job and how hard he was working to make a good impression. Being a dishwasher wasn't as easy as it sounded, and he struggled to keep up with the demand. He liked his boss. Seth Gunderson was a big Swedish guy who didn't put up with any nonsense. Anson claimed he didn't mind that, because he knew where he stood.

He also told her that if he continued to work extra hours, he could have the reimbursement monies paid by the middle of the summer. As soon as that happened, they could see each other again. She noticed he didn't refer to any of his troubles with this other guy, Tony.

Six months, Allison reflected. It would be six very long months, but she could wait.

The last part of the letter was the best. Anson wrote how difficult it was to see her every day and not be able to talk to her. In French class, he said, he found it almost impossible to keep his promise to her father. But he'd do it because of everything her father had done for him. He told her that some nights he dreamed about her and always woke with a happy feeling inside.

She dreamed of Anson, too. She hated knowing it would be another six months before they could see each other. Anson was of legal age now and she would be soon. All of this seemed so junior high and yet, at the same time, it was the only way they could be together and not alienate her parents.

She sighed heavily as she folded the letter and slipped it back inside the card. She ran her finger over the embossed image—an old-fashioned picture of cupids and flowers. It was an expensive card bought at a specialty store.

Even when he was putting aside almost every penny he

earned in order to pay restitution to the town, he'd bought her a lovely Valentine card. There'd been no need to purchase the best one available, but that was what he'd done.

Her heart was so full of love for him that she wanted to weep. Then, out of the corner of her eye, she saw a sudden movement, a flash of darkness. She rose from her bed and hurried to the window.

Anson.

He wore his long black coat and a black knit hat that covered his ears.

Anson walked across the yard and stood on the other side of the window.

She smiled and he smiled back, her eyes looking into his.

He pressed his bare hand to the cold glass. She pressed her hand to his. Through the glass they mouthed "I love you" to each other. Seeing him, reading his card and letter—it was the best Valentine's gift she'd ever received.

Thirty-Three

Maryellen Bowman sang a soft lullaby as she finished bathing Katie and dressed her daughter for bed. Katie stuck her feet in her footed pajamas, chattering happily, the volume of her comments rising when Jon walked into her room. He wrapped his arms around Maryellen's waist, resting his palm against her still-flat stomach. It was a sweet gesture acknowledging the baby nestled in her womb.

"Let me read to Katie tonight," he offered.

Maryellen agreed. She'd had a busy day at the gallery and was exhausted. She'd experienced this same fatigue when she was pregnant with Katie—and the baby she'd miscarried, too. She felt as though all her energy was used up by eight o'clock. Jon never complained, but she worried that she wasn't giving her husband enough attention.

"Come to bed early tonight," she suggested, caressing the side of his face. "I miss spending time with you."

"You'll be asleep."

"I won't be if you wake me up."

Jon slowly grinned. He knew exactly what she meant and what she wanted. They hadn't made love since Christmas morning, and Maryellen craved the intimacy. She was well aware of the reason Jon so often delayed coming to bed. He was afraid their lovemaking might distress the pregnancy, but there was no indication of any problem. She felt fine, and other than the fatigue, she was perfectly healthy.

"Is it…safe? I mean, are you farther along now than you were with the other baby?"

Smiling, she nodded. She'd miscarried at nine weeks and was currently entering her fourth month. Jon took over with Katie, letting their daughter choose her favorite book—*Goodnight, Moon* at the moment—and then settling in the rocking chair with her on his lap. In the meantime, Maryellen prepared for bed. She fell asleep almost immediately and woke some hours later, when her husband joined her. She'd chosen a low-cut, silk gown that he'd given her a year ago on Valentine's Day.

"What time is it?" she asked, rolling onto her back.

"Eleven," he whispered, moving closer to her.

She yawned sleepily. Slipping her arms around his neck, she brought his mouth down to hers. His kisses were deep and probing, and his lips devoured hers with urgency.

"Oh," she sighed softly. "What took you so long?" she whispered, excited by the way her nipples hardened at his touch.

Their lovemaking was exquisite, painstakingly slow and filled with passion and tenderness. Afterward, Jon held her and kissed the tears from her face. Her emotions seemed so close to the surface; that was another effect pregnancy had on her. She felt everything more intensely. In the aftermath of their lovemaking, she was so moved by Jon's devotion to her and their family that she began to cry.

"Why are you crying?" he asked between kisses. He followed one stray tear to the edge of her mouth and kissed her again.

She was breathless when he finished. "I love you so much."

"I love you, too...and Katie. And this baby."

"I know you do," she whispered, but that didn't stop the flow of tears. Jon held her in his embrace and with her arm draped over him, she returned to sleep.

At some point during the night, she felt Jon get out of bed. He often stole away for an hour or two and then came back. Most of the time she was only vaguely aware that he'd left. One night, his leaving had stirred her awake and she'd climbed out of bed and gone to see if he was ill. Maryellen had found him sitting in the living room, reading the Christmas card that had accompanied the gift from his father. He'd turned on only one small lamp. Deep in thought, he hadn't noticed she was there, and rather than disturb him, she'd returned to bed alone. A small crack had developed in the wall Jon had built blocking out his parents. One tiny fissure. She prayed that eventually the relationship would be restored.

The next morning, Jon was whistling and in a cheerful mood. Come to think of it, Maryellen was in a good mood, too. A *very* good mood. Jon had a cup of herbal spice tea waiting for her when she came downstairs, dressed for work. Katie sat in her high chair banging her cup and looking pleased with herself.

"What time will you be home tonight?" Jon asked as he walked them to the car.

He asked this same question every morning; it was part of their ritual and the answer never changed. "Same as usual," she promised.

Jon placed Katie in her carrier and buckled her in, kissing the top of her head before climbing out of the rear seat. "Have a good day," he said and she saw the reluctance in his step as he rounded the car to kiss her, too. "I wish you didn't have to go into town." This was a familiar complaint.

"I wish I didn't, either."

Jon kissed her, but rather than giving her a token peck on the cheek, he kissed her passionately.

"Wow, what was that for?" she asked, fluttering her eyes, hardly able to catch her breath.

Jon chuckled. "I'm not sure," he responded. "I guess it's because I'm a satisfied husband."

"I plan on keeping you that way."

"You do?"

"Definitely." She got inside the car and watched as Jon walked back to the house, his steps lighter now.

By one o'clock Maryellen hadn't had a chance to eat her lunch. The gallery was doing a robust business, much to her delight. Fortunately, Lois showed up to relieve her, and she went into the back room to warm the soup delivered by the Potbelly Deli nearly an hour earlier. While the soup du jour, beef barley, heated in the microwave, she took a washroom break. That was when her happy world went into a downward spiral. She was spotting.

For a minute or more she sat there, her head spinning. This couldn't be happening. Not again. Perhaps it was the lovemaking, but the doctor had reassured her on that score. Terror clawed at her as tears sprang to her eyes.

Not wanting to alarm Jon prematurely, she called her mother at the library. "Mom," she said fervently, "I need you."

Her mother seemed to know instantly what was wrong. "Is it the baby?"

"Yes. I don't think I can drive."

"Do you want me to take you to the medical center?"

The tears came in earnest now. "I don't know."

At that point, Grace took over the decision-making and decided Maryellen should see her regular physician. Dr. De-

Groot's office was nearby and the receptionist promised to get them in as soon as Maryellen arrived.

"I've called Jon," Grace told her when she picked up Maryellen at the gallery.

"No," she cried. She didn't want him to worry unnecessarily.

"Sweetheart, this is his baby, too. He's on his way."

"Was he upset?" Maryellen knew he'd blame himself for this, although she felt certain their lovemaking had nothing to do with it.

"Jon's only concern was for you and the baby."

"You told him I was fine, didn't you?"

"Of course I did."

Her mother walked her into the physician's office and Maryellen was quickly ushered into a cubicle. Grace stayed with her until Jon got there and then announced that she'd be out in the waiting room.

Before her mother left, Maryellen hugged her. "I love you, Mom." She feared she didn't say it often enough. She'd been blessed with a wonderful mother, and she knew this was a difficult time for Grace because of the breakup with Cliff.

Grace returned her hug. "Love you, too, sweetie."

Once her mother had left, Jon sat next to Maryellen and held her hand.

"I'm so sorry," she said, trying not to break into sobs.

Her husband drew her close. She knew he was struggling with emotion, too. If she lost the pregnancy, Maryellen was afraid there wouldn't be another. Jon would refuse to risk it. She wasn't sure she could go through this again, either.

Reading her chart, Dr. DeGroot stepped into the cubicle, and smiled at the two of them, holding hands, clinging to each other physically and emotionally.

With his nurse at his side, he examined her carefully.

"Am I losing the baby?" Maryellen cried, unable to keep silent.

He shook his head. "If you mean are you miscarrying, the answer is no."

"Is the baby safe?" Jon asked.

"For now."

Maryellen didn't like the sound of this. Involuntarily she stiffened and tightened her hold on Jon's hand.

"Your cervix is weak and there's a danger you'll lose the child unless you have complete bed rest for the next five months."

Maryellen gasped. "But how can I?" Katie demanded constant care and like a typical two-year-old was into everything. In addition, Maryellen had a job and with her employment came an insurance package that covered medical care. Jon was self-employed and had no benefits.

"If you want your baby to live, you'll find a way," Dr. De-Groot insisted. "I can stitch up the cervix and that'll offer some protection, but you'll need to stay in bed and off your feet."

"This is my fault," Jon said. "I…we made love last night."

"It's impossible to know for sure, but frankly I doubt that's the cause," Dr. DeGroot told him. "However, you'll need to abstain from lovemaking until after we deliver your baby."

Maryellen nodded and so did Jon. He raised her hand to his lips and kissed the back of it.

"We'll be fine," he assured both the physician and Maryellen.

She didn't know how that could be true.

"I'm not sure Lois is ready to take over the gallery," she lamented after Dr. DeGroot had left.

"She doesn't have a choice," Jon said, unwilling to yield.

Maryellen knew he was right, but she couldn't help worrying. How was Jon going to be able to work, take care of her and look after Katie, too?

Jon kissed her forehead. "All you need to think about," he whispered, "is taking care of yourself and our baby."

Maryellen attempted a smile. He was trying to set her mind at ease, and she was grateful for that, but even his loving words weren't proof against her doubts and fears.

Thirty-Four

Linnette could hardly imagine Cedar Cove without a medical clinic. She hadn't worked a shift yet during which she wasn't on her feet for the full eight hours. She loved her job and was responsible for a variety of cases.

She'd adjusted to life in Cedar Cove surprisingly well. Naturally, it helped that she was familiar with the town, since her parents had lived there for six years. And making friends with Gloria Ashton had boosted her sense of welcome.

Thursday afternoon, Dr. Timmons walked into a cubicle, passing within inches of her. He nodded politely and she smiled back. They worked side by side nearly every day and he'd been guarded but friendly. He always treated her with respect. But not once—not even one time—in all the weeks they'd worked together had he given any indication that he'd be interested in seeing her outside the clinic. Linnette had finally accepted the truth, finally stopped deluding herself. It was all too apparent that Chad had no romantic interest in her.

Linnette wanted to kick herself for being so coldhearted and callous toward Cal Washburn. Despite the fact that her mother had arranged their initial meeting, she liked him. His stuttering didn't bother her. What did bother her was how much she enjoyed his company—and his kisses. She was still thinking about it. In the weeks since their last date, she hadn't *stopped* thinking about Cal and where their relationship might have headed if she hadn't been so eager to cast him aside.

Her behavior upset her so much that she'd talked to her father about the strong attraction she felt for Cal. In retrospect, Linnette was happy to get advice from her dad; her mother would've said *I told you so* a dozen times.

Her father's advice, however, had left her slightly confused. He'd said something about fate stepping in, putting Cal in her path. When she did see him she'd apologize, which she wanted to do anyway—she just wasn't sure how or when. She hoped he'd ask her out again. The only alternative would be to make the first overture. She didn't know if she could.

"There's a man who needs stitches in the surgery," Sally Lynch, the LPN, said.

Linnette grabbed the man's chart. She'd taken one step into the small surgery when she read Cal's name on the computer printout. Just a few seconds earlier, he'd been foremost in her mind. She remembered what her father had said, and her heart started to beat fast. If it was meant to be, Cal would come back into her life.

And here he was!

Maintaining a calm facade, she pulled the curtain aside and discovered that the palm of his left hand had been sliced open. The wound had been prepped and was ready to be sutured. It was an ugly cut and no doubt painful.

"Hello, Cal," she said, moving into the room.

He closed his eyes and turned his head; he didn't acknowledge her greeting.

Ignoring his lack of warmth, she sat down on the stool to

examine the cut. "I think we're looking at ten or eleven stitches here." She glanced at his face. "Do you want to tell me how you did this?"

"No."

Linnette had the feeling that, given the opportunity, he would gladly have walked out the door. She wasn't about to let that happen.

"Actually, I was hoping I'd run into you," she said, reaching for the needle to numb his hand.

"I b-bet," he muttered from between clenched teeth.

Linnette waited until she'd finished giving him the Novocaine. "I feel I owe you an apology."

"None n-n-necessary."

"You were nothing but kind to me and I was exceedingly rude."

He didn't comment one way or the other.

The first suture went in without a problem. "I've felt badly about it ever since," she said, tying off the second stitch.

He remained uncommunicative while she continued to speak in even tones that belied her physical response to him. She wasn't sure how to tell a man who worked in a barn how badly she missed his scent. She didn't realize it until she caught a whiff of fresh alfalfa and what she suspected was a combination of man and horse.

Neither of them spoke during the next three sutures. Linnette wanted to ask if he'd thought of her at all, but she feared the answer even more than the question. After the cold way she'd treated him, he didn't want anything more to do with her; she was convinced of it. Still, she felt she had to say something else.

"I, uh, wondered if I'd see you again," she said as she tied off the last of the sutures.

Once more he left her comment hanging. She wrapped the

wound and gave him instructions on taking care of it. Cal worked with his hands so he'd have to be extra careful to keep the cut clean and protected.

In his eagerness to escape, he all but vaulted out of his seat when she stopped speaking.

"Cal," she said sternly before he could bolt.

Exasperated, he turned back. "What?"

"You'll need a follow-up appointment."

"Why?"

"I'll need to remove those stitches and inspect the cut."

He whirled away, prepared to leave again.

This time Linnette stepped in front of the door, blocking his exit. "It's important to have that looked at in about a week." He stood no more than a foot away. His presence nearly overwhelmed her and she thought her heart might stop beating. He seemed to be staring straight through her. She hoped he was; then he'd know she was sincere. If her eyes told him anything, she wanted it to be an apology—wanted him to know she regretted the things she'd said and done at their last meeting.

Neither moved until it became apparent that there was someone on the other side of the door. Linnette shifted as Sally came into the room and nearly collided with Cal.

"Sally, Mr. Washburn will need a follow-up appointment," she said, her throat so tight the words came out sounding strangled.

"Uh, sure thing." Sally regarded her closely. She knew as well as Linnette did that such appointments were handled by the receptionist and not the nursing staff. "Come with me, Mr. Washburn."

"I'll see you later," Linnette forced out the words as Cal walked past her.

Again he didn't respond to her or the unspoken plea evident in her remark.

When Cal strode into the waiting area, with Sally trotting behind him, Linnette felt she needed to sit down. Strangely, she yearned to run after him and demand to know if he'd kissed other women the way he'd kissed her. It was a ridiculous question and since she'd already made a fool of herself once today, she figured that was her limit.

Once she regained her composure, she walked out to the receptionist's desk and looked over Marilyn's shoulder. "Did Cal Washburn make a follow-up appointment?" she asked.

"The man who came in with the cut hand?"

"That's him. He didn't, did he?" Linnette wasn't sure why she bothered to ask. She would've been shocked if he had. Cal had made it as plain as possible; he wasn't interested in seeing her again.

"No," Marilyn said. "Sally tried to talk him into it, but he said he could take the stitches out himself."

"Linnette."

Chad called her and, surprised, she turned to face him. "I was hoping to see you when you've got a free moment."

"Right now is fine," she said and even managed to sound professional.

Chad touched her shoulder, guiding her to the side of the hallway that led to the cubicles and the surgery. "I've been meaning to talk to you for a while now."

He didn't quite meet her eyes, which told her this wasn't going to be a pleasant conversation.

"Is there a problem with my work?" This was her immediate concern, although she couldn't think of a single incident in which her ability as a P.A. might be questioned.

"No, no, nothing like that." Still he hesitated. "Perhaps we could get a cup of coffee after work."

Had he asked her this as little as three weeks ago, she would've leapt at the suggestion.

"Is tonight convenient?" he murmured.

"Ah…I guess."

"Hey, you can't go back there." Sally's voice rang down the hallway.

Linnette spun around and saw Cal.

His eyes narrowed as he read the physician's name tag.

Linnette straightened. Chad had kept his voice low in order to talk privately and she'd leaned close so she could hear him. Anyone happening upon them would've assumed they were deep in conversation—a confidential, perhaps even intimate, conversation.

"No p-problem," Cal said, and with that he wheeled around and walked out the door.

Once more Linnette resisted the urge to run after him. She hated to let this relationship go, but no longer felt she had any other choice.

Thirty-Five

On Valentine's Day, Grace drove out to visit Olivia rather than head home to an empty house. Jack had recently returned from the hospital where he'd had bypass surgery, and poor Olivia had her hands full. Apparently Jack wasn't a good patient, which came as no surprise to Grace. Or Olivia either, Grace assumed.

She rang the doorbell and waited a few minutes before Olivia answered, flustered and unkempt, which was completely unlike her. She stared at Grace and her small bouquet of red carnations and seemed about to burst into tears.

"Looks like you've had a rough day," Grace said sympathetically.

"You don't know the half of it," Olivia muttered under her breath.

Jack sat in the living room, arms crossed and eyes flashing defiance.

"Ah," Grace said, glancing from one to the other. "Did I come at a bad time?"

"No," Olivia insisted.

"Yes," Jack countered.

"Perhaps I should come back later?"

"Absolutely not," Olivia said, glaring at her husband.

Jack sighed his capitulation. "You might as well stay."

"Jack Griffin!"

"Sorry, Grace." He rolled his eyes. "I just wonder if you know how stubborn your best friend can be."

"Olivia?" Grace feigned shock. "Never."

"Et tu, Brute!" Olivia mutttered.

Grace handed her the flowers and while her friend retreated to the kitchen to find a vase, she sat down across from Jack. "A little overprotective, is she?"

He snickered softly. "How'd you guess?"

"I know Olivia."

"She's become my shadow. I can't even take a—use the bathroom without her running after me to make sure I'm not going to keel over."

"That's a natural reaction, don't you think?" Grace asked. "She nearly lost you, in case you've forgotten."

"She's suffocating me."

Olivia poked her head around the kitchen door. "Are you talking about me behind my back?"

Grace wasn't about to lie. "Of course."

Olivia frowned. "Don't listen to him. Jack's trying to do too much too soon."

"I'm following doctor's orders," Jack shouted. He turned his attention to Grace again. "Tell her to go back to work. I need some breathing space."

Grace disagreed. "Let her fuss over you. She needs to do that."

Jack regarded her, then slowly shook his head. "I suppose you're right."

"Grace, would you like a cup of tea?" Olivia called.

"Please."

"I'll take coffee," Jack said.

"Green tea is better for you."

He started to argue but apparently changed his mind. "Whatever you think, dear."

This time Olivia came all the way out of the kitchen. She pointed at Grace. "What did you say to him?"

Holding back a smile, Grace said airily, "Oh, just that you love him."

Olivia's eyes narrowed. "I'm reconsidering that. In all my born days, I've never known a man as pigheaded as Jack Griffin."

Grace would hear none of it. "You're crazy about this man. You love him—you can't help loving him."

To her surprise, Olivia laughed. "I do, and he knows it."

A smug look came over Jack. "The thing is, I love her, too." He held out his hand to Olivia, who clasped it firmly. "I'm sorry, sweetheart."

"Me, too." She sniffled, then abruptly went back to the kitchen.

"We argue," Jack said. "I don't think she's used to that."

"She isn't," Grace told him. Her friend, the judge, liked order and control; she rarely raised her voice or lost her cool. Marrying Jack had changed all that.

"But we make up, too," Jack added. "That's the best part." He jiggled his eyebrows for effect.

Grace smiled. Her friend's marriage might not be perfect, but she'd never seen Olivia happier. Jack was exactly the kind of man she needed in her life—irreverent, confrontational and fun.

"The tea will be ready in a minute," Olivia said from the kitchen.

Jack's eyes softened and he seemed to have forgotten that Grace was in the room. After a moment, he said, "I was sorry to hear about you and Cliff."

Rather than comment, Grace nodded. It still hurt to think about Cliff. Much as she wanted to, she couldn't dismiss him completely from her thoughts. In time, she reasoned, that would get easier.

"Things just didn't work out," she said as if it were a minor occurrence.

Olivia returned then, carrying a tray with three filled cups and a plate of oatmeal cookies.

"None for you," she announced to Jack the instant his eyes widened with delight.

"This is cruel and unusual punishment," he growled.

"The doctor wants you down twenty-five pounds."

"Who made you the diet police?"

"I did. Do you want to argue some more?" she asked as she passed him a cup of tea.

"No, but it's downright mean of you to tempt me."

Olivia sighed. "All right, you can have one cookie."

As soon as Jack set down the tea, he grabbed Olivia about the waist and pulled her onto his lap.

She let out a squeal of protest, then threw her arms around his neck. "Do I need to remind you we have company?" she asked.

"Am I embarrassing you?" Jack asked his wife.

"Terribly."

He grinned as if that had been his purpose all along. "Good."

Olivia struggled into an upright position, patted her hair and then gave Grace her tea with an air of refinement.

Grace stayed long enough to drink her tea and have a cookie and then left. On her way home, she fought a deepening depression. This was Valentine's Day, and she was alone again. She'd been alone for the last four years, but this year it felt a hundred times worse. Dan had never been much of a gift-giver. He'd made a few attempts over the years but she couldn't recall a single Valentine card he'd given her, or flowers.

Buttercup and Sherlock were at the door to greet her. They always showed great enthusiasm about having her home and she rewarded them both with lots of praise and attention. After filling their dishes, she turned on the television. She wasn't interested in any of the programs, but the TV provided company, the sound of people talking and laughing.

When the doorbell chimed an hour or so later, she didn't know who it could be. She wasn't expecting anyone. Opening the front door, she saw Cliff, and her breath caught. After a slight hesitation, while she fortified her resolve, she opened the door.

He waited on her porch, a bouquet of red roses in hand. At this time of year, Grace knew those flowers must have cost a fortune.

Without a word, he opened the screen door and stepped into the house. He held out the roses. "Can we talk?"

The desire to welcome him back into her life felt like an undertow, about to drag her beneath the waves. She took a deep breath as they just stood there, inside her front door. "I love you, Cliff—but no."

Her answer appeared to shock him. "You won't even talk to me?"

"Why? So you can apologize and then two weeks or two months down the road repeat the same behavior?"

"No," he said. "It won't happen again. You have my word on that."

She wanted to believe him, but she couldn't.

He must have felt her indecision. "I love you, Grace."

"I'm sure you do, but you don't trust me."

Cliff removed his Stetson and studied the floor. "I told you what my marriage was like."

"And I've told you I'm not Susan. I made a mistake and I've paid dearly for it. I'm sorry, Cliff, truly sorry, but I think you should leave." Her voice faltered, but her determination didn't.

He nodded, replacing his hat. "When you said we were through, I thought breaking it off completely might be for the best. What you said was right on target. The way I treated you wasn't intentional—but in a sense it was. I see that now. I suppose I was hoping you'd put an end to the relationship...."

His honesty hurt, but she kept her chin high and didn't comment. He confirmed everything she'd suspected.

"Then you were out of my life, and I was more miserable than before. Every day I found myself missing you so much. I had a hole in my heart and in my life. I realized I was the biggest fool on earth to let you go." He paused, shaking his head. "Lisa and I talk every week. Sometimes she knows me better than I do myself. She said if I let you walk away, I'd regret it the rest of my life."

"So Lisa prompted this?" Cliff loved his daughter and listened to her when he would listen to no one else.

"No," he said quickly. "She was just telling me what I already knew." Before Grace could speak, he told her, "Lisa isn't the only one. Cal said either I patch things up with you or he's quitting."

Grace managed a half smile. "I don't believe that for a moment."

"Believe it. If you turn down my proposal, Grace, I might as well not go home."

Tears filled her eyes. If Cliff Harding was proposing to her on Valentine's Day, she didn't think she'd ever forgive him for being so romantic. He made it almost impossible to say no.

"I love you, Grace," he whispered. "I can't live without you any longer. I tried, but nothing seemed any good. I'm working hard—and for what? I don't need the money. At the end of the day, I walk in from the cold and the house is dark and lonely. That's the way I feel without you."

Grace closed her eyes rather than look at him.

"I want to love you, live with you, travel with you."

She longed to say yes, she really did, but she was afraid....

"You said, when you made dinner on New Year's Day, that you were going to ask me to marry you. I'd give anything to have been here. I'd give anything to have the chance to hear that proposal because, my darling, the answer is *yes.*"

His reminder was the dash of reality she needed. "I didn't get to ask you, remember?"

"I do, and I'm sorry every day for being such a jackass. Then again, I'm just old-fashioned enough to do the asking. Grace Sherman, I love you and I want to marry you. Will you be my wife?"

She pressed her hand to her mouth and blinked rapidly. Loneliness had been her constant companion since Dan's disappearance. Here was the opportunity to end that. Without his saying it, she knew that if she refused, she'd never see Cliff again. He'd leave, and it truly would be over.

"Will you?" he asked, his eyes pleading with her.

Grace sobbed once and nodded. "Yes, oh, yes." Before she could draw another breath, she was in Cliff's embrace, crushing the roses between them. He kissed her until she was weak in his arms, and then whispered in her ear, "I hope you don't believe in long engagements."

She laughed and hugged him tight. "I was thinking the very same thing."

Thirty-Six

Cecilia met her friend Cathy for lunch on Saturday afternoon at the Pancake Palace. They served a really nice meal for a reasonable price. Cecilia had been feeling low all week and was badly in need of a pep talk.

Cathy was waiting for her when Cecilia walked in. She sat toward the back of the room in a booth, waving vigorously. Her four-year-old son wasn't with her, which surprised Cecilia.

"Where's Andy?" she asked as she slid into the booth. Seven months into her pregnancy, there was no disguising the fact any longer. There wasn't an inch to spare between her protruding belly and the table. In another few weeks, it'd be too tight a squeeze and she wouldn't be able to sit in a booth anymore.

"Andy's with friends on a play date," Cathy explained. "I have all afternoon free, so after lunch we can do something fun." She seemed almost giddy at the thought.

Cecilia wished she shared her excitement. To hide her mood, she reached for the menu tucked behind the napkin canister. Nothing looked appetizing but she made a decision.

"What do you think?" Cathy asked. "Shopping? A movie?"

"Either would be great," she said, forcing some enthusiasm into her voice. "You decide."

"Shopping then," Cathy announced.

"That sounds perfect." Already Cecilia felt better. "The mall or the commissary?"

"The mall," Cathy decided. "We won't be as likely to run into someone who'll want to tag along."

"I wouldn't mind, you know." Cathy was such a cheerful person to be around that she naturally attracted people.

"Not today," her friend said. "You and I need quality time together. That's what Andrew always says about him and me—but most of *our* quality time is spent in the bedroom." She smiled as she said it.

The waitress came for their order; Cathy asked for the seafood salad and Cecilia ordered the turkey wrap with a cup of vegetable beef soup. As soon as the woman had brought their drinks—sparkling water for both—Cathy folded her hands on the table and leaned forward.

"Okay, what's wrong?"

"What makes you think anything's wrong?"

Cathy studied her carefully. "I can see it in your eyes. Besides, when you phoned, you didn't sound very happy."

"I'm not," Cecilia confessed.

"Ian and the baby again?"

"He refuses to decide on a name," Cecilia blurted out. "It's ridiculous, and oh—he's just so frustrating."

"He knows the baby's a boy. So what's his problem?"

"I've been after him for weeks to give me suggestions for names and he just ignores me. Finally I sent him a list of my favorites and he ignored that, too." This was the one thing Cecilia disliked about e-mail. Whatever he didn't want to answer, he simply ignored.

"What are you going to do?" Cathy asked. "Wait until after the baby arrives? You can't call him Baby Randall for the rest of his life, you know."

"I do know. I told Ian he had his opportunity and if he wasn't going to make any suggestions, I'd choose the name I liked best without him."

"So," Cathy said, her eyes sparkling with curiosity, "what name have you chosen?"

Cecilia placed her hand on her belly. "Aaron. Aaron Randall has a good sound, don't you think?"

"I like it," Cathy said, testing the name on her tongue. "Aaron Randall. Yes."

"Ian's middle name is Jacob and I thought we'd use that for the baby's middle name, too."

Cathy nodded her approval. "Does Ian have a problem with Aaron Jacob?"

She sighed. "For weeks he refused to discuss names and when I told him fine, I'd do it without him, he didn't respond. But the minute he heard the name Aaron he went nuts. I told him about it when he called last week," she added.

"Why doesn't he like the name?"

Cecilia was embarrassed to repeat what he'd said. "He doesn't want a name that begins with the letter *A*."

"That doesn't make sense," Cathy muttered, and then her eyes widened. "Oh. He's upset because Allison's name began with *A*?"

"Exactly." The waitress delivered their meals and Cecilia thanked her with a smile.

"Isn't that being a little superstitious?"

Cecilia nodded. "He's so afraid, and it's really starting to bother me. I like the name Aaron. When I first went back to school, I had a teacher at Olympic College who encouraged me. If it hadn't been for Mr. Cavanaugh, I would've dropped out."

"His first name was Aaron?" Cathy guessed.

Cecilia took a bite of her wrap, which was actually quite tasty. "He became my advisor and steered me toward the bookkeeping classes. I think he must be a friend of Mr. Cox's, too, because I was hired after Mr. Cavanaugh suggested I apply for the position." The math professor had been more of a father to Cecilia than her own, and she wanted him to know how much his encouragement had meant to her. She kept in touch with him, sending a Christmas card each year. She'd mail him a baby announcement and thank him again for his kindness.

"Ian had his chance to name the baby." Cecilia tried a spoonful of soup. "I tried and tried to get him to discuss names and the only reaction I got was that he didn't like Aaron."

"Well, like you said, he's afraid."

"I'm going to be fine," she insisted, as though she had to convince herself as well as Cathy. "The baby will, too." She'd already begun to think of the baby as Aaron, and the name was a perfectly good one.

Half an hour later, Cecilia and Cathy left the Pancake Palace and drove to Silverdale, to the Kitsap Mall. Neither of them had much extra money, so they just browsed in the baby departments. Cecilia did buy some little undershirts that were on sale.

"I'm concerned about Allison Cox," Cecilia said as they passed a record store and saw a display of DVDs. "I think I told you. She's fallen for this kid who looks like he's stepped right out of *The Matrix*."

"There's something highly attractive about a bad boy," Cathy said and although she was teasing, Cecilia knew it was true. The attraction was certainly there for Allison.

"I thought you told me they aren't allowed to see each other."

"They aren't, and it's killing Allison. She comes in after school and moans on and on about how hard this is. I listen and try to be sympathetic, but that boy is bad news. I'm just grateful Mr. Cox put his foot down."

"So what's your concern?"

Cecilia swung her small plastic bag. "Mr. Cox and Anson have an agreement and, when that's fulfilled, Anson can see Allison again. The poor girl's living for that day. I'm afraid she's setting herself up for a big disappointment."

"You're borrowing trouble," Cathy told her as they strolled past a display of baby furniture. "But on another subject, what do you hear from Rachel Pendergast these days?"

"Not much," Cecilia said. As soon as Rachel had learned that Nate's father was a United States Congressman, she'd broken off the relationship. Cecilia still planned to go to Rachel for her haircuts, but it'd been two or three weeks since she'd talked to her.

"I take it she's running scared."

"Yeah." Cecilia paused to run her hand over the side of the display crib. She already had Aaron's room set up and had purchased a used crib from a secondhand store. Everything was prepared and waiting for her son, although she hadn't bought many new things.

"Don't you wonder how young parents can afford all this?" she mused aloud.

"They can't. This is for grandmas to buy," Cathy said with a smile. "After Andy was born, Andrew and I flew home to visit my parents, and they'd bought a crib for him to sleep in while we were there. A brand-new one! Andrew and I bought a secondhand crib that he painted white. I did the best I could with decals, but it didn't look half as good as any of these. We got a real kick out of the fact that my parents had a brand-new crib and we had a used one."

They left the mall after a couple of hours and no other purchases. Cathy needed to get back to pick up Andy. Cecilia headed home, then changed her mind and drove to the cemetery where Allison was buried.

Cecilia made sure the gravesite was always well maintained. In the first year, she'd visited at least once a week and brought flowers. These days she didn't come as frequently, but her daughter was never far from her thoughts.

Cecilia stooped down and with her gloved hands brushed some wet leaves from the grave marker. "Hello, sweetheart," she whispered. "It's Mommy and your little brother." The baby moved inside her as if to add his own greeting. "Your daddy's being stubborn again." She nearly choked on the words, surprised by the emotion that rose inside her whenever she talked to Allison. "Don't worry, though," she whispered. "We'll be all right." She straightened, placing both hands on her lower back. A moment later, she returned to the car, her head bent against the February wind.

Thirty-Seven

Jack rolled his leather chair up to his desk and sighed at the sheer pleasure of getting back to work. Damn, this was where he belonged. He inhaled a deep breath, glancing around the busy newsroom.

Olivia had made a real stink about his returning to the office. He'd placated her as best he could and promised he'd work only a half day. If he wasn't home by noon, he was afraid she'd send the sheriff after him. Troy Davis would do it, too. He'd probably delight in hauling Jack out of the office in full sight of any and all onlookers.

His assistant editor, Steve Fullerton, came up to his desk, carrying an insulated coffee cup. "Listen, Jack. I need to talk to you about the Lifestyle feature. We couldn't get the photos and…" He grinned widely. "Hey, I'm glad you're back."

"Thanks." Jack was embarrassed by the fuss his staff had made. His desk was covered with flowers and cards, and they'd hung a banner overhead with gold letters that said Welcome Back. It was nice to know he'd been missed.

By ten, he was completely immersed in the routine of getting out a daily paper. It seemed as if he'd never been away. He wrote an editorial and praised the quick response of the local EMTs who'd saved his life. His fingers flew on the keyboard. He'd always composed his best editorials under time constraints; in fact, Jack had spent most of his career under the gun and thrived with the pressure—or so he'd once believed. This recent scare made him rethink that assumption.

At noon, the Lifestyle article had to be dumped, they needed to come up with something new and there was a one o'clock deadline. Olivia would be furious if he stayed longer than he'd promised. He weighed her anger against his inclination to pitch in with everyone else. Jack was still trying to decide what to do when Bob Beldon strolled in.

"Jack," Bob said, heading straight for Jack's desk. "I was in the neighborhood and thought I'd stop by, see how you're doing."

Jack frowned. Bob *just happened* to be in the neighborhood. Not likely. He knew this visit was no accident. "Olivia sent you, didn't she?"

A chagrined look spread over Bob's face and he nodded.

"That's what I figured." Leave it to his wife.

"She said I was to drag you out of here kicking and screaming if necessary. You aren't going to make me do that, are you?"

Jack groaned in protest, but Bob was the best friend he'd ever have in this life. He knew when he was beat. Grumbling under his breath, he turned off his computer, then stood and reached for his jacket. He just hoped his wife and his friend knew how hard it was for him to walk away in the middle of a crisis.

The staff looked on in disbelief. He'd never abandoned them, never left before every deadline was met, every detail attended to. Steve Fullerton actually started a round of applause, and Jack gave a mock bow, waving on his way out the door.

"See you tomorrow, old man," Steve called. "Try to stay alive for another few days."

Jack wouldn't admit it, but he was exhausted. During his recovery, Olivia had insisted he take a nap every afternoon. In the beginning he'd defied her because he resented being "ordered around like a kid." Little good that did him, since he fell asleep anyway, and always slept at least an hour.

"What am I supposed to do with myself now?" Jack muttered as he and Bob went to the parking lot.

"I thought I'd invite myself over so the two of us could play a few games of cribbage. It's been a while."

The last comment was a reminder that Jack had been working too hard for too long. The job hadn't started out like that, and yet within five years he'd managed to work himself into a heart attack.

"Cribbage sounds like a fine idea," Jack said. "Just promise to be gentle with me. My skills are pretty rusty."

"No mercy," Bob teased. "For once, I have the advantage and I'm taking it."

"Oh, so that's how it's going to be." Jack laughed. It felt good to be with his friend, who was also his AA sponsor and all-around mentor.

Fifteen minutes later, the crisis at the office was forgotten as Jack stared at the cards in his hand, deciding which two to discard. He chewed on the end of a toothpick, a habit Olivia detested, and set aside the six and the three.

The phone interrupted his concentration. "Ten bucks says that's Olivia checking to see if I'm home," Jack muttered, glancing over the top of his cards.

Bob chuckled. "You're on."

Jack grabbed for the receiver. "Yes, sweetheart?"

Olivia gave a small gasp. "How'd you know it was me?"

Jack held out his palm to his friend, indicating that Bob should pay up. "Lucky guess," he answered his wife. "I'm home, and my baby-sitter's doing a fine job of looking after me."

"Bob is *not* your baby-sitter."

"Am I required to nap this afternoon?"

She ignored the question. "How did it go at the office?"

"Great, really great." He dared not let her know how much he loved being back at work. The frantic pace stimulated him. Afternoon naps—even if he needed them—didn't.

"Are you tired?"

He smothered a yawn. "No way. I'm sitting here in the middle of the day playing cutthroat cribbage with Bob Beldon. There's nothing else I'd rather be doing."

Not true. He'd rather be at work—or making love to his wife—but that was another area that appeared to be taboo since his surgery. The only time he'd mentioned the possibility, Olivia was the one who damn near had a heart attack. Absolutely no sex. Apparently even talking about it was off limits. As far as he could figure, he'd been cut off for the rest of his natural life. Sex wasn't all, either. He hadn't seen a piece of red meat in weeks.

"See how you feel after Bob leaves," she suggested. "You sound a little cranky."

There she went again, treating him like a five-year-old. "Shouldn't you get back to work?" he asked, hoping to get her off the phone before he lost his temper.

"Not really—I'm on my lunch hour."

"You're interrupting our game," he said. He suspected Olivia had given Bob instructions on how long he should stay. Although Olivia's actions were prompted by love, everything she'd said and done since the surgery felt like a noose being tightened around his neck.

"Have a good afternoon, sweetheart, and I'll be home soon after five."

He wanted to tell her not to rush on his account, but it wouldn't do any good. Olivia was on a mission and unfortunately that mission was to save him from himself.

Jack replaced the receiver, closed his eyes a moment in an effort to reduce his blood pressure, then picked up his cribbage hand.

"So how'd you know it was Olivia?" Bob asked, placing a ten-dollar bill on the coffee table.

"She's smothering me with attention."

"I don't know," Bob returned with a skeptical look. "I wouldn't mind Peggy giving me a little extra TLC."

"You'd mind this." That was all Jack was willing to say on the subject.

True to her word, Olivia was home at twelve minutes past five. Jack knew for a fact that the drive from the courthouse to Lighthouse Road took exactly eleven minutes. That meant she was out the door at the stroke of five, in her car and racing away from the office.

Jack sat in front of the television. He found daytime TV asinine. It seemed largely populated by the stupid and the shameless. One more talk show or courtroom program and he was going to leap off a bridge.

"Hi," she said, coming through the front door. Studying him for any signs of—what?—she removed her gloves and hung up her coat. "Did you have your nap?"

Jack clamped his jaw rather than comment.

"Is there anything I can get you?" she asked next.

"Yes." His response was automatic. "I want a kiss. A real kiss."

She hesitated for only a moment. "All right."

"None of that peck-on-the-cheek stuff, either. I want—no, I *need*—a kiss from my wife."

"Jack...I don't think this is a good idea."

"I happen to believe it's a mighty fine one." Slowly he got up from the chair. If she wouldn't come to him, he'd go to her.

Olivia must have recognized the determination in his eyes because she backed away from him until she could go no farther. Pressed against the wall, her eyes wide with alarm, she whispered, "Jack..."

He didn't allow her to finish. She stiffened when he brought his mouth to hers and kissed her for all he was worth. Her lips were soft and pliant, and it wasn't long before he felt her relax. She sighed; soon her arms were around his neck and they were completely caught up in each other.

Jack was just beginning to wonder how difficult it would be to unfasten her blouse and free her breasts. He loved the feel of Olivia's breasts; the weight of them in his hands was about as close to heaven as he figured he'd get. Suddenly the oddest thing happened.

Olivia started to weep.

These weren't ordinary tears, either. Her shoulders heaved with sobs as she clung to him, kissing him as though she couldn't stop. A moment later, she was crying so hard she had to pull away in order to breathe. With her head against his chest, her arms circling his middle, she continued to weep.

"Olivia?" he asked anxiously. He'd never seen her cry like this, never known her capable of this heart-wrenching kind of grief. His hands were in her hair as he tried to comfort her.

"I almost lost you," she managed to say between hiccuping sobs. "Jack, oh Jack, please, please, don't ever do that to me again."

He closed his eyes and tightened his hold on her.

"All I could think about was losing you… I kept remembering the day Jordan drowned and…don't leave me, Jack! Don't leave me, I love you so much."

"I would never leave you," he assured her, still stroking her hair.

"I couldn't stand it."

"Never," he promised. "I'll never leave you, Olivia." And, God willing, he'd keep his word.

Thirty-Eight

"Roy, would you fill the water glasses?" Corrie called from the kitchen. Their company was due any minute, and she was decidedly flustered.

They were having the Beldons over, and cooking for someone like Peggy Beldon was a challenge. Peggy's skill in the kitchen was worthy of her own cooking show on the Food Network. What did one serve a culinary virtuoso?

After days of flipping through cookbooks, Corrie chose baked halibut with wild rice and fresh green beans. Dessert was coconut cake, using Charlotte Jefferson's recipe. With this cake, Charlotte had apparently won the blue ribbon in the Kitsap County Fair five years running. Corrie didn't doubt it. If the cake tasted half as divine as it looked and smelled, even Peggy would be impressed.

"Done," Roy said, holding an empty water pitcher in his hand. "Anything else you need me to do?"

Corrie stepped back and surveyed the dining room. The presentation was elegant, if she did say so herself. A fresh flower arrangement sat in the middle of the mahogany table, which was covered with a pale-yellow linen cloth. Matching napkins were folded into the shape of birds about to take flight. Corrie had picked up this neat trick watching a Martha Stewart show a few years back. The simplicity of it had attracted her. Their very best china and silverware were laid out for their guests.

The doorbell chimed, and Corrie drew in a calming breath. She didn't know why she'd worried so much. It wasn't a competition, and Peggy wasn't critical. She supposed her own perfectionism was the culprit; that and her desire to make sure their friends had a wonderful time.

Roy welcomed the Beldons. After he'd taken Bob and Peggy's coats, they all gathered in the living room and Corrie brought out an appetizer. It was an easy recipe she'd gotten off a package of cream cheese. You started with fresh Oregon shrimp mixed with cocktail sauce and heaped it all on a block of the softened cream cheese. Small crisp crackers were arranged around it.

Roy took a bottle of white wine from the refrigerator and poured three glasses. Bob had a soda. It didn't seem to bother him that wine was served, although Corrie was sensitive to the fact that their friend was a recovering alcoholic. Bob had assured them it wasn't a problem the last time they'd had the Beldons to dinner, which was—oh, she was embarrassed by how long it'd been. The night of the fruit basket, as she always thought of it now. Last October…

They toasted one another and made small talk for a while, just catching up on life.

"Do you ever hear from Hannah Russell?" Roy asked. He sat next to Corrie, his arm draped around her shoulders.

Hannah was a young woman who'd lived with the Beldons the previous year. Her father had died two years earlier at the Thyme and Tide, and his death had shaken the entire community—especially when it was revealed to be no accident, no natural death. Max Russell had been murdered. No one was more shaken than Bob, who appeared to be a suspect at the beginning.

Even now Corrie didn't understand all the connections. She knew Max and Bob had served together in Vietnam; Dan Sherman had been with their unit, too. So was a fourth man, now a colonel. The men had held on to a terrible secret—a massacre in a remote village. They'd all been involved and, needless to say, none of them had ever gotten over it. They'd handled that unbearable memory in different ways. With Bob it had been drinking....

Dan was the first to die. His death, however, had been a suicide. Then Max was murdered, and there were all sorts of questions and misconceptions regarding his death.

The shocking truth about Max's death came later, when it was learned that his own daughter had killed him. No one had been more stunned than Peggy, who'd befriended the girl and welcomed her into their home. The Beldons had let Hannah live with them, helped her find employment, encouraged and supported her.

"I haven't talked to Hannah in months," Peggy said, and her words rang with sadness. "I've written her any number of times, but she never answers. The last I heard, she'd been taken to California to await sentencing for her mother's death." Hannah had initially tried to engineer her father's death by having a friend tamper with his car, but it was her mother who'd died.

"Peggy was in court when Hannah accepted the plea agreement." Bob shook his head in confusion. "Somehow Hannah blames us for her arrest."

Peggy bit her lip. "I still find it hard to believe that Hannah could murder her parents."

Roy didn't respond, and Corrie knew why. Her husband

was the one who'd long suspected the girl's involvement in the murder. The only reason Hannah had come to Cedar Cove was to keep track of the investigation. Meanwhile, she'd fooled people by acting timid and vulnerable, a little girl lost.

"Max's death wasn't the only mystery in this town," Bob commented, sipping his soda. "As I recall, the last time we were at dinner here, someone left a package at your front door."

Peggy brought her hand to her throat. "You frightened us because you thought that fruit basket might contain a bomb or something."

Roy's smile was forced. "I remember."

"Did you ever find out who was responsible?"

Corrie looked at her husband.

"Not yet," was all Roy would say.

"I hope this wasn't confidential, but Corrie told Peggy you'd been receiving anonymous postcards," Bob said. "Don't tell me that's still going on?"

"The most recent one arrived on Valentine's Day," Corrie answered when it seemed that Roy wouldn't. The subject made them both uncomfortable. The card had actually been a valentine and the message inside had read: ROSES ARE RED, VIOLETS ARE BLUE, I KNOW WHO I AM— DON'T YOU?

Bob frowned and shook his head. "Don't you have a clue who's doing this?"

Roy nodded. "We have an idea."

Just then the oven timer buzzed. The timing couldn't have been better as far as Corrie was concerned. "I believe that's our cue to move into the dining room."

The evening was enjoyable and they lingered over drinks until Bob suggested cards. Roy set up the card table while Corrie got out the deck. They played pinochle, the women against the men. After the first game they paused for coffee and dessert, and Corrie promised to write out the coconut cake recipe for Peggy. They were just finishing when Linnette arrived.

Their daughter seemed surprised that her parents had guests. "Oh, sorry," she mumbled. "Hi, Peggy, Bob. I didn't realize Mom and Dad had company."

Corrie immediately knew that something had upset her. "Should I call you later?" she asked.

"No need," Peggy said, reading the situation perfectly. She carried her empty cake plate and cup to the kitchen. "It's time Bob and I went home."

"It is?" Bob glanced longingly at the card table.

"Yes," Peggy said pointedly. "It is."

Corrie had to smile. The men were finding it difficult to end the evening with the women having won the first round. They'd soundly beaten her and Peggy last time, so she considered this poetic justice.

Roy and Corrie walked their guests to the front door while Linnette helped herself to a slice of cake. Whatever was troubling her must be serious if her diet-conscious daughter had resorted to cake.

After heartfelt farewells, Corrie returned to the kitchen.

Roy faked a yawn. "I'll go up to bed and leave you women to talk."

"No, Dad, this involves you, too." Linnette gestured with her fork to the empty chairs across from her.

Roy pulled one of them out and stretched his long legs. "What's up?"

"Gloria Ashton."

Roy turned to his wife. "Who's she?"

"Linnette's neighbor," Corrie reminded him.

"And friend," her daughter added. "A good friend, too."

"Then what's the problem?" Roy asked, his voice impatient. He was a lot more accommodating with his clients than his children, Corrie thought, and she resisted the urge to kick him under the table.

"Does it have to do with Chad?" she asked.

"Oh, yeah, the doctor fellow," Roy muttered.

Linnette lowered her head and nodded. "He asked me to have coffee with him after work a week ago, and I agreed." She frowned and then shrugged her shoulders. "Basically, he wanted to tell me he's dating Gloria."

"Your neighbor," Roy put in, although by this point, he knew darn well who Gloria was. "Why should he have to ask your permission? It's none of your business."

"Which is exactly what I told him."

Now Corrie was getting confused. "I must've missed something here. Last I heard, you'd decided pining after Chad was a waste of time."

"Big waste," Linnette concurred. "I told Chad if he wanted my permission to date Gloria, he had it. I felt that his asking me was junior-high stuff. Then Chad explained that Gloria's refused to go out with him because she and I are friends."

It sounded like the kind of thing that happened in high school, all right. "Why would she do that?" Roy demanded.

"I don't know. I tried to talk to her," Linnette said, "but she wouldn't listen. She said men are a dime a dozen." Their daughter sent her father a tentative glance. "Sorry, Dad."

"Continue," Roy urged, waving off her apology.

"Gloria said good friends aren't that easy to come by, and I agree. I told her it doesn't matter to me that she's interested in Chad, but she said she didn't want to risk losing my friendship over a man."

"And Chad blames you?"

Linnette sighed. "I feel guilty about it and yet why should

I? I went so far as to tell Gloria that if she didn't go out with Chad, I would—and that was the worst thing I could've said."

"Does Chad get a say in this?" Roy murmured.

"Not really," Linnette said. "Okay, he does, but I don't care if he asks me out or not."

"Would you care if Cal did?" Corrie inserted triumphantly.

"Cal?" Roy repeated. "Does every man you date have a name that starts with the letter *C?*"

"Cute, Dad, very cute."

"You didn't answer my question," Corrie said.

"Yes," she admitted with another deep sigh.

"Have you seen him since he was at the clinic?"

Linnette shook her head. "I doubt I will, either."

"Don't you need to take out those sutures?" In Corrie's opinion, this was the perfect excuse.

She shrugged. "Someone needs to. Either Cal will do it himself or Cliff Harding."

"You could always go to him," Corrie suggested.

"Is there a reason my presence is necessary here?" Roy asked in a bored voice.

"Yes, Dad, there is. When I asked you about Cal, you said if I was supposed to see him again, fate would send him back into my life. That's what happened with you and Mom, right?"

"Right," Roy agreed.

"Fate *did* bring him back, and this time I refuse to make the same mistake. I don't know what'll come of it, but I'm willing to find out. He isn't a doctor with a lot of degrees, and I doubt he has a large income, but he's about all the man I can handle."

Delighted, Corrie smiled, but when she looked at Roy, she noticed that her husband wasn't quite as pleased.

Thirty-Nine

Maryellen was at her wits' end. Jon had set up a makeshift bed for her downstairs. Now, what had once been their living room had become the center of her universe—and her prison. The doctor didn't even want her climbing stairs. Worse, Maryellen couldn't lift anything that weighed more than a few pounds, which meant she was unable to hold her own daughter.

Fortunately, her sister was looking after Katie during the day, and Maryellen didn't know what they'd do without Kelly's help. Jon handled all the childcare plus most of the housework at night, and that was difficult enough.

Every morning he drove Katie into town and then he drove back in the afternoons to pick her up. In the meantime, Maryellen was trapped in the house, restless, bored and desperately afraid any unnecessary movement would bring on premature labor.

Her life assumed an unsettling routine. Jon woke by seven, came downstairs and put on coffee, then went back upstairs to dress Katie. After giving Katie her cereal, he brought Maryellen a cup of herbal tea. They tried to spend a few minutes together with Katie before he took her to Kelly's. It was early spring, so ferns and early flowers were starting to emerge, and the opportunity for interesting nature shots was at its prime. Jon was often away from the house for hours. He needed to work in order to earn the money they desperately needed.

Maryellen knew he didn't want her to worry about finances—as if that could be avoided. Naturally she was concerned. Without her working, they were forced to live on a single income. Jon's sales increased every year, but he wasn't yet at the level where he could support himself, let alone a wife and two children. Maryellen had encouraged him to quit as chef for The Lighthouse restaurant and devote himself to his career. Her plan had worked well until now.

The front door opened and Maryellen set aside the novel she was reading. Her attention had been wandering all morning; the hours dragged on endlessly. Jon walked into the house carrying the backpack in which he kept his camera equipment.

"I'm home."

She tried to smile.

"How are you feeling?" he asked as he slipped off his boots.

"Cranky," she moaned. "You can't imagine how awful it is to stay in bed like this." Every place she looked, there was something that needed to be cleaned or finished, folded or put away. Jon tried, but he couldn't manage everything on his own.

"How about if I make lunch?" he suggested.

"I'm not hungry." She appreciated the offer and knew Jon was trying to please her. The fact was, she didn't have much of an appetite these days. Why would she? The most exercise she got was walking to the downstairs bathroom and Dr. DeGroot had suggested she cut back on those visits as much as possible.

"You barely touched your breakfast," Jon reminded her. He sat on the edge of her bed, his eyes revealing tenderness and care. "I'll make your favorite—a toasted cheese sandwich and tomato soup."

She smiled; for his sake she'd try to take a few bites.

Jon kissed her cheek and moved into the kitchen. "Did anyone phone while I was out?"

"No." Maryellen crossed her arms. For the first couple of weeks, she'd received daily calls from Lois, needing advice or guidance. Those calls had stopped. Apparently her assistant, or one-time assistant, was comfortable as manager of the gallery now. Her mother usually tried to call during her lunch hour, and Maryellen was thankful for the distraction. But the library was often hectic around noon and her calls had dwindled down to maybe three a week.

"Did you hear from your mom?" Jon asked as if reading her thoughts.

"Not today." Grace helped Maryellen as much as possible. Her mother, however, had a life of her own. Now that she was engaged to Cliff, Grace spent every spare minute with him. Maryellen wasn't sure when the wedding was scheduled to take place. Soon, she suspected. It was doubtful she'd be able to attend, which depressed her further.

"My vacation pay is up this week," she said as Jon came back five minutes later with a tray. She didn't want to be the bearer of bad news, but it was important her husband realize there'd be no more checks. She worried constantly about the fact that they were about to take a financial freefall. Worse, they'd have to pay the medical insurance premiums, which were hefty. Maryellen felt grateful to have some continuing coverage from her job, but the benefits were limited.

"I know," Jon said as if it meant nothing. "We'll manage."

"How?" She gazed at the diamond ring he'd given her for

Christmas. How she wished he'd put that money in the bank, instead. They were on the brink of financial ruin, and here she was, sporting a huge diamond ring.

"Where's your faith, Maryellen?"

"My faith?" she repeated. "In you? In God?"

"In both," he stated calmly. He rested the tray of soup and sandwiches on her lap and sat next to her. "I know this is hard, sweetheart, but we'll be fine."

Maryellen had taken over the bill-paying and she wasn't sure Jon grasped how tight things really were. How close they'd already come to not meeting their obligations—and now with the insurance premiums to pay...

"Only thirteen more weeks until the baby's born."

If he meant that to be encouraging, it had the opposite effect. Thirteen weeks sounded like forever.

"Eat," he said, pushing the cheese sandwich toward her.

For the baby's sake, Maryellen took one small bite. Then another. Jon had to coax her every time. She didn't mean to be such a problem, and sighed, feeling wretched. Caught up in her own miseries, she hadn't noticed that Jon's mood wasn't any better than her own.

"Is everything okay, honey?" she asked anxiously.

His face immediately relaxed as if to reassure her. "Of course."

"You'd tell me if it wasn't, right?"

"I would," he promised.

But Maryellen had to wonder. And the more she did, the guiltier she felt. "I've been horrible all day, haven't I?"

"Not at all." He dismissed her question with a shake of his head.

"I have, and don't tell me otherwise."

Jon grinned, but Maryellen could tell it was forced.

"Tell me," she insisted.

He shrugged. "Why? So you'll be more depressed?"

"Jon," she cried. "We're a couple—a team. We shouldn't hide the way we feel from each other. Communication is the key. You're the one who told me that, remember?"

She set the tray aside, unable to eat any more.

Jon looked away from her and into the distance. "I went to see Seth Gunderson about working part-time. We could use the money, and I don't care what hours he gives me."

Maryellen hated the thought of Jon postponing his photography, but they were going to need a steady income.

"Seth was pleased to see me. He said he'd take me back anytime."

"That's good news, isn't it?"

"It was—until I found out the only hours available were at night."

"Oh." Maryellen couldn't cope with Katie alone.

"Seth understands I need daytime hours, and he said he'd talk to the day chef and see if he'd be willing to trade shifts for a while."

"That would be wonderful." Maryellen tried to sound positive. At the same time, she realized that if Jon worked all day he wouldn't have a chance to continue his commercial photography business. It was a lose-lose proposition.

"We'll be just fine," he said again, but the comment fell flat.

Maryellen swallowed hard. "Would you hold me for just a moment?" she asked. Everything seemed better when she was in her husband's arms. There she found comfort and peace. With her head against his shoulder, she could anticipate the future and remember that at the end of this enforced rest, they'd have a second child. Katie would have a little brother or sister. A little more than three months from now, this would all be over. What she needed to do was keep her gaze focused on the future and not their present circumstances.

Jon's hand caressed her back, and she sighed, content for the first time that day. "I've been thinking," she murmured, carefully broaching the subject.

"That's a dangerous sign."

Maryellen felt her husband's smile. "I've been trying to come up with another way. We need help, Jon."

"I'm managing."

"Yes," she agreed, "and you're doing a wonderful job. But it's only been three weeks, and you're already exhausted. Taking care of Katie and me, cleaning the house, shopping, cooking, plus trying to work and sell your photographs. You're worn out." She couldn't begin to imagine what would happen if he added a forty-hour week at The Lighthouse to his schedule.

"You think I'm tired, do you?" He nuzzled her neck, but it was more affectionate than provocative. Anything remotely sexual was off limits until six weeks after the birth.

Maryellen hugged him close. "You *are* tired. I am, too."

"Yes, sweetheart."

"We do know people who could help."

He knew immediately who she meant. "If you're going to suggest what I assume you are, then save your breath." Jon broke away from her and stood up.

"Jon, would you please be reasonable about this?"

"You want me to call my parents."

That was exactly what she wanted. "They'd leap at the opportunity to spend some time with us." His father and stepmother were desperate to win back his love and would do anything to help if the chance arose.

"I'm not asking them for a damn thing," Jon said forcefully, "and I absolutely forbid you to contact them."

"Forbid?" she repeated, raising her eyebrows. *"Forbid?"* The temptation to retaliate in anger nearly overwhelmed her, but she maintained a calm facade. When she spoke, Maryellen chose her words carefully. "I'm going to ask you to rephrase that, Jon, because I have to believe you didn't mean it the way it sounded."

Her husband started pacing. "*Forbid* wasn't a good word. I'm sorry." He hesitated, then walked to the picture window that overlooked Puget Sound. "But knowing how I feel about them, I would hope you'd take that into consideration."

"I already have."

His back was to her, his hands in his pockets. "Have you been in touch with them?"

Maryellen sighed. "I mailed the last photos you took of Katie and included a note that said I was pregnant."

"When?"

"At Christmas." Then she remembered she'd also sent a thank-you note. "I...I wrote after Christmas, too—a short note to thank them for the gifts." Even then she'd felt guilty, as though with this small act of kindness she was somehow betraying her husband.

Jon turned to face her. "At one time I needed my parents and they failed me. I vowed I'd never ask them for help again."

Maryellen knew what was coming.

"I can't do it. I'm sorry, Maryellen. I'd rather work twenty hours a day than ask my parents to lift a finger to help me. I simply won't do it."

The decision was his, and nothing she could say would change his mind. "Okay."

He eyed her skeptically. "Are you angry with me?"

She shook her head. "No, you said it earlier—we'll be fine."

"You won't go behind my back?"

She'd done that once and regretted it. "No."

Jon came back and sat down next to her. "It's no wonder I love you as much as I do. You and Katie are the best thing that ever happened to me."

Despite what he said she'd done for him, Maryellen knew it was Jon's love that had redeemed *her* life.

Forty

Friday evening Grace arrived at Cliff's an hour later than she'd planned. She felt exhausted and worried and guilty all at once. Maryellen needed her; Cliff wanted to set the date for the wedding and she was scheduled to leave for a library conference first thing Monday morning. With all these demands, she didn't feel she was much help to anyone.

Cliff walked out to the car to meet her, and Grace swore if he said one word about her being late, she'd burst into tears.

He opened the car door and instantly sensed something was wrong. "Bad day?"

She nodded as she climbed out. "I drove to Maryellen's to see what I could do for her," she said. The house was a disaster, her daughter's spirits were low, and Jon seemed about to collapse under the burden of his responsibilities. He was cooking again, too, whenever The Lighthouse needed him to cover a shift. To top everything, Katie had the flu, which meant the little girl needed constant care. She clung to Maryellen and wouldn't allow Grace to hold or comfort her. "I stayed and did a couple loads of wash, and cleaned up a bit, but Cliff, they're in bad shape."

"Is there anything I can do?"

He was sweet to offer. "I don't know. Offhand, I can't think of anything." She shrugged. "Perhaps bring them dinner one night."

"Consider it done."

Grace was seriously thinking about not going to the conference and spending the time with her daughter, instead. She'd hate to cancel; the money for her to attend had come out of their tight library budget and no one else could take her place on such short notice. The thought of wasting the round-trip ticket to San Francisco, plus the conference fee, depressed her.

"I don't know what to do," Grace said as she slid her arm around Cliff's waist. Together they walked toward the house.

"I don't suppose now would be a good time to ask you to elope, would it?"

He couldn't possibly know how tempting that was. "Maryellen and Kelly would never forgive me." Olivia wouldn't, either, but she didn't mention her best friend. Of the three, Olivia would be the most sympathetic.

"Lisa would feel the same way," he admitted grudgingly. "I had no idea it was so difficult to schedule a wedding. I hate this waiting. I can see us six months from now, still searching for the perfect date, working around everyone else's schedule."

"Maybe we *should* do it," she said, thinking out loud. "Elope, I mean."

Cliff came to an abrupt halt and dropped his arm from around her waist. "You aren't just saying that, are you?"

Grace supposed she'd meant it more as a comment than a suggestion, but then realized how badly she wanted to end this craziness and—just marry him. "Olivia could perform the ceremony."

"We can get the license Monday morning."

Then she remembered she was flying out on Monday. "Oh, no—I've got that conference."

"Where is it again?"

"San Francisco."

Cliff smiled. "All the better. We'll be married there."

That sounded perfectly wonderful, if not for one minor detail. "Cliff, I'm attending a huge library conference."

"We'll go on a real honeymoon later."

"You're serious?"

"Are you?" He studied her as if he wasn't sure.

"I...I was just thinking I might have to forget about the conference altogether. Maryellen and Jon need my help, and I'm feeling guilty about not doing more."

"Can you cancel out at this late date?"

"Well, yes, although it's a problem. And, Cliff, I *want* to go. I have workshops scheduled each day, plus there's a banquet one night and I'm even on a panel about literacy."

"Then you *should* go. Why don't we hire a housecleaning service to help Maryellen out? We'll arrange it for Monday. And we'll have The Lighthouse send out a few meals. Then there's no need for you to feel guilty—and you and I will go to San Francisco."

Grace stared at him. "You are a miracle worker," she said.

"Aw, shucks, ma'am," he muttered with fake modesty.

When she laughed, he said, "You do have some free time during the conference, don't you?"

"Some. On Wednesday afternoon." She'd hoped to steal away and do a little sightseeing.

"Some is enough. We won't need much."

"But—"

"Are you looking for an excuse to get out of this?"

"Absolutely not."

"Good, because I'm going to make it happen. Wednesday afternoon it is, March eighth. Don't you worry about a thing."

They weren't even inside the house yet, but she threw her arms around his neck and kissed him hard. "We're running away to get married!" Cliff lifted her off the ground and with a shout of jubilation, whirled her around and around.

Cal came out of the barn and gave them an odd look. He stood there, apparently waiting for an explanation.

"We're getting married," Grace told him when Cliff set her feet back on the ground.

Cal grinned. "I...th-th—figured as much."

"Next week," Cliff added.

Cal straightened his hat. "You got that m-m-mare coming from Ken-tuck-ky."

Cliff's smile slowly faded, but then he shook his head. "You can handle her. You'll have to, because I'll be in San Francisco with my bride."

"Y-yes!" Cal laughed and nodded. "Go!" he yelled, waving them off.

Cliff wrapped his arm around her waist. "If we waited for the perfect time, it could take years. I, for one, am not willing to wait a minute longer than necessary."

"Are we going to tell anyone?"

"And risk the wrath of the entire universe?" he teased. "Lisa will probably hire a hit man and I know your daughters won't be thrilled with us, either. That's the risk we'll have to take. As far as I'm concerned, no one needs to know we're married until we decide to tell them."

"But if we don't tell everyone we're married, I won't be able to move in with you."

"Why not?"

"I can't let my family assume we're living together."

"If I had my say, you'd be living with me now."

"Cliff!"

"All right, all right," he said, opening the front door to let her into the house. The fire in the fireplace warmed the room, welcoming her, and she glanced around at the log walls, the simple, solid furniture, the old-fashioned braided rug. This would be her home....

"We'll announce that we're married when we return and let the chips fall where they may," he said.

"Good." That solved that. "We'll schedule a wedding reception at a date convenient to all."

"That'll be years from now."

"Okay," she amended, smiling. "We'll schedule the reception when it's convenient to most." Then, because it was impossible to contain her excitement, Grace turned into Cliff's arms and kissed him again.

"Wednesday can't come soon enough for me," he murmured, his voice husky against her ear.

"Do you know how long the waiting period is in California?" she asked. It was three days in Washington State, and she didn't want any last-minute problems if it happened to be longer in California.

"No," Cliff said, "but I'll find out. Now don't worry—we're getting married, come hell or high water."

Dinner—a beef stew—was warming in the Crock-Pot, and Grace set the table. She felt as if she was walking on air. Every now and then, she'd catch Cliff's eye and they'd share a smile. Once, Grace broke into giggles of delight. She felt so light-hearted, so…happy.

Cliff disappeared into his office after dinner and returned about twenty minutes later. "I went on-line and there's no waiting period in California."

"Great!" All their plans were coming together.

"And while I was at it, I booked my flight." His eyes shone. "It's the same one as yours."

"How'd you know?"

"Easy. You told me when your flight was leaving, so all I had to do was check the airlines for that departure time."

Cliff said he'd ask Cal to drive them to the airport early Monday morning. That meant everything was settled. "Have I told you lately how brilliant you are?" she asked in an admiring voice.

"I am, aren't I?" he said, sounding smug. "If it means I can marry you next week, you'd be amazed at how smart I can get."

Cliff put in a DVD; she hardly noticed what, nor did she care. They sat together in front of the television. Cliff's legs were stretched out, his boots propped on the coffee table. He'd slipped his arm around her shoulders and her fingers were linked with his. In a matter of days, she would be this man's wife....

Cliff leaned down and rested his cheek against her hair. Sighing, he asked, "Are you enjoying the movie?"

She had a vague impression of car chases and lots of action. What she enjoyed wasn't the movie, but being with him. "Not really. Why?"

"I'm going to need help reorganizing the bedroom."

"Now?"

"Might as well, since you're moving in with me the minute we get back from San Francisco."

"What about my house?" All of a sudden she realized that their decision to elope brought immediate consequences.

Cliff shrugged. "That's up to you and the girls. Keep it, sell it, rent it—do whatever you want as long as you promise you won't live anywhere but with me."

"Cliff, what about Buttercup and Sherlock?"

"They'll adjust to a new home." He seemed so confident. "Hey," he muttered, "you're not having second thoughts, are you?"

When he was looking at her like this, his eyes intense with love, there wasn't a thing in the world that concerned her.

"No—but I don't know anything about horses."

"You don't need to."

"What about my job?"

"Do you enjoy working?"

"I love it."

"Then keep your job." He frowned. "Are you *sure* you want to do this?"

Laughing, Grace grabbed his shirt collar and brought his mouth down to hers. Then she kissed him with everything she had. "Does that answer your question?" she asked.

Forty-One

Linnette pulled onto the side of the road and looked at her MapQuest printout. According to the directions, Cliff Harding's ranch, where Cal Washburn was employed as a trainer, was right here. She wasn't sure what she'd expected, but it wasn't this massive piece of property. The field in front was bordered by a white fence that stretched as far as the eye could see. There were a dozen horses grazing, their bodies sleek and beautiful. Linnette could tell they were valuable.

The barn was huge, with what appeared to be an apartment above it, and the house, set back at the end of the drive, was a two-story log building with plenty of windows for light.

Stopping to check the address was just an excuse, a stalling tactic. Linnette knew she'd taken a big risk in coming out here to talk to Cal. A *very* big risk. He could slam the door in her face or tell her to get out. She didn't think that would happen, though. More likely he'd be completely indifferent to her. That was, after all, what she deserved. But it didn't matter; she had to do this, had to explain.

Even now, on the verge of seeing him, she wasn't sure what she'd say. She hoped inspiration would strike when she needed it, because this was probably the most difficult conversation she'd ever had. She didn't want to be attracted to Cal, but she hadn't been able to get him out of her mind. She refused to accept that he didn't feel the same way about her. He couldn't kiss her like that and feel nothing.

Sitting by the side of the road wasn't going to accomplish anything, so she started the engine and entered the driveway that led to the house. Linnette had expected some sort of activity but the house looked deserted. The only vehicle in sight was a battered pickup. Just her luck to get up her courage to come all this way and find Cal wasn't home.

Deciding to explore, she parked close to the house and, dropping her keys in her coat pocket, walked to the barn. The doors were open and, as she approached, she heard Cal talking. Apparently there was someone with him.

Linnette suddenly realized he wasn't stuttering. The hair on the back of her neck went up. Was his speech impediment some kind of stunt? If so, she was not amused.

Hands swinging at her sides, Linnette marched into the barn.

Once she'd gone all the way inside, she saw that Cal *was* alone. He crouched beside a huge horse—a stallion, judging by certain obvious signs—and was examining the beast's hoof, talking all the while. His back was to Linnette, so he didn't see her.

The stallion, however, did and reared his head, alerting Cal to the fact that someone else was present.

Cal straightened and glanced over his shoulder. When he saw her, he dropped the horse's foot. The stallion didn't take kindly to such neglectful treatment; he snorted and pawed the ground.

As if to apologize, Cal removed his glove and stroked the animal's nose.

Linnette noticed that the bandage was off, and she grimaced at the risk of infection.

Without a word, he grasped the stallion's halter and led him into a stall.

"You weren't stuttering," she said when he came out.

He stared at her. "I d-d-don't with a-a-animals."

"Just people?"

He nodded, then shrugged, suggesting he didn't understand it himself.

For a moment she'd nearly forgotten the true purpose of her visit. "How's the hand?" she asked in a concerned voice.

Cal looked at it as if he'd forgotten, and again answered with a shrug, a quick lift of his shoulders.

"What about those stitches?"

"I t-took care of it."

"I can check it, if you like." The moment she said that, she knew giving him a choice was a mistake. "You've kept it clean, haven't you?"

"I don't need your help."

He felt strongly enough about that to be able to speak without a single hesitation.

"I know, but I was in the area and thought I'd stop by." He'd probably see through that weak explanation, but it was the best she could do.

"Un-in-n-n-vited?"

Linnette gestured carelessly, as though she often stopped by people's homes unannounced, welcome or not. Refusing to give him an opportunity to argue, she stepped forward. "Let me see your hand."

At first he seemed about to refuse. She peered around the dimly lit space. The inside of a barn wasn't the best place to examine a cut. "Is there someplace else we could go so I could take a look at this in the light?" she asked.

He nodded reluctantly, then led her to the stairs and without a word, headed up to what must be his apartment. When she reached the top, he let her inside. The apartment was surprisingly spacious and modern. However, it was badly in need of a woman's touch. The windows had no blinds or curtains; the furniture was bulky and dark. The only photographs were of horses, the only decoration a pillow at the end of the sofa.

Cal pulled out a kitchen chair for her and went to the sink. He lathered his hands with soap, drying them on a kitchen towel. Then he sat down in the chair next to hers and laid his hand on the table, palm up. He smelled of fresh hay and leather—the scent she'd noticed on him the night he'd kissed her. It had acted like a powerful aphrodisiac then. It did now.

To disguise her attraction, Linnette examined her handiwork. The cut had healed nicely. "You took good care of it," she said, and smoothly ran her fingers over his palm. At the feel of her skin against his, Cal bristled. She chose to ignore his revulsion at her touch. "I don't see any infection."

"N-none," he agreed.

She looked up long enough to smile. Long enough to let him read the message in her eyes. The regret, the fear of rejection, the apology. He had to understand that she hadn't found it easy to come to him like this.

"I'm enjoying my work at the medical clinic," she said casually, disregarding his impatience. "I've seen a variety of cases. It's something different every day."

Cal didn't comment.

"Working with Dr. Timmons has been interesting."

Cal seemed to tense at the mention of the other man.

"Have you ever done anything you regret?" she asked. She didn't give him the opportunity to answer, for fear of what he'd say. Perhaps he regretted having kissed her.

"I met Chad at the hospital while I was training in Seattle," she said. "I was attracted to him then, and I felt elated when I discovered he was going to work at the clinic, too."

He didn't react, didn't respond.

"I know now that my attraction to him was a schoolgirl crush. His interests lie elsewhere and—and as a matter of fact, so do mine." She held his gaze for an extra-long moment. "Cal," she said, her voice dropping to a whisper. "I am so sorry for the way I treated you—so very sorry."

He still didn't respond, and she read the indecision in his eyes, as if he wasn't convinced he should trust her.

"I knew almost immediately," she continued, bending her head. "You kissed me and I was afraid. I know that sounds idiotic, but I was. I didn't *want* to be attracted to you. I didn't want to feel the things I did when you touched me." She exhaled and hoped he sensed how much it had cost her to be this honest. "I even went to my dad and talked to him about you. He said I should let it rest."

"H-he's a w-w-wise man."

Linnette pretended not to hear him. "Dad said I should wait to see if you came back into my life. A couple of weeks after that, you were in the clinic with this cut." She didn't add how absolutely delighted she was to see him, despite his injury. That injury had been the working of fate, the fate her father had alluded to.

"Timmons?" he asked, his eyes narrowed.

She wasn't sure what he wanted to know. "Oh, you're asking about Chad and me?"

Cal nodded.

"Chad did ask me to have coffee with him that one time— the day you were in the clinic." She emphasized that this had happened only once. "He's dating a friend of mine now. Well, actually, that's a problem, too. Gloria's apparently told him she's not interested, but I know she is." Linnette sighed. "Sometimes relationships get rather convoluted."

He snorted softly.

Having said everything she could think of, she met his eyes and smiled boldly. "Now that I've explained, what are you doing tonight?" She felt a bit like Indiana Jones stepping into thin air.

"W-working."

"Oh. Friday night, then?" She was working late, which meant they wouldn't have dinner until most people were in bed, but she didn't care.

"C-can't."

She was beginning to get the message. "I see." That was pretty much what she'd expected. Linnette had given this her best shot and it hadn't worked. She stood up, prepared to leave. But then… Linnette didn't have a single excuse for her brazen behavior. Cal had more or less told her to go; he couldn't have made it plainer. He wasn't interested in seeing her again. So what did she do? What *could* she do?

She kissed him.

Judging by his reaction, Cal was as shocked as she was. At first he kept his mouth tightly closed and seemed about to push her away. But he didn't. Instead he moaned in welcome and parted his lips as he settled his arms around her waist and brought her onto his lap. Then he gave himself over to the kiss. His hands were in her hair and a moment later they were sliding beneath her sweater. Linnette moaned between kisses at the way her nipples instantly tightened at his touch. He continued kissing her as he found the clasp to her bra and unfastened it, groaning as his hands cupped her breasts.

Breathing hard, Linnette broke off the kiss and raised her head. Her mind took a few seconds to clear. When it did, she saw Cal watching her. His eyes were warm with desire—no doubt a reflection of the desire in her own.

"I—"

"Sh-h," he whispered back. He was still caressing her breasts. "You're beautiful. I knew you would be."

"You're beautiful, too."

Cal grinned and kissed the side of her jaw. "You can apologize anytime you want." His words were gentle and coaxing and fell sweetly on her ears.

"It would be very easy to let you take me to bed."

"It would be easy for me, too."

She wasn't ready to make this commitment. Her body was, though, and she felt a little alarmed at how quickly he could lower her inhibitions.

"I can't."

He closed his eyes and nodded. "We know one thing," he said after a while. "We're certainly compatible in some areas."

Linnette smiled to herself as he refastened her bra and tugged down her sweater. That was when she realized that Cal didn't stutter when he talked to horses—or when he made love to a woman.

Forty-Two

Cecilia looked up from the computer screen, blinked and then reread Ian's e-mail. According to her husband, the *USS George Washington* was coming back to Bremerton shipyard a full two months ahead of schedule. This was too good to be true!

All at once Cecilia couldn't sit still. In her joy and excitement she hurried to the phone and dialed Cathy's number. The line was busy but a computer voice informed her that for a mere seventy-five cents, it would ring through when her friend was off the line. Cecilia didn't have the patience to wait nor was she willing to squander a single penny.

She paced and tried again five minutes later. The line was still busy. Because she needed to talk to someone and soon, she dialed Rachel Pendergast's home number. It rang twice and then Rachel answered.

"Oh, hi, Cecilia," she said. She sounded pleased to hear from her. "Have you had the baby?"

"Not yet."

"You're due soon, aren't you?"

"Next week."

"How are you feeling?"

The answer to that was pregnant. Very pregnant. But what she said was, "I feel great, better than great. I'm feeling *fabulous*. Do you know why? Ian's coming home!"

This news was greeted by a short silence. "Just Ian? I mean, he isn't arriving by himself, is he?"

"The entire aircraft carrier is on its way back to base." Ian hadn't told her why, Cecilia explained, but he probably couldn't.

"In other words, Nate will be back, too." Rachel had kept in touch with Cecilia, Carol and Cathy, even though she'd broken off her relationship with Nate Olsen.

"I thought I should give you a heads-up," Cecilia said. She suspected from everything Ian had told her that Nate wasn't going to drop this relationship without a fight.

Rachel sighed. "Thanks for letting me know, but I don't think it'll be a problem. I doubt I'll be seeing Nate."

"He might change your mind." Cecilia hoped he did. She liked Rachel, and she'd only heard about Nate through her husband, but Ian spoke highly of the warrant officer. It was a shame that Rachel had let her insecurities come between them.

"Nate's a wonderful man, but I'm not the right woman for him."

"Shouldn't he be the one to decide that?" Cecilia asked and then sighed. "Sorry, that's none of my business."

"This is really good news for you, isn't it?" Rachel said, ignoring Cecilia's comment. "This means Ian might be home when your baby's born."

"Yes, if he hurries." She didn't know the exact day and time the *George Washington* was scheduled to dock.

"You're feeling all right?"

"Oh, yes." True, she was extra-tired at night and tended to

go to bed earlier than she did when Ian was home. The baby was constantly active, kicking and stretching. She rubbed her hand over her belly, communicating her love to her son.

"Keep me informed," Rachel said.

"Of course."

They said their farewells and as soon as they'd ended the call, Cecilia dialed Cathy's number again. This time the phone rang, and Cathy picked up on the first ring.

"Cathy!"

"Cecilia!"

"Did you hear?" they cried simultaneously and then burst into peals of laughter.

"You first," Cathy said.

"I got an e-mail from Ian."

"Andrew sent me one, too."

"I have the strongest feeling Ian will be with me when Aaron's born," Cecilia said happily.

"You're keeping the name?" This had been a silent battle of wills between Cecilia and her husband. He hadn't agreed to the A-name. At the same time—once he'd retracted his original objections—he hadn't disagreed, either.

"After all these weeks, the name's comfortable to me." The last thing Cecilia wanted was to argue with Ian over a name when he finally got home. Suddenly another thought struck her.

"Cathy," she cried. "Oh, my goodness, Ian's never seen me pregnant before."

"Not true," her friend insisted. "And if you recall, he's the one who got you in this condition."

"Yes, I know, but *really* pregnant."

"Pregnant is pregnant."

Cecilia smiled at Cathy's teasing. "You know what I mean. He's never seen me this *big*."

"He's going to love it, seeing your belly swollen with his baby. Andrew was so loving with me before I delivered Andy. He hardly let me go to the bathroom by myself."

Cathy had miscarried two babies before Andy. None of the doctors had been able to tell her what had gone wrong with those first pregnancies and she'd lived in fear that she'd miscarry the third one, too. But she'd successfully carried Andy to term.

"Everything will be different this time," Cathy said confidently, answering Cecilia's unasked question. "Just you wait and see."

"My due date's only a few days away. I couldn't bear it if Ian was so close and couldn't be with me."

"If he can't, you know I'll be there."

Cecilia whispered her thanks, more grateful than ever for Cathy's friendship. "Hold tight, Aaron, hold tight," she told her unborn baby after she'd hung up the phone.

Three hours later, as Cecilia got ready for bed, her back began to ache. Rubbing it as she walked into her bedroom, she had a feeling that her son had decided he wasn't going to wait for his daddy.

By midnight, there was no doubt she was in labor. Logging onto the computer, she sent her husband an e-mail to let him know. She timed the contractions, pacing through the apartment as she did. When they were five minutes apart, Cecilia phoned Cathy.

"Now?" Cathy screamed, so excited she woke Andy. "I'll be right over. Don't move, breathe deeply and don't worry. I'm on my way." Without a pause, phone pressed to her ear, she shouted instructions to her son to get his suitcase and his teddy bear. "I'll be there in twenty minutes," she promised Cecilia.

Sure enough, Cathy rolled up in front of the duplex

precisely twenty-two minutes later, after dropping off her son at Carol's place. She had a basket of soothing musical CDs, lotions and fruit chews. There were snacks, too, in case Cathy got hungry during the labor.

Shortly after her arrival at the hospital, Cecilia was prepped and brought to the labor room. Cathy was with her, wielding a stopwatch and clutching the CD player. Roy Orbison crooned softly from the side of Cecilia's bed.

She raised her head and laughed. "Somehow, I don't think this is a good time to hear 'Pretty Woman,'" she joked.

"I disagree. If Ian was here he'd say you're beautiful, and he'd be right. You are, Cecilia, and you're about to have your baby." Cathy squealed with delight and Cecilia smiled.

But she stopped smiling as the pain overcame her. She lay back on the pillow and closed her eyes, trying hard to let her body flow with the contraction instead of fighting it. Cathy started counting off the seconds in a slow, even tone.

With Allison, Cecilia had labored for nearly fifteen hours in a room by herself, with only a nurse to check on her from time to time. When Allison was born, her cry had been weak and barely audible.

By contrast, Aaron Jacob Randall made his appearance ten hours after Cecilia had entered the hospital. He gave a loud, lusty squall as he was born, pink and perfect. He didn't like the bright lights and made sure everyone in the room heard about it. Nor did he appreciate having a suction tube stuck up his nose.

"He's certainly got a good set of lungs," Cathy said, squeezing Cecilia's hand. Tears streamed down her face and Cecilia's, too—tears of joy. She strained to see her son.

"What about his heart?" she pleaded. "Is his heart okay?"

The attending physician smiled over at her. "He looks just fine, but we'll run all the tests and let you know right away."

"Thank you," she whispered, exhausted.

"You did so well," Cathy said, brushing the wet tendrils from Cecilia's forehead. "You were incredible—no epidural or anything."

"I'm exhausted."

"Sleep," Cathy urged. "I'll take care of letting everyone at your office know. Plus Carol and Rachel."

"Thanks. Sleeping certainly won't be a problem." Already her eyes were drifting shut. After a few minutes, Cecilia was hardly aware of the activity going on around her. She knew Aaron had been placed in a tiny bed in her room and was sleeping at her side, swaddled in a pale blue blanket with a blue knit cap on his head.

Cecilia wasn't sure what time it was when she woke. Her first thought was that she'd given birth to her son. She'd so badly wanted Ian with her, but that hadn't been possible. Slowly she opened her eyes and discovered that her son's tiny crib was empty. Half-raising herself, braced on one elbow, she saw her husband sitting beside the bed, cradling Aaron in his arms.

Cecilia blinked, afraid her imagination and desire had conjured him up. "Ian?" she tried tentatively.

He glanced at her and Cecilia saw that his eyes were bright with tears.

"It *is* you. Oh, Ian, Ian, I can't believe you're here. How... when?" Her tongue kept tripping over itself in her happiness.

Her husband gave her the brightest smile she'd ever seen. "The *George Washington* had a transport that was headed home. The chaplain talked to my CO after I learned you'd gone into labor. I don't know what he said or did, but he got me on that transport."

One day Cecilia would personally thank him.

"So this is our son," Ian said, gazing at Aaron. The baby

wrapped his tiny hand around Ian's finger and held on. "He's perfect," Ian whispered, nearly overcome with emotion. "I talked to the pediatrician and she put Aaron through a test they do on newborns—the Apgar, it's called—and he scored a ten."

Cecilia sighed, relieved and grateful.

"I'm holding our baby," her husband said in awe. "Our Aaron."

Ian had never gotten the opportunity to hold Allison. "I'm so sorry I didn't make it for the labor," he told her.

"Next time," she assured him.

Ian's head came up. "Next time?" he repeated.

"Aaron needs a little sister, but we'll talk about that later."

Her husband grinned. "Aye, aye, Captain. At your service."

Forty-Three

It was Saturday afternoon. Allison Cox walked out of the JCPenney store in the Silverdale Mall with two of her best friends, Kaci and Alicia. The St. Patrick's Day displays were still up and the entire mall was decorated with an Irish theme. She was joking and laughing with her friends, having a good time, when she heard her name.

"Hey, Allison."

She stopped abruptly when she saw Anson, shocked that he'd spoken to her. He wore the same long black coat, noticeably shabbier now. His hair was messy and his boots untied. He didn't look good. And normally he worked on Saturdays. Why was he here?

Without a word to her friends, Allison joined him. She knew something was terribly wrong even before he spoke.

"Ditch your friends," he said, eyeing Kaci and Alicia, who were a few paces behind her.

She sucked in a breath. "I can't do that."

"Fine." He turned and walked away.

"It's all right," Kaci said, hugging Allison briefly. "Go. Meet us at Waldenbooks at three."

Allison nodded gratefully and hurried after Anson. He was walking through the mall at such speed that she had to run in order to catch up with him.

"Anson, stop!" she called.

He turned around but didn't smile when he saw her.

"What happened?" she asked. Clearly something had, otherwise he would never have spoken to her. He'd kept his word to her father. "Why are you here?"

"To see you. Eddie told me you'd gone to the mall. I took the bus." He looked past her, his eyes hard as flint. "I lost my job."

"The Lighthouse laid you off?" That didn't make sense. Her father had checked on how he was doing, and Seth Gunderson had said Anson was conscientious and diligent in his work habits. There was even talk of promoting him from dishwasher to working as a prep cook. Her father seemed pleased that his faith in Anson had been well placed.

"Does this have anything to do with Tony?"

Anson frowned. "Who told you about him and me?"

"My dad. Mr. Gunderson mentioned that the two of you weren't getting along. Is he involved in…in getting you fired?"

"Probably."

"Did they give you a reason?" she said, her hand on his sleeve. Anson was so cold and angry and with his whole Goth regalia, including the heavy pewter cross he wore around his neck, people obviously found him menacing. Shoppers gave them a wide berth as they stood outside the food court.

Anson refused to meet her gaze. "They said it was reduction in force."

"Maybe business slacked off," she said, thinking quickly. "That happens, you know."

"It was an excuse." His eyes narrowed as he spoke.

"Do you think there was another reason?" she asked softly, her hand still on his arm.

For the first time he looked directly at her. But this boy wasn't the Anson she knew. He was irate and resentful, and she felt as though every bit of his fury was directed at her. Allison nearly dropped her hand and stepped back.

"Mr. Gunderson thinks I took something that didn't belong to me. He thinks I took cash out of his office."

Allison had the sudden urge to sit down. She walked over to an empty table and pulled out a chair. Anson followed.

"You didn't do that." She refused to believe Anson was guilty of such a thing.

Pain flashed from his eyes but was immediately shielded. "That's not what Seth Gunderson believes."

"He talked to you?"

Anson nodded. "He talked to everyone."

"Did he have any proof?"

"How could he?" Anson asked hotly. "I didn't do it."

Allison reached for his hand, curling her fingers around his. She needed to touch him, to reassure him. At first he resisted and tried to pull away. Then he entwined their fingers, holding onto her as if she were the only solid thing in a world that was crumbling. Allison didn't know what to say that could make this better.

"What can I do?" she asked after a while.

"Nothing," he said and swore. "I wouldn't go back there if they begged me to. I worked my butt off for that restaurant and then they treat me like—"

He didn't finish. He didn't need to; Allison knew what he intended to say.

"I'll talk to my dad," she suggested. Her father had been willing to help Anson before. Once she explained the situation, he would again. She hoped.

"No." His voice was harsh. "Not this time." He laughed. "Your father can't do a damn thing for me. I was the obvious suspect, you know. Mr. Gunderson knows I was responsible for setting the park shed on fire. If they were going to accuse anyone, it would be me—and why not? I've been in trouble. I was a convenient scapegoat."

"But it's not right!"

"Not everything is right, Allison. You live in this comfortable world where everything turns out perfectly. It isn't like that for everyone. You've got parents who care about you. You've got a home and a future. Some of us don't."

"You have a future. We all do." Her fingers tightened around his. "We each make our own."

His eyes met hers as he digested her words. "I just don't have the options you do."

"Do you know who did it—stole the money, I mean?"

He hesitated. "No, but I have my suspicions."

"Who? Tony?"

"Tony said I made everyone look bad because I worked hard and put in extra time. He was hired before me and then Mr. Gunderson talked to the chef about training me to be a prep cook. Tony didn't think that was fair."

She'd report this to her father and have him talk to Mr. Gunderson. "My dad and Mr. Gunderson are friends."

Anson shook his head. "No. I'll take care of this in my own way."

"What are you going to do?" she asked, afraid of what he might do in this state of mind.

"I don't know yet."

He had a wild, disheveled look and she suspected he hadn't slept in a long time. "Have you been home?"

He shook his head. "Mom's brought home a new friend." His lips curled in a half snarl. "We don't get along. To put it mildly."

Anson didn't need to spell it out for her; his home life was dreadful. Allison frowned. His problems seemed huge, over-whelming. "I'm so sorry," she whispered.

"Yeah, right. Like I said, some of us were dealt a lousy hand."

She wanted to take away his burdens. She knew that was impossible, and the ache in her heart increased.

Allison glanced at her watch. Kaci had to be to work by four and Allison didn't want to make her late.

Anson stood abruptly and checked his watch, too. "I gotta go."

"Where?"

He shrugged, his gaze focused elsewhere.

"When will I see you again?"

That, too, was answered with a shrug, as if he didn't know. As if it didn't matter.

Allison tried to brush aside her disappointment. "I need to know," she insisted.

"Why do you care?"

"I care," she whispered. "I care more than you'll ever know."

"Don't," he said starkly. "You're wasting your time."

"I'm not," she told him. "Just promise me you won't do anything stupid."

"Like what?"

"I don't know. Anything. Please, Anson, this is too impor-tant. Everything will work out in the end. I'm sure of it."

He snickered as though he found her attitude amusing. "Things like this don't work out for people like me. It's time you learned that."

He walked away without looking at her again.

She had a sick feeling in her stomach. But as much as she wanted to run after Anson, she couldn't.

That evening, Allison could barely eat dinner. As soon as the meal was over, she escaped inside her room. Twice now, Anson had come to her bedroom window and she hoped he would again. They needed to talk.

Sitting on her bed, writing in her journal, Allison poured out everything that was in her heart. She was terrified for Anson and angry about what had happened. She wanted to help him. If she spoke to her father, he might be angry that they'd broken their word. And Anson didn't want him to find out he'd been fired....

At nine her mother tapped on her door.

"Come in," Allison said. She thrust her journal under a pillow and sat cross-legged.

Rosie Cox walked into the room and sat on the end of the bed. She touched Allison's shoulder. "You've been very quiet this evening. Is something bothering you?"

Allison nodded and stared down at her pale-pink comforter. "It's Anson," she whispered.

"Are you sad because you two can't see each other yet?"

She nodded rather than confess that she'd seen him and, more than that, spoken to him. All at once Anson's burden became too much for her and silent tears began to course down her face.

Her mother held her close, murmuring soothing words, and Allison remembered that Anson had said some kids were dealt a better hand in life than others. He was right; she had been. Until she'd gotten to know Anson, she hadn't realized how lucky she was to have two parents who loved her.

Her mother gently stroked her hair. "Is there something you want to tell me?"

"You'll be upset with me."

"I'll risk that," her mother whispered softly.

"Anson and I talked." She waited a moment, fearing a reaction. Her mother didn't comment, so Allison continued. "He got laid off from his job. Mr. Gunderson thinks Anson took some money, but he didn't! He wouldn't. He tried so hard to do everything right, and now he's been treated unfairly. He's so hurt and angry." She swallowed hard. "I'm afraid of what he's going to do."

Her mother didn't say anything for a long time. "Do you want your father to talk to him?"

"I don't know. I suggested talking to Dad, but Anson wouldn't hear of it. I tried to tell him everything'll work out." She lifted her head and looked at her mother. "He laughed at me. He said that wouldn't happen for him. He won't ask Dad for help because he doesn't want Dad to be disappointed in him. Mom, he didn't do it!"

"I'm so sorry," her mother whispered.

"I don't know how to help him."

Her mother sighed. "Unfortunately I don't either."

"We have to do *something*. You can ground me, take away my computer privileges, not let me drive, do anything you want. I don't care how you punish me—I'm talking to Anson." Allison was willing to make any sacrifice. "He needs me, and he needs you and Dad, too."

"Allison…"

"I'm serious. I…I love him. Go ahead and laugh if you want, but I mean it with every fiber of my being."

Her mother sighed. She didn't say Allison was being melodramatic, as she often did. Instead, she drew Allison close. "I know you have feelings for this young man. I'll talk to your father and see if there's anything we can do."

Allison felt hope suddenly rise in her.

"I'm not making any promises," her mother added.

Allison understood. But now, at least, Anson had someone who'd stand up for him.

Forty-Four

Olivia, who'd finished court for the day, sat at her desk, finishing up some paperwork. She squinted at the computer screen and decided it was time to update the prescription for her reading glasses.

Jack phoned to tell her he was home from the office; he was working eight-hour days, with no overtime. He'd promised to make dinner, which should be interesting. He almost always got to the house before her these days and had taken an unexpected interest in cooking. He favored salads with lots of fresh vegetables and an occasional surprise such as dried cranberries or chopped pecans.

Grace and Cliff were married now and Olivia was delighted for her dearest friend. They'd snuck away without even hinting that they intended to elope. When she'd first heard the news, Olivia had been disappointed. Had she known, she would have found a way to join Grace in San Francisco. But given time, Olivia saw the wisdom of Grace and Cliff's decision.

Her friend had moved in with Cliff, bringing Buttercup and Sherlock, who seemed to be adjusting nicely to their new quarters.

As she began to read her next brief, a knock sounded at her office door. It was Deputy Mike Lusk. "There's a man asking to see you, name of David Rhodes. Says he's your stepbrother. Should I bring him over?"

Olivia hesitated briefly, then said, "Please. Show him in."

The deputy nodded. "I'll wait outside until you're through."

"I'd appreciate that."

Soon, an attractive man, probably in his midforties, was escorted into her chambers. He smiled widely when he saw her. "Judge Olivia Griffin?" he asked, extending his hand.

She nodded and they exchanged brisk handshakes.

"I'm David Rhodes, Ben's son. It appears we're related!"

Olivia remembered hearing some story about David; however, whatever it was didn't immediately come to mind. She did recall that her mother and Ben had joined him in Seattle for dinner. Her mother had raved about the restaurant and the wonderful meal they'd had. Olivia also had a vague memory of something Justine had said; apparently she'd met him, too.

"I was hoping for a few minutes of your time, if that would be possible." He didn't wait for a response but walked into her office and immediately sat down in the guest chair.

"Of course," she said, her tone a little ironic. "Make yourself comfortable." She glanced at her watch. "I told my husband I'd be home by five-forty-five, so we can talk for ten or fifteen minutes."

"That's fine." He leaned back, crossing his legs, and surveyed the room. The cut of his suit told Olivia it was expensive, possibly cashmere. The polished loafers, the silk tie—this was a man who liked to spend money.

"What can I do for you?" she asked, getting directly to the point.

"Ah, a woman who prefers to skip the small talk." He smiled approvingly. "I like a no-nonsense attitude."

His charm left her cold, although she could see why some people were swayed by it. David Rhodes was probably an experienced manipulator who relied on good looks and superficial wiles. "As I explained, I have an appointment."

"But it's with your husband."

He sounded as if he thought she didn't need to worry, since it was only Jack. Olivia was almost sure she didn't like Ben's son and tried to remember what she'd heard. With Jack's heart attack, she'd missed a lot of details during the last two months.

"I've been to Cedar Cove twice now," David said conversationally. "This is a tight community, isn't it? People know people, neighbors talk to neighbors. It's that sort of town."

"We think of ourselves as the kind of place anyone would like to call home."

He nodded. "A good PR line," he said, but before she could respond to his cynicism, he forged ahead. "I imagine you know the other judges fairly well."

"Yes…" she said hesitantly.

"The sheriff, too."

"We're proud of our low crime rate." Cedar Cove had its share of crime; no community was immune. But Olivia liked to think she didn't need to lock her door when she left for the day. As a matter of habit she did, but often wondered if it was necessary.

David clasped his hands loosely together. "I can understand why Dad enjoys life in Cedar Cove as much as he does. We had no connections to this town when he moved here, so my brother and I were both surprised. We assumed he'd want to live in Seattle, but Cedar Cove seems to have all the benefits of the big city."

"We're only a ferry ride away." It was the best of both worlds, in Olivia's opinion. She enjoyed small-town life and yet she could take advantage of the cultural opportunities Seattle provided.

"Dad has certainly fallen for Cedar Cove—and your mother," David said.

"We love your father. He's given my mother a new lease on life," Olivia murmured.

David gestured toward her. "That brings up another matter," he said, grinning. "My father married your mother, which makes the two of us stepbrother and sister, right?"

"I guess it does." Olivia wished he'd get to the point. She'd worked with enough attorneys to recognize that this wasn't a social visit. David Rhodes wanted something.

"I've never had a sister before," he said, and there was a quality of wonderment in his voice that got on her nerves. This guy should be in community theater.

"You'll meet Steve later on," he told her.

"I'm sure I will." She glanced at her watch again, hoping he'd take the hint.

"I was thinking we should all get together for Easter," David suggested. "It's too late to arrange a full family gathering this year," he added quickly. "But maybe next year. We could invite both sides, get to know each other."

"I'll keep it in mind." Olivia was fast losing her patience. "Is there something I can do for you?" she asked pointedly.

David took an audible breath. "As it happens, there is," he said in a confidential tone. "I was in town a few weeks back and due to a misunderstanding—well, it's not important to discuss the details." He shook his head, implying that he found all of this distressing. "I ended up leaving in a rush, and I'm afraid I was driving above the speed limit." He laughed, as though embarrassed to trouble her. "I was pulled over by a deputy. Unfortunately I must've given him the wrong impression."

That meant his problem was more than a speeding offense. "What happened?" Olivia asked.

"The officer—now, I'm sure he was only doing what he thought was his duty—"

"He gave you a ticket." She'd leave him to fill in the blank. At least now she knew what this was about. David Rhodes wanted her to fix the mess he'd gotten himself into.

"Actually, this must've been one of your junior officers," David said. "He was a little too eager to get his quota, if you know what I mean."

"We don't have ticket quotas in Cedar Cove." She didn't work in traffic court, but she knew the system.

"The officer apparently took a dislike to me, I'm sorry to say. I didn't help matters, I suppose," David admitted with a look of chagrin. "I thought he had a bad attitude. Anyhow, one thing led to another—and now it's a bit of a disaster."

"What was the ticket for?" Olivia asked, tired of having to ferret out each kernel of information.

"Speeding—but I wasn't speeding," David insisted. "I have a signed statement here from a mechanic that states my speedometer was faulty." He extracted a folded sheet of paper from inside his jacket and held it out.

"David," she warned, "put that away. I don't want to see it. Just tell me what else you were charged with."

He heaved a sigh. "Negligent driving," he confessed. "It was a simple misunderstanding that got out of hand. I can't even begin to tell you what this'll do to my car insurance rates. Normally I'd just pay for the ticket and be done with it. But it's going to be more difficult than that. My insurance company is threatening to cancel my policy and then I'll have to find another one, and my rates will skyrocket."

"You haven't paid the ticket?"

"No. You see, I'm experiencing a bit of a cash flow problem at the moment. I figured it'd be fifty bucks or so and if it was, I'd pay it and write off the entire matter. Unfortunately, the fine is more than three hundred dollars—and then there's this dilemma with my insurance company. I need this whole thing to go away. The best way to make that happen is to throw myself on the mercy of the court." He laughed lightly. "Then I learned that my very own sister is an influential member of the Kitsap County Court."

"I see." Boy, did she.

David shook his head, as though embarrassed to trouble her with anything this trivial. "I was hoping you'd help me out. A brief conversation with the Traffic Court judges…"

Olivia relaxed in her chair and crossed her arms. "I'm afraid it doesn't work like that."

"You just said you were friendly with the other judges."

"Yes—on a social basis. It doesn't mean I can or will involve myself in any situation that would contravene the law. My relationship with my fellow judges can't help you."

"Of course it can," he argued. "You talk to them, and my little issue with the Cedar Cove sheriff's department will go away." He leaned close and lowered his voice to a whisper. "All you have to do is snap your fingers."

"No. I can't do it." She spoke slowly, deliberately. Olivia couldn't make her position any plainer than that.

His jaw tightened. "In other words, you *won't* help me."

"There's no *other words* about it. I don't know how the judicial system works wherever you live, but we don't fix traffic tickets here in Cedar Cove. If you broke the law, I suggest you step forward and deal with the consequences of your actions."

Olivia found her stepbrother to be a decidedly unpleasant man, despite his glib and rather overstated charm. Then it clicked. "Just a minute here," she said, bolting to her feet. "*You're* the one my daughter was telling me about."

"Hey, hey," he said, raising both hands. "I haven't dated any women in this town—and definitely not your daughter. Who is she, anyway?"

"Justine Gunderson. You were at her restaurant."

His smile faded. "Your daughter owns The Lighthouse?"

"My daughter and son-in-law."

David's eyes went hard with a look that set Olivia's heart pounding. "Your daughter took that check right out of my hand," he said from between gritted teeth. "She interfered in something that was none of her damned business."

She suddenly remembered exactly what she'd heard about David Rhodes. She rose from her chair. "You were trying to cheat my mother out of five thousand dollars."

David leapt to his feet. "It was a *loan,*" he insisted, his eyes on fire. "I fully intended to pay her back in two or three weeks. She's a lovely woman, kindhearted and generous. Apparently none of those traits were handed down to anyone else in the family."

Olivia wasn't going to allow him to insult her in her own office. "I think it's time you left, Mr. Rhodes." She walked around her desk and opened the door. "Officer Lusk," she called.

Mike Lusk walked purposefully in her direction. "Would you kindly escort Mr. Rhodes out of this building?"

Mike stepped forward and planted his hands on his wide belt. "This way, Mr. Rhodes."

"Hell of a way to start off our relationship," David snarled as he moved past her.

"I sincerely hope, Mr. Rhodes, that we never have a relationship. Now kindly leave me and my family alone."

"You're going to regret this."

Olivia smiled. "You know what? I doubt it. Oh, a word of warning—if you show up in my office or my courtroom again, I'm going to throw the book at you."

Mike's eyes widened and Olivia realized she'd probably divulged too much. "Thank you, Officer Lusk," she said formally.

Olivia shut down her computer and reached for her coat and purse. Once she got home—late—she'd tell Jack everything that had happened.

Forty-Five

Roy hadn't shared his suspicions with Corrie. He needed to deal with this in his own way. After all, the postcards had been addressed to him and him alone; only with the fruit basket had the messages started coming to Corrie, as well. But all communication had ceased after Valentine's Day. There'd been nothing in any form for weeks now.

It didn't matter; he knew. Furthermore, *she* knew that he knew, which was, he suspected, why he hadn't received any further postcards or anything else.

He'd discovered she had been adopted and raised in California. Then he'd run into a dead end. But her recent actions in the Puget Sound area had given her away. His first break had come when he'd finally talked to the florist who'd taken her order; from then on, things began to fall into place.

"Roy?" Corrie interrupted his thoughts Saturday morning as he sat at the breakfast table. "You're very quiet."

Roy set aside the morning newspaper and reached for his coffee as Corrie slid a plate of scrambled eggs in front of him. "I was reading the paper."

"Considering how long we've been married, do you seriously believe I don't know when something's bothering you?"

He shook his head. She could always tell.

Corrie sat across from him, placing her elbows on the table. "How long have you known?"

"A while," he returned casually.

"Then what are you waiting for?"

"I don't know. I hate to admit this, but I'm a little nervous. It's me she's angry with, you know." He was sure of this. And much as he wanted to take responsibility, wanted a relationship with his unknown daughter, he had trouble accepting the changes that would come into his life. Linnette and Mack would need to be told and that worried him. He hated the fact that his children might think poorly of him or their mother.

"What you're feeling is guilt," Corrie whispered, her voice shaky. "I feel it, too, although intellectually I know I shouldn't. Giving this child up to a loving family was the very best choice I could've made. I loved her, but at the same time, I knew I wasn't capable of caring for her on my own."

What bothered Roy wasn't simply guilt about the adoption. It was his own failures. "Corrie—"

She cut him off. "I'm the one who made the decision, the one who signed the adoption papers. I don't know why she singled you out. She has no reason to be upset with you."

Roy made a pretense of eating, acting as though this was a normal morning conversation. "Before we seek her out, we have to discuss it with Linnette and Mack."

Corrie scooped up a forkful of egg, but didn't take a bite. She lowered her head. "I agree." Then she glanced up and smiled. "I called Mack last week." She raised her head to look at the kitchen clock. "He should be here in an hour."

After all these years, Roy shouldn't be surprised by anything his wife did. In this instance, however, her sense of timing was uncanny. "What about Linnette?" He'd always been close to his daughter, and confessing his failures to Linnette, and Mack, too, wasn't going to be easy.

"I thought we should tell them one at a time." She met his eyes. "Is that the way you'd like to do it?"

He nodded. Telling his children… This, above everything else, would be the most difficult part of the whole situation.

Mack arrived at nine. Roy didn't know what Corrie had said to persuade him to drive from south Seattle to Cedar Cove this early in the morning. Generally, Mack avoided his father. And thinking back over the last few years, Roy accepted the blame for their estrangement.

He wasn't completely sure when this rift between them had started—when Mack was in high school probably. Roy had wanted his son to play football the way he had; Mack chose soccer. In his disappointment, Roy had refused to attend any of Mack's games. That had been childish, and he regretted it deeply. From then on, their relationship had degenerated into a clash of wills. It almost seemed as if Mack had made a point of provoking his father. Corrie's heartbreak was something else Roy laid at his own door.

Mack stood awkwardly in the living room, hands tucked in his pockets. "Mom. Dad." He acknowledged each one with a curt nod. "You wanted to talk to me?"

Corrie nodded and indicated he should sit down. Mack did, perching on the outer edge of the chair, presumably in case he needed to make a fast getaway. He was a fine-looking young man, Roy thought, studying his son as though he were a stranger. As tall as Roy was himself, he had curly hair, which he wore longer than Roy liked—no doubt why Mack had chosen that style.

Roy looked at Corrie and she looked at him. They should have discussed the best way to broach the subject beforehand.

He understood why they hadn't. Talking about their first daughter was just too painful.

"Your mother and I have something to tell you," Roy announced, sitting beside Corrie on the sofa.

She reached for a tissue and wadded it tightly.

Mack went very still. He frowned. "Are you two...splitting?"

Roy shook his head. "Never," he said, taking Corrie's hand. "Your mother's stuck with me for the rest of our natural lives."

That seemed to reassure their son, who smiled briefly.

"Before we explain why we asked you to come over this morning, there's something I need to say first." Roy cleared his throat. This seemed to be the day for difficult conversations. "I love my wife and I love my children."

Mack shrugged, seemingly indifferent.

"What I'm attempting to tell you, Mack, is that I love you. You're my son. My only son. I know we've had our differences over the years, and I blame myself for those. From the time you were a teenager, I gave you the impression that you were a disappointment to me. You weren't. And you aren't. I expected you to live up to what *I* felt was your potential— not that it was my right to determine what you should be or do. But despite everything, you followed your own path. That took grit and character." He paused and looked away. "I'm proud to call you my son."

Mack stared at him hard, as if he wasn't sure what to say.

Roy stood, extending his hand. Mack met him halfway but it wasn't a handshake they shared, it was a hug. By the time Roy sat next to Corrie again, his eyes were moist, and he saw that Mack's were, too.

Corrie didn't pretend to hide her own tears, which streamed down her face unchecked. "There's...more," she said after a few moments.

"More?" Mack glanced at Roy, who nodded.

"There's something else you need to know," Roy said, studying his hands. "It isn't easy to say this."

Mack leapt to his feet. "You've got cancer!"

When Roy shook his head, Mack subsided into his chair but still looked apprehensive.

"You mean this father-son thing doesn't have anything to do with…why you asked me to come over this morning?" he asked.

"No, but what I'm about to tell you will come as a shock." And he launched into the whole story.

Their news did astound Mack. He held up his hand and stopped Roy halfway through. "You mean to say you got Mom pregnant when you were in college?"

Roy nodded.

"He didn't know," Corrie explained hurriedly. "I never told him."

"She couldn't." Roy wasn't willing to let Corrie take all the responsibility for this. "And that was my fault. But it doesn't matter now. We want you to know you have a sister who was given up for adoption."

"Wait." Once again Mack was on his feet. He clutched his head with both hands, as if to hold all his thoughts inside. "*She's* the one who's been sending you those postcards?"

"We believe so," Corrie said quietly.

"Another *sister?*"

"Yes."

"I have two older sisters," he whispered, obviously finding this hard to take in. "Does Linnette know?"

"Not yet."

Mack continued to gaze at them in astonishment. "When do you plan on telling her?"

The relief Roy felt at revealing this part of his past with

Mack made him want to finish what they'd started. "Let's do it now," he suggested.

"I'll phone Linnette," Corrie said, sharing his eagerness.

While she was in the kitchen, Roy and Mack sat in the living room, still a bit awkward with each other.

"I've been doing some hiking in the Olympic rain forest," Mack remarked.

"I always enjoyed hiking myself," Roy said, and then added tentatively, "perhaps one weekend the two of us could do a day hike. There are some great ones in this area."

Mack grinned. "I'd like that."

Corrie returned from the kitchen. "Linnette has some kind of arrangement with a friend this morning. But she said if we came right away, she's got half an hour."

They piled into Roy's car and he drove to the apartment complex on the Cedar Cove waterfront. Their daughter met them at her front door.

Linnette noticed the changed relationship between Roy and Mack immediately. "Hey, you guys," she said as the three of them gathered in her living room. "What's going on?"

"Prepare to be surprised," Mack said, exchanging a grin with Roy. "You'd better sit down."

"It must be good news," she said, glancing from one to the other with a puzzled frown.

"It's *wonderful* news," Mack said.

Linnette spread her hands wide. "Then tell me!"

"We have a sister," Mack blurted out.

Reacting the same way as her brother, Linnette was instantly on her feet. *"What?"*

Slowly, refusing to omit any detail, Corrie and Roy told their story for the second time that morning.

Linnette sat dumbfounded, hardly able to ask questions. "I have a sister?" she repeated. "We have a sister?"

"I wanted to tell you," Corrie said. "A dozen times, at least, I tried. But you always seemed to have something going on in your own life and I didn't want to burden you with more."

"Oh, Mom, I can't imagine you going through this alone. You were so young…."

That sufficiently elevated Roy's guilt. When Corrie answered their daughter, she didn't blame him, nor did she discount how agonizing a time it had been.

"I was fortunate to have supportive parents," she explained. "They never pressured me one way or the other when it came to deciding my baby's future. Mom and Dad backed me one hundred percent."

The doorbell chimed. "That's Gloria. We were planning to go shopping at the mall."

"I'll get it," Roy said. He was closest to the front door.

Gloria's eyes widened when Roy let her into the apartment. "I believe we've met," he said, extending his hand. "I'm Linnette's father—and yours." He heard the gasp behind him as his family took in what he'd just said.

Gloria gave him a slow smile. "I wondered when you'd figure it out."

Roy hugged her, nearly choking on emotion. Then he turned to face his family, one arm around Gloria's waist. "Corrie, this is our daughter."

Corrie rushed forward, tears flowing down her face, and threw her arms around Gloria. "Oh, baby," she murmured. "My baby."

"Gloria," Linnette said in a shocked voice. "You? It's you?"

Gloria, who was weeping now, nodded. "You can't imagine how excited I was when I discovered you were my new neighbor. It seemed like fate when you moved in practically next door."

"I felt a bond with you from the beginning," Linnette told her.

Gloria wiped the tears from her cheeks. "Now you know why."

"How did you find us?" Corrie asked.

"Through my grandmother. Apparently she knew your mother and, when Gran heard Corrie was pregnant, she approached your mother on behalf of her daughter and son-in-law. It was a private adoption."

"I should've known that," Corrie whispered, "but I was so lost in my own pain I didn't pay much attention."

Roy reached for her hand and gripped it hard.

"My mother never said a word," Corrie said, frowning, "not even in her journals. Perhaps she was afraid I'd read them one day—which I did."

"What made you come and look for us?" Mack wanted to know.

Gloria looked at him, then stared out the window, unseeing. "My parents were killed five years ago in a small-plane accident. Dad loved to fly, and the three of us had scheduled a day trip to Fresno, where Dad was hoping to buy property. I had to cancel at the last minute, not knowing I'd never see my family again." Fresh tears gleamed in her eyes. "My grandmother, who was my only surviving relative, helped me bury them." She swallowed hard and waited before continuing her story. "Losing her daughter devastated Gran. When she knew she was dying, she told me I had another family and that I should look them up. She couldn't bear the thought of me being alone." There was another pause. "She died a week after telling me."

"So you were able to track us down easily enough. But why did you address the postcards to me?" Roy asked.

Gloria glanced down. "I was hurt and angry. I saw my

original birth certificate and realized you hadn't signed off on the adoption. My grandmother said you weren't in the picture. I felt you'd abandoned my mother, so I wanted you to wonder—and worry." She paused, swallowing hard. "I don't feel that way anymore." Her gaze slid to Corrie. "You love her and—your children. I see that now. I know I should've gone about this differently. But once I started mailing the postcards and everything, I didn't feel I could stop until you found me. Do you understand what I mean?" At Roy's silent nod, she said, "It was wrong and I apologize for that."

Linnette stood and walked over to Gloria, placing both arms around her. "Right or wrong, I'm so grateful you found us," she breathed. "You can't imagine how much I've always wanted a sister. Do you remember, Mom?"

"Yes," Corrie whispered, still fighting her emotions.

"At first I wasn't going to do it," Gloria said, facing Corrie. "I figured you hadn't wanted me, so I didn't want you—which wasn't true. However, I wasn't planning to intrude on your life. But then I learned you'd married my father and that I had two full siblings."

"It took me a while to work it all out," Roy said. "Still, I—"

"Just a minute," Mack interrupted. "Aren't you in police work? Just the way Dad used to be?"

Gloria nodded.

"Hey, Dad," Mack said. "You finally got your wish. One of us followed in your footsteps."

Roy smiled. He had his family with him. His whole family.

Forty-Six

Grace stopped at the house on Rosewood Lane on her way home from the library. It was the Monday following Easter. Little by little, she'd moved most of her possessions to Cliff's house—clothes, books, important papers. Saturday morning, Cliff had brought his truck and they'd packed up the last of her things, except for the larger pieces of furniture. He wanted her completely moved into his home. However, Cliff had suggested she not leave the house vacant much longer, fearing it would invite vandalism. Grace thought that was unlikely, since there wasn't much crime in Cedar Cove—but then she remembered that incident of arson in the park.

Her husband—she wondered if she'd ever grow accustomed to thinking of Cliff as her husband—was right. It was time to reach a decision, hard though that would be. The small house on Rosewood had been her home for more than thirty years, and she found placing it on the market a painful and difficult prospect. But Grace was afraid that renting it out would be too much extra work for her and Cliff, and she didn't want that.

Kelly had been born while she and Dan lived in this house.

Both Maryellen and Kelly had attended elementary school around the corner. The girls had gone through the traumatic teen years here. When they'd grown up and moved away, Grace and Dan had briefly experienced the empty-nest syndrome.

The neighbors on Rosewood Lane were her friends. When Grace had gone back to school for her degree in library science, Mrs. Vessey across the street used to baby-sit the girls after class until Dan got home from work. Mrs. Jennings down the road had two daughters the same age as Grace's. They still compared notes. These days their conversations were mostly about gardening.

Her rose garden. That was something else Grace didn't feel she could leave. Working on her roses had brought her such comfort in those early months after Dan's disappearance.

At the thought of her dead husband, Grace grew teary-eyed and sad. Kelly and Paul had recently announced that they were expecting another child. Dan would have loved his grandchildren. He'd loved both girls; she'd never doubted that, although he'd felt closer to Kelly. He'd been alive when their youngest daughter learned she was pregnant with Tyler. Until Dan's body was found, Kelly had refused to let go of her belief that he'd return, with a perfectly logical explanation of where he'd gone and why.

That was never to be. The demons that haunted Dan had been merciless and unforgiving. How she wished he could have talked to her about his ordeal in Vietnam. Perhaps then, the outcome might have been different.

His suicide was her life's greatest tragedy.

Because Dan was on her mind, Grace went out to the garage, which had been her husband's domain. She missed not having Buttercup at her side.

As she walked through the garage, turning on the lights,

Grace remembered the day she'd discovered that Dan had destroyed the last Christmas gifts she and the girls had given him. At the time she'd been filled with rage and grief, incapable of understanding why he'd done something so cruel. She'd assumed he hated her, hated his life with her. She'd assumed wrong. The person Dan hated was himself. She understood now that Dan hadn't considered himself worthy of those gifts. Because of that, he'd repeatedly turned his back on any good thing life had to offer.

Most of what was in the garage had belonged to Dan. Grace didn't know what to do with his tools or the expensive tree-cutting equipment. Sell it, she supposed. Other than a few photographs—and her memories—this was all that was left of her dead husband. Kneeling on the cold concrete, she peeked inside a couple of the cartons and saw books and old magazines. How sad that Dan's legacy to his family was reduced to a few cardboard boxes.

"I thought I'd find you here." Cliff's gentle voice came to her.

Startled, she glanced up, surprised to find it dark outside. "What time is it?" she asked.

"Almost eight."

"No!" She couldn't believe she'd been in the garage so long. It felt like only a few minutes. Unable to resist checking her watch, she confirmed that Cliff was right.

"Is there anything you need to take back to the house?" he asked.

She shook her head. "This was Dan's stuff."

Cliff stepped into the garage. "You're wondering what to do with it now?"

Grace smiled, grateful her husband understood. "I could always give it to the girls, I suppose." Although what Maryellen and Kelly would do with it was another question.

"That isn't really the problem, is it?" Cliff said softly. He looked around, although she was sure he'd been here a dozen times. "You don't want to let go of the house, do you?"

When he said this, she recognized her reluctance for what it was. "No," she confessed. "No...I can't. Not yet."

"Then keep it."

"You don't mind if we rent it? Even though dealing with tenants is a bother..."

"Grace, no. Of course I don't mind. It's your home to do with as you wish. And if we choose the right tenants, it won't be much bother."

She felt a great sense of relief and slipped her arms around Cliff's waist, hugging him close. "Thank you," she whispered.

"For what?" He sounded amused.

"For loving me."

"That, my dear," he said, lifting her chin so she could look into his eyes, "is the easy part."

"I love you so much." Her feelings for him, and her lingering grief over Dan, brought her close to tears.

His arms circled her. "I know you do." He kissed her forehead. "Are you ready to come home now?"

Grace nodded. Home, she told herself, was wherever Cliff was.

With his arm about her waist, he led her out of the garage. "You haven't had dinner, have you?"

"No." Now that he mentioned it, she realized how hungry she was. At that very moment, her stomach growled as if to verify the fact.

"Do you want to stop somewhere in town and eat?" he asked.

She smiled gratefully. "That's a wonderful idea."

Despite not having reservations, they decided to try The

Lighthouse, which was doing good business for a Monday night, if the packed parking lot was any indication. When they got inside, Justine seated them immediately—to Grace's pleasure and gratitude. As they ordered a glass of wine, she noticed Cal and Linnette McAfee. They sat not far away, their heads close together. This was definitely a romance in the making. Grace wasn't sure what had happened, but all at once those two seemed to be a real couple.

"What's going on between Cal and the McAfees' daughter?" Grace asked in a low voice, leaning toward her husband.

"I don't know," Cliff answered. Their eyes met above the menu and Cliff raised his eyebrows. "I asked Cal the other day and he pretended not to hear. I guess he doesn't want to tell me. I'm sure you've noticed he's a very private person."

"I thought he wasn't interested in Linnette."

Cliff shrugged. "That's what he's been saying for months, but from all appearances, his feelings have changed—a lot."

Grace didn't see much of Cal these days. By the time she left the ranch to drive into Cedar Cove, he was already busy with the horses, either in the barn or one of the pastures. In the evenings, Cal gave the newlyweds their privacy. Grace hadn't said more than a few words to him in the two and a half weeks since they'd returned to the ranch.

"Judging by the way he's acting, I'd say he's in love," Cliff said in a low voice.

"What makes you so sure?" Grace asked, although she shared his suspicion.

Cliff's mouth twitched. "Cal Washburn walks around with a dopey look most of the time." He hesitated, and a smile lit up his face. "As a matter of fact, so do I."

Her husband's words warmed her heart. "Me, too," she whispered. "Me, too, Cliff."

Cliff set aside his menu and reached across the table for

her hand. She was grateful he'd read her mood so accurately. She needed this time just for them, in a place that was neutral, that wasn't her house or his.

Seeing that they were ready to order, the waitress hurried to the table, pad in hand. Grace chose the halibut in shrimp curry sauce, and Cliff asked for a T-bone steak.

Both dishes were excellent. Grace was thrilled that Cedar Cove had such an outstanding restaurant. She was proud of Justine and Seth and the success they'd made of this enterprise. Having worked as a commercial fisherman, Seth knew good fish and seafood, and served only the freshest. She could see that owning a restaurant was demanding, but so far the couple's marriage seemed to be withstanding the pressures. Grace hoped that wouldn't change.

When they'd finished, Cliff paid their bill. "Ready to leave?" he asked.

Grace told him she was. While Cliff retrieved her coat, she saw that Cal and Linnette were lingering over coffee; Grace smiled at them but they were completely absorbed in each other.

In the parking lot, where she and Cliff had both left their vehicles, he insisted on checking her car. She followed him home, arriving a minute or two after him. He waited for her outside the house while she parked in the space he'd cleared in the garage. When she joined him, Cliff placed one arm around her shoulders. Yawning, he covered his mouth with the other hand.

"Is that a hint, Cliff Harding?" she teased and playfully elbowed him in the ribs. He had a vigorous sexual appetite, although they were still a bit shy with each other. She knew exactly what he meant—he wanted to go to bed…and not because he was tired.

"Well, I guess you could say so."

She laughed and slipped her arm around him, resting her

head on his shoulder. "It's late, isn't it? We should've been in bed hours ago."

"Yes—extremely late. So we'd better get a move on."

Grace smiled to herself. After all, she wanted the same thing her husband did.

Forty-Seven

Cecilia woke from a sound sleep at Aaron's first cry. She groaned inwardly and glanced at the clock-radio on the nightstand—4:10 a.m. It'd been four hours since she'd last nursed. Aaron was hungry again and he wouldn't return to sleep until he'd been fed.

Ian rolled over when she climbed out of bed. "Need any help?" he asked sleepily.

"No thanks, sweetheart." It wasn't as if her husband could give Aaron his breakfast. Breast-feeding was a new experience; she'd never had the opportunity to nurse Allison. She'd pumped her breasts, wanting to believe that her milk would somehow provide the sustenance to pull Allison through her medical crisis. Sadly, it hadn't.

Carefully lifting Aaron from his crib, she shushed the newborn, who was crying hard enough to wake the neighbors. Cecilia soothed him with gentle whispers as she changed his diaper and settled in the living room rocker. Singing softly to him, she unbuttoned the front of her nightgown and gave a slight gasp when her hungry son latched onto her nipple.

Ian's barely discernible laugh caught her attention. "I have a strong son," he said, walking into the room. He was barefoot and wore only the bottom half of his pajamas.

While Cecilia rocked and nursed the baby, Ian sat across from her.

"You don't need to get out of bed for this," she felt obliged to tell him.

"I know. I wanted to. It's been two weeks now, but I don't think I'll ever get tired of watching you nurse our son."

She brushed the tiny wisps of hair away from Aaron's sweet face and gazed down at him in utter amazement as tiny milk bubbles formed at his mouth.

"From the first moment I saw you, I thought you were beautiful," Ian whispered.

"Oh, honey, stop." His compliments embarrassed her.

"You were," he said with a sigh. "But you've never looked more beautiful than you do right this minute."

His words filled her heart. "Thank you," she whispered.

He seemed about to say something else, but paused, as if caught up in the emotion of the moment. After a while he said, "I've been thinking about us finding a house to rent. Maybe with an option to buy."

She smiled at him quickly. "I'd like that. Where?"

Ian shrugged. "Cedar Cove. I want our son to have a real yard to play in and a neighborhood with other families, other kids. Living in a duplex is fine for you and me, but we have a baby now who'll need room to grow. What do you think?"

"Let's start looking today!"

"I'll check with a rental agent to see what we can find."

Cecilia nodded, excited by the idea.

As soon as Aaron was satisfied, he fell asleep. Holding him over her shoulder, Cecilia rocked for several minutes until she felt she could place him in his crib again without fear of waking him.

Ian crawled into bed and pulled aside the covers so she could join him. Cecilia curled up against her husband, but after a few minutes, she shifted away in an effort to get comfortable. Ten minutes later she was back.

"Want to tell me what's on your mind?" Ian suggested when her restlessness didn't end.

"I don't want to keep you awake," she protested.

"It's either you talk or you wake me every time you roll from one side to the other. I might be on leave, but I still need my sleep."

"Sorry."

"Talk," he insisted.

"It's Allison Cox," Cecilia said reluctantly. She hadn't intended to mention this to Ian, but the girl had been in her thoughts ever since yesterday afternoon, when she'd stopped by the house to visit Aaron. Allison had confided in her and spent the better part of the afternoon unburdening her woes.

"I know you're not too keen on this new boyfriend of hers."

"No," Cecilia murmured. "I'm not."

"She isn't planning to run away and marry him, is she?" Ian asked in a sleepy voice.

"Not that I know of." But Cecilia was afraid that whatever Anson requested, Allison would do.

"Then it can't be too serious."

"Don't bet on it." Cecilia nestled more comfortably in the crook of her husband's arm. "I'm telling you, Ian—this kid is trouble."

"Is he hanging around Allison a lot?"

"Apparently not. He had some sort of confrontation with her recently and she hasn't seen him since." Cecilia paused, biting her lip. "He hasn't shown up for school, either, which worries her."

"Did she try to find out where he is?"

"I asked her, and she started to cry."

"And?" Ian pressed when she didn't immediately continue.

"According to Allison, Anson's mother claims she hadn't seen him for a few days, which she doesn't happen to think is any big deal. Can you imagine that? Anson's eighteen now, but it shouldn't matter what age he is. If he's living at home and he disappears, then the woman should be concerned."

"Surely he has friends."

"Allison says he runs with a rough crowd." This didn't surprise Cecilia; kids like Anson and his buddies weren't the type of friends she wanted Allison to have, but she dared not let the girl know that.

"Hasn't anyone checked with these guys?"

"I suspect Allison has. But if she found out anything, she didn't say."

Ian was silent after that.

"Allison's really worried, and I don't blame her. She asked her father to talk to Seth Gunderson."

"About what?"

Cecilia realized she'd never filled in this part of the story for Ian. "Back in December, Mr. Cox spoke to Seth on Anson's behalf."

"That was good of him."

"Mr. Cox was the one who recommended Anson for the job, so he feels responsible for what happened. He wanted to hear what Seth had to say."

"What did he learn?"

This was where it became confusing for Cecilia. "Well, Mr. Gunderson said he wasn't a hundred percent positive that it was Anson who took the money, and because he couldn't be sure, he laid off another of the kitchen staff, too. Both had opportunity. Naturally, Allison believes the other guy did it. She says this Tony was out to get Anson because he made Tony look bad."

"How?"

Cecilia gave a small shrug. "Supposedly because Anson was such a hard worker."

"That certainly gave Tony a motive, didn't it? And Anson, too—if he thinks Tony's been on his case, maybe spreading rumors about him."

"That's exactly what I figured," Cecilia agreed. She couldn't blame Seth Gunderson for laying off Anson. He had the motive, the opportunity and the reputation.

Her husband was quiet for several minutes. "That's all true," he finally said, "and I wouldn't totally rule him out, but in my opinion, the kid's gotten a bad break."

"He isn't right for Allison," Cecilia insisted.

Ian was quiet again, and then he said, "You know, I'm glad you didn't listen to the people who told you it was a mistake to go out with a Navy guy."

"Oh, Ian." She turned into his embrace. "I'm glad, too."

She was. Not only that, her husband had given her something to think about.

Forty-Eight

Rachel laughed at Jane's joke as they walked out to the parking lot after work on Saturday. It was the shop's busiest day and she'd been on her feet for almost ten hours; she was exhausted. Laughter was a good release, even if the joke had been silly and a little off-color.

The parking lot was dark, only fitfully illuminated by nearby streetlights. Approaching her car, keys in hand, Rachel stopped abruptly when a tall, lean man came out of the shadows. Terrified, she couldn't move.

Until the man spoke.

"Rachel, it's Nate."

She felt instantly weak until the anger kicked in, rescuing her. "You scared me out of ten years of my life," she snapped. "What do you think you're doing, hiding in the shadows like that?"

"Sorry."

"You should be!"

He held up both hands. "All I wanted to do was talk. I wasn't interested in starting World War Three."

"You should've thought of that before you came sneaking

up on me." Just then, Jane drove by and slowed down as if to check out the situation. As soon as she recognized Nate, a gigantic smile formed and with a wave, she drove off.

Undeterred, Rachel went on. "You're lucky I didn't gouge out your eyes with my car key." The anger concealed her elation. Rachel didn't want to be this happy, and that made her feel even angrier at herself for reacting to him. "Furthermore," she added in a flustered voice, "why *are* you lurking in the shadows like…like some stalker?" She inserted her key in the lock and yanked open the door.

"Like I said, I came to talk to you." He didn't back down. They stood several feet apart—which was too close. Far too close.

"I love you, Rachel. I can't help it. I was going to let you have your own way, but I couldn't do it."

She wished he hadn't said that. Every time he opened his mouth she weakened a little more. "This is not a good idea."

"I happen to think it's an excellent idea." He advanced one small step toward her.

Heart pounding, Rachel held out her arm. "Stop right where you are."

"No."

"I'll call for a security guard."

Still he came. "You do that."

"Nate…no." But he reached her and gently took her by the shoulders and brought her toward him. She couldn't fight him. Instead, the minute he touched her, she swayed into his arms as if she belonged there. When he kissed her, she had to grab his shirt collar just to remain upright.

"Rachel, Rachel," he murmured between kisses that left her clinging and breathless. "Why did you shut me out of your life?"

If he hadn't said anything, she might have forgotten, at least for the length of another kiss. But, no, he had to go and remind her why a relationship was impossible.

She forced herself to pull away, then dragged in a deep breath and prayed she could get enough oxygen into her brain to think clearly.

"Oh, no, you don't," he protested. "I'm not letting you go that easily."

"Nate—it won't work."

"Who says?"

"I do."

"Then you're wrong. I love you."

"You don't even know me." He was making this more difficult than it had to be. "I'm just another way to thumb your nose at your family. I…refuse—don't you dare kiss me again! Oh… Oh." The fight went out of her as his mouth found hers. His kisses were hungry and demanding and each seemed more potent than the one before. Her knees wobbled and her heart fluttered and if she didn't do something soon, they'd end up at her house, in her bed….

"Let's get out of here," Nate said, his breathing uneven.

"No." Where she found the strength to deny him anything, she didn't know. "I told you, this won't work."

He gripped her shoulders and his eyes bore into hers. "I'm only going to say this once, so listen carefully."

At his touch she was dumbfounded.

"Do you understand me?"

Somehow, she managed to nod.

"Good. Rachel Pendergast, I love you. I am my own person. I always have been. I love my parents, but I won't allow them to dictate my life. My father is a congressman. I'm a Warrant Officer in the United States Navy. It's a job I enjoy and a rank I earned by my own merit. Understand?"

Again she nodded.

"My father doesn't tell me what to do—or who to love. I make my own decisions. Got it?"

"Yes, but—"

"No *buts*. I love you."

Rachel hung her head. "Don't love me. Please, don't love me."

He lifted her chin so she couldn't avoid meeting his gaze. "Sorry, it's too late."

"But…"

"Are you going to argue with me?"

"I…oh, Nate." She threw her arms around him. "I missed you, too—so much."

He sighed deeply, and slipped both arms about her waist, lifting her off the ground. "It took you long enough."

"I'm frightened," she whispered. And she was. If they permitted this relationship to continue, the time would come when she'd have to meet his family. It went without saying that they wouldn't approve; there was absolutely nothing to endear her to his parents. No status, no wealth, no education to speak of. She'd been raised by an aunt who'd died when she was nineteen, and she'd been on her own from that point forward. Dogs at the pound had a better pedigree than she did.

"I don't have any family," she said, ashamed to admit this to a man who had such an important one.

"You've got me."

"Do I?" She sighed. "Why do you make this so hard? Why won't you just let me go?"

"Because you're worth keeping. Now, no more arguing. We're going to talk."

Reluctantly she agreed. He drove them to the Pancake Palace, where they sat in one of the old-fashioned booths. They couldn't stop staring at each other. When the waitress came, they both ordered coffee and banana splits, but the ice cream melted and the coffee grew cold before they even noticed it.

Finally Rachel reached for her spoon, then put it down again. "All right. Seeing that you're the one with the big ideas, where do we go from here?"

"Right where we left off when I shipped out."

"And where was that?"

"We were dating. You were my girl, and I was your bachelor prize."

She rolled her eyes. "Nate, that sounds like something out of a 1950s movie. I should be wearing saddle shoes and a poodle skirt, and we should be listening to Bobby Darrin."

"I'm sure they have some Bobby Darrin on the jukebox here," he murmured.

"What about Bruce?" she asked.

"I think it might be a good idea if you told him you won't be seeing him anymore." Nate leaned all the way over and pressed his lips to hers. "You've already got one steady," he said. "You don't need two."

Steady? Sandra Dee and Frankie Avalon were going to waltz in here any minute.

Still, she knew what Nate meant—and she knew he was right. Jolene would be unhappy, but Rachel's confused relationship with Bruce simply couldn't go on.

Forty-Nine

Allison woke to the sound of a light tap on her bedroom window. Her heart flew to her throat and she gasped. It could only be Anson. She didn't care what time of day or night it was, she had to talk to him. In her eagerness to get to the window, she nearly fell out of bed.

Sure enough, Anson stood there in the yard, his shoulders hunched against the cold March wind. In the faint moonlight she could see that he wore his black coat and watch cap and was peering into the darkened room. When she approached the window, he stepped back. Without question Allison opened it for him.

"Anson," she cried. "Where have you been? I've been worried sick about you." It was two weeks since she'd seen him, that day in the mall. He hadn't been to school. None of his friends seemed to know where he was. He'd vanished; no one had seen him anywhere. When she broke down and phoned his mother, Mrs. Butler didn't show any interest or concern.

Anson didn't answer nor did he climb inside her bedroom, as he had the last time he'd visited her in the middle of the night.

"Come in," she urged. "It's cold." She moved aside, but he remained out in the wind and the cold. "Anson," she said, "get in here! You must be half frozen."

"No!" He shook his head wildly. "The only reason I'm here is to say goodbye."

"Goodbye?" Her mind was spinning. "Why? Where are you going?"

He shrugged as if that was of no significance. "I don't know yet."

Allison rubbed her hands up and down her arms, shivering with cold. "Come in. We need to talk."

Again Anson refused. If anything, he moved back another step.

"Please," she added softly.

He considered it for a moment. "I can't," he finally muttered. "I can't."

"Why not?"

He seemed to steel himself against her. "Like I said, the only reason I'm here is to tell you I won't be seeing you anymore."

The shock of his words felt like a slap across her face. "You don't mean that! You can't mean that." She swallowed down the hurt and disappointment. "I love you."

"Well, don't," he said sharply, as if her confession had angered him. "In case you haven't figured it out yet, I'm a loser. I'm not going anyplace but down."

"That's not true!" But Anson wasn't listening.

"I don't want to drag you down, too," he said.

"Don't say that," she argued hotly, furious that he'd say it about himself. "You're *not* a loser. You're not." She suspected he was just repeating what his mother had told him all his life.

"Your dad's a good guy," he said. "Thank him for me, all right?" He started to turn away.

"Don't go." She leaned out of the window and grabbed for him. She would've fallen onto the ground if Anson hadn't caught her. Once she was in his embrace, practically dangling from the window, she wrapped her arms around his neck and kissed him. At first he resisted and attempted to shove her away. But soon he was returning her kisses. Then, apparently reaching some decision, he tore his mouth from hers and pulled back.

"Please," she begged. "Come in so we can talk about this properly. Don't walk away from me—not like this."

Reluctantly he nodded. While he climbed in through the bedroom window, Allison found her thick fleece housecoat and put it on. Shivering, still shaking with cold, she tied the sash around her waist.

Anson sat on the end of her bed, his head lowered. "Nothing you say is going to change my mind."

"You love me," she whispered, kneeling on the floor in front of him. "Don't deny it, because I know it's true."

He closed his eyes, a tortured expression on his face. "I shouldn't have come," he muttered. She suspected he said it more for his own benefit than hers.

She placed her hands over his. "I'm so grateful you did. You can't leave me. I won't let you." She got to her feet. "If you go, then I'm going with you." There was no alternative, she decided, no other choice. "Wherever you go, that's where I want to be."

"No." The word was chilling in its intensity.

"Anson, you've *got* to listen to me. This is all because of what happened at The Lighthouse, isn't it?"

He refused to answer, refused to look at her.

"My dad believes you. I believe you. Doesn't that mean anything?"

He seemed to think about it, then shook his head. "Don't

you see? This is how it is—everything I touch turns to dust. I thought it'd be different with you, but it's not. I'm getting out of here before I screw up your life, too." He scrambled to his feet and started for the window.

"But you don't know where you're going," she said in a hoarse whisper. Then she remembered something else. "You *can't* leave," she told him. "You'll be breaking the terms of your plea bargain. You have to stay in school, remember?"

"I was supposed to have a job, too."

"Yes, but—"

Anson shook his head again. "It's too late to worry about that. If they find me now, I'll probably get jail time. I'm out of here."

A dozen questions rose at his response. She didn't ask a single one because she was afraid of the answers. "What will you do for money?"

He turned back and gave a harsh laugh.

"Anson?" She'd never heard him sound like that before, and it frightened her. Her stomach knotted as she realized there was a reason Anson had chosen to leave Cedar Cove tonight. *"What have you done?"* she whispered.

"It's better if you don't know." His eyes softened as he looked at her one last time. "Goodbye," he whispered, stretching out his hand to touch her face.

"No!" She hurried to the window, but he was too fast. He moved with an agility that belied his size. "How will I know where to reach you?" she called out as he walked across the grass.

Anson didn't answer. His hands were buried deep inside his pockets, his shoulders bent. She stayed where she was until she lost sight of him, and in her heart she knew she'd never see him again. Eventually the tears came, flooding her eyes and rolling down her cheeks. She closed the window and crawled back into bed.

Allison didn't fall asleep for hours. Her pillow was damp with tears when she woke Saturday morning, again to the sound of knocking—but this time it was someone pounding at her bedroom door.

"Allison," her mother said, opening the door. "It's after ten."

She sat up in bed and rubbed her eyes. She often slept in on the weekends.

"There's someone here who wants to talk to you."

Her first thought was that it might be Anson, but she realized that it wouldn't be.

"Who?"

"It's Sheriff Davis." Her mother's expression was serious, and Allison's stomach immediately tensed.

"Why does he want to see me?" Even though she asked, she knew the answer. This had to do with Anson.

"Your father's talking to the sheriff now. I suggest you get dressed right away and join us."

Allison nodded and although she appeared outwardly calm, her heart clamored hard. This was what she'd feared most—that Anson would get into trouble again.

By the time she'd put on jeans and a sweatshirt and brushed her hair, Allison was shaking. Whatever Anson had done, if he was caught, it would mean the fire in the park would now be part of his permanent record. It also meant her father would never allow her to see him again.

The sheriff set down his coffee mug when Allison entered the kitchen. He sat at the table with both her parents.

"This is our daughter, Allison," her father said, motioning that she should sit down. "Allison," he said, looking straight at her. "Sheriff Davis has some questions for you. It's important that you answer him honestly and directly. Do you understand?"

She lowered her head and whispered, "I will."

"Hello, Allison," Sheriff Davis said pleasantly. "I hear you're friends with Anson Butler."

She nodded.

"I'm wondering when you last saw him," the sheriff said next.

The minute Anson left, she knew he'd done something he shouldn't have. He'd as much as said so. His chilling laugh echoed in her mind.

Her father leaned toward her. "Please tell Sheriff Davis the truth."

"Last night," she whispered, knowing her parents would be outraged that she'd let him into her bedroom in the middle of the night.

"When?"

"About two this morning."

"You snuck out of the house?" This outburst was from her mother, who was clearly upset.

Allison shook her head. "No. Anson came to me."

"At the house?" her father clarified without apparent censure. But his eyes let her know he wasn't pleased, although he kept his voice even.

Allison sighed. "He tapped on my window and woke me up. He—he came to say goodbye."

"Did he say where he was going?"

"No. He said he didn't know."

"Do you have any idea where he is now?"

She shook her head a second time.

"You're sure he ran away, though?" her father said, pressuring her for more information.

"He hasn't been at home or at school. I asked around and no one's seen him."

"Where's he been keeping himself?" This came from the sheriff.

"I don't know." Allison wished she did. All week she'd wondered and waited to hear from him. The thought of Anson living on the streets made her want to weep all over again. His mother wasn't any help; she didn't even seem to care.

"Do you know whether he had any money?" the sheriff asked.

She hesitated, but for only a second. "He didn't say."

Sheriff Davis exchanged a look with her father.

"What did he do?" Allison had to find out.

"At this point we don't know that Anson did anything," Sheriff Davis said, his words measured and flat. "He's what we consider a person of interest."

"Interest in what?"

Again her father and the sheriff exchanged that ambiguous glance.

"About one this morning, The Lighthouse restaurant burned to the ground."

"Is it arson?" she cried.

"We don't know for sure," the sheriff said, "but the indication from the fire chief is that the fire appears to have been purposely set."

Allison gasped. "Anson would never do that!"

"He burned down the shed in the park," her father reminded her. He placed his hand on her shoulder as if to lend her strength.

"I don't care," she said, shrugging off his comfort and leaping to her feet. "He wouldn't do that."

"Seth Gunderson laid him off."

"Mr. Gunderson thought Anson had taken some money from his office, but he didn't."

"Anson was angry."

"You would be, too," Allison shouted, "if you were unjustly accused of—something." Her voice broke. She couldn't believe The Lighthouse was gone. It'd become a Cedar Cove landmark.

"As I mentioned, we're not certain that the fire was arson," Sheriff Davis said in an obvious attempt to calm her.

"But you're already trying to frame Anson!"

"Allison." Her mother spoke her name softly. "No one's going to frame him for anything."

"All I want to do right now is talk to Anson," the sheriff assured her.

Allison didn't believe him. She was convinced the sheriff and her parents considered him guilty. She recognized that he must have done *something,* but he hadn't burned down The Lighthouse. Despite any evidence or suspicion to the contrary, she knew one thing: Anson was innocent.

Justine Gunderson stared at what had once been their restaurant, her arms tight around her son to ward off the cold wind gusting from the cove. Leif was peacefully asleep, thumb in his mouth. Seth stood a few feet apart from her, answering the fire chief's questions. The stench of fire invaded her nostrils, clung to her clothes and hair. Smoke wafted up from the ashes of what had once been their dream—their restaurant, their investment and sole source of income. Even now, staring at the charred remains, it was hard to believe The Lighthouse was no more. All that survived of the structure was a blackened skeleton and a pile of rubble. With a jolt she recognized the twisted metal frame of a photograph—the picture Jon Bowman had given them when they opened the restaurant.

After a few minutes, Seth returned to her side and took Leif from her arms. Their son was still asleep so he'd be spared seeing this. Justine felt numb with shock. She couldn't cry, could barely think.

"It was arson," Seth whispered.

This was as unbelievable as the fire itself. "Who...who would do such a thing to us?"

Seth shook his head. "I don't know."

"How?"

"The fire chief says it was started near the kitchen. We were supposed to think it was a grease fire."

This whole situation was becoming more unreal by the minute.

"Whoever did it was stupid," he said grimly. "Or else they wanted to be caught."

That, at least, was encouraging. Justine wanted whoever had done this to be caught, too. Wanted that person to face his—or her—day in court, to receive the maximum sentence.

"The fire chief asked if we had any disgruntled employees," Seth murmured. He, too, seemed to be in shock.

"Do we?" Seth was the one who handled the hiring and firing, plus the scheduling of staff. Justine had enough to do working as a hostess and keeping their financial records straight.

"Anson Butler was pretty angry when I laid him off." Seth's voice was hoarse, and he hardly sounded like himself.

Justine remembered now that Seth had laid off two employees recently. "What about the other kid?"

"Tony Philpott," Seth told her. "He seemed to take it in stride. I hear he's already got another job."

"Oh."

"The police want to question Anson. He's missing. They're looking for him now."

Justine leaned close to her husband. "I hope they find him."

Seth nodded. He placed his free arm around her shoulders, and pulled her against him. "We'll get through this."

"Of course we will," Justine said. She just didn't know how.

Fifty

With a heavy heart, Maryellen set down the phone after talking to Kelly. She felt like weeping. Nothing was going right. Bedridden and miserable during this difficult pregnancy, she counted the days until she could get on with her life again.

With Maryellen unable to work and contribute to their finances, their budget was stretched to the breaking point. Jon was working as hard as he could to fill orders and make new photographs available. It was tax season, though, and sales of nonessential items were notoriously bad at this time of year.

When Jon wasn't developing and printing his photographs, he'd been cooking whatever hours Seth Gunderson could give him at The Lighthouse. Until last weekend, when it burned to the ground in the biggest fire in Cedar Cove's history. Everyone in town was sick about losing The Lighthouse. The money from Jon's job at the restaurant was gone now, too. They were back to first base financially.

As it was, Jon was working constantly to support the family, plus taking care of her, Katie and the upkeep on the house. Her husband was worn out, and Maryellen didn't know how much longer he could continue this killing pace. The baby, the fire and now this problem with her sister.

Kelly was pregnant, too, but unfortunately she'd been experiencing terrible bouts of morning sickness. She spent the first half of every day bent over a toilet. Paul had put his foot down; taking care of Katie was simply too much for her, he'd said. Maryellen understood. Her sister wanted to help and felt dreadful about letting everyone down, but she just couldn't look after Katie anymore.

Now Maryellen had to tell her husband that, in addition to everything else, he'd have to supervise their two-year-old daughter. At best, he'd have a ninety-minute reprieve when Katie went down for her nap. Most afternoons she only slept an hour.

As Jon walked downstairs from his small office, he entered the living room—and obviously realized that something was wrong.

"What is it?"

Maryellen patted the empty space next to her on the bed.

"That bad?" he said as though this was a joke.

"You'd better sit down," she said, trying to smile. She suspected the effort was unconvincing. "That was Kelly on the phone."

"Katie's all right?"

"Katie's fine." It was everything else that wasn't.

Jon sank down on the foot of her makeshift bed. "The baby?"

Maryellen rested her hand on her stomach. "If all the kicking is any indication, I'd say this baby has more energy than the two of us combined."

Jon relaxed and reached for her hand. She'd seen little of him while she was pregnant with Katie, and they both wanted him to share as much of this pregnancy as possible. Maryellen wished it could be a more positive experience.

"Things will improve soon," he reassured her.

"I know," she whispered, struggling with what she had to tell him.

He took her gently in his arms. "Do I need to remind you how much I love you? Without you and Katie, I'm nothing."

Maryellen leaned back and took in a deep breath. "Kelly's pregnant."

"I know," Jon said, his voice puzzled. They'd talked about the two cousins being born within a few months of each other. Paul and Kelly were ecstatic about this second pregnancy. She'd had difficulty getting pregnant the first time and there would be almost six years between the two children.

"She's been suffering from severe morning sickness again." Kelly had the same problem when she was pregnant with Tyler. "So…"

Jon tensed, as if he knew what was coming. "She can't watch Katie anymore."

Maryellen nodded wearily. "She hated to tell me. Kelly feels terrible about this. But chasing after a two-year-old while she's feeling so sick—she just can't do it."

Silently Jon stared into the distance. This was one more burden. Maryellen didn't dare make the obvious suggestion. In their last letter, his father and stepmother had offered to help. Yet the one time she'd brought up the subject, Jon had rejected the idea in no uncertain terms. She couldn't, wouldn't, do that again.

"I've been trying to think of what we can do," she whispered, attempting to focus on a solution. "I could keep an eye on Katie in the mornings. It won't be easy, but I'll manage."

"Katie is walking and exploring and into everything," Jon muttered. "There's no way you can watch her and protect this pregnancy."

"But you—"

"I'll take her with me. I used to do that, remember?"

Maryellen nodded, but they both knew Katie had been an infant in those days. He'd had a special backpack to carry their daughter when he went on his photographic excursions, and young as she was, Katie had loved those times with her daddy. Maryellen could still picture it.

"My mother can help." Even as she spoke, Maryellen knew that wasn't possible. Grace was a newlywed with a demanding job. Her mother already came to the house two or three times a week. It was the best she could do, but it wasn't enough. She and Cliff had arranged for a cleaning crew one day the previous month, plus some prepared meals, and Maryellen had been so grateful. But they couldn't expect that kind of gift again. Cliff and especially Grace had done enough for them.

"We can't ask Grace to do any more than she already is." Jon said aloud what Maryellen had been thinking.

"I know…." Tears filled her eyes. The worry and stress were more than she could handle.

"Maryellen…"

She covered her face with both hands and bent her head.

"Sweetheart, it'll be all right."

"No, it won't."

"I'll get a mortgage on the land."

"No!" she insisted. This land, an inheritance from his grandfather, was everything to Jon. If they lost it, he'd be devastated.

Her husband was silent for a long time. Finally he stood up and walked away.

"Jon?" she said when she saw that he was returning upstairs. "Where are you going?"

"To make a phone call."

"To whom?"

He turned and looked over his shoulder. "I'll contact my family, Maryellen. It's what you want me to do, isn't it?"

She didn't answer him.

"Do I have a choice?" he said quietly.

"I'm sorry!" she choked out. "But it's not my fault—I didn't make any of this happen, so don't be angry with me."

"It's what you want, though, isn't it?" he persisted.

It was, but only because it made sense to give his father and stepmother an opportunity to rebuild their relationship with Jon, their only living child. And because Maryellen needed the help. Jon did, too.

He sighed and wiped a hand down his face. "They can't stay with us, understand?"

She nodded.

"And they're only welcome until the baby's born."

She swallowed hard. "You're going to tell them that?"

"Damn straight I am. I don't want them anywhere near me. This isn't for me, Maryellen. The only reason I'm doing it is for you, and for our daughter and our baby."

Tears streamed down Maryellen's cheeks. She hated being this emotional. "Call them if you want," she managed to say between sobs. "Only don't be upset with me. I can't bear it if you're angry. I just can't bear it."

Jon came back downstairs and was immediately at her side. He gathered her in his arms and let his shoulder absorb her tears. "I'm not mad at you," he whispered into her hair. "I'm furious with myself."

"But why?"

"Mostly because I can't be the man you need me to be. You think I should forgive them for what they did. Hard as I try, Maryellen, I can't."

Her arms went around him and they clung to each other. Somehow, they'd get through this time, with or without his parents' help.

* * *

Roy McAfee stood in front of the charred rubble that had once been The Lighthouse restaurant. It made him sick to his stomach. His son stood on one side and Gloria on the other.

"Sheriff Davis told me the arson investigator says the fire was deliberately set," Gloria said, hands on her hips as she surveyed the damage. Slowly she shook her head, as if it was difficult to take in the scene before her. Roy felt the same way.

Arson. Roy hated to hear that. This wasn't the sort of thing you expected to find in a quiet community like Cedar Cove. The article in *The Chronicle* reported that the Gundersons were in shock and that no decisions had been made yet. They didn't know at this point whether or not they were going to rebuild.

"Is there a suspect?" Roy asked his daughter.

Gloria nodded. "A person of interest—a high school boy. He started a fire a few months back and was recently let go from the restaurant."

"The shed in the park?" Roy remembered reading about that, but the boy's name had been kept out of the paper.

Gloria nodded again.

"Does he have a motive?"

"Sheriff Davis seems to think so. The money box is missing, too."

Roy tried to remember what he'd heard about the toolshed fire. "What does the kid have to say?"

"He's a runaway," Gloria informed him.

"Dad," Mack said, "didn't you have a teenager visit the office last Monday?"

Roy nodded. His son had connected the dots even before he had. "The Coxes' daughter wanted to hire me," he murmured thoughtfully, "to find her boyfriend." The high school girl had been saving for a vehicle, but was willing to lay down every penny if Roy could locate the missing boy. Roy had been touched by her devotion—but not once had she mentioned that this boyfriend was in a heap of trouble. Well, she should save her money. The law had far better resources than he did. If she insisted on spending her money, he'd suggest a good attorney.

"The kid's name was Anson Butler," he said.

That got Gloria's attention fast. "Butler came in to see you?"

"No, his girlfriend. He's the one who's missing."

She held his look. "He's also the one who's wanted for questioning about the fire."

Raising his eyebrows, Mack kicked at the ashes. "I suppose now's as good a time as any to let you know I've been a volunteer with the Kent Fire Department for the last couple of years."

"Is that so?" It was Gloria who showed the most interest.

"Yeah," Mack said with a careless shrug. "I enjoy it."

"I hear the Cedar Cove fire department has two paid openings," Gloria said. "You might want to apply."

Mack looked at Roy, as if seeking his approval.

Roy nodded solemnly. "I wish you would."

His son grinned. "In that case, I will."

Roy squatted down and picked up a handful of ashes. He had his family with him now. Gloria, the daughter he'd never known, and Mack, his formerly estranged son. Linnette had already moved to Cedar Cove and if Mack got a job with the fire department, he'd be living here, too.

He let the ashes run through his fingers and wondered if Anson knew that Allison was prepared to give up everything she owned in order to find him. He hoped that, one day, the kid appreciated what she'd been willing to sacrifice on his behalf.

Straightening, Roy looked over the scene one last time. He knew losing the restaurant had come as a devastating shock to Seth and Justine Gunderson. Even with the evidence right before his eyes, he found it difficult to believe anyone would purposely set out to do them harm. Who had started the fire remained to be seen. Troy Davis considered the teenage boys Seth had recently laid off—especially Anson Butler—his prime suspects; Roy thought that was a little too convenient. But if it wasn't a disgruntled employee, then who?

Roy hadn't had a chance to talk to Seth or Justine yet, but he was thinking he'd stop by their home at 6 Rainier Drive sometime soon.

* * * * *

We hope you visit Cedar Cove again –
drop in at 6 RAINIER DRIVE,
Seth and Justine's home.
Find out what they plan to do about The Lighthouse
– and follow the investigation that reveals
who burned down the restaurant.

Catch up with the newly married Grace and Cliff,
Ian and Cecilia and the rest of your friends in Cedar Cove!

Read on for a sneak peek!

One

Justine Gunderson woke suddenly from a deep sleep, with the vague sense that something was wrong. A moment later, she remembered, and an intense sadness pressed down upon her. Lying on her back, she stared up at the dark ceiling as the realization hit her yet again. The Lighthouse, the restaurant she and Seth had poured their lives into, was gone. *Gone*. It had burned to the ground a week ago, in a blazing fire that lit up the night sky for miles around Cedar Cove. A fire started by an unidentified arsonist.

Without bothering to look, Justine knew her husband wasn't in bed with her. Only a week had passed since the fire, but it felt like a month, a year, a lifetime. She didn't think Seth had slept more than three or four hours at a stretch since that shocking phone call.

Folding back the sheet, she climbed slowly out of bed. It was barely four, according to the digital readout on the clock radio. Moonlight filtered through a gap in the curtains, creating patterns on the bedroom walls. Justine slipped her arms into the sleeves of her robe and went in search of her husband.

As she'd suspected, she found him in the living room, pacing. He moved ceaselessly, his angry strides taking him from the fireplace to the window and back. When he saw her, he continued to walk, looking away as though he couldn't face her. She could tell he didn't want her near him. She barely recognized this man her husband had become since news of the fire.

"Can't you sleep?" she asked, whispering for fear of waking their four-year-old son. Leif was a light sleeper and although he was too young to understand what had happened, the child intuitively knew his parents were upset.

"I want to find out who did this and why." Fists clenched, Seth turned on her as if she should be able to tell him.

Tucking her long, straight hair behind her ears, Justine sank into the rocker in which she'd once nursed their son. "I do, too," she told him. She'd never seen Seth this restless. Her strikingly blond husband was of Swedish extraction, a big man, nearly six-six, with broad shoulders to match. He'd been a commercial fisherman until soon after their marriage. That was when they'd decided to open the restaurant. The Lighthouse had been Seth's dream, and with financial assistance from his parents, he'd invested everything—his skill, his emotions, their finances—in this venture. Justine had been at his side every step of the way.

In the beginning, while Leif was an infant, she'd kept the books and handled the payroll. When their son grew old enough for preschool, she'd assumed a more active role, working as hostess and filling in where needed.

"Who would do this?" he demanded again.

The answer eluded her just as it did him. Why anyone would want to hurt them was beyond her comprehension. They had no enemies that she knew of and no serious rivals. It was hard to believe they'd been the target of a random firebug, but maybe that was the case. So far, there'd been little real progress in tracking down the arsonist.

"Seth," she whispered gently, stretching her hand toward him. "You can't go on like this."

He didn't respond, and Justine realized he hadn't heard her. She longed to ease his mind, to reassure him. Her fear was that the fire had destroyed more than the restaurant. It had stolen Seth's peace of mind, his purpose and, in some ways, his innocence. He'd lost faith in the goodness of others and confidence in his own abilities.

Justine's innocence had been devastated one bright summer afternoon in 1986, when her twin brother, Jordan, had drowned. Justine had held his lifeless body in her arms until the paramedics arrived. She'd been in shock, unable to grasp that her brother, her twin, was gone. He'd broken his neck after a careless dive off a floating dock.

Her entire world had forever changed that day. Her parents divorced shortly afterward and her father had quickly remarried. To all outward appearances, Justine had adjusted to the upheaval in her life. She'd graduated from high school, finished college and found employment at First National Bank, then risen to branch manager. Although she'd had no intention of ever marrying, she'd been dating Warren Saget, a local builder who was the same age as her mother. Then she'd met Seth Gunderson at their ten-year high-school reunion.

Seth had been her brother's best friend. She'd always felt that if Seth had been with Jordan that day, her brother might still be alive, and her own life would've been different—although she wasn't sure exactly how. It was ridiculous to entertain such thoughts; she recognized that on a conscious level. And yet…it was what she believed.

All through high school she'd barely spoken to Seth. He was the football hero, the class jock. She was the class brain. And never the twain had met until that night nearly six years ago, when she'd run into him at the reunion planning meeting. Seth had casually mentioned that he'd had a crush on her during their high-school days. The look in his eyes told her he'd found her beautiful then and even more so now.

They hadn't experienced an easy courtship. Warren Saget hadn't wanted to lose her and made a concerted effort to pressure her into marrying him. He'd instinctively understood that Seth was a major threat. Warren bought Justine the largest diamond she'd ever seen, promising a life of luxury and social prominence if she agreed to be his wife.

All Seth had to offer Justine was a twenty-year-old live-aboard sailboat—and his love. By that time, she was so head-over-heels crazy about him that she could scarcely breathe. Still, she struggled, unwilling to listen to her own heart. Then, one day, she couldn't resist him anymore….

"I'm calling the fire marshal this morning," Seth muttered, breaking into her thoughts. "I want *answers*."

"Seth," she tried again. "Honey, why—"

"Don't *honey* me," he snapped.

Justine flinched at the rage in his voice.

"It's been a full week. They should have some information by now, only they're not telling us. There's something they don't want me to know and I'm going to find out what. If I have to bring Roy McAfee in, I will!" He looked directly at her then, probably for the first time since she'd entered the room.

"Seth, I like and trust Roy," she said, referring to the town's only private investigator, "but the fire department's already investigating. So is the insurance company. Let them do their jobs," Justine said in a soft voice. "Let the sheriff do his."

Splaying his fingers though his hair, he released a slow breath. "I'm sorry, I don't mean to take my frustration out on you."

"I know." Justine got up and walked into his arms, pressing her body against his, urging him to relax. "Come back to bed and try to sleep," she said.

He shook his head. "I can't. Every time I close my eyes, all I can see is The Lighthouse going up in smoke."

Seth had arrived a few minutes after the fire trucks and stood by helplessly as the restaurant, engulfed in flames, had quickly become a lost cause.

"I can't believe it was Anson Butler," Justine said, thinking out loud. She'd liked the boy and had trusted him—which, according to her friends and neighbors, had been a mistake.

"You don't *want* to believe it's him," her husband returned, the anger back in the clipped harshness of his words.

That was true. Seth had hired Anson several months earlier. The teenager was paying off court expenses because of a fire he'd set in the city park. He'd had no explanation for why he'd burned down the toolshed. All Justine really knew were the few details Seth had divulged at the time he'd taken the boy on.

To his credit, Anson had turned himself in to the authorities and accepted full responsibility for his actions. That had impressed her husband, and on the recommendation of their accountant and friend, Zachary Cox, who'd become something of a mentor to the boy, Seth had agreed to give Anson a job.

At first the teenager had made an effort to prove his worth. He'd shown up early for his shifts and put in extra hours, eager to please his employer. Then within a few weeks, everything had fallen apart. Tony, another dishwasher, had taken a dislike to Anson and the two had exchanged words. From what she understood, they'd also gotten into a shoving match once or twice. As a result of their animosity, the tension in the kitchen had increased. Seth had talked it over with Justine and she'd suggested they separate the two boys. Seth decided to make Anson a prep cook. Tony didn't like the idea of Anson getting a promotion, while he'd been on staff longer and remained a dishwasher.

Then money had gone missing from the office and, although others had access to the money box, both Tony and Anson had been seen entering the room. When questioned, Anson claimed he'd been looking for Seth because a supplier had a problem. Tony insisted he needed to talk to Seth about his schedule. Both boys were suspects, so Seth felt he had no choice but to lay them both off. The money was never recovered. Seth blamed himself because he'd left the safe open, lockbox inside, while he was briefly out of the office.

A week later, The Lighthouse had burned to the ground.

"We don't have any proof it was Anson," Justine reminded her husband.

"We'll get proof. Whether he's the culprit or somebody else is. We'll find whoever did this." Seth's hard mouth was set with determination and his body tensed.

"Try to sleep," she urged again. Despite his reluctance, she led him back to their bedroom.

Together they slipped under the sheets and she moved her body close to his. Seth lay on his back, eyes open, as she slid her leg over his and draped her arm across his powerful chest. He held her tight, as if she were the only solid thing left in a world that had started to crumble. Kissing his neck, Justine purred in his ear, hoping that if they made love, the restlessness in him would ease and he'd be able to relax. But Seth shook his head, rejecting her subtle offer. She swallowed down the hurt and tried not to take it personally. All of this would be over soon, she told herself; soon everything would be back to normal. Justine *had* to believe it. Without that hope, despair would encroach, which was something she had to avoid at any cost. She fought to maintain a positive outlook, for her husband's sake and for the sake of her marriage.

When Justine woke again, it was morning and

Leif was climbing onto her bed, wanting breakfast. Penny, their cocker spaniel-poodle mix, followed him, eyeing the bed.

"Where's Daddy?" she asked, sitting upright, rubbing her hand tiredly over her face.

Her son dragged his teddy bear onto the bed, blue eyes soulful. "In his office."

That wasn't a good sign.

"It's time we got you ready for school," Justine said briskly, glancing at the clock. Quarter to eight already. Leif's preschool class was held every morning, and even though their own schedules had fallen apart, Justine and Seth had done their best to keep Leif's timetable consistent.

"Daddy's mad again," the four-year-old whispered.

Justine sighed. This was almost a daily occurrence, and she worried about the effect of so much tension on their son, who couldn't possibly understand *why* Daddy was mad or Mommy sometimes cried.

"Did he growl at you?" Justine asked, then roared like a grizzly bear, shaping her hands into make-believe claws. With Penny barking cheerfully, she crawled across the mattress after her son, distracting him from worries about his father.

Leif shrieked and scrambled off the bed, racing for his bedroom. Justine followed and laughingly cornered the boy. Leif's eyes flashed with delight as she set out his clothes. He insisted on getting dressed on his own these days, so she let him.

After saying a perfunctory goodbye to her husband, Justine delivered Leif to preschool. When she pulled back into the driveway, Seth came out the door to greet her. The April sky was overcast, and rain was imminent. The weather was a perfect reflection of their mood, Justine thought. A sunny day would've seemed incongruous when they both felt so fearful and angry.

"I talked to the fire marshal," her husband announced as she got out of her car.

"Did he have any news?"

Seth's frown darkened. "Nothing he was willing to tell me. The insurance adjuster's taking his own sweet time, too."

"Seth, these things require patience." She needed answers as much as he did, but she certainly didn't want the fire marshal to rush the investigation.

"Don't you start on me," he flared. "We're losing ground every day. How are we supposed to live without the restaurant?"

"The insurance—"

"I know about the insurance money," he said, cutting her off. "But we won't get anything for at least a month. And it isn't going to keep our employees from seeking other jobs. It isn't going to pay back my parents' investment. They put their trust in me."

Seth's parents had invested a significant amount

of the start-up money; Seth and Justine paid them monthly and she knew Mr. and Mrs. Gunderson relied on that income.

Justine didn't have any solutions for him. She recognized that he was distressed about more than the financial implications of the fire, but she had no quick or ready answers. "What would you like me to do?" she asked. "Tell me and I'll do it."

He glared at her in a way she'd never seen before. "What I'd like," he muttered, "is for you to stop acting as if this is a temporary inconvenience. The Lighthouse is *gone*. We've lost everything, and you're acting like it's no big deal." Justine recoiled at the unfairness of his words. He made it sound as if she was some kind of Pollyanna who wasn't fully aware of their situation. "Don't you realize the last five years are in ashes?" he railed. "Five years of working sixteen-hour days and for what?"

"But we *haven't* lost everything," she countered, hoping to inject some reason into his tirade. She didn't mean to be argumentative; she simply wanted him to see that although this was a dreadful time, they still had each other. They had their child and their house. Together they'd find the strength to start over—if only Seth could let go of this anger.

"You're doing it again." He shook his head in barely controlled frustration.

"You want me to be as angry as you are," she said.

"Yes!" he shouted. "You *should* be angry. You should want answers just like I do. You should—"

"More than anything," she cried, her own control snapping, "I want my husband back. I'm as sick as you are about everything that's happened. We've lost our business, and to me that's horrible, it's tragic, but it isn't the end of my world."

Her husband stared at her, incredulous. "How can you *say* that?"

"Maybe you're trying to lose your wife and son, too," she yelled, and before she could change her mind, she slipped back inside the car, slamming the door. Seth didn't try to stop her and that was fine with Justine. She needed to get away from him, too.

Without waiting for his reaction, she backed out of the driveway.

Welcome to Cedar Cove –
a small town with a big heart!

When family court judge Olivia Lockheart
causes a scandal by denying a couple's divorce,
the whole town starts talking about it.

Meanwhile, her daughter Justine must decide
if she should stop waiting for love and accept
a marriage of convenience.

And Olivia's best friend, Grace, wonders if her
own husband is having an affair.

In Cedar Cove, nothing stays secret for long.

Welcome to Cedar Cove –
a small town with a big heart!

Grace Sherman's life was happy and untroubled –
until her husband just disappeared.

But life can – and does – go on. Cedar Cove is
abuzz with talk of weddings and babies. Romance
is blossoming between friends, and there are
troubled relationships to solve.

And will Grace ever find out what happened
to her husband?

www.mirabooks.co.uk

MIRA

Welcome to Cedar Cove – a small town with a big heart!

Recently divorced Rosie and Zach's unusual custody arrangement means that they will be moving between each other's places, not the kids!

Will Judge Olivia stay with Jack, the local newspaper owner, or get back together with her ex-husband?

And who is the mysterious man who died at the local bed-and-breakfast?

In Cedar Cove, it won't be a mystery for long!

www.mirabooks.co.uk

Welcome to Cedar Cove –
a small town with a big heart!

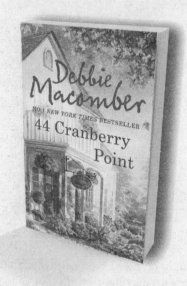

It turns out that the man who died at the
Thyme & Tide bed-and-breakfast was called Max.
But why did he come to Cedar Cove –
and who killed him?

In other news, Jon and Maryellen are getting
married. And Maryellen's mother, Grace, has
more than her share of interested men.
But who will she choose?

www.mirabooks.co.uk

Welcome to Cedar Cove –
a small town with a big heart!

Poor Justine and Seth! Their Lighthouse restaurant was burnt down and the prime suspect is an ex-employee who disappeared after the fire. This kind of crisis is not good for a marriage…

In the meantime, Cal from the local ranch is now rescuing wild horses. But what could this mean for his new relationship with Linette?

www.mirabooks.co.uk

MIRA

Welcome to Cedar Cove –
a small town with
a big heart!

There's so much gossip to catch up on
in Cedar Cove.

Make time for friends. Make time
for Debbie Macomber.

www.mirabooks.co.uk

MRS MONEYPENNY'S CAREERS ADVICE FOR AMBITIOUS WOMEN

'Mrs Moneypenny puts my hectic life in perspective – she is funny and wise, and above all, very very busy'
SARAH BROWN, author of *Behind the Black Door*

'Equal parts provocative, hilarious and wise – this book is a timely antidote to the pervasive power of male networks. It's guaranteed to get a girl's career moving'
LYNDA GRATTON, professor of Management Practice at London Business School and author of *The Shift*

'Want to get ahead? Then just do what Mrs M. tells you'
MERRYN SOMERSET WEBB, Editor-in-Chief, *Moneyweek*

'Beware, reading this book in bed will keep you awake! Warmth and wisdom shine through this tour de force of the joys, trials and tribulations of trying to have a fulfilling career as a woman'
JAN HALL, headhunter and partner at JCA Group

'Mrs Moneypenny's advice is tough, but spot on. Aim for the top. Jettison guilt. Outsource like a madwoman. Success requires sharp heels – and a sharp mind – but if you're willing to work hard, it is there for the taking'
LAURA VANDERKAM, author of *All The Money In The World* and *168 Ho*

C800506801

'The message of this career-advice book for women is blunt: to get to the top, you need to do all the things that men do to get there, and then some. Mrs Moneypenny dispenses valuable advice on making connections, what sort of education to pursue, financial literacy and saying 'no'; a difficult one for women'
USA Today

'If you follow the advice of Mrs Moneypenny I'm sure it will pay dividends'
Bookgeeks.co.uk

'If you want to reach the top there's no better way than following the example and lessons of those who have gotten there before you. Take Mrs Moneypenny's advice straight to the top'
BARBARA CORCORAN, star of ABC's *Shark Tank*, founder of the Corcoran Group

'Mrs Moneypenny covers the career basics and more. As a mother, sister, aunt, manager and friend this is a book I'll recommend to all the women I care about'
MARYANNE B. RAINONE, Senior Vice President and Managing Director, Heyman Associates

'Straightforward, to the point, idealistic and pragmatic: wonderful woman'
CRISTIANA FALCONE, World Economic Forum